S0-BDM-910

Dani was writhing in the same fever of love that possessed her lover. Her hands were wandering wildly over him, clutching and tugging, seeking all of him. Her fingers aided his as they undid the collar of her dress.

Then a sound outside of her seemed to echo, distantly, the pulse of her own blood hammering in her ears. It grew louder, an insistent beat that cut like jagged ice through the opiate of love.

They were coming straight this way. Along the same trail she and Adam had taken.

"Adam — Adam . . ."

She was struggling against him now.

"Adam! He will kill you! Oh God, Adam, get away from here! Get away now!"

But it was too late . . .

Fawcett Gold Medal Books
by T. V. Olsen:

BLIZZARD PASS

BONNER'S STALLION

CANYON OF THE GUN

THE HARD MAN

McGIVERN

RED IS THE RIVER

T.V. OLSEN

FAWCETT GOLD MEDAL • NEW YORK

A Fawcett Gold Medal Book
Published by Ballantine Books

Copyright © 1983 by T. V. Olsen

All rights reserved under International and Pan-American
Copyright Conventions. Published in the United States by
Ballantine Books, a division of Random House, Inc., New York,
and simultaneously in Canada by Random House of Canada
Limited, Toronto.

Library of Congress Catalog Card Number: 82-90859

ISBN 0-449-12407-X

All the characters in this book are fictitious, and any resemblance
to actual persons living or dead is purely coincidental.

Manufactured in the United States of America

First Ballantine Books Edition: March 1983

To
PHYLLIS LUXEM
who helped start it all

If men will give challenges,
they must expect consequences.

THOMAS PAINE

O, it is excellent
To have a giant's strength
    but it is tyrannous
To use it like a giant.

SHAKESPEARE, *Measure for Measure*

❧ *one* ❧

The Challenge

☸ *one* ☸

HUDDLED WITH HER daughters on a transverse seat of the old Studebaker wagon, Selma was too wet and chilled and miserable to pay much attention as Elof checked the team, bringing the vehicle to a halt. Then she heard Axel, out ahead of the wagon, start to curse with a steady, rising fury. Peering into the rain-lashed darkness, she couldn't make out a thing till a tortured rope of lightning played over the scene.

Selma saw a wide churning stretch of water and the black outlines of naked trees rimming it. Out in the middle of that stormy lake where no lake should be, she saw, a moment before the afterwash of light faded, the shapes of buildings jutting up forlornly.

"Flooded, by God!" her husband said. Again he swore bitterly.

"Stop that!" Selma said sharply. "The children, you *dumskalle!*"

Axel continued to curse, but more quietly and in Swedish.

"How could this be?" she said impatiently. "Are you sure it's the right place?"

"*Ja*, damn it! Of course I'm sure."

Axel Holmgaard tramped back to the wagon and stood for a long moment facing his family. His arms hung loose at his sides, but his fists were knotted, his shoulders hunched with anger. Those fists were like hams; he looked massive and bearlike in his wet bulky mackinaw.

But though Axel was a large man, rawboned and slab-muscled, standing six feet three in his bare feet, he had less of the clumsy hugeness of a bear than the rangy spring-sinewed bigness of a catamount. At forty-six he still moved like one too, despite a gray grizzling in his flaming thatch of red hair. He had the long squarish face of his Scandinavian ancestors; a Quaker beard rimmed his mastiff-like jaw.

Standing in the lightning flashes like a slouch-hatted Thor, he swept his family with blue eyes that held a volcanic glare: his four grown sons, one on the driver's seat and the others standing beside the team; his wife; his grown daughter; and two young twins shivering on the wagon's back seat, hugging each other for warmth. The wagon had no cover. All of them were drenched to the skin except for the twin girls, Julia and Erika, who were wrapped together in the family's only oilskin slicker. Also fairly dry were their supplies and belongings, heaped in the wagon bed and covered with an old tarpaulin.

"We only can make the best of it," Selma said practically. "We can't just sit like this or we'll catch our death. We have axes; there are trees. You can make us lean-tos, can't you, for shelter?"

"*Ja*," Axel growled.

He gave brusque orders to his sons. Elof was to unhitch the horses and tend them; Rudy was to help the women; Arvid and Lennart were to get out their hand axes and follow their father. He growled the commands. Each boy except Rudy took them in the same surly spirit.

With Rudy's help, Selma unrolled a piece of dry canvas beneath the wagon. It would serve as shelter for the children and womenfolk until the lean-tos had been set up.

Rudy straightened up from the task, giving his mother a quiet smile.

Six feet tall and strongly made, he was still lighter of build than his father and brothers. His face was thin and finely boned;

of the Holmgaard men, he was the nearest to being handsome. If anything robbed him of that, it was the brooding Holmgaard look that bordered on wildness. Just a touch in Rudy's case, but it was enough. Of all the children, Rudy alone shared his mother's heritage of black hair and brown eyes—attributes of what they called a "black Swede" in the old country.

"There you are, *Mor*," he said. "Now I'll rustle up some dry wood. You and the girls try to stay as warm as you can, meantime."

Selma nodded, smiling a little as she watched her eighteen-year-old walk away into the rain. "Come," she told the others briskly. "Crawl under the wagon and lie down. Come, children...."

Rudolf was a good boy, Selma thought as she knelt beneath the wagon, adjusting the old slicker around the shivering twins. Never complaining, always giving a lift to her own spirits when the going was roughest. The dark temper that seemed to lurk in so many Swedes had seemingly been left out of Rudy. And out of his sister Dani, too. Oddly, though they were the brightest and most sensitive of the children, they were also the steadiest.

The near darkness was fitfully illumined by flashes of lightning. Both the seven-year-olds, Julia and Erika, were sniffling fretfully. They sat between their mother and big sister, who glanced over their heads at Selma, lifting her tawny brows with a faintly comical grin.

Not quite as tall as her mother, built along more delicate lines, Dani was fair-skinned and gray-eyed. Her slim face, with its high cheekbones and exquisitely molded planes, had an arresting loveliness that went beyond the bloom of youth. True even here and now, though Dani was as wet and chilled as any of them. Her lips quivered with cold; strands of her white-blond hair had escaped her perky pug and were matted wetly to her cheeks.

Dani never had to feign her sunny nature, as Rudy sometimes did. He had a grave and thoughtful side that his brothers lacked. Dani, a year younger than Rudy and just as sensitive in her way, seemed to wear a kind of gentle armor against life's worst. Yet Selma sometimes worried that the girl's tender

5

and sunny outlook made her too trusting, too prone to see the good even where there wasn't any.

Lying beside them under the wagon box, Selma absently comforted the children, stroking their heads and mildly shushing them, as she gazed out into the slanting veil of rain. Now and then she heard Axel's voice out in the dark, giving his sons gruff orders above the rustle of falling water. Flickers of lightning continued to outline those dark buildings and the rain-pocked lake that covered the level ground surrounding them.

Det förbjude Gud! What a disappointment! To look forward through the weary hours of dark to the arrival here, to a cozy roof and a warm fire, only to find your future home partly under water.

What could have happened since Axel had seen this place last fall?

During the winter they had just spent in Minnesota, snow had fallen heavily. Maybe it had been just as deep in this northwestern corner of Wisconsin, and the spring meltwater combining with heavy spring rains had raised the river so high. Maybe in time the water would go down. But what a thing to be welcomed by. And what had happened once might happen in the future. Were they to look forward to being flooded out of their home again and again?

A tired discouragement had sunk clear to Selma's bones, along with the chill wetness of this night.

She'd had misgivings from the first about their moving to Wisconsin, but had tried not to voice them too stridently. She was an outspoken woman (too damned outspoken for her own good, her father used to say even when she was a girl), and it had been hard to follow her husband's decision as a dutiful wife must. Not that a more passionate argument would have done much good. Axel Holmgaard was as strong-willed for a man as she was for a woman, and law and custom gave him the voice of authority.

At the same time, Selma had to admit with a wry honesty that she most resented Axel's stubbornness when it clashed with her own. Even during their courtship, she'd sometimes thought they were more at war than in love.

Axel and the boys came trudging back to the wagon, dragging a number of spruce trees and pine saplings. They trimmed

6

off the limbs, cut the trunks into ten-foot lengths, and lashed them together with cords to form a twenty-foot-long lean-to, thatching it with the densely needled boughs. On the soggy ground beneath they spread the big tarp that had kept their things dry; it effectively shut out the ground dampness. The rain had begun to slack off, dwindling to a slight drizzle, by the time the shelter was finished. The Holmgaards transferred their gear from the wagon to the lean-to. The children, who had escaped a soaking, were put to bed in a snug cocoon of blankets.

Rudy had obtained a good supply of dry wood by kicking apart a half-rotted deadfall. He got a fire started under a sheltering pine and built it to a roaring blaze. The grown-up Holmgaards gathered around it, gratefully thawing their numb bodies and soaking up its warmth.

"Pa," Lennart said slowly, "the river warn't this high last fall, was it?"

It was not a bright question, but then nobody expected Lennart to come out with anything bright. The big surprise would be if he ever did. Something had been left out of Lennart. It showed as much in his dull eye and thick clumsy body and groping speech as in the things he said. He was twenty-two years old and hadn't grown in his mind since he'd turned twelve.

Axel cleared his throat angrily, but managed to make his reply merely gruff. "No, Lenny. It was way down. It shouldn't be this high now, not even from the thaw."

"Well?" Elof said impatiently. "Just what'n hell is it then, Pa?"

"Watch your damn talk," Axel growled.

It was a rote order; Elof had been swearing openly since he was five. Axel, who'd never made much effort to curb his own language, had been scolding and whipping him for it for all of sixteen years. Quite uselessly.

Axel scowled, tugging his beard and shaking his head. "I don't know. I just don't know. It's too damn dark to tell anything now. When it gets light enough, we'll have a look around."

He tipped his face to the sky. By now the rain had died to

7

a fine misting. "Let's get into dry clothes, all of us. Then we'll get some hot food in our bellies."

It was a welcome suggestion. For better or worse, this was the end of a rough journey. The start of a new life.

✿ two ✿

AXEL HOLMGAARD HAD come from Sweden in 1881, at the age of seventeen. Like many another immigrant youth, he'd been a second son who'd bitterly watched an older brother fall heir to all their family's holdings. That was the law in the old country, and Axel and his brother had never gotten along; he would not stay to work his ancestral soil for mere wages, largess of a brother who despised him. Axel had taken passage for America, and he had never looked back.

A restless foot had carried him from the logging camps of Michigan to the gold camps of Colorado, but in a few years his wanderings had come to an end. Like hundreds of immigrant Swedes, Selma Gotberg's family had settled in Douglas County, Minnesota, and it was here, in the summer of 1886, that Axel had come to work in the wheat harvest. Very soon he and the sixteen-year-old Selma were wed. Within a couple of months she was carrying Arvid. And there was no question of Axel's satisfying his familiar wanderlust when it came on him once more.

Selma's father was generous, turning over a developed piece

of his farm to the young couple. Over the years Axel had added to it, buying up a choice forty acres to the west of him and another forty to the north. When Emil Gotberg had died six years ago, he had willed all his property to his daughter and her husband. So the Holmgaards had owned a fair-sized and thriving farm—until three years ago.

Hail had flattened their wheat one year; locusts invaded it the next. That bad second year had been capped by a miscarriage, Selma's first in twenty-three years. It was as if the Almighty had chosen to visit the plagues of Egypt on them, one after another.

The series of misfortunes had softened Selma's resistance to Axel's mutterings about pulling up stakes and shaking the dust of this damn jinxed place from their feet. (He was as confirmedly superstitious as he was nonreligious.) The dormant wanderlust in him had started to revive—no uncommon thing with men in their forties. He became increasingly irritable, his occasional outbursts of temper more frequent.

Selma had realized that her man's growing discontent must be satisfied or it would spell ruin to their life together. On her part—though it would be hard to tear up her roots, to leave the home and the friends she knew—no really strong ties bound her any longer. Both her parents were gone; her three sisters had all married and moved far away; no family remained to her, except the one she and Axel had made together.

She'd urged her husband to go away for a while, to travel as much and as far as he wished and not to come back until he'd found what he wanted. Axel had been quick to seize on the suggestion, though all his travels had confined him to the Middle West, as if he were reluctant to venture far from home. His laboriously scrawled letters had kept the family posted on his wanderings.

Within three months he'd returned to tell them he had found the place he was looking for. It was in Sayer County in northwestern Wisconsin, a farm with a quarter section of largely cultivated land on the Ottawa River. The country was a near wilderness and heavily wooded, reminiscent for Axel (who always bemoaned the lack of real woods in Douglas County) of the well-forested district in Sweden where he'd grown up. The soil and growing season were right for hay, potatoes, rutabagas; there was plenty of logging in the region, so a man would have no problem finding work in the winter. The farm's owner, George Slocum, had it up for sale, and his asking price of $1,800 had been unusually low. In that year of 1909, even cut-over lands that boasted no improvements at all were selling for between two and ten dollars an acre. But Slocum, anxious to try his fortunes in the far West, had no wish to delay or dicker about the price.

Returning to Douglas County, Axel had lost no time in making inquiries. He'd quickly determined that by putting their own farm on the market, they could easily meet Slocum's price and have a sizable sum left over. However, it was late fall by then. Getting settled into a new place would be trying enough without the hardship of enduring snow and cold. They'd made as good a sale of the old place as Axel had predicted—stressing a proviso that their family might remain in residence on it till the following·April. To this the buyer had agreed. With the necessary cash in hand, Axel had departed for Wisconsin to close the deal with Slocum.

Back in Minnesota once more, he had waited impatiently through the winter, which had been uneventful except for the auctioning off of the bulk of their household goods and farm equipment. Even before the date arrived on which they were to evacuate the old farm, the Holmgaards were on a train to Minneapolis. There they'd switched to an eastbound train that would carry them to Winterfield, the county seat of Sayer County. A few belongings came with them. Most of the things they'd kept had been crated up and left with a neighbor who'd promised to ship them along once the family was settled in.

They had arrived in Winterfield on a murky day in the spring of 1910. At a livery stable Axel had obtained a wagon and team to carry their gear and to spare the women and kids a long walk. They'd set out on the road to the Slocum farm. It was little more than a rough-hewn trail that Axel called a "tote road"; he'd said it had been cut out years ago by loggers for the purpose of hauling supplies to their camps in the woods. Barely wide enough to accommodate a wagon and team, it was ungraded and bumpy; in places it was churned to a thick oozing mud.

Jolting over the rough trace, the wagon had flung Selma

and the girls this way and that. For most of the dreary journey they had elected to walk. They'd still had half the distance to go when the icy pelting rain had begun.

The family's spirits picked up quickly after they changed to dry clothes and crouched around the fire, wolfing down the bacon and biscuits and black coffee that Selma prepared. She put a kettle of water on to boil, then began chopping up meat and vegetables on a flat board. She would keep them bubbling over a low fire all night, and there would be a savory stew for breakfast.

As they'd been impatient to see their new home, they'd delayed in town just long enough to purchase adequate grub for a few days. They would need to lay in many more supplies, and soon.

Axel, starting to glower and mutter again, was working himself into a conviction that dirty work was afoot. *Helvete!* That damn river couldn't have risen this high in the course of a normal spring. *Ja,* something dirty was afoot, and somebody had to be responsible. He meant, by God, to find out who—

"Aw, come off it, Pa," Elof said lazily.

Axel swung toward him. "What? What did you say?"

Elof stood by the fire, holding his hands to it. He gave Axel a faint crooked grin. "I said, come off it. First you get that jinx stuff in your head, now it's some'un's out to get you."

"Well," Axel said ominously. He tramped over to Elof, halted, and set his fists on his hips. "Just what is it *you* call it, sonny? Come, speak up. Tell us all about it."

Elof yawned. "Come on, Pa. Jesus, it's Ma Nature showing the vote, that's all."

The color came up in Axel's face; his beard jutted.

Instinctively, Selma opened her mouth to give Elof a sharp reprimand—then closed it in resignation. Any intercession by her would only heap fuel on the fire. Periodically and quite deliberately, or on mere whim, Elof would provoke his father. But *Gud bevara,* why did it have to be now? In a moment or so the two of them would be in a shouting match that nothing could head off. Or would it go beyond that? Selma only prayed it wouldn't.

"You will make apology for that," Axel thundered, *"now!"*

Elof widened his eyes. "For what?" He gave a loud sneeze, sniffled, and wiped his nose. "Damn, I do believe I have took a chill. Better turn in before I catch my death. 'Scuse me, folks."

He turned his back on them and tramped away toward the lean-to shelter. Cursing, Axel bent and picked up a large piece of wood from the stack of dry punk Rudy had gathered.

Selma cried, *"No!"*

Axel threw the light but solid chunk with a savage overhand heave. It caught Elof between the shoulder blades hard enough to stagger him. He gave a pained grunt, then caught his balance. He turned slowly around, rubbing his back.

A wolfish smile touched his lips.

"Now that wasn't very damn friendly, Pa," he said mildly. "You ain't trying to start up a ruckus with me, are you?"

"It is started!" Axel roared, stalking toward him. "You have got too big for your britches again, sonny, and now it is Axel Holmgaard going to show some votes!"

Elof laughed, edging away from him in a half crouch.

Elof's eyes held a light of battle; he'd never looked quite so cocky and confident. He'd displayed these tendencies since he was a small boy, but as many times as Axel had punished his insolence, it had only grown more biting and provocative. It was a cheerful rather than a mean insolence, but Selma always feared it would lead to worse.

Axel came to a halt, his eyes narrowing. "So," he said between his teeth. "It is to fight you want. It's been a long time, eh?"

"Too blamed long, Pa." Elof grinned. He shucked off his coat, tossed it aside, and beckoned with outstretched hands. "C'mon, ole fellow. Ain't gonna keep me waiting, are you?"

Elof still lacked his full and solid growth; he was lighter than Axel but just as tall, and his rawboned build showed plenty of the same rangy power. He had the same luxuriant thatch of red hair as Axel, and had lately cultivated a silky mustache whose ends drooped past his mouth. Both Arvid and Lennart were stocky and pale-haired; only Elof was a younger image of his father. But he had even more of that wild Holmgaard look.

With a growl that held more satisfaction than anger, Axel

shrugged out of his mackinaw and flung it to Selma as she came up to him. She caught at his arm. "Please! He is not a boy anymore. You could get hurt, one of you. Maybe both."

Axel shrugged her hand away. "Go on, stand off. A long time he has wanted for a good licking. While he eats my food and lives under my roof—"

"What roof?" Elof jeered.

"—he will show respect," his father went on grimly, and began to roll up his sleeves. "There's only one master to a family. This he will learn."

Resignedly, she moved back to the fire. The others stood as they were, watching with a curious show of differing reactions. Rudy appeared sober and concerned; Lennart wore a vaguely interested half grin; Dani's lips were pursed with distress; Arvid looked simply indifferent.

Axel moved in stolidly, as willing as always to wade right into anything that confronted him and take his share of punishment if he could give some back.

Long ago, Selma had realized this was something of a pose on Axel's part. He was a man's man, all right. He liked a good fight, and he never hesitated to tangle head-on with anything that brooked his displeasure. All the same, he fought with calculation. He thought on his feet, and he thought fast; he could move just as fast, in spite of his rangy bulk.

Axel was anything but a stupid fighter. Elof knew it. Rather than close at once with his father, he circled around and away from him, not relaxing that wide taunting grin.

How often those two had fought through the years! It had started with a small boy defying his father and repeatedly getting whipped for it. Next there'd been a teenage Elof, fighting back and always getting beaten bloody. It had been two years since they'd last fought. Elof had been nineteen then, and he'd fought better and harder than ever before. But after taking that beating, he hadn't again provoked his father to the point of a physical exchange. Selma had wondered if he might be biding his time. Now she had the answer.

Elof looked very confident as he made a sudden rush at his father. Then he stepped abruptly to one side, wheeled in and pounded a fist into Axel's kidneys, and wheeled out again. Axel grunted with the blow. As quickly as Elof spun away, it wasn't quickly enough. His father's fist caught him across the neck with a solid wallop that almost knocked him off his feet.

Elof staggered for balance and recovered it. He plunged back into the fray at once, piling into Axel with a savage flurry of blows that drove the older man backward across the clearing. There was nothing panicked in Axel's retreat. He hunched his shoulders and protected his head with his crossed arms. Only a few of Elof's windmilling punches found a vulnerable spot.

Then he dropped his arms suddenly and ducked forward, seizing Elof around the waist. Axel jerked him completely off his feet in one powerful heave, and whirled him around and flung him away. Elof landed on his side with a ground-shaking thud and kept rolling.

He rolled into the fire. With a yowl of pain and rage he scrambled out of the blaze, scattering red coals in every direction. The back of his shirt was smoking. He spat blood from a cut lip and looked at Axel.

"That's the last time you'll do that, Pa," he said softly.

"I ain't even started," Axel rumbled. "Come on, sonny, you wanted it. Come and get it all."

Elof put his head down and charged. Axel made no effort to evade him. But the punch he threw at Elof's head skidded off without slowing his momentum. Elof barreled full-tilt into his father and they crashed to the trampled earth. They rolled over and over, grappling and gouging.

"Stop it!" Selma shouted. "That is enough! You fools, you *dumboms!* You want to kill each other?"

She might have yelled down the wind with as much effect.

Axel had rolled atop his son, pinning Elof by sheer weight and beating at him with those big sledging fists, yet with little effect. The blind full tide of Axel's rage made him clumsy. Elof managed to protect his face with one hand and slug back with the other.

Selma whipped off her shawl, wrapped it around her right hand, and strode over to the kettle of boiling water that Elof's fall had left slightly tilted among the coals. Selma grabbed the metal bale in her wrapped fist, hoisted the kettle, and carried it across to the struggling men.

Swinging the kettle not quite above the combatants, she

seized the skirt of her coat in her free hand and grasped the lip of the searing-hot vessel. She tilted it suddenly.

A gout of steaming water splashed the ground alongside the tussling pair. It splattered both of them.

Axel and Elof scrambled apart, letting out yells of real pain.

Axel got to his feet, clutching at his soaked right sleeve. *"Gud in himmel,* woman!" he bellowed. "What the hell are you about? Is this a pig-butchering, you got to throw hot water around?"

"Ja!" Selma blazed at him. "Two pigs are butchering each other, so I scald the pigs! Maybe it will take all your hair off, eh? Now—you are through with it, or you want more?"

She held the kettle in a threatening manner—and she was angry enough not to bluff. Axel glared for a long moment, chewed the edge of his mustache, and muttered an expletive. He stalked away to the fire. Selma set the kettle down and looked at Elof, who had rolled to a sitting position. The boiling water had drenched most of his left arm and side. He was grimacing to fight back groans of pain.

"So. You will not learn," she said coldly. Maybe you'll never learn. But *Gud bevara* that you think you'll make trouble and not pay. Always there is something to pay.

"All right, Ma. All right!" Still grimacing, Elof got gingerly to his feet. "But Jesus, you burned me something fierce. I am gonna lose me some skin for sure."

"You are lucky at that." Her tone did not relent, but she added, "Come along. I'll put something on it."

"Hey, Pa," Elof called as he followed his mother to the lean-to. "That was pretty close, huh?"

Axel was standing by the fire, mildly swearing as he rolled up his soaked underwear sleeve to inspect his scald burn. He glanced toward Elof. "Pretty close, sonny." Axel was always tranquil after letting off a head of steam. "But you got a ways to grow yet, eh?"

"That's all right," Elof said cheerfully. "I'm still gonna beat hell out of you one of these days, old man."

Axel gave a shout of laughter. "Hah! That will be the day!"

Selma said to Elof in a low fierce voice, "Hush now! For shame! To speak so in front of your sisters! Get off your shirt. Sit down."

Grinning, Elof peeled off his shirt and collapsed on the ground tarp under the lean-to. He winked at the tittering twins. Selma got out a small flat can labeled *Dr. Godbold's Balm of Gilead*, knelt beside Elof, and began vigorously to rub the tarry-looking salve over his scalded arm and side.

"Ouch! Jesus, Ma, take it easy. Come on, hey . . . ouch!"

"If you don't like it," she said grimly, "you know what you can do."

A cocky grin tipped his mustaches. "Yeah? What?"

"Pack your things and leave. You are of age. And I'm sick of all your monkeyshines. If it is not one thing, it's another. The last couple of years, it's been the drinking and the girls. Now this!"

Elof chuckled, swiping a finger across her chin. "Buck up, Ma. Fat chance of me finding any booze or lovin' way out in these woods. About Pa, though—I won't make no promises. I vowed a long time back I was gonna whip hell out of him one day. Reckon I'll just stick around till I do."

Selma slapped a final smear of salve on his arm, fetching another yelp out of him. "So. You think you'll ever be that good a man?"

"Dunno yet." Again his sly grin crinkled Elof's face. "But man oh man, am I gonna have me a bushel of fun finding out."

He gave her a quick kiss on the cheek, grabbed up his shirt, and walked back to the fire, humming jauntily. Selma's face softened; a smile twitched the corners of her mouth. For all his mischief, Elof had a way about him. Easy to see why he'd never lacked for willing female company during various escapades.

The fire was crumbling to dull glimmers as the family rolled into their blankets with all their clothes on. The girls were installed under one side of the long lean-to, the boys under the other, and Axel and Selma settled into a space between them.

Axel laid a big hand on his wife's stomach. "You are still mad, *käresta?*"

She pushed his hand away, murmuring, "Don't, *dumskalle*. This is not a bedroom."

"Well?"

"No. Well, a little mad."

"That passes."

Selma yawned; she blinked at the dark roof of logs overhead. "Axel, what will we do? Our place is under all that water. What if—?"

"Hush. We will sleep. Tomorrow we'll see what to do."

She felt for his calloused hand under the blanket. When his voice had that sound to it, deep and calm and comforting, it always had one sure effect. It dispelled all doubts. Holding his hand tightly, she dropped off to sleep.

ಸ *three* ಸ

LIKE ANY FARM family, the Holmgaards were used to rising at what town dwellers regarded as an ungodly hour. Well before sunup, when the darkness had given way to enough gray light to see by, they were rousing themselves.

Rudy was the first to roll out of his blankets. He crawled from under the lean-to and stood up, stretching the cramps out of his muscles as he gazed about at the surrounding country, which the night and storm had shut off from view. The land Pa had bought covered a quarter section, or one hundred and sixty acres, and even in this vague morning light he could get a rough idea of where most of it lay in each direction.

Pa had said the Ottawa River formed the east boundary of their land. Apparently the house and outbuildings had been built close to the river. But it was hard to tell exactly where the riverbed was, for the overflow had spread across much of the flat ground surrounding the buildings. Besides the rambling one-story house, there was a snug-looking barn, a woodshed, a chicken coop, and a pigpen. A little to the west, an A-frame root house had been dug into the slope of a small hillock. This was the only piece of ground that formed an island above the flooded area.

The rain had ceased hours ago. The water lay bright and glassy in the light of dawn.

Off north of the place, the watery stretch ended at the bottom of a broad-loaf-shaped ridge, well timbered and flat at its summit. The land to the west inclined upward. As near as Rudy could tell, about seventy acres of it had been cleared, but probably no more than forty acres had ever been cultivated. More land had been cleared to the south; it was lower and flatter, and a lot of it had been covered by the flowage. At its far end, a ragged edge of woods rose above the water level, cutting off the view in that direction so completely that you couldn't tell how far the inundation reached.

What was clear, though, was that not only the house site but a large chunk of their whole quarter section lay a foot or more under water.

Axel saw the same thing a few moments later, as he emerged from the makeshift shelter. When he perceived how far onto his land the water had ranged, he swore just once, almost tonelessly. His rage was burning low and steady, still intense but under control. He'd accepted the bitter facts. If the situation held any more surprises for him, they wouldn't catch him off guard.

Axel began tramping away toward the south, skirting the edge of the flood.

"Pa!" Rudy called after him. "Where you going?"

Without slacking his pace or glancing back, Axel growled, "To find what makes the water high."

"Can I come along?"

Axel made a brusque motion of assent with one hand. Rudy hurried after him.

By now the others were rousing from their blankets, sleepy and grumbling. "Hey!" Selma called now. "Where do you two go? Don't you want breakfast? The stew is ready."

"It will keep!" Axel snapped over his shoulder.

He kept walking so fast that Rudy had to stretch his own long legs to stay alongside him.

"What you think's doing it, Pa?" he asked. "Beavers?"

"Not beavers, not on a river this deep and wide. More likely a tangle of driftwood got caught on a snag and a lot more piled behind it and now the river is blocked." More than an afterthought made him add grimly, "Beavers ain't all that make dams."

"Oh—you mean men?"

"*Ja.* Lumbermen. That old tote road we took to get here— it was never used except by Slocum, anymore. That was last fall. But there been wagons on it already this spring. The ruts show. Maybe there was sleds using it last winter, too."

"What does that mean?"

"It means likely someone's started a logging operation up the river a ways." Axel shut his jaws with a snap. "No more talk. Use your head; keep your eyes open. All I tell you, you can tell for yourself."

Rudy fell silent, smarting a little as they tramped along.

He was a daydreamer. As with most daydreamers, a good deal slipped by him that wouldn't escape a more observant eye. Axel, who noticed practically all tangible details of everything, didn't understand that. Not an imaginative man, he tended to discount the importance of anything outside his own ken. He wasn't even aware of the fundamental differences that Rudy easily perceived and accepted. For Axel, it all boiled down to being competent in the things a man was expected to know. Either his sons cut the mustard or they didn't, and he never awarded any of them A's for effort. With Dani and the twins, it was different. Axel didn't expect them to be anything but girls; if they were lucky they might one day be women as good as their mother.

He and Rudy tramped into the line of jack pines that had cut off their view to the south. The shining cut of backed-up river had spread into this grove of stunted, gnarled trees. As the land tended lower, the water got deeper and spread out wider, flooding the jack-pine trunks up to a depth of two or more feet. They had to circle wide around the flowage.

They emerged suddenly from the jack-pine growth and came onto a wide overgrown meadow. This was old timberland that had been logged off twenty or thirty years ago. Second-growth wilderness had partly reclaimed it. The loggers had taken only the giant pines; where these had grown, nothing but rotting stumps and brambly overgrowth remained. It gave Axel and Rudy an unobstructed view of the landscape for quite a ways.

Axel came to a stop, letting out a muttered oath.

Not over forty yards ahead of them and to their left a solid-looking dam stretched across the river. It was newly built, all right. The sawed planks and butt ends of the unpeeled logs that comprised it had a fresh-cut look.

As they advanced across the cleared area, holding to the edge of the water, Rudy got a better look at the obstruction. Being new to logging country, he'd never seen anything just like it. About seventy feet across, the dam consisted mostly of a central span built of massive squared-off logs. Three sluice gates made of rough boards were set in a row of vertically grooved frames at the top of this section. The pink light of sunrise glinted on the iron wheels that could be used to raise or lower the gates. At either end of the dam a sturdy wing built of heavy planks extended from the main section to the river-bank, meeting it at an out-slanting angle.

On the downstream side of the dam, water that seeped over it added to a brisk flow. A maze of boulders cluttered the shore-line. Before the dam had been thrown up, the river above this point had boiled over rock-fanged rapids. Probably logs driven from upstream had snagged on the rocks and other logs would back up behind them, forming monumental jams. Log drives would be hung up for days or weeks. To move logs over such stretches of whitewater, a dam must be erected to create a high level of water. When the logs reached this part of the stream, the dam could suddenly be opened. The rush of water would sluice the logs through the dam and far downstream.

In his breakdown of this bit of primitive engineering, Rudy hadn't paid much attention to the good-sized shanty that stood on high ground some yards west of the dam.

Now he took better notice of it. The logs that formed its walls had been somewhat squared by adze and drawknife; the plank roof was covered with tar paper. Like the dam itself, the building had a new raw look. It commanded a good view of the dam and the cleared area around it for a distance of maybe two hundred yards.

And it was occupied. Smoke began to puff from a tin stack on its sloped roof. Someone was laying a breakfast fire.

Axel hadn't paused after his first sight of the dam. He'd kept tramping straight on, jaw set and eyes narrowed, toward the shanty.

Its plank door opened now. A man stepped out. He was shirtless, wearing a pair of stagged trousers whose ragged edges, crudely cut off lumberjack-style to avoid being entangled in machinery, revealed the legs of his red flannel underwear. He yawned prodigiously, combing a hand through his mussed black hair. His other hand held a rifle that was pointed carelessly downward.

"Hey," he called lazily. "What you fellas looking for?"

Axel came to a stop about a hundred feet away, studying the man with a flat, hooded gaze. "Maybe," he said, "I'm looking for you. This dam, it's yours?"

"Naw. Uh-uh." The man grinned slowly. "I help build her, though."

A slight and wiry fellow with an impudent long-jawed face, he had a funny accent. French, it sounded like. When he grinned, his face had the sly feline look of a bobcat's. It was bisected by a pair of dapper mustaches.

"I'm Axel Holmgaard," Axel said quietly. "I own the farm here. This is my son Rudy. Now maybe you say who you are."

"Sure. I am name' Jean LeBoeuf. They call me Canuck John. It's easier to say, eh?"

"So. Then can I ask what the hell you do here?"

"Ha, me?" LeBoeuf lifted his shoulders, grinning. "I'm a watchman. This one here . . ."

He tipped his head backward. A hulking figure of a man filled the doorway of the shanty, then stepped out beside LeBoeuf.

"This one is name' Bear Roback," chuckled LeBoeuf. "He watches too. Ha ha, some fella he is, eh?"

Rudy stared.

The second man was close to seven feet tall. He was so huge-boned that although he looked hard as oak, with great slabs and bands of muscle showing against his shirt and pants, he'd probably tip the scales at three hundred pounds. His arms were long and apelike, with great spatulate hands. Roback's head was entirely hairless, lacking even eyebrows, and his skull and jaw were malformed and oddly elongated. His small eyes

23

were deep-set under a shelving ridge of brows; no glimmer of expression showed in their pale flatness.

If Axel was remotely impressed, he didn't show it. "You are watchmen, so. What do you watch?"

"Is it not plain?" LeBoeuf said amiably. "Bear an' me watch a dam."

"*Ja*, why?"

"Ah. You maybe know, m'sieu, that the big lumber companies, they have the feuds going. It is always so, *n'est-ce pas?*

"Sometimes threats are spoken. Blows are struck, guns are fired. Sometimes, even, dams are blown up with dynamite. It is a common thing. In the spring when the logs come down, it is ver' common. That is why we are here to watch the dam."

"Working for who?" Axel's voice was quiet, but his throat muscles stood out like cords.

"The Gannett Logging and Boom Company." LeBoeuf inclined his head in a mocking bow. "It owns pinelands up the river, if you did not know. Now these are opened for logging, and the first drive will come down the river to Winterfield in a few days. The dam, it must be ready for it."

"That's just fine," Axel said slowly. "Only this dam, the wing of it rests on my land."

"Ah? Per'aps so, per'aps no." LeBoeuf thoughtfully scratched his crotch, then showed all his teeth in a smile. "But, M'sieu Home-gar, that is no affair of ours. We have the orders. That is all we do, carry out the orders. And now I think I mus' tell you, you are trespassing the hell out of land belonging to the Gannett Logging and Boom Company."

"To me—"

"M'sieu, I do not argue. I tell you what I am told to say. *Mais non*, I do not argue. A man can shoot a trespasser."

Canuck John LeBoeuf raised the rifle ever so slightly, and still he smiled, but Rudy felt a sudden coldness. You didn't have to guess why a man like this one had been picked to guard a dam. The reason showed in his eyes and face. Given the excuse, he would kill without a second thought.

Without a word, Axel turned and headed back toward the camp, his strides long and angry.

Rudy had to half run to keep up with him. "Pa—what are you thinking?"

"I think," Axel said very softly, "that Farmer Slocum has gone and slipped one over on Axel Holmgaard."

⚜ *four* ⚜

SELMA HAD KEPT the stewpot at a low boil all night, getting up now and then to tend it. Now she dished out bowls of stew and filled one for herself, glancing once in a while toward the jackpine woods that had swallowed Axel and Rudy. Everyone shivered a little in the chill dawn as they wolfed down stew and coarse rye bread. Arvid and Elof had built up the fire, and the girls huddled around it as they ate.

"Top o' the morning, folks!"

Elof, startled by the voice, sprang to his feet.

The man had approached the camp so silently that his sudden appearance had gone unnoticed. He was standing at the edge of a poplar grove a little northeast of the camp. He came trotting across the clearing, his step bouncy. He had a small pack slung over his shoulders; a rifle swung in his fist.

Coming up to the fire, he said cheerfully, "Can a man be asking a bite to eat? Smelled your cooking a half mile off."

He had a woodsman's look. His trousers and brush jacket and old felt hat were well worn and much patched, faded to neutral colors that blended with hues of the leafless woods.

26

Instead of the high-laced boots favored by most outdoorsmen nowadays, he wore thick-soled moccasins of cured hide that came to his knees and were tied in place over his trouser legs by rawhide thongs.

Selma returned the greeting politely. She filled another bowl, glancing curiously at the newcomer as she bent above the kettle.

He, in turn, was sizing up all of them and their camp with small eyes that were tough and merry and a remarkably vivid blue. He was a man of about her own age, which was forty. His body was stocky and thick-trunked. He had a look about him, and a way of bearing himself, that was keen and hard and resilient. Such a man might tramp all night and still be fresh for breakfast. Perhaps he'd done so. He was a curiosity for sure, and she didn't think he belonged to the usual run of woodsmen.

Quite suddenly, he turned his eyes full on Selma. He smiled broadly; his teeth were bright and clean.

His face was broad and good-natured, ruddy with its deep weathering, and his hair and short beard were a curly blue-black. Hair so black and eyes so blue were a combination that seemed most commonly found among the Irish; his strong, lilting accent sounded Irish.

She handed him a bowl of stew and a spoon.

"Ah . . . my thanks to you, mistress. Tom O'Dea's the name, and I live down the river a piece. Went out for a bit of hunting upriver yesterday and got caught in the storm. Not that I mind the wet, but I laid up under a sheltering rock and kept me warm the night long. Smelled your fire this mornin' and also your good cooking."

The boys came forward one at a time and gave Tom O'Dea a handshake and their names. Selma introduced herself and Dani and the twins. O'Dea replied firmly and pleasantly to each one. Then he seated himself on an old stump and began to spoon up the stew.

"Ah," he observed between mouthfuls, "this here's eating as fine as it smelled, Mistress Holmgaard."

"Thank you. Would you care for some coffee? It's starting to boil."

"Aye, it smells like a lovely brew."

O'Dea gave her a boldly appraising glance as she handed him the tin cup of coffee.

She was more amused than disconcerted; being the object of men's admiring looks was nothing new to her. Selma's sharply chiseled features had never been conventionally pretty, and as a girl she'd had reason to envy other, smaller and daintier girls. But she knew with some pride that few of those girls could have stood up to the rigors of hard living as she had. Her strong firm-fleshed body had been dragged down hardly at all by work and childbearing. Her skin remained clear and unlined; the contrast of black hair and dark eyes to her milky Scandinavian coloring was as eye-catching as her tall full figure.

All the same, she felt rather too aware of O'Dea's appreciative stare, a more brash and assured one than most men would dare. If she were twenty years younger and less used to it, she would find it hard not to blush.

"Well, well." Smiling a little, he shifted his glance to the flooded buildings. "I heard there was a man named Holmgaard bought old George's place. Your husband, ma'am?"

Selma said yes, and explained that Axel and their youngest son were off investigating the rise of water on their land. O'Dea came over to the fire and refilled his cup from the big coffeepot at the edge of the coals, smacking his lips.

"There now!" he exclaimed. "That's a lovely brew. Nothin' on earth like your true Swede-made java. Or would you folks be from Norway?"

"No, from Sweden. My husband and me were. All the children were born over here. We lived in Minnesota till now."

"Is that so? Most of your immigrant folk in this part of Wisconsin are Norwegian. With the Krauts and Polacks running good seconds. There's a salting of the Irish and our fellow Celts, Scots and Welsh y'know. Some Canucks—them's your French-Canadians—but they come here mostly by way o' Maine, with the logging crews. Even most o' your first-generation immigrants settled here before the turn o' the century."

"But it is the same as everywhere else, I think," Selma said. "The country belongs to the Yankees."

"Don't it always?" Once more he appraised her with those

tough lively eyes. "Can't beat your old Americans, your New Yorkers and New Englanders, for taking over a place. But they been on the American ground long enough to send down roots and bend the native soil to their own. All the know-how is theirs, and all the wealth, too. And that's the whole game anywhere, mistress."

"It does seem so."

"Well," he said contentedly, "it's still a mighty open country, the top o' Wisconsin is. Room for new settlements, new kinds o' people like yourselves. Not too many, ye'll forgive me for hoping. Below Wausau now, that's about a hundred miles southeast o' here, they cut off all the big trees long ago. All o' Wisconsin south of Wausau went to farmin' country a long time ago. Some cities o' goodly size down there. Around Milwaukee, Racine, Kenosha, ye'll find as thriving an industrial region as America can boast. But way up north here, why, it's a halfway wilderness yet. Nothing but a few sawmill towns here and there, and most of 'em will not outlast the big-tree logging, which is near done for. Places like Rhinelander and Merrill and Winterfield will go on 'cause they got other industry. There is also your summer resorts to bring in some money. But you can't crop the land on a big scale this far north. Your growing season's too short, and your sandy and pine-loam soil is too acid. Hay and potatoes is about all it's good for."

"Ah?" Selma raised her brows. "You don't paint a happy picture for us farmers."

"Oh well"—O'Dea made a deprecating gesture—"you'll be making out if you keep your croppin' ideas modest. Stick to spuds and rutabagas and corn for market produce. Raise the fancier truck for your own use. Marsh hay'll do for your cows to eat. You'll raise your share o' problems, too, and being such a far piece from town and no good road on hand will add to 'em, I fear. But you got a strapping crew o' kids to help, you and your mister, and that's no small thing." He grinned. "If you can keep 'em at home. Anyway, it'll be a millenium before the northern woods changes a deal."

"That is satisfactory to you, Mr. O'Dea," she observed.

"Nothing but the truth, ma'am. Up in this country a man can still live as the soul of him lists and beg no man's favor."

O'Dea spoke leisurely between sips of coffee as he relaxed on the deadfall, his legs outstretched and crossed one over the other. He was the image of not quite slovenly contentment. For all his woodsy look there was nothing shy or reclusive about him—and he surely was a talker. Maybe he was enthralled by the sound of his own words. Selma could see how a man might become so, living a free but lonely life in the woods.

Elof came over to the fire to dish up his third helping of stew. He gave O'Dea an oblique look. "You say you live down the river a ways?"

"That's right, me boy. About two miles below yez. Got me a cabin on a bluff and a garden o' sorts and a paddock full o' goats I raise. That and some trapping in the winter is me sole source o' income. It's plenty and to spare. My needs ain't many."

"I guess not. Sort of shy on lady company, ain't you?"

O'Dea returned Elof's grin with an indulgent one of his own. "Oh, I had me a wife some years back. Chippewa woman she was, rest her soul."

"Hey. You been a squawman, huh? How was it?"

Selma said warningly, "Elof!"

"C'mon, Ma. Just wondered how a man comes to matching with a squaw."

O'Dea's grin tightened a little, but he said agreeably, "No secret about it, and not much to the telling. Got myself born in the Bloody Third Ward o' Milwaukee. Back before the great fire o' '92 wiped it out, that part o' the city was like a bit o' the auld sod uprooted, if ye didn't know. Bein' the oldest son of an Irish Catholic family means responsibility is supposed to be your middle name, and responsible is a place I never took to. Run away to the woods when I wasn't much more'n a tad, clear up to Lake Superior. Was just about starved when I come across this band o' Chippewas. They took me in and I stuck with 'em. That was, let's see, spring o' '87. Anyways, the band used to move all over Wisconsin and upper Michigan, and I went where they went. To the sugar bush in the spring, to the river camps in the summer. To the wild-rice beds in fall, to the huntin' grounds in winter. Ah, a great life it was."

Feeling a kind of challenge in his declaration, Selma said, "But you left it, Mr. O'Dea?"

"To be sure, ma'am. Your Indians was getting too set up with white men's ways. Got to sinking roots on their reservations at Red Cliff an' Lac du Flambeau an' Lac Court Oreilles—instead of roaming where they listed. Made new ways for 'emselves, and I liked the old ones best." O'Dea talked on as he dug out a stubby pipe and chewed the stem. "I'd married my Chippewa princess, chief's daughter she was, and we departed from the band. Had three kids before she died bearing a fourth. Then the second two got took by diptheria and there's only the oldest left, my girl Swan. She's hired out to a family near town. Works for her keep and gets her rightful schooling. And there's all of it."

Elof, obviously bitten by a curiosity bug, said, "Huh. Ain't you ever felt the urge to get hitched again?"

"Niver. Oh it's well enough, marriage is. But it's by keeping his feet loose and his fancies free that a man truly lives. Me, I may now pull stakes when I please and come or go when I please. There's a price, me boy, to keeping your soul free. It's first to keep your fancies free."

That, Selma thought grimly, was hardly the sort of advice Elof needed. His fancies were already too free for his own good.

Glancing toward the jackpines now, she saw Axel and Rudy come tramping into sight.

The expression on her husband's face told Selma two things. First, he was angry as the devil about something. Second, and typically, he was already setting his teeth into the problem. When she introduced the two of them to O'Dea, Axel took bare notice of the newcomer. His handshake was perfunctory, his response a gruff and abstracted mutter.

As she handed him a bowl of stew, Selma said, "What is it?"

Slowly, in a brooding and absent manner as he ate, Axel told of what he and Rudy had found. Tom O'Dea paid a mild attention as he took out a pocketknife, opened the small blade, and began to scrape at the inside of his pipe bowl. When Axel had finished, everyone watched him expectantly. But he gave no clue to his thoughts as he paced restlessly up and down, eating his stew.

It was Arvid who finally said, "What'll you do now, Pa?"

"Go to the sheriff about it. I'm pretty damn sure a side of that dam rests on my land. That's something."

Not looking up from his pipe, O'Dea said placidly, "So it is. So it is, Mr. Holmgaard. But what's the good in seeing the law, d'ye think?"

Axel glowered at the visitor. "The good is, I'll have that thing out of the river. If part of it rests on my property, it's part mine. And that damn well gives me a say on it."

O'Dea grinned and raised a finger. "Ah, that may not be quite the case. In fact, if ye'll forgive my saying so"—he chuckled mildly—"not by a dam site."

"What the hell are you saying?"

"Well now, the law's a bit sticky on this point, Mr. Holmgaard. But I know a man's got to get a franchise from the state o' Wisconsin to build a dam across a navigable river. You can be sure the builders o' this one got their franchise—they'd not miss a thing like that. Now you get tampering with a legal dam across a Wisconsin waterway, it's state law you'll be butting against and it's the muckymucks in Madison you'll have to reckon with."

Axel's eyes narrowed to blue slits. "You're saying they can plant a dam on my land and flood it to boot and there's nothing I can do?"

O'Dea shrugged. "Legally, I don't reckon. Oh, a man can sue 'em for damages. But I don't know just what good that'll do either. Ye can try."

"Who are these people? This—company?"

"The Gannett Logging and Boom Company?" O'Dea pulled a pouch of shag from a deep pocket and started to fill his pipe. "The Gannetts own half the blasted county. Or used to. Old Dave Gannett come from Maine in the early seventies. That was right after the federal gov'ment completed its survey of northern Wisconsin and put up tracts of federally owned land for sale at a dollar twenty-five cents an acre. Tryin' to promote settlement and development. A lot o' folk back then, ye see, still thought the northern woods was such sorry country they might's well give it back to the Injuns. Which ye'll forgive me for wishing they had.

"Anyways, old Dave was one o' the first to take the full measure of both the problems and the promise. Wasn't nary a white man's road up in here then, and no good-sized rivers to drive logs to the sawmills down south. But the big timber was here and plenty o' demand for it, what with all the settlement and building on the plains after the Civil War.

"Well, Dave Gannett come up and took a long squint at this country, and invested most of what he had in buying up the best pinelands available. Lot o' folk thought he was crazy. But Dave had taken note of some rapids on the Paradise River where a big dam could be laid across to make a boomage— that's a storage lake for logs—out o' some nearby marshes. Also a fine waterpower to run your sawmills. Took him five years o' haggling to persuade the Midwestern and Northern Railroad to extend a spur line northwest to them rapids. They finally agreed to do it in exchange for half the pinelands Dave had bought up, plus a heavy freight fee on goods shipped in or took out on their rails.

"That's how the town o' Winterfield started at the Paradise Rapids. Dave Gannett's town. It become a supply center for a great passel o' logging camps, most of 'em owned by Gannett. The logs they cut got drove down the tributary streams into the Paradise and then downriver to Winterfield. At the peak there was eight sawmills going day an' night turning out rough-cut lumber. Dave Gannett owned three of 'em himself an' also the planing mill that finished the lumber off. The railroad brought supplies in and carried out the finished lumber.

"When the big trees along the driving streams was all cut, the lumbermen extended operations farther into the woods and run in a narrow-guage railroad to bring the logs to Winterfield. By the time the big trees was almost played out, at the start o' the century, the Gannetts was rolling in wealth. Had money to invest in bringin' new industry to their town, and that they did. Old Dave is gone, died in '03. But his family carries on."

Axel scowled. "So. I was told it is mostly cut-over land in this county. If the logging's petering out, why do these people now build a dam here?"

O'Dea shrugged, swiping a match alight on his pants and

holding it to his pipe bowl. "Oh, there's still sizable parcels of virgin pine here an' there. Not many big enough to log at a profit, but some. One of em's up the Ottawa River mebbe five miles above your place. It was bought up a long time back by a firm that went bankrupt and niver got to logging it. So the Ottawa River got used for log driving above these rapids hard by your place. But it was bound to happen, soon as that fine big tract upriver got opened for logging. Which it was last year, after it got put up for public sale—the Gannetts underbid some other outfits that took a shine to it. That's why you got a dam on your doorstep and a couple o' timber beasts guarding it."

"Against who?" Axel demanded. "The companies that bid against those Gannetts and lost?"

"Just so. The logging game gets that rough betimes, dams get blowed up out o' sheer spite. O' course," O'Dea added amiably, "they might be thinking a certain farmer would try the same, and for good reason. Man, that George Slocum sold ye a pig in a poke. Ain't you guessed as much?"

Axel nodded, his face bitter and musing. "It is plain. Slocum knew a dam would be built here. That's why he sold me the place so cheap—eh?"

"Seems so. Georgie was ever a sly one for seizin' an advantage, but he wasn't no fighter. He'd long thought of going West anyways, and it's nothing he'd think of getting his stake at another fellow's expense." A kind of neutral amusement touched O'Dea's voice. "No native 'ud been taken so, but you was new to these parts and a natural mark. Ye should have inquired around before you put up money—'less you aimed on growing crawdads an' lily pads."

"I took it for what it looked to be," Axel said coldly. "A good piece of land and a good buy. Why should I think of anything like this?" He let his heavy shoulders lift and settle. "What is done is done."

"Spoken like a Viking. A bow to the fates, eh?" Grinning, O'Dea picked up his rifle and lounged to his feet. "Well, I'll be on me way. Nice meeting you folks. Reckon I'll be seeing

you again if"—his brows rose with a quizzical impudence—
"you mean to stay around."

Axel's gaze swept the faces of his family. *"Ja,"* he said
quietly. "We are here to stay."

﷼ *five* ﷼

AXEL DECLARED HIS intention of driving to Winterfield at once. Unwilling to take their visitor's word on the matter of the dam's legality, he wanted to check with the sheriff. After that, Axel said vaguely, he had other things he meant to do. Typically, he didn't enlarge on his plans to the family, and being familiar with his stubbornly close-mouthed moods, nobody asked.

Selma dragged him out of his own preoccupations long enough to point out that they would need to get some things in town: tents for shelter and additional grub supplies. She would accompany him and attend to these matters, and she would need the boys' help. So the whole family might as well come along. Glumly and impatiently, Axel agreed. Arvid, the quiet one, elected to stay behind. He didn't like towns. Neither did Lennart, who became miserably nervous in the bustle and traffic of one.

When the horses had been harnessed and hitched, Selma climbed to the wagon's high seat beside Axel. He growled the team into motion. They jolted toward town on the old tote road.

Rudy and Elof tramped behind the wagon. Dani and the twins tramped ahead of it, slogging through the muddiest places till a sharp word from Selma ended their romping.

The road skirted past the west edge of the Holmgaards' land and ran north along the river—so Axel had guessed—to the Gannetts' logging camp. Just south of the dam, the Ottawa made a sharp bend to the southwest, and the road followed its west bank much of the way to Winterfield. Here and there it detoured deep into the woods to avoid marshes along the river bottom.

Axel said the road had been carved out of the woods many years ago for use by logging crews below the Ottawa Rapids. Afterward only George Slocum had used it; he'd kept it free of brush, but had done nothing to improve it. Neither had the Gannett Company's loggers, who must have merely extended it north of the rapids last winter. The old trace had never been graded except to whittle down any obstructions that might stall wagons or sleds. Some log corduroy had been laid down in boggy places, but the trail was extremely bumpy. Luckily their wagon was a sturdy one. They had bought the vehicle and team of horses from the Winterfield livery stable owner just before leaving town. It had been a hasty purchase, but Axel knew his equipages and his team animals. The wagon had seen a fair amount of use, but Axel had said it was all the better for that, being "seasoned" now.

The country they passed through was attractive enough. Selma could understand why it had seized Axel's fancy. She too had a particular liking for wooded places—just as others preferred to live on open land or in cities or villages. And these were pleasant woods, not overly wild. The scars of old logging showed in decaying stumps and skeleton heaps of slashings, but a lot of dense forest remained. The loggers had left untouched the smaller evergreens, balsam and spruce and cedar, as well as the dense stands of hardwood trees, mostly birch and soft maple and white oak. Gnarled jack pines and straight young poplars, always the first stage of a returning forest, had sprung up on much of the cut-over land. There were rambling belts of meadow overgrown with blackberry brambles and the crisp brown stalks of last year's bracken.

Selma had drawn up a list of the kind and quantity of grub

supplies they would need. Enough to last at least a month. She needed some tools to start a truck garden. They would need other tools and some heavy equipment for farming, but that was Axel's province. No need to concern themselves with furniture and the like till they had a house to furnish. Before leaving Minnesota they had auctioned off to neighbors most of their household goods, mainly the bulky pieces that would be hard to transport. They'd brought with them on the train only a few clothes and bedclothes and other personal belongings, and these would suffice for now.

The road made a wide detour around a flat swamp where nothing grew but sphagnum moss and a few runty tamaracks. Then it climbed back to high ground and swung within sight of the river. As Selma was wondering where Tom O'Dea's place might be—for he'd said he lived a couple of miles down-river—they came in sight of a sizable cabin and its outbuildings. Situated at the brow of a pine-covered bluff overlooking the river, the place merged almost invisibly with the dark pines. It had a snug and ground-hugging look, as if the buildings were as much a part of the hill as the mossy glacial boulders scattered across its flanks.

Just as its owner was like part of the country he roamed. He was home now; smoke eddied from the cabin's stone chimney.

"That is where Mr. O'Dea lives," Selma observed.

"A ridge runner," Axel grunted contemptuously. "He better not take to hanging about our place. I didn't like the looks of that smart-mouth mick."

Selma smiled inwardly. She was sure they hadn't seen the last of Mr. O'Dea.

It was noon before they approached Winterfield; in all that distance on the old road they saw no other sign of habitation. The tote road ended a little north of the town, debouching onto a turnpike that had a firm gravel surface. It appeared to be well traveled by wagons and a very few automobiles. At this point the highway closely followed the Ottawa River, and the Ottawa curved almost due west till it poured into the southward flow of the Paradise. At their confluence the two rivers formed a pocket of land that was Winterfield's south side. The city's south and west sides were bounded by the riverbanks.

A few dwellings were set along the Ottawa's west bank north of the town outskirts, and the road passed close by them. Pigs and chickens roamed freely in the yards and into the road. They took grunting, squawking indignant flight from the occasional passing car or a blat of its bulb horn. With several autos attaining the reckless speed of twenty and more miles an hour, some of the team horses panicking at their approach, dogs setting up a fearful racket in nearly every yard they passed, the Holmgaards rode through a cheerful bedlam that contrasted with the sylvan quiet of the woods they'd just quitted.

Many people in the wagons that passed them waved or called out greetings; so did people out tending to their yard chores. This was a friendly country, like the farm district where they had lived in Minnesota. Selma felt a lift of spirits. The town had seemed a very depressing place when they had arrived late yesterday. It had been dark and chilly and the weather had driven people indoors.

They were nearing the edge of town when Elof swung a long stare at a house they were passing. A girl was sitting on the porch peeling potatoes. She looked part Indian and she was very pretty. But she had the bold and roving look that you associated with outright tarts. The smile she flashed in reply to Elof's grinning stare seemed actually wanton.

Selma knew that voicing a reprimand would do no good. It would only amuse Elof—or prompt him to some harebrained act of defiance. As he'd grown older, any attempts to curb his antic impulses had proved more and more useless.

All the land adjacent to the town had been pretty well cleared off during the thirty years of Winterfield's existence; it was level enough to allow for expansion as the town grew. But apparently Winterfield had done little growing in recent years. Even toward the edge of town few new buildings were in evidence. The surrounding sand flats from which trees and brush had been cleared were overgrown by sweet fern and blueberry bush. Winterfield's rise had coincided with the logging boom; when that had subsided, the town's growth had all but ceased.

Still, it was a pleasant and bustling community. More than a village or small town, less than a real city. A mild traffic of wagons and drays and a handful of automobiles flowed along the main street. The avenues were unpaved and uncobbled, but were surfaced with a dirt-and-sawdust composition that had packed down hard and smooth. As in other towns of the time, sidewalks of planks or bricks were being replaced by concrete ones. But Selma noted a puzzling fact: The wooden walks were pocked almost to shreds by thousands of tiny holes, and the newer stretches of concrete were badly chipped.

She asked Axel about it.

"Lumberjacks' smallpox," he grunted. "Them timber beasts wear steel calks on their boots. They come riding logs down the river in the spring, down to the sawmills, and then there's all kinds of hell-raising goes on in town. Messed-up sidewalks is the least of it."

A steady whining roar of noise seemed to hang over the town. Yesterday Axel had said it came from the sawmills along the shore of the boomage lake north of town. At one time Winterfield had boasted eight mills that had run day and night; now all but two of them were closed down. This infernal racket was just a sample of what used-to-be. A logging town, Axel had said firmly, was no damn place to live. Each mill was equipped with a big sawdust burner where wood scraps and tailings were disposed of. When the wind was right, the burners would sweep the town with acrid clouds of smoke and, not infrequently, showers of sparks. The hazards of this situation needed no explaining. A lot of the stores along the street were frame buildings scoured by years of weathering to a tinder-dry look.

A murky funnel of smoke was pouring from somewhere beyond the buildings toward the east side of town. Dani said, "Is that one of those burners you told us about, Papa?"

Axel shook his head dourly. "People told me that is a factory for making paper. Logging ain't such a big thing as it used to be, so they built that stinking thing to keep the town going. Plenty towns in the north of Wisconsin, anywhere there's pulpwood and waterpower to be had, have built up paper mills. Worse than any sawmill they are. Damn near as noisy and stink up the country a hundred times worse."

He brought the team to a stop in front of Sam Overland's General Merchandise Store.

"Buy what you need," he told Selma. "I have business with the sheriff, and now I will get to it."

The county courthouse was a two-story building at the end of Main Street. It was set back on a winter-withered square of lawn fronted by handsome basswood trees and a neatly trimmed hedge. Axel angled across the lawn to the side door with a black-lettered sign SHERIFF above it and went down a short flight of stairs to a basement corridor. His heavy work shoes rang hollowly on the concrete floor as he tramped down the hall and turned through an open doorway into a gloomy cement-walled room. Dimly lighted by two small high basement windows, it was plainly furnished with a filing cabinet, a pair of rolltop desks, several chairs, and a telephone on the wall.

Two men were seated by the desks, idly talking. One, a youngish fellow with pale red hair and freckles, wore rough woodsman's clothes. He was so long and angular that his whole lank frame seemed to drape itself into accordionlike pleats to the contour of his chair and the desk on which his legs were propped.

"Hoddy," he said, not stirring a muscle.

Axel nodded briefly. He shuttled his glance to the older man, whom he assumed was the sheriff. Immense and porcine of build, this man filled his chair, his shapeless and rusty black suit bulging with ridges of hard rather than soft fat. His jaw shelved like a vise out of his comfortable wreath of chins; for comfort's sake he wore no collar. His eyes were green and cold and shrewd.

"Hello there," he said affably, extending a hand but not troubling to rise. "I'm Joe Pleasants, sheriff o' this county. This here's Monty Harp, my deputy. Something I can do you for?"

Axel said his name and shook hands with both men. Not wasting words, he told how he had purchased George Slocum's farm, paying good money in good faith for land that was now flooded. Sheriff Pleasants nodded placidly; he laid a hand as broad and flat as a seal's flipper on his desk and gently drummed his fingers. Obviously none of this was news to him.

Meaning that, by now, Axel thought grimly, the whole country knew how a dumb Swede had got himself suckered.

"Well now, that's some story, Mr. Holmgaard. Just what is it you want from me? You want to sue Georgie Slocum for fraudulent dealing, I'm afraid you are out of luck. He's gone from the country and didn't leave no forwarding address. Wouldn't do much good no ways. Afraid you got taken proper and the condition is binding."

"I didn't come for that," Axel said coldly. "A wing of that dam rests on my land. I understand this family, these Gannetts, they have a license for such a dam."

"That's right." The sheriff's chill eyes blinked solemnly. "That waterway belongs to the state, Mr. Holmgaard, and you don't go fooling with any dam that's built across it."

"Whose dam is it?"

"Beg your pardon?"

"I say, who does this dam belong to, then? If the river belongs to the state, is the dam theirs? If it does not, whose is it?"

"I don't quite follow—"

"Maybe, if part is on my land, it belongs half to me."

The sheriff heaved forward in his chair with a soft "I'll be damned" and clapped both big hands on his knees. "Ain't that some question now." He chuckled; his chins shook. He glanced at his deputy, who grinned and shrugged one shoulder.

"I dunno," Pleasants said amiably. "Could be a real hair-splitter. But the Gannetts been franchised by the state legislature and they built the dam. That gives 'em a right, way I look at it. I reckon the courts would too."

"I see," Axel said and added without a pause; "Possession is nine tenths of the law, eh?"

"Well, that goes without saying."

Axel dug a flat can out of his pocket. He unscrewed its lid, took out a pinch of pungent *snus*, and stowed it between his gums and cheek. He closed the can and held it in his hand, gazing at it. "I take it you won't do nothing," he said quietly.

"Not won't, mister. Can't."

"All right, can't. What you think I should do?"

Pleasants shrugged broadly. "Hell, I dunno. You might try settling out of court with 'em."

"You think that will do any good?"

42

"You want a flat yes or no, I'd have to say no." The sheriff paused, isolating his next words. "Since old Dave Gannett passed on seven years ago, his three sons have took over. Leastways that's how it's supposed to look. There's Beau and Adam and Shadrach, and you'd have to say Beau is the only one of 'em as tough as his pa was. But it ain't him, or any of 'em, you'd really have to deal with. It's their ma. Dave's widow. Letitia Gannett is the real head o' the family, of all the business dealings, everything. And she has one hell of a shrewd adviser in her brother Saul. Reckon you'd have to say Saul Peregrine plots the course, Mrs. Gannett gives the orders, and her son Beau carries 'em out." Pleasants glanced at his deputy again. "Would you say that's about how it stacks up, Monty?"

Harp nodded lazily. "Right on the bean."

"This woman, Mrs. Gannett," said Axel. "Is she tough too?"

"Tough as an old shoe," the sheriff said promptly.

"But a lady, Joe," drawled Harp.

"Right down to her toes." Pleasants' chair creaked to a massive shift of weight. "Mr. Holmgaard, now here's my advice. Don't you get fooling with that family. The Gannetts are used to doing things their way. Own half this town, and I mean literally. A good share o' the folks in it work for 'em. Friends o' theirs hold most public offices in the city and the county. They got other friends down in Madison, important friends. You got any idea at all of going up against 'em, like trying to secure payment for damages, I suggest you drop it. You're just a hard-luck farmer, Mr. Holmgaard. Can you afford a drag-out fight in the courts? Can you even afford to hire legal help? Do you figure any of it would do you a lick o' good? My advice, forget it. You still got a jag o' land, some of it cultivated, and there's more you can put under plow."

"I got a house full of water, too," Axel declared flatly. "Along with a barn and other buildings."

"Tear 'em down. Set 'em up on higher ground. Hell, man—be a sight cheaper in the long run."

Axel looked from one man to the other; he raised his shoulders and let them settle. Now you have been told, he thought.

You know what you knew you would get from the law, and that is nothing. Now you can do what you have to for yourself.

"Thank you for the advice," he said. "There's one more thing I would ask you. Where does the county register of deeds have his office?"

℞ six ℞

AS SELMA MADE her choice of grub supplies, Rudy and Elof carried the kegs and sacks of groceries out to the wagon. Most of her selections were dry staples in bulk—beans, flour, coffee, dried fruits, and the like. She also took her pick of three large canvas tents and some gardening tools. Afterward she ran an expert eye over the loaded wagon bed and gave a satisfied nod.

"That's good. Now we'll wait for your father. Maybe there'll be things he will want to pick out for himself."

Elof shifted from one foot to the other, hands on his hips. "Pa could be quite a while getting his business settled," he said idly. "Ought to give us time for a look around the town."

Selma raised an eyebrow. "Oh? What do you have in mind? You want to take us all to the drugstore for a soda, Elof?"

Rudy rubbed a hand over his mouth to hide a grin. Ma hadn't missed the byplay between Elof and that Indian-looking girl they'd passed on the edge of town. Elof was honing to get back to his old tricks—knowing full well that Ma was onto him and not the least abashed by it.

"Nope," grinned Elof. "Not even to a saloon for a drink. I just thought we might each of us look around on our own." He spoke the last words over his shoulder; he was already tramping away down the sidewalk.

"If you don't get back when it's time to leave, we'll go without you!" Selma called after him. If he heard her, he gave no sign. With a slight shake of her head, she glanced at Rudy. "Well, Rudolf. You want to look around too?"

"I'd like to, *Mor*. If that's all you'll need me for."

"Yes, that's all. Go on." Her gaze swiveled to the twins. Julia and Erika were seated on the store stoop gnawing on licorice sticks to which she'd treated them, their mouths bracketed with sticky stains. "Come along, children. We'll have a soda."

"Can I go with Rudy, Mama?" Dani tossed her head, her blue eyes sparkling. "There's so much to see in a new town!"

"*Ja*, but see you stay close to your brother. Don't go traipsing off by yourself. A rough town like this, it's no place for a girl alone."

Flanked by the twins, Selma quartered across the street to Blankenship's Drugstore.

Dani took Rudy's arm, saying gravely, "Do you mind squiring a sister about town?"

Rudy looked down at her with a grin. "Hate it."

In fact he was proud of Dani, of her quiet loveliness and fine ways and nice disposition, pleased to be seen with her. Of his brothers and sisters she was the one nearest him in age—just a year younger—and the only one with whom he could exchange anything like real confidences. They'd always been close, even as toddlers, when a rivalry for parental affection would have been taken for granted. But all the Holmgaards felt the same about Dani: She was the apple of their eye, the gentle and loving and bright-spirited one.

Rudy would have liked to explore the north outskirts of Winterfield, where the sawmills were; he was curious about their operation. But he knew Dani was eager to window-shop along the main street. So they loitered along the sidewalk, peering at the wares in each display window.

They came to a stop in front of a store whose sign proclaimed: JANE'S DRESS SHOP—DRESSES AND MILLINERY MADE

46

TO ORDER. Dani exclaimed over a row of hats ranked in a display case.

"Oh Rudy . . . can we go inside?"

He smiled ruefully. "We can't afford to buy any frills, kid. I wish we could."

"I know. I just want to look at everything."

Rudy followed her into the shop, looking about him with a twinge of discomfort. The place smelled of dress goods; the walls were lined with shelves stacked with ready-made garments and bolts of cloth. Behind a counter an attractive middle-aged woman was ringing up a sale on the cash register while she chatted with a lone customer. The door to a back room was open, and through it he glimpsed a long cutting table, a Singer sewing machine, and a couple of dressmaker's dummies.

Dani's attention was taken by a display stand of ladies' shoes at one end of the counter; she ran her hands over them, exclaiming softly. Rudy wished he could buy her something. But all the coin he had in pocket wouldn't pay for a paper of pins.

"Thank you, Rachel." The middle-aged clerk handed the customer her change. "Do you think you can manage all those packages by yourself?"

"I think so, Jane."

The customer had made quite a number of purchases. Picking up the wrapped parcels one by one, she was having trouble balancing all of them in her arms. As she turned from the counter, she dropped a bundle. Rudy walked over and bent to pick up the package, yanking off his cap as he straightened up.

"Here you are, ma'am."

She smiled at him. "Thank you. Will you lay it on the counter, please? I am afraid I'll have to make two trips to get all these things home."

"Perhaps the young man will help you carry your bundles," the proprietress said.

Rudy hardly heard her. He was gazing at the customer, at her beautiful smiling face above the stack of parcels she clutched. She had skin like new cream. The smooth coils of her hair under a small hat seemed to contain gold of sunlight, though no beam of sun touched it. Her eyes were deep and alive, full

47

of sea-green lights. She wore a dove-gray suit that was demurely tailored to the fullness of her bosom and hips, the slimness of her waist.

As he realized how he was staring, Rudy's face went warm. "Yes, ma'am. Be pleased to give you a hand."

"If it wouldn't be a terrible imposition..."

"No ma'am, not at all." He looked at Dani a bit sheepishly. "Uh... would you mind...?"

"Go ahead, Rudy." Considerate of his embarrassment, she hardly glanced away from the shoes. "I'll wait for you here."

Warmly blushing, Rudy gathered up all but one of the bundles in his long arms. The woman called Rachel took that one; she held the door open for him as he marched out of the shop. Afterward she fell into step beside him, turning left on the sidewalk and moving a little ahead to guide him.

"I am Rachel Merrick," she said. "I haven't seen you about, have I?"

"Not likely, ma'am. I'm Rudolf Holmgaard. Just came on the train yesterday with my family. We are settling a ways up the Ottawa River."

"Oh yes. I'd heard that a Swedish family had bought Mr. Slocum's farm." She gave him a smiling look over her shoulder. "Is the young lady your wife or sweetheart? Or, as I'd guess, your sister?"

"I didn't know it showed that much."

"Well, the differences *are* quite striking, Mr. Holmgaard. But yes, there's a family resemblance."

Rudy managed to make answers readily enough, but he felt tongue-tied. He couldn't remember ever seeing a woman so radiantly beautiful (even if she was a little old—he guessed twenty-eight or twenty-nine). Rudy's favorite reading was the Sherlock Holmes stories; to cudgel his brain away from his shyness, he tried to draw some deductive conclusions about Rachel Merrick. Her husband must be an important man in Winterfield. Her clothes were fine, and she could afford to buy a lot of them. Her manicured appearance indicated that menial chores in her home were handled by domestics.

Yet the side street onto which she now led Rudy seemed to be anything but a prosperous neighborhood. She stopped by a gate set in a rickety fence that fronted a big rambling frame house. It looked as if it had been jerry-built in sections whenever its owner or owners could afford to add onto it.

Rachel held the gate open for him and closed it behind him. She peeled off her gloves as she went ahead up the flagstone path to the wide veranda. As she took a key from her reticule, he noticed that her left hand was ringless. Both hands were reddened and worn enough to prove she didn't evade her share of housework.

Rudy gave up on any further Holmesian deductions.

She unlocked the door and admitted them to a large and well-lighted parlor. Its furnishings, appropriately genteel if a bit shabby, didn't fit the image of a wealthy widow or single woman. No lace-woven antimacassars were in evidence, but several ashtrays were. And a definitely masculine flavor was lent the room by trophy heads of deer and black bear and a collection of antique weapons mounted above the mantel of a huge fieldstone fireplace.

As though she sensed his puzzlement, Rachel said casually, "I let to boarders. Most of them are single men without families who own a business or practice a profession in Winterfield. This way, please."

They passed through a doorway hung with beaded portieres and into a dining room with a long oaken table flanked by eight leather-bottomed chairs. At her direction Rudy deposited the packages on the table. "Thank you very much." She unpinned her hat, turning a dazzling smile on him. "Surely you'll accept a cup of coffee before you leave? It's the least appreciation I can show for your help."

Rudy said yes before he remembered that Dani was waiting. But the millinery displays should occupy her attention for a while—no need to hurry. He followed Rachel Merrick into the kitchen, where a woman, standing with her back to them, was scrubbing an enormous roasting pan in an oversize sheet-metal sink. She didn't bother to look around, but the smooth round arms bared by her rolled-up sleeves showed she was young.

Rachel said, "Sit down, Mr. Holmgaard," as she went to the big Monarch range and felt the coffeepot for heat.

Rudy seated himself at the kitchen table. When she set the mug of coffee before him, apologizing because it wasn't quite fresh, he took a sip and said it was fine: hot and strong, the way he was used to it.

There was a low whine and a sudden pawing at the back door. Rachel went to open it. A gangly large-footed black pup who looked to be predominantly retriever came bounding in. He scampered around Rachel, his hindquarters squirming with abject pleasure. She gathered him up in her arms.

"Honestly," she said with a laugh, "I don't know what to do with you! You don't take to housebreaking worth a darn."

The woman at the sink swung around to face them. Rudy saw she was only a girl, his own age or a little younger. Sturdy and thick-waisted in a shapeless dress, she had a round face with a thin mouth and features that were sharp and stern. Her skin was ruddy and moist from the steamy dishwater. Her bright pale eyes told of a temper that was too strong for the hired girl she obviously was.

"That dog!" She pointed at the pup with a scouring brush. "He has made his last mess on the floor while I work here. I tired am of cleaning up after him. He will go or I go."

She had a thick immigrant accent much like that of newly arrived Scandinavians Rudy had known in Douglas County. Along with making v's of her w's, she pronounced "that" and "the" as "zat" and "ze," which argued that she was from some German place. Anyway, she wasn't much to look at and was a crosspatch to boot. Rudy went back to watching Rachel Merrick over the rim of his cup.

"Now, Lotte," she said in gentle reproval, "I know Otto is a stray. But it's you who took him in and fed him—even gave him a cute name."

"*Ja*, a mistake it was! I tell you, no more dog messes I clean up! If *you* to clean up for him would like, *fräulein*..."

Rachel grimaced. "Not really. But I can't just turn him out. Mr. Holmgaard, does your family own a dog?"

"No, ma'am. Pa had a couple hounds for hunting, but he sold 'em to a neighbor before we left Minnesota."

"Then perhaps you'd care to take this one? He's yours for the asking—and he should make a first-rate hunter."

"Ha!" Lotte gave a short laugh. "A good messer he makes."

"Sure," Rudy said with a grin. "Can't matter how he messes

around our place, 'cause Ma wouldn't let him stay in the house anyway."

When Selma and the twins left Blankenship's soda fountain and came back to the wagon, none of the others had returned. Selma glanced up and down the street. She saw Dani standing in front of a millinery store, talking with a young man.

The two of them were chatting animatedly, as if they were old friends. The man was big and handsome and well-dressed; he was smiling broadly. Dani gave a quick light laugh to something he said.

Selma's lips thinned. "Get in the wagon," she told the children. "Wait for me."

She walked briskly up the sidewalk toward her daughter and the stranger. Before she reached them, the young man gave Dani a slight bow, tipped his "summer straw" to her and strode away up the street, twirling his malacca walking stick in one hand. Dani stood looking after him a moment. Then she turned, her face pensive and smiling.

Seeing her mother, she blushed in confusion.

"Oh . . . hello, Mama."

"So. Who is your friend?"

"Just a . . . young man I met. I was coming out of the store and bumped into him and . . . we started to talk."

"For shame, Dani Holmgaard! To carry on so—talking and laughing on a public street with a man you have not properly met. The very idea!"

"I'm sorry, Mama." Dani's cheeks were pink. "I didn't think . . . he seemed so nice and I didn't think of any harm in it."

"Ha! I bet he's nice, all right," Selma said grimly. "He's a real dandy fellow, that one."

"But he did introduce himself, Mama. His name is Adam Gannett."

Gannett. The name of the rich family that O'Dea had said owned the town and had built that dam. Selma said, "Hm. Well, where's that brother of yours? Where did he go off to?"

"Oh, Rudy . . . here he comes now," said Dani, relieved by the diversion.

Rudy was coming along the sidewalk toward them. He wore

a strange look, a look that was dreamily bemused and far from unhappy. He was carrying a gangly black dog in his arms.

"So!" Selma exclaimed. "Where do you traipse off to and leave your sister?"

Rudy smiled. "Don't scold, *Mor*." He unloaded the black pup in Selma's arms. "See, I have a dog for us."

"Augh! He's licking my face—take him back! And answer me, please."

When he'd explained that he had helped a lady carry some packages to her home and she had given him the dog, Selma said, "Well, that's all right. It's how you were raised, to do a courteous thing. But Dani, you should not have—"

"Oh mama, he's so cute!" Dani had gathered the wriggling pup into her arms. "Can we take him along? Can we keep him?"

Selma nodded wearily. "I suppose so. But he must stay outside the house. If we ever have a house."

Rudy, wearing that moonstruck expression again, headed back toward the wagon, walking ahead of his mother and sister.

I have never seen him look just so, Selma thought wonderingly.

Dani walked beside her, cooing over the pup as she cuddled it. Selma said quietly, curiously, "This lady he helped. Was she very pretty?"

"She is beautiful, Mama." Giving her a quick glance, Dani laughed. "Oh, you think Rudy... but she is old."

"M'm. As old as your mother, you think?"

"No, um"—Dani hesitated—"not as old as you, Mama."

Selma laughed.

Axel was waiting by the wagon as they came up to it. He wore a strange look, too—a look that was still preoccupied and determined, but oddly cheerful now. Something he'd learned or decided on must have turned his grimness to pleasure.

Selma didn't feel relieved. She knew her man: He hadn't yet got rid of whatever was so intensely on his mind.

"Come," he said briskly. "Let's be going home. Where did you get the dog?" Selma explained, and he merely nodded. "All right, we can use a dog. Where is Elof gone to?"

"Who knows? Axel, I want to ask—"

"*Helvete!* Let that damn boy walk home by himself then. We're not waiting."

He gave Selma a hand into the wagon, swung onto the seat beside her, and took up the reins. With Julia and Erika riding in the wagon bed among the supplies, Rudy and Dani walking behind, they drove out of town.

"Axel," Selma ventured again, "did you see the sheriff? What did he tell you?"

"Not much I didn't know. From him we get no help. But I think I got the answer."

When he did not go on, she said impatiently, "Answer to what?"

"What I will do about that dam." Axel's beard split in a slow grin. "After I seen the sheriff, I went to the register of deeds and looked up our land. I wanted to be sure I was right. And I am. The plat shows that on the part of the river when the dam is, the west side of it is sure as hell inside our line."

"Very good," she said tartly. "So?"

Behind them the twins were tussling among the boxes and barrels, raising their voices in a squabble. Selma turned on the seat, giving them a sharp reprimand. She noticed the long wooden crate in the wagon bed just behind the seat. It was nothing she had bought.

"Mr. Holmgaard, what is that box?"

Axel had his *snus* out. He took a pinch of it before replying. "Guns," he said tersely.

"Guns?"

"Winchester rifles. Five of them. And a couple of Colt revolvers."

"*Gud bevara!* So many guns—but why?"

"Because we will need them. The boys and me will need guns."

"For hunting?"

"*Ja.* Something else, too."

Axel's beard was jutting in the stubborn way she knew, his eyes flicking small blue lightnings. Selma's mouth went dry. And she felt a quiet fear, cold and crowding, rise into her throat.

❧ *seven* ❧

THERE WAS NO sign of life around the log shanty as Selma approached it, picking her way across the brambly cut-over land close to the dam. The place drowsed in the noonday warmth; no smoke came from the cabin's stack. A small window was set in the front wall to the right of the door, but light reflections on the dingy glass made it impossible to tell whether anyone was watching her from behind it.

Selma shifted the weight of the basket on her arm. She kept walking steadily, a nervous chill running along her spine. She was doing this at Axel's insistence. He could be very insistent when he was bitten by the bug of one notion or another.

When she was less than a hundred feet from the shanty, the door opened. A dark wiry man with a little mustache came out. He would be the Canuck Axel had described—the man named LeBoeuf. He was carrying a rifle.

"You," he said. "Stop there."

Selma came to a halt.

"What is it you want?"

She let her shoulders lift and fall. "I want nothing. Today I baked bread and rolls and I have brought you men some."

"Why? Eh?"

She managed to smile. "Why not? It's the neighborly thing." She lifted a clean white cloth that covered the basket, tipping it enough to show him the golden-crusted loaves inside. "We have plenty for ourselves—and I thought you would like some."

LeBoeuf studied her for a long moment. "You are Mrs. Home-gar?"

"Yes."

"Pardonnez-moi, madame. I fail to comprehen' why your husband who talk so tough when he is here, why he send you with food."

"Nobody 'sent' me. I bake today, I know two men who live alone do not eat very well, so I tell my husband I think it's neighborly to take them some good eating."

"Ah, *oui.* That is ver' thoughtful of *madame.*" LeBoeuf touched his mustache with a finger. "And Mr. Home-gar does not object?"

"Oh. He is grumpy, sure, but he is always grumpy." She set the basket on the ground and straightened up. "Here, I will leave the food. You leave the basket out and I'll pick it up tomorrow."

LeBoeuf watched her with half-lidded eyes. Behind him now loomed the brutish face and giant form of his companion, a man as awesome as Rudy (who had a gift for making such things vivid) had described him to her. Both of them regarded her in silence.

Trying not to seem uneasy, Selma gave them a slight, pleasant nod and turned, heading back the way she'd come.

When she entered the line of jack pines and was hidden from the men's view, she came to a stop. She pressed a fist over her pounding heart. The way that Canuck John LeBoeuf had looked at her! Axel had guessed he was the kind of fellow who would fancy himself a lady's man. But he was something more or less than that. He looked at a woman as a predatory animal might.

Hard on that thought came a rush of anger at her husband.

She'd found Axel's scheme distasteful from the moment he'd proposed it. Of course it had done no good. Axel didn't threaten or cajole; he merely hammered at a point with a steady, untiring persistence till he had his way. You could yell and argue, but rarely could you outlast him. Once Axel's mind was set on a thing it was easier, finally, to just give in and get it over with.

Even so, Selma had raised bitter objections.

Could he really believe those men would be so dumb as to fall for such a simple trick? They would, Axel had insisted; it would just take time and patience. The big fellow was a brainless hulk of muscle; the other one could be gulled by a woman. Axel wanted to handle it so nobody would get hurt. If the guns came out, there might be shooting. Where there was shooting, there might be killing. Did she want to risk that?

Of course she didn't, Selma had said indignantly.

The words had committed her. Only afterward had she come to realize how Axel had used a kind of emotional blackmail on her. Forcing her help by letting her know his only alternative would be to use violence. He might be bluffing, but she didn't think he was. She knew just how mulish he could be. Also, he was too tightfisted to invest so much money in an arsenal of guns just to make a bluff.

Gud bevara! All this fuss over a few acres of flooded land!

Selma passed through the belt of jack pines and walked slowly back to the camp.

Along with the guns he'd bought, Axel had purchased some hammers, nails, crowbars, saws, and other carpentry tools, as well as bags of cement and mortar. Since their return from town yesterday, he and the boys had been engaged in tearing down Slocum's house and outbuildings, wading out into a couple of feet of water to do so. The work was proceeding quickly. The roof and walls and partitions of the house had already been dismantled and carried to dry land. Now the men were tackling the barn.

The dam as such was an evil that Axel had decided to accept. He was following Sheriff Pleasants' suggestion that he relocate the buildings on high ground. The place he'd chosen was a pleasant wooded rise to the north. It overlooked the river to the east, the rolling fields and pasture to the west.

Axel, his trousers rolled high on his legs, left off work and came tramping out of the water to meet her.

"Well?" he demanded.

"Well what?"

"What did they say, anything? How did it go?"

"I guess it went the way you want," Selma said coldly. "The Canuck thanked me very politely. You keep slogging around in that icy water, you'll be coming down with the croup, all of you."

Axel tipped back his head. He watched a bald eagle swooping above the river, the sun hitting its snowy cap. "Sure, *käresta*. We'll knock off in a little while. By God, but it's turned out a fine day, eh?"

After Axel called a halt to the day's work, he and the boys thawed their numb limbs by the fire and discussed what to do with the rest of the day. Most of a long golden afternoon still lay ahead. They decided that a little hunting would be just the ticket. Besides, all of them were anxious to sight in and try out their new rifles. There was no complaint from the women; any game the men could bring in would be a welcome addition to the larder.

Which, Elof thought complacently, would dovetail with his own plans.

He'd been mulling over an excuse to get away from the place this afternoon. Not that it made a hell of a lot of difference—if he felt like going off somewhere, he'd do so anytime it suited him. Still, he'd scandalized Ma enough times in the past that by now he might be pretty near to overstepping her limits of toleration.

A small grin touched Elof's lips as he inspected his rifle. The old man didn't really give a hoot what shenanigans he pulled so long as they didn't interfere with work to be done. Ma was the morally righteous one. Never intolerably so, for Selma's sternness was leavened by a healthy streak of humor. But it wouldn't hurt to play his cards close to the belly.

The four boys and their father headed into the woods in a group, the pup Otto frisking at their heels. But they didn't stay together long. Axel's attention was on Otto, whom he meant to train for hunting. He headed upriver, calling the pup to follow; Lennart tagged along with them. Elof and Rudy and Arvid worked down the river a short distance, holding close to its bank. Finally Arvid suggested they strike off toward a range of hills on their far right.

"Suits me," said Rudy. "Elof?"

Elof yawned and shook his head. "You boys go along. I'll mosey on down the river a ways."

As soon as his brothers were out of sight, Elof shed any pretense of looking for game. Slinging his rifle across his shoulder, he cut over to the tote road and set off south along its muddy trace at an easy stride. He shouldn't be too late. Even if he was, that little breed would wait for him. She couldn't have much of anything else to do.

Elof gave a mild chuckle. He'd fallen into a jackpot of luck there. That little number was hot for a trot. And he was just the boy to ride her to a fare-thee-well.

After parting from his family yesterday, he'd lost no time getting back to the house on the town outskirts. The girl was still dawdling on the porch, peeling potatoes. Elof had struck up a conversation with her right away. Swan O'Dea was her name, and to Elof's prompt question she'd replied that, yes, she was Tom O'Dea's daughter. Right now she was hired girl for the Stevenses, who lived in this house, and meantime she rather irregularly attended classes at Winterfield High School. Elof had asked if she got to see her pa often. Not very often, Swan had said. All her father cared about was roaming the woods and otherwise living as it pleased him. Slyly, Elof had wondered aloud whether *she* ever visited her pa. Once in a while, Swan had answered, flirting the lashes of her bronze-colored eyes at him.

She was a saucy little number. Her drab sack of a dress wasn't designed to show off her figure, but hinted at its lissome fullnesses all the same. Maybe one day she'd go all to suet the way a lot of Injun and breed girls did. But right now every inch of her was prime filet.

Elof had blandly suggested that they might see a bit of each other next time she came visiting her pa. Swan hadn't responded with a strict yes or no. Tomorrow, she'd obliquely observed, was Sunday and her day off; she might consider taking a walk to visit her parent. Only thing was, she never knew for sure whether he'd be home or not. Elof, giving her a long, foxy look from the corners of his eyes, had said that was all right. Calling on Swan's daddy wasn't exactly what he had in mind. Maybe they could meet upriver a ways from O'Dea's cabin. There was a big mossy boulder at the first bend in the river above where her daddy lived—did she know the place?

She knew it.

Elof whistled as he tramped along. He let out a loud, happy "Goddamn!"

Hearing a distant shot now, he remembered that his brothers were hunting and he was supposed to be too. He took a few shots at such casual targets as willow catkins and old pinecones before it occurred to him that Swan's daddy, if he were at home, might be minded to investigate anyone firing off a gun near his place. O'Dea had impressed Elof as a pretty sharp shamrock. Easygoing, but just possibly capable of a wicked retribution against any bird he caught honeyfuggling his little girl. No point inviting trouble from that quarter.

After curving away from the river for a short distance, the road swung back toward the Ottawa's broad channel. When he was a few hundred yards north of the pine-covered bluff where O'Dea's cabin stood, Elof left the road and waded through heavy brush till he came to the huge moss-covered boulder at the edge of the river. A deep bend in the channel cut off any sight of the boulder and the area around it, while the thick trees and brush gave the riverbank at this point a kind of sylvan seclusion.

Great place to meet a girl. Elof's mind was seasoned to strategems of that sort.

Only Swan wasn't there.

The jubilation hardly had time to ebb out of him when he heard a sharp splash, surprisingly close and made by something heavier than any river fish. He peered upstream, scanning the willow-choked bank from which the sound had seemed to come. For a moment he was puzzled. The bank was so densely mantled with brush, he could just make out the churning ripples of the splash at water's edge.

Then he caught a glimpse of something else: a gold-colored flash in the water. In a moment the girl's head bobbed into view. She threw back her wet hair and began swimming upstream along the bank with clean easy strokes. Graceful as a golden eel, she was quickly lost to view.

Elof grinned.

She had come here and waited—and the gunshots had alerted her to his approach. Staying out of sight, she'd watched till he was near enough to identify, then had gone for a swim. Close by, of course, and making enough noise to draw his attention. Okay with him if she wanted to play that kind of game.

He moved along the bank to the willow thicket and found Swan's clothes in a tidy heap on the ground. Quickly stripping down to his drawers, he plunged down the steep bank into hip-deep water. And scrambled right out again, stifling a yell. Jesus—its icy grip was enough to paralyze a man! The lesser chill of the shallows in which he'd been wading half the day hadn't prepared him for anything like this.

Elof eased back into the water by cautious degrees, cursing between his clenched teeth as he immersed himself to the neck. The water gripped his torso and limbs like icy bands; the up-forcing chill congealed the blood in his head till he thought his eyes would pop. Then as he moved arms and legs, treading water, he felt his veins start to thaw a little. He should, Elof thought with a teeth-chattering grin, be able to tough it out just long enough anyway.

The Ottawa was wide and placid at this point—easy to swim against its sluggish current. Elof struck upstream along the bank, pushing his way wherever he could behind the leafless willow switches that overhung the water, for he hoped to catch sight of Swan before she saw him. Birch points thrust into the river every few yards, cutting off whatever lay beyond; he could come on her quite suddenly.

Just ahead and around a shelving point, he heard a lively splashing. Marshaling his faculties with difficulty, for the bands of cold were eating into his marrow, Elof plunged noiselessly beneath the water. He paddled carefully around the point, keeping submerged as he strained to make out objects through the amber glow, sunshot with greenish-gold rays. Swan's body would be a gleam of paler gold by which he would discern it.

But he saw nothing of the sort; his lungs were on the edge of bursting. Hell! He'd have to come up. He burst to the surface with a mighty snorting and peered around, blinking his eyes clear. Where the hell *was* that girl?

The probable answer had barely registered when Elof felt a tug on his ankle. It was strong enough to yank him under. He kicked free and floundered back to the surface, strangling on water as she popped up beside him, splashing still more water on his face.

Elof was too ribaldly good-humored to mind being fairly if temporarily bested. He took up the game with a lusty will. They splashed and tussled with the abandon if not the innocence of children. Wasn't every day a man got to water-wrassle with a bare-ass beauty like Swan O'Dea; it was so much fun he nearly forgot his carcass was going icily numb.

Swan backstroked away from him, giggling. "You're turning blue!" She turned and swam back downriver, and Elof started to follow her. Then, feeling a surge of cramps grab his limbs, realized he'd better get out of the water right away.

He floundered out on shore just as Swan, maybe fifty feet ahead of him, lifted herself onto the bank close to the willow thicket. For a moment she stood on the open bank, smoothing her long dripping hair back from her face. Elof forgot he was damn near frozen. She was lovely in the sunlight; it washed the pale gold flexings of her full, slimly muscled body with wet highlights. Then she ducked out of sight into the thicket. Though she hadn't even glanced in his direction, he knew the momentary pose had been deliberate.

By the time Elof reached the willows, Swan was dressed. Or partly so, having pulled on her skirt and shirtwaist. Now she sprawled on the bank in the sun, hands folded behind her head. Elof, clad only in his soaked drawers, dropped down beside her. His teeth were chattering like castanets. The sun's warmth left his chilled flesh untouched.

"You want a rubdown?" Swan asked.

"S-s-sure."

"Roll over."

He flopped onto his belly and felt her strong quick hands go to work, massaging his back and sides with what seemed an instinctive skill. Elof folded his arms under his chin and shut his eyes, giving himself to her devilishly deft touch and to the prickling pleasure of renewed circulation.

"That's great," he grunted. "You always take your clothes off when you meet a guy?"

She gave him a stinging slap on the short ribs. "I take 'em off to swim, smarty. You were so late, I didn't think you'd be here."

Elof grinned. "You knew damn well I'd be here."

"Huh. You think what you want."

"I always do. That's enough rubbing—thanks." He turned onto his back and let the sun soak into him now.

Swan lay on her side, propping her chin on one hand. The other hand hovered over his chest, fingertips brushing the hard ridges of muscle. "Mm," she murmured, "where'd you get all those nasty bruises?"

"Had a fight with my old man."

"You fight with your *pa?*"

"Sure. Don't everybody?" Elof added gravely, "It was self-defense. He's a pretty mean old bastard."

"He does this to you and you stay on? Don't you ever think of leaving?"

"Huh-uh. Not till I can kick hell out of the old man."

She laughed. "Oh God, you really are crazy! You know that?"

Elof opened his eyes and winked at her, saying lazily, "Don't tell anybody," as he let his sultry gaze assay and appreciate her: the damp cling of her waist and disarranged skirt, the wanton sprawl of her legs. He closed a hand over her bare ankle and pulled her foot to his mouth. He kissed her toes and ran his lips up her leg. She giggled and yanked her foot away.

"Your mustache tickles."

"It's supposed to. Ain't you ever heard of a Swedish tickler?"

He rolled up on his elbows and leaned above her, smiling into her eyes. He bent to her mouth, tasting its soft moving wetness and the delicate searching of her tongue, which seemed oddly tentative and innocent, like a child taking a cautious yet sensuous pleasure in a new toy. Momentarily he wondered if she really were the seasoned flirt she'd seemed. The abrupt answer came as his weight pressed her tighter to the ground. She gave his jaw a jarring clout with the heel of her palm.

Elof jerked his head back. He glared at her, rubbing his jaw. "What the hell was that for?"

"It's too easy for you, Mr. Smart. Don't think you're going to get it so easy."

But her body was quiescent, not resistant, beneath him. Her voice was throaty; her eyes were half shuttered, and her smiling lips were poppy-red and swollen. Elof's temper went up like a flag.

"All right, you damn little teasing klooch," he muttered. "I'll get it rough then—rough as you want to make it."

His arms went around her with bruising force; his mouth drove fiercely onto hers. It muffled Swan's scream; her lips broke against her teeth; she tried to fight. But the struggle was a short one.

She managed to sink her teeth into his lip, but a single cuff jarred her loose. Then she ceased to fight, realizing that resistance would only make the whole business that much more painful.

He turned gentle now that he could afford to, unbuttoning her waist and sliding it off the smooth golden shoulders, fumbling her skirt away. Her body remained lax, unresisting and unresponsive. For a moment, as he drew back to tear off his drawers, Elof filled his eyes with her wild and tawny beauty. Her eyes were as inexpressive as black stones.

He bent to the pouting hills of her breasts. Teeth and tongue worked with a patient skill on two sepia nipples until they grew pebble-round and hard. A soft whimper trickled from her throat. Her whole body arched feverishly to his kisses, then to his hand as it roved across a satiny swell of haunch and a flat smooth belly and finally sought the crisp black-furred nexus to her womanhood.

In the hot and hungry fusion of their bodies, time and place melted away and the world itself was forgotten. . . .

Afterward, as they lay quietly in each other's arms, side by side, Swan was the first to speak. "You're awfully strong," she murmured against his cheek. "You didn't seem so strong in the water."

"As you may have gathered, water ain't my element."

"No." She giggled, tracing a finger along the line of his

jaw. "Now I know your element. Wow, do I. You're just about the best ever. Are all Swedes that good?"

"We're like everyone else, honey. Some are, some ain't. What do you mean, 'just about the best.' That the voice of experience or what?"

"Well . . ." She drew back a little and plucked a grass stem. Closing her white teeth on it, she smiled archly. "I've had boyfriends, you know."

Elof grinned. It had been plain at their first meeting that she was no unplucked blossom. "No kidding."

"Sure. One in particular, too."

"Is that right," he said lazily.

"Ain't you going to ask who?"

"Honey, I don't give a rat's ass who."

He yawned and settled on his back, dropping a forearm across his eyes against the sun's glare, liking its even warmth on his bare hide. Swan said in a faintly annoyed voice, "Well, you better."

"Yeah, why?"

"He's *jealous*. Very jealous. Why, if he found out what you just did . . ."

Elof gave a grunt of laughter. "All by myself, huh?"

"Go on, smarty, laugh! He's handsome and he graduated from the University of Wisconsin and he's *rich!* And he'd do anything for me, anything I ask him. Don't you *laugh!*"

She gave him an angry jab in the ribs. Elof went on laughing. "Oh kid, you're something," he said between chuckles. "You really are. All right, you got this rich cluck on a string, who is he?"

Swan hesitated. But anger pushed her to a quick reply. "He's Shadrach Gannett, that's who."

Elof lifted his arm, eying her quizzically. "Gannett? You mean one of those . . . Say, you handing me a lot of bushwah?"

"I am *not!* You want to prove it, just go tell Shad Gannett about this and see what happens!"

"Every little thing, huh?" Elof said amusedly. "Sure that's what you want?"

Swan drew back a little, giving him a superior, pitying smile. "Go on, laugh. Shad will believe what *I* tell him, Mr.

64

Smart. If I do, you can bet he'll mop up the ground with you. You'll be lucky if that's all that happens!"

Elof yawned. "Now I'm scared. Seven feet tall, is he? He's going to marry you, I suppose."

"Yes!" ·

"What makes you think so?"

"Because he *promised,* that's why! He's not like you. He's a *gentleman!*"

Elof stared at her for a long moment. Jesus, he thought unbelievingly, she can't really be that dumb.

Possibly she wasn't. People could inveigle themselves into believing the goddamnedest things if they wanted those things badly enough. You could call Swan O'Dea a tease and a doxie and just about any term society applied to "that kind of girl." But Elof, who didn't give a hoot in hell about society or its rules, had learned—with a kind of sad and instinctive wisdom that went beyond his years or his upbringing—that the labels people got pinned on them had little to do with the sum of human needs that drove them. Swan had her personal needs like anyone else. If that included persuading herself that a rich boy would make her his wife, why deny her the privilege of her illusions? The final truth would be bitter enough to swallow.

Elof reached out and took her hand. "Ah hell, don't mind me. I'm sure your boy is a real gent. I like you, kid. Don't you ever settle for anything but the best."

A shadowy hint of doubt—or fear—glided out of Swan's face. Her eyes changed and softened. "I like you too, Elof," she whispered.

Suddenly, swiftly, she was bending above him. Her lips feathered damp little kisses over his face till he stopped her mouth with his own. The touch of hands on bodies was warm and gentle at first, then hot and urgent.

This time their lovemaking was unhurried and languorous and tender.

✿ eight ✿

EVERY DAY FOR three more days Selma brought the two watchmen by the Gannett Logging and Boom Company dam a gift of something to eat. The first day it was a savory stew; the second day, more fresh-baked bread prepared in a Dutch oven; on the third, she brought a pan of fudge.

She would call out cheerily, "Don't shoot—it's only me," or something of the sort. LeBoeuf would step out of the shanty, touching his mustache like some obsolete gallant, and proffer a winning witticism or two. Selma would good-naturedly return his sallies, but their suggestive nature and the way he looked at her made her feel smudged and shamed.

She hated the fellow, she hated her part in this miserable deception, and she almost hated Axel for badgering her into it. After the fourth time she flatly declared to him that she would have no more of it, she was finished, she would not do it another time. "You will," he replied positively. "You have to, *käresta*. Otherwise it's been for nothing."

And resignedly she knew that she would. But as things turned out, it wasn't necessary.

The spring weather brought a tonic-like warmth to each day. The nights were still bitter cold, but the Holmgaards passed them pleasantly enough, installed in three new tents with plenty of warm bedding. Axel and Selma occupied one tent, the girls another, and the third one sheltered the four boys.

On this seasonally cool morning all the Holmgaard men were at work over on the high knoll that was the site of the new house. Laboring like beavers, they'd completely dismantled the old buildings and salvaged all the sound planks and timbers. Already they had put in a footing for the new house and were at work gathering fieldstones and mixing mortar and laying the foundation. It was remarkable how much they had accomplished in a short time.

Their appetites were incredible too; Selma and Dani spent much of every day preparing huge meals. As they lacked a house, there was no other housework to be done except the once-a-week laundry. Selma would have mostly enjoyed it if not for having to take food to the watchmen each day.

Thinking of going through it another time had her in a cross mood.

Today was wash day. Selma had stuffed part of the week's load of dirty clothes in a kettle of water and brought it to boiling over the open coals. Lately the vermin had got into all their garments, and this was the time-honored way of cleansing them of pests. Nits and lice, lice and nits, she thought furiously as she used a stick to turn the clothes over and over in the seething water. She was thinking more of certain people than of vermin.

Dani came up and touched her arm. "Mama . . ."

Selma straightened, wiping a straggle of wet hair back from her forehead as she looked toward the southward line of jackpines.

Coming jauntily toward their camp was Canuck John LeBoeuf, an empty pan swinging in his hand. She shuttled a glance toward the knoll where Axel and the boys were laying masonry. Axel too had noted LeBoeuf's approach, and he had left off work and was watching.

Selma felt a quickening of her blood. This was what Axel had waited for. The time when LeBoeuf would feel bold enough to leave the shanty and his companion and come visiting the pleasant woman who brought him food.

She wiped her hands on her apron, forcing a smile to her lips as Canuck John came up. He bowed from the waist and held out the fudge pan. *"Bon jour, madame! Très bon—*the sweet was very good. I return your dish myself. And this," turning a sensuous look on Dani, "is your so-lovely daughter?"

"Yes, this is Danielle."

"Danielle? Elle est ravissante! But that is a French name."

"It is Swedish, too. We call her Dani." Selma had enormous difficulty holding the smile. "Wouldn't you like some coffee, Mr. LeBoeuf? We have some fresh."

"Bien."

She went to pour the coffee. LeBoeuf's dark eyes were casually watchful; he wore a pistol in a holster on his hip. His gaze moved toward Axel, who had left the knoll and was coming this way at his loose rangy walk, not hurrying. The boys went on working, apparently paying no attention to anything else. Selma handed LeBoeuf the mug of coffee. He took it with a word of thanks, accepting it with his left hand while his right rested on his hip near the pistol.

Axel was mopping his brow with a bandanna as he came up. He said a pleasant "Hi there" to LeBoeuf, otherwise hardly seeming to notice him. The Canuck might have been an everyday caller. Looking at his wife with a grin, Axel said, "It moves right along, the work. I'll have a cup of that coffee myself."

Standing a few yards from him, LeBoeuf nodded a brief response and sipped his coffee. His narrow face held a hard-eyed alertness, just a touch of caution, and an amused insolence that edged on contempt.

"Well, m'sieu. I see you make the best of things, eh?"

Axel shrugged. "What else can a man do? Thank you, *kä-resta.*"

He too accepted the cup from Selma with his left hand, still wiping his sweaty face with his right, and then idly stuffing the bandanna back in his hip pocket under the skirt of his coat.

When the hand came out, it was holding a Colt .45 revolver that was pointed at LeBoeuf's belly.

Axel took the upper hand just that simply. With a gesture so easy and natural you wouldn't have guessed he'd practiced it for hours. LeBoeuf was covered and helpless before he knew it.

"Now, monsoor"—Axel's voice was deep and ugly—"you stand like you are and don't bat an eye, eh?"

"Say . . . what you think you're up to?"

Axel tramped over to him, lifted the Canuck's pistol from its holster, and stepped back. "Lay down on the ground, mister. On your face. Stretch out and be quiet. Do like I tell you!"

LeBoeuf hesitated only a moment. It must have been clear to him from the way he'd been tricked that Axel was at pains to avoid bloodshed. But he couldn't miss the thinly checked wildness in Axel's face. LeBoeuf went down on his face; he sent Selma a look so fierce it made her stomach flutter.

He said one word, spitting it out: an epithet she didn't know.

A quiver of repugnance ran through her. *"Ugh, du fan,"* she murmured. "You nasty devil!"

Axel laughed coarsely. A kind of triumphant exuberance lighted up his face. He looked at the boys as they came hurrying up now. Both Elof and Arvid were carrying rifles. The twins had been playing with Otto by the water; now they too came up, wide-eyed and a little fearful.

Axel looked at Dani. "Go on." He made a little shooing motion. "You know what to do."

Dani nodded, her face pale. She and Elof and Arvid walked away, heading for the belt of jackpines that cut off view of the dam and its guard shanty beyond.

"What is this?" LeBoeuf demanded in a husky, furious voice. "What the hell you think you're doing?"

"Not 'think,'" Axel corrected him. "We are doing it. She'll tell your big friend Mr. Roback you took sick all of a sudden, you fell down and had a fit, you're in great pain. She'll tell him to come quick. He's not too quick in the head, eh? Not too smart. So right away he will come to see. The boys will hide in the trees. When he comes into the trees they will be waiting, they will get the drop on him. Then . . ." He chuckled from the deep well of his pleasure. "Then we got both of you."

LeBoeuf turned his head and spat. "So you will have both of us. *Peste!* You damn crazy squarehead! What you think that gets you?"

"Why," Axel said gently, "it gets me the dam."

Seeing to the captives' needs was no great problem. All day

they were tied to a tree close to where Axel and the boys were laboring on the new house. Occasionally they were freed to stretch their legs, tend their needs, and eat their meals, all under the surveillance of a watchful and armed Holmgaard son. At night they were trussed up with both rope and wire, and always one of the boys was on watch.

Now the family would await developments.

Trying to get out of Axel just what he had in mind was like pulling teeth. He'd always had a secretive, closemouthed streak in his nature, and was given to revealing his plans only by grudging degrees.

After capturing Canuck John LeBoeuf and Bear Roback, taking effective possession of the dam, he blandly observed that there was damned little else he could do.

But didn't he mean to tear down the dam?

What? Destroy a dam licensed by the state of Wisconsin? *Gud* forbid!

Well then, would he open the sluice gates and drain their flooded land?

No, that didn't accord with Axel's plan either. He had made that plan with great care and would not deviate from it.

So then, what of the prisoners? How long did he intend to hold LeBoeuf and Roback?

That was hard to say; even LeBoeuf was unsure when his company's log drive would begin. But it should be soon, as the last threat of recurring winter seemed past. LeBoeuf and Roback would be held till then.

Wasn't that illegal—the equivalent of kidnapping them?

Not at all. The pair had trespassed on Holmgaard land; they were damn lucky to be alive. At which point, Axel declared, he'd had enough of damn-fool questions. What this family could use, by God, was a shot of trust in the man who was the head of it.

That didn't leave much to say. He had it all figured out.

Long ago Axel had tempered his latent streak of wildness for Selma's sake, to become a sobersided family man and provider. She knew how he'd chafed at times against these restraints. Yet it was the sort of bondage that a man must expect to live with lifelong—and merely grumble about when it suited him. Breaking away from their old life in Minnesota seemed to have stirred up a long-suppressed part of the man's being, as natural to him as the color of his hair.

By evening, Selma's patience had frayed to shreds. She decided to have it out with him. The kids had retired to their tents. She and Axel stood by the fire and wrangled. Mildly at first, but soon the talk became heated.

"Damn it, woman," he growled, "I done it like I said I would. Took that dam without shedding a drop of blood."

"But if you keep on like this, there is bound to be bloodshed. I think what you want to do is see how far you can push things and get away with it."

"What? What kind of fool talk is that?"

"Men," she said bitterly. "You are all like boys. Putting a chip on your shoulder. Or drawing a line in the dirt and daring the other man to cross over it."

"Jesus, woman! Where do you get such damn-fool notions? Look—I got good reasons. Slocum put over a bad turn on me. And them Gannetts ruined a lot of our land for use."

"But there's a good chunk of it not flooded," she argued. "Enough so there's plenty of it never got cultivated by Slocum himself. Isn't it enough?"

Axel grunted, "No," and started to swing away toward their tent.

But she confronted him, hands on hips. "And what about us? Axel, it is not a matter of right or wrong. It is a thing of good sense against bad judgment. Don't you think what you could bring down on all our heads?"

"Agh, Christ. Nothing is going to happen."

She folded her arms, lips compressed. "All right. Say what you think *will* happen. Tell me."

"I told you enough," he said irritably.

He tramped around her, lifted the tent flap, and ducked inside. She walked slowly back to the fire, feeling more helpless and frustrated than before.

⋇ *nine* ⋇

SHORTLY AFTER SUNUP four days later, they knew the log drive was under way. Rudy was the first to spot the logs coming from upriver—slim easy-running logs that had broken away from the main drive and were riding the sluggish current far in advance of their fellows.

Axel gave a couple of orders. Elof was to take his rifle and occupy the guard shanty. Rudy was to take LeBoeuf and Roback into the woods and hold them out of sight there.

Yesterday the last stone of the new house's foundation had been mortared into place, and now they would let the mortar season for a while before laying the joists and floor planks above it. So, said Axel, sounding very humorous and relaxed, they had all earned a holiday. Today they would just stand around and watch the "river pigs" at work.

It was better than the circus—eh?

Though her stomach was churning with worry, Selma found a high excitement in watching the activities of these "white-water men."

The logs began to arrive in thick flotillas, rolling and jostling and grinding together as they poured into the flowage behind the dam. Herding them along were men armed with peaveys and pike poles, and they were a marvel to watch—cat-footing from one log to the next as they poled the big sticks across the flowage. The men's calked boots gave them burrlike grips on the huge cylinders. The balance and agility they showed in riding that shifting, tumbling mass was almost unbelievable.

The children were entranced by the sight, but not much more so than their elders. For most of the day the Holmgaards—except for Rudy and Elof—watched the spectacle with unflagging interest. They idled up and down the riverbank between their camp and the dam, now and then exchanging jocular comments with the river drivers.

By late afternoon the storage pond back of the dam was crowded with logs from one bank to the other and as far upriver as you could see. The men began to knock off work, heading back upriver. Axel explained that the log drive was followed by a pair of big rafts called "wanigans." One of them carried tents and blankets and grub; the other raft bore the cook's shanty. These would tie up back of the drive and the men would make camp there.

"Don't they quit work pretty early?" Selma asked.

Axel rubbed his beard. "Mostly they work till after dark, from what I been told. I guess the next thing is to begin sluicing the logs through the dam and they are waiting till tomorrow to start."

The two of them were standing on the open ground between the guard shanty and the dam. Long streaky shadows fell across the river; the flotilla of logs was gilded by the gold light of a dying day. Gold, all right, for the ones who owned such a treasure as this. It must contain enough sawplanks to build a whole town. Some of the logs, from their enormous size, had probably been hundreds of years in the growing. It was awesome and a little shameful to contemplate—the colossal reaping, and no doubt also the colossal waste, that this harvest represented. In a way, it was like mocking God.

To Selma's question, Axel said he couldn't really be sure, but he reckoned there were several tens of thousands of feet of logs backed up at this place. A mighty heap of money on the hoof, you might say.

One man did not return upriver with the others. He came striding along the great float of logs as briskly and easily as if he were on a Sunday promenade. Earlier Axel had pointed this fellow out as the drive boss. He'd seemed to be everywhere at once, shouting orders in the rich brogue of Erin, working twice as hard as any other man.

When he came to the dam, he sprang lithely atop it and crossed its length to where the Holmgaards were standing. He tramped up the bank, tipping his battered felt hat to Selma. A short thick-chested man, he had a twinkling Irish charm that reminded her of Tom O'Dea. Sweat matted his straight brown hair to his big head and stained his red flannel shirt with great blotches. He wore a curious pair of pants—a shouting green-and-red plaid stagged off at the calves. Probably this was to prevent snagging or wet cuffs—or whatever.

"Greetings, folks. I believe I've heard your name—if ye're the people that just settled here. Holmgaard, is it?"

"Axel Holmgaard. This is my wife, Selma."

"Pat Delaney." He shook hands with both, then clapped his hat back on his head and ran a satisfied eye across the lake of logs. "A foine sight, eh? And quite a job moving 'em this far down the river, I'll be telling the world."

"But worth it," Axel said idly. "What the Gannetts will make off of it, I mean."

"Aye..." Delaney gave him a keen glance. "A hard thing for you people, I'm thinking—the flooding of your place. I see you've tore down your buildings and are building anew. A divil of a shame, that."

Axel smiled. "Think nothing of it."

Delaney slowly nodded. "Well, if ye'll excuse me, I'll be wanting a word with our watchmen."

He started to walk toward the guard shanty, but Axel's voice halted him. "Don't bother. They ain't in there."

"Oh?" Delaney's head swiveled around quizzically. "I wondered why they hadn't appeared all day. Can ye be telling me where those two lunkheads are?"

Axel told him.

Delaney, his face ruddy with anger, tramped slowly back to them. He tipped his head to stare up hard-eyed at Axel. "Can a man be asking what the hell you think you're about?"

"It's simple. This shack of yours stands on my land. So I took it. Part of that dam rests on my land. So I am claiming my share of that, too."

"Are ye now!" A heavy vein beat in Delaney's temple. "And just what the divil do ye mean by that?"

"I mean by that, your company is going to pay over to me, Axel Holmgaard, ten cents on the hundred feet for every log they drive through this dam. Didn't I tell you it's simple?"

"Ten cents on the . . . ! Jasus, man, you must be loony!"

"Ten cents on the hundred feet," Axel repeated stolidly. "No haggling and no compromises. And no checks, either. It will be that, cash on the line."

Delaney let out a short explosive laugh. "The divil! Beau Gannett wouldn't pay ye toll like that if you put a gun to his head!"

"Well, *ja*. In a manner of speaking, that will be the way of it."

"Huh?"

Axel turned his head toward the shanty and shouted "Elof!" When there was no response, he cleared his throat and fairly roared it: "Elof!"

After a moment the door of the shanty scraped open. Elof stood there with a rifle in one hand, the other smothering a prodigious yawn. "Went to sleep," he explained with an unabashed grin.

"*Ja*, you would," Axel grunted. "Mr. Delaney, this is my boy Elof. You—say hello to Mr. Delaney."

"Hoddy," Elof said.

"Now you see the way of it," Axel said quietly. "I have four boys. From now on they take turns on guard here. Look around you, Mr. Delaney. See what a good place your company has set this shack for me? A man inside can see out windows all four sides. Nobody can sneak up by day and not be seen by him. On all sides he can see hundreds of feet across this cleared land. The dam he can see and all around it and a long ways up and down the river. Anyone tries to open one of them sluice gates, the man in the shack can shoot him and not even show himself." He paused. "You see how it is?"

Delaney shut his jaws with a snap. "Is that so. Now I'll be

telling you something, bucko. Tomorrow at sunrise I am coming to open them gates."

"I would not try it if I were you."

"Can a man be asking what the hell you'll do about it?"

"Trespass on that dam and you'll find out. Try it yourself or send another man—it will be the same to me. You are already trespassing on my land, Mr. Delaney, and I will thank you to get the hell off it."

Without another word Delaney turned and tramped away down the riverbank. Abruptly he halted and looked back at Axel, saying coldly, "What about them men of ours you've kidnapped?"

"They trespassed too," Axel said gently. "Kidnapped? I don't think that stands up. A man can *shoot* a trespasser. All I did was tie 'em up and hold 'em."

Delaney's eyes narrowed. "Ah, I see the way of that. You held LeBoeuf and Roback so there'd be no warning given us. So we'd push the drive this far and then you could hold it up."

"You're a sharp fella, Irish. That's it, and now I'll turn 'em loose. You can have 'em back with my compliments. How's that?"

Delaney said an oath and stalked away. Watching him go, Selma said anxiously, "Will he do like he said?"

"Try to," Axel said. "He's that sort. He'll be here at sunrise. So will I."

Rudy stifled a yawn, trying to blink away a fog of tiredness. He shivered against the chill mist that overhung the river, vaguely shrouding the dark massed hulks of the logs. It was nearly dawn; he'd stood guard by the shanty since relieving Elof at midnight. It was a cold and tense and monotonous duty that had taken a toll of his nerves. He could barely resist a temptation to sink to the ground and fall asleep.

But Pa would be along soon. If Pa caught him in even a mild doze, there'd be hell to pay. Rudy wondered dully just how far the old man would go if Delaney showed up to open the sluice gates. Pa could be almighty cautious at times; at other times a stubborn fever took him and he might be capable of anything. Elof was like that, only more lighthearted about it. Elof was *enjoying* this business.

Just maybe, under his grim composure, so was Pa.

A sound of feet tramping along the riverbank drew Rudy alert. He saw a man's dark form loom out of the mist; his fists tightened around his Winchester.

"Pa?"

"Me all right," Axel said gruffly. "Go to camp now. Get some sleep."

"Mind if I wait with you?"

Axel merely grunted, his usual sign of assent.

Suddenly Rudy was no longer tired; the arousal of his nerves roughened from weariness to a real excitement. He wouldn't have gotten a wink of sleep anyway, wondering what was happening with Pa.

They stood together on the high bank. The minutes inched by. Rudy was starting to muffle yawns again when a pinkish glow began to suffuse the mist. Sunup—or close to it.

A faint noise from the river's far bank. A crackling of brush. A deer coming to drink? No, it was a man's measured tread.

Rudy saw his stumpy figure move along the shore and swing with a quick stamp of calked boots onto the dam's top. He had a crowbar in his hand. He strode along the narrow obstruction to the first sluice gate and jammed the crowbar into the wheel.

Axel levered his Winchester. In the still dawn, the sound was like a Chinese firecracker going off.

"Leave go of it, Irish," he called.

For answer Delaney gave a powerful heave on the crowbar.

Axel raised his rifle and put his eye to the sights. "You are playing with fire, man!"

"Ye damned scut!" Delaney shouted. "To hell with ye! To hell with ye!"

The roar of Axel's Winchester echoed across the water and back.

Rudy heard the bullet scream off the iron wheel and then a howl of pain from Delaney. He staggered back, letting go of the crowbar. It slipped out of the wheel and fell in the water on the dam's downstream side.

So did Delaney, almost. He fought for balance and recovered it and crouched atop the dam, yelling curses. He was holding onto his left arm with his right hand. The ricochet must have creased him, but no more than that; his oaths held more of rage than pain.

Axel levered the Winchester again.

"That was for openers," he said in an iron voice. "Next one will go through your shoulder."

"It's a bluff you're making, Holmgaard! A goddamn bluff!"

"No. I shot at the wheel. Next I shoot at you. Believe it."

Delaney believed it. He turned and strode off the dam. On the far bank he yelled, "If I had a gun, Holmgaard! If I had a gun! But it's a sorry day for you, all the same. The sorriest of your life!"

He slogged away into the growing dawn.

Rudy looked wonderingly at his father. He knew Axel was no Dead-eye Dick with rifle or pistol, not even in practice. "Pa...did you shoot at that wheel?"

One of Axel's rare guffaws twinkled in his eyes and twitched his lips before it left his mouth. "No, at his arm. But he didn't need to know that, did he?"

❧ *ten* ❧

AXEL SAID THEY shouldn't have to wait long on a reprisal. In fact, it should come before the next day was out.

He was actually deriving enjoyment from the whole thing. With that realization, Selma's worry increased. She had stomach and bowel upsets; so did the twins.

The day dawned cold and windless. The kind that put a dull gray stamp on your mood even if you had no worries at all. Axel laid out the dimensions of a new barn well downslope from the house foundation, and he and the boys went to work excavating for another footing.

Selma thought maybe a decoction of herbs would help soothe the stomach and quiet the nerves. She mentally reviewed the herbal lore her mother had brought from Sweden. Many of the best medicinal herbs to be found in the old country didn't grow wild here, but a surprising number did. She ticked off possibilities. Rue, bracken, goldenrod, yarrow. All were good, but they were seasonal plants; she needed leaves or flowers to make an effective decoction. Nothing was leafed out in this month of April.

She thought of the maple tree. There must be sugar maple in the area, and its inner bark made a fine tea that would open a body's humors.

Taking a basket and a knife, Selma crossed their cleared land to its north end and entered the woods. Otto followed her, tagging at her heels or frisking ahead, setting up a clamorous barking at each glimpse of a chipmunk or a chickadee. After passing through a belt of oak, she came on a good-sized motte of sugar maple. They must tap these trees for sugar water next spring, she thought; it was now a month too late for catching the sap flow.

If we are still here next spring.

She chose a young sapling and trimmed away sections of its smooth gray bark to get at the greenish layer over the cambium. She peeled off small pieces and dropped them in the basket at her feet.

Suddenly Otto made noises.

Selma looked quickly over her shoulder. The pup was standing behind her, stiff as stone. A ridge of hair bristled along his spine as he faced the trees at her back, giving out low steady growls.

"Call off that big bad watchdog o' yours, mistress," said a cheerful voice. "It's naught but your friendly neighborhood skulker. Divil the dog, though! Nobody'll be stealing up on ye while he's about."

Tom O'Dea came out of the trees at his noiseless stride. He had come quite near and made no sound; even when she had peered among the leafless trees she hadn't seen him, he made such a blend with their trunks.

"Oh . . . Mr. O'Dea, you scared me. Otto, be still!"

"And I'll be apologizing for it." O'Dea dropped on his hunkers, rifle across his knees, and smiled at her. "Gathering barks, I see. Medicine? I thought so. Your old-country ladies are as great for that as your Indians. Well, and what's the word with you folks?"

Selma told him what Axel was up to.

O'Dea gravely shook his head. "He's seizing a bobcat by the tail, your man is. Sure and it'll be interesting to see what develops. But no great pleasure for you, mistress, eh?"

Selma said, "No," and was again too aware of his bright brash glance.

She was wearing a coat against the day's coolness, but somehow didn't believe that either coat or heavy skirt would entirely proof her against that look of his. Though his tone was proper enough, she thought there might be a hidden implication behind his addressing her as "mistress."

Cautiously Otto sidled up to O'Dea and sniffed at his knee. O'Dea scratched the pup behind the ears.

"It's a fine figure of a woman you are," he said idly, "for having all them grown kids and a pair o' young'uns beside."

She murmured, "Thank you," feeling a hot confusion wave across her face.

"There now—" He got up and walked over to her, smiling a little. "It's embarrassing you I am."

"I . . . I don't know. Do you always talk so to a married woman?"

"Ah no—no. Not if friend husband's about."

His laugh was so open and disarming, such a flow of genuine mirth, that Selma couldn't help but smile in return.

Yet she knew very well that a current of meaning ran beneath his words. It was disturbing in more ways than one. O'Dea wasn't at all like Canuck John LeBoeuf; his manner made a woman feel flattered rather than tainted.

It might be no more correct to feel one way than the other. But it *felt* like a difference.

"I'm a clean man, mistress." Exactly as if he were answering an unspoken query. "Dunk meself in the river every day, every day o' the year no matter what the weather, and scrub meself to the quick."

"Do you say so?"

"I do." He grinned at her. "Keep my clothes as clean as can be too. There—" He held his sleeve a couple inches from her nose. "See?"

It was true. He smelled faintly of pine pitch and a little more strongly of wood smoke, both odors clean and not unpleasant—no more than a man's clothing might soak up in any day of roughing it. Selma caught up her thoughts with a deepening confusion. He should not be such a forward man. Of course there was no sin in just listening to him. But she did not want to listen anymore.

She picked up the basket, saying briskly, "Well, I have all I need of barks. Now, Mr. O'Dea, do you go your way or will you come to our fire and have coffee?"

"Why, mistress, don't be thinking I'll pass up an offer of your coffee."

His tone was bantering and more than a little amused. As though he sensed her thoughts. He fell into step beside her, and they walked back through the grove, Otto scampering around their feet.

As they emerged from the forest and started across the cleared area toward the camp, the dog raced suddenly ahead of them, barking more vociferously than he had at any time.

"You've other company than me," said O'Dea. "When a mutt barks like that, it means visitors. Ah, and there they are."

Two men on horseback were coming into sight off the tote road.

Axel and the boys had left off work and were walking to meet them, and all were carrying their Winchester rifles. Selma came to a stop. Her mouth went dry; a wordless flare of dismay rose in her throat.

"The fat one's the sheriff, Big Joe Pleasants," O'Dea observed. "Skinny man is his deputy, Mr. Monty Harp. Now then, mistress. Wouldn't you be hearing what they and your good husband have to say to one another?"

O'Dea's hand on her elbow was gently urging, and to its pressure she continued walking, her steps leaden and reluctant.

The two men had halted and dismounted a little distance from the camp, and Axel tramped stolidly to meet them, the four boys flanking him two to a side. All of them looked grim and ready except for Elof, who wore a contented grin. Rudy would have doubts about some moral niceties of this business. Arvid, stolidly practical, had briefly stated that he felt they were buying into unnecessary trouble. But both were unshakably loyal to Axel and whatever course of action he might take.

Though five armed men were coming straight at him, the sheriff's fat face showed nothing at all. His deputy looked almost bored.

Selma felt a sudden vibrant anger at all of them. Men!

Always their prattle of laws and rights, but through all of it playing their stupid games. Good God! Did they ever quit being boys?

She and O'Dea had stopped a short way off. Axel gave them a frowning glance, then looked back at the sheriff.

"Well, Mr. Holmgaard," said Big Joe Pleasants. "I'm afraid you have kicked up a little bit o' dust."

"I meant to."

"Yeh, well—" The sheriff took a folded paper from his pocket. "This here is an injunctional order sworn out by Mr. Beau Gannett. It restrains you from interfering any further with the driving of logs on the Ottawa River by the Gannett Logging and Boom Company."

Axel took the paper from his hand and tore it across and let the pieces fall to the ground.

Big Joe Pleasants cleared his throat. "Now that ain't going to get you nowhere. Mr. Gannett will just swear out a warrant for your personal arrest."

"Maybe, just in case, you brought that warrant along too?"

"Maybe I just did."

"Maybe you'll have better luck serving that one. Try it."

"Let's talk this over, Mr. Holmgaard."

"Sure. You talk."

The sheriff squatted down on his massive haunches, and after a moment Axel settled on his heels facing him. It lent a deceptive reasonableness to the scene. Selma thought it was just more of their masculine posing.

"You a citizen of this country, Mr. Holmgaard?"

"I got my papers."

"Ever fight for it—in the Army, I mean? Cuba or the Philippines or maybe the Boxer thing?"

"*Ja.* I joined up in '98."

"Well, sir. You think enough of your country to fight for it, you ain't the sort to fly in the face of its laws, are you?"

"What I fought for then," Axel said slowly and deliberately, "was me and mine. That's what I fight for now. Don't talk to me like I'm a simple snorkie, sheriff." A taut edge touched his voice. "Possession is nine tenths of the law. I said that and you agreed. Well, I possess that dam now. I got all the right to it they have."

"Let's see now," Pleasants said patiently. "You took over that shack o' theirs. Okay, that's within your right, I checked it out and the shack's on your property. Fine. But Mr. Holmgaard, that dam ain't in the same case."

"The hell it ain't," Axel thundered softly. "I got anyway a halfway claim, and that's as much as theirs."

"No, sir. I don't know who that dam *belongs* to, strictly speaking. But the operation of it, now that's something else." The sheriff put out a broad flat hand with index finger pointed, tapping the finger on Axel's knee for emphasis as he talked. "No franchise for operating a dam, or even half a dam, has ever been granted to you. That authority can only come from the state o' Wisconsin, and the state granted it to the Gannett family and their assigns and heirs. One end o' that dam being on your property don't give you no right whatever to tamper with it."

"Nobody is tampering with a dam," Axel said quietly. "I am not pulling it down, not blowing it up. I am stopping logs from going through it, that is all."

Monty Harp, looking more bored than ever, shook his head. "But that ain't your right either, Mr. Holmgaard," he drawled. "The Gannetts are the duly enfranchised party with the only say-so about that dam's use."

"That's right," said Pleasants. "They can stop you or any other party from sluicing a log through and be within their rights. You *ain't.*"

"Well, that might be a big question. Big enough to take to court. Maybe they should do that." Axel spoke mildly, but his voice was hardening. "That paper I tore up. If I didn't obey that, you got along an arrest warrant to show me. Is that right or not?"

"All right. Yes."

"To put me in jail just long enough for them to finish a log drive."

Big Joe Pleasants shrugged. He heaved to his feet, dusting off his pants. "You're a calculating man yourself."

"Is that so?"

"What's stuck in your craw, mister, ain't a piddling piece o' land you got underwater. What it really is, you seen how you could hold the Gannetts up for a goodly piece o' money.

Hell. You wanted them two guys moved out of that shack on your land, you could of come to us. We'd of moved 'em. But you had to do it your way."

Axel shrugged. "How would I know you'd do anything? You said it yourself. All local officials are in the Gannett pocket."

"Bullshit," the sheriff said evenly. "All right, I said it. But I never chirped when any Gannett said cricket. You could of tried me. Wouldn't of cost you nothing to try me. Or would it?"

"You tell me."

"Sure. Tell you what you goddamn well know better'n anybody. You could of took this thing to court without showing a gun. Tied the Gannetts' hands for a spell without all this fuss. But you *wanted* that drive of logs pushed down here so you could stall it. They can't push the logs back upstream, and they can't get 'em out o' here any other way 'cept by crossing your land. Right now you got 'em over a barrel that could cost 'em plenty—and make you more money than you'd see in five years o' farming."

"Maybe that's so." Axel's lips curled off his teeth, and his grin was not pleasant. "But what are you going to do about it, sheriff? That's the real question. Just what the hell are you going to do about it?"

Pleasants shook his head, wearily. "I have had my say. Let's go, Monty."

They watched the lawmen ride away into the trees.

Axel gave O'Dea a curt nod. "Let us have some coffee. Do you have any on the fire, *käresta?*"

Selma was glad to have something to do, anything to do, after what she'd just witnessed. She dumped the grounds out of the big coffeepot, rinsed it out, and poured in Triple X and a half gallon of water, and set it by the fire.

As they waited for it to brew up, O'Dea said idly, "See here. If it suits ye, I can keep an eye out for any trouble that comes your way. After what's just passed, it might be a handy idea."

"Why?" Axel demanded.

"My house overlooks the road from town. When I ain't there, I am roaming the woods hereabouts, and altogether it's

85

damned little I miss. Don't tell me you couldn't use an ally like that."

Axel repeated "Why?" in a flat cold voice.

O'Dea gave his breezy chortle. "Fair enough. Why indeed? Well, I've met courtesy in this camp. I've eaten your grub and drunk your coffee. Ain't that enough? No? Well then—I'm a free-living man and it's something of an outlaw I am in my heart. Betimes I itch to give the law the back o' me hand. Man, any movement o' men in the woods'll be hard to get past me. I can get to ye ahead and give ye warning."

"*Ja*—and what are you fishing for?"

"God, you're a muley squarehead!" O'Dea roared, laughing. "All right, I'm fishing for another cup o' that java your mistress brews so lovely. Satisfied?"

However he disliked O'Dea, Axel was far too practical not to give a grudging assent to the offer of help. But he grumbled about it after O'Dea departed, wondering "what that damn mick is doing something for nothing for."

Selma discreetly made no comment. She had a pretty fair idea why.

❧ *eleven* ❧

THE NIGHT WAS still except for the muted gurgle of the river behind the guard shanty. A fine mist of rain was drifting down, but it made no sound and was hardly visible. Rudy sat by the shanty's propped-open window and kept a watchful eye on the open ground.

That took some doing, because he was bored half to death. Also tired after a day's work on the new house. Only the prospect of action and the suspense of waiting for it kept him in anything like a semblance of wakefulness.

Pa was pretty sure something would happen soon. The logging company was bound to attempt some kind of retaliation. Whoever occupied the shanty controlled the dam—it was at this vantage that any strike would come. And it was almost bound to come at night.

Rudy yawned. What was it now? Midnight or close to it. Sitting in total darkness, he couldn't have checked a watch even if he owned one.

However, it was surprisingly clear outside, as if a full moon lurked behind the gray-black overcast. Light glistened on the smooth wetness of boulders and on the bark of isolated trees. Rudy could make out shadowy details of the landscape all the way to the distant fringe of woods.

So far he'd seen nothing out there of any interest. But Pa's warning to keep a particularly sharp lookout tonight had him tensed for just about anything.

Axel had speculated that the sheriff himself was virtually helpless—unless he called in all his constables from outlying townships, deputized others, and formed a posse. Axel was confident it wouldn't go that far—that Pleasants wouldn't carry it to a shooting war. Neither would the Gannetts. They would capitulate. Maybe not right away. Axel was sure they would try the enemy's defenses first.

But finally they would be willing to reach an agreement.

Pa had flatly refused to speculate on what might develop if the Gannett family took the matter to court and the court ruled against him. He didn't believe it would happen, that was all. He was savoring this gamble—and its rewards if he could bring it off successfully.

Rudy turned his head toward the room's inner darkness. He said softly, "Arvid?"

No answer. No sound at all from the unseen bunk in the corner.

Rudy grinned. Arvid always slept the sleep of the dead, not even snoring. He could sleep through anything. Yet when awakened for his watch, he'd be ready at once, alert to his duty.

Arvid had Pa's bulk and was as stolid as a bull. He took everything in easy stride and didn't give much of a damn about anything outside of the family and his daily work. At least not so that it showed: He never had much to say. If he had any interests at all, aside from very occasionally joining Elof on one of his drinking-and-wenching bouts, you'd never know it.

Pa had wanted two of them on guard duty tonight, just in case. By now the Gannetts would know of the sheriff's back-off—and they might not waste any time.

Rudy shifted his butt on the hard stool and huddled deeper into the warmth of his Mackinaw coat. He was as cold and uncomfortable as he was tired and bored. But discomfort was helping keep him alert—along with a squirrelly feeling in the pit of his stomach.

Another hour passed.

Boredom freighted Rudy's mind like a lead weight. His thoughts drifted, and his chin slumped to his chest. He fought himself back to wakefulness. But the same thing happened again. . . .

A noise brought him bolt upright. Bewilderedly, he shook a fog of sleep from his brain. What was it?

The sound came again. A stealthy tapping on the door. Taking a sweaty grip on his rifle, Rudy eased to his feet and sidled over to the door, crouching to one side of it.

"Who is it?" he asked hoarsely.

"Me," came Axel's impatient voice. "Open up."

Rudy slipped the latch and Axel pushed inside. Rudy couldn't make out his father's face, but felt a flush of guilty heat in his own.

Axel said harshly, "You should of spotted me from the window. You two been asleep or what?"

"Arvid is. It's my watch. I, uh . . . guess I sort of dozed off."

"Jesus." Axel's tone was thick with disgust. "Ain't one of you dumbhead kids that don't pick the wrong time to pound his ear. All *right*. Listen now. I have got Lennart and Elof in position. They are laid up down along the riverbank. I am going to be there too."

"What for, Pa?"

"Because the feeling gets stronger and stronger. After the thing with the sheriff today, I think them Gannetts will hit us right away. Just a feeling . . . but I could not sleep, thinking on it. So now, tonight, we will all wait."

"All right."

"If anything happens," Axel went on grimly, "you and Arvid be damn sure you don't shoot any of *us*. Remember, we will all be laid up by the riverbank."

Axel was slipping back out of the door as he spoke the last words. And he was gone.

Rudy took his place at the window again. He felt very keyed-up now. Every once in a while Pa had premonitions. Like as not they'd prove correct to one degree or another. Nothing really mystical about it, Rudy thought matter-of-factly. If a man set up all the prospects of an event by his own actions, wasn't it pretty near bound to happen?

After a little while the misting rain began to slack off. The moon stayed behind the overcast, but there was a bit more light now. Rudy's eyes were starting to ache from watching.

Then it came.

He saw movement at the edge of the woods, and they were coming out of the trees. He counted five of them—moving furtively across the cut-over, keeping widely apart as they came, using stumps and clumps of brush for cover. They were just bent-over shadows; you couldn't make out anything else. But that was enough.

Rudy stepped back from the window and fumbled his way to the bunk. He shook Arvid awake. Both of them returned to the window. Pa and the other boys were watching too, Rudy swiftly explained. He and Arvid wouldn't open fire yet—let Pa make the move.

A roar of gunfire split the night.

It came from the riverbank on either side of the shanty, as Pa and Elof and Lennart opened up. The shadows coming across the clearing all melted to the ground. Apparently none of them was hit. Briefly, they returned fire.

Rudy was held motionless by the sudden flare of violence. His nerves seemed frozen. The blast of Arvid's rifle almost at his ear shocked him into action. He began shooting at the gun flashes almost blindly, hardly thinking of what he was doing.

Lever the Winchester, fire, lever and fire again. The close interior of the shanty reeked with the stink of burned cordite.

Rudy heard a man yell out there. One of them must have been hit. But the shadows were up now, retreating in a run—all five of them.

That's all there was to shoot at. Shadows. And these were already merging again with the trees. As suddenly as it had begun, it was over. Shot echoes died into silence.

Rudy's knees felt boneless. Abruptly he dropped onto the stool, scrubbing a wet hand over his face.

Arvid said, "Hey kid—you okay?"

"Ah—okay? Sure."

I shot at men, he thought. Maybe I even hit somebody. Lord Almighty. Maybe . . .

Selma turned drowsily in her blankets, careful even when only half awake not to brush against the tent wall. Moisture had soaked into the canvas, and the fabric was heavy with water. It did not drip, but anything dry that touched it was drenched by a quick cold runnel. It was very annoying and one more reason, besides the difficulty of keeping warm in a drafty tent, she'd be glad when their new house was ready for occupancy.

In spite of her days being filled with work, Selma had slept poorly these last few nights. She would constantly doze off only to jerk awake.

Sleepily she put out an arm, wanting the touch of Axel's solid bulk. But her groping hand found nothing. Instantly she was fully awake and sitting upright, her heart pounding. His place in the blankets was empty.

Then she heard gunshots.

Selma flung the blankets aside and scrambled to the tent flap, throwing it open. She peered in the direction of the dam, cut off from her view by trees. There was a whole fusillade of shots now. From the girls' tent voices rose in querulous fright. No sound from the boys' tent, and she knew where they would be.

Selma groped at the head of Axel's blankets where he kept his guns. The Winchester was gone, but her hand closed over the hard-rubber grips of his Colt revolver. She pulled on her shoes and then, revolver in hand, stepped outside.

A touch on her arm made her wheel around, swinging the gun.

"Mama!"

It was Dani. Her voice was hushed and scared.

"What can we do, Mama?"

"Nothing." Selma's own voice sounded hollow against the pulse in her temples. "Pray maybe. And wait. There's nothing else to do."

Dani went back to her tent to comfort the whimpering children. Selma stayed where she was, the mizzling rain clammy on her face. Fully dressed but coatless, she was hardly aware of the chill and damp.

No more shots came.

Unable to wait any longer, Selma started forward, gun clutched wetly in her fist. Then she stopped. Three dark figures were coming across the soaked ground. To her husky call of "Axel?" her husband's voice gave a gruff reply. Selma's knees went weak with a flood of relief.

In a moment he came tramping up to her, saying roughly, "What's this—eh?" And took the gun from her hand. His arm around her shoulders propelled her toward their tent. "Who you trying to be? A warrior woman, eh? A Walkyrie?"

Elof and Lennart had returned with him; they were tromping over to their tent.

"Was nobody hurt?" Selma said urgently. "Axel!"

"Nobody."

"Are you sure?"

"Nothing. Not even a scratch."

They had reached their tent. Axel motioned her to enter, then ducked inside behind her. "Arvid and Rudy will keep guard the rest of tonight," he said. "But I don't think they be back."

Selma heard a metallic clank as he fumbled with the coal-oil lamp. A match was struck and the lamp wick touched; a saffron glow spread through the tent. She turned from securing the tent flap to see him eyeing her scowlingly; water dripped from the tip of his beard.

"You are wet," he said almost accusingly.

"*Ja*, so are you."

"At least I had a coat." Axel shrugged out of the moist garment and tossed it aside. "Come now." Kneeling in front of her as he reached for the neck of her dress. "Out of those wet clothes."

"You too."

He didn't object as her hands moved deftly down the front of his shirt, undoing it.

"Mr. Holmgaard, I want to know what happened out there."

"Not much. There was about five of 'em made a rush on the shack. We was ready."

"Who? Who were they?"

92

"Didn't make out no faces. We shot close to 'em to scare 'em off. They scared off damned easy. Shot back a few times and then ran." A harsh chuckle stirred his chest. "Just some lumberjacks got handed guns and got sent to take back that shanty. Maybe they got slipped a few dollars for the job, but I guess it wasn't near enough. That's how they thought."

"You are lucky nobody got hurt."

The clutch of her fear had loosened. Now anger and chagrin were coming to the fore, but it was hard to keep them uppermost. His hands had unbuttoned her dress to the waist, and now they slipped inside it and moved with a slow, caressing certitude.

"No, *dumskalle*. Not tonight."

"Ah. Maybe you wouldn't say that if your Irishman was about, eh?"

Furious, she seized his hands and thrust them away. "You! What do you mean by that!"

"I see how he looks at you," Axel growled. "You think I ain't got eyes in my head too?"

"That is not my doing—how he looks!"

"You don't lead him on a little, eh?"

"No! And if you think I do, you can—"

"I believe you." He smiled a little. "You are damn nice to look at when you get mad . . . *käresta*."

The big hands were inside her dress again, continuing their movements, gentle and knowing and unhurried, teasing up the hungers of her woman's body that he knew as well as his own.

She moaned softly, throwing back her head. "Oh *Gud—Gud!*" And then: "Put out the lamp, *dumskalle*. Put it out."

Axel reached for the lamp and momentarily held it in one palm, watching her with eyes in which warm blue lights kindled. "You know, sometimes I forget you're still a pretty good-looking old woman."

"You're not bad yourself." The dryness of her mouth made it hard to shape those whispered words. "The lamp . . ."

In a moment the light died away. Selma struggled with her clothes, her fingers awkward with haste. In the hot drumroll of her blood, the flaming tingle of her skin, the rainy chill on her nakedness was scarcely noticed. She lay back on her blankets, cupping her hands over the deep mounds of her breasts.

Slightly flattened by her lying down, they peaked at the nipples with a bigness of tension.

"Mister," she whispered. "Oh mister. . . ."

The small noises Axel made pulling off his clothes seemed abnormally loud. Suddenly he was a warm naked presence bending above her in the dark, unseen and not yet touching, yet known by every sense of her being.

And then, abruptly and hotly, there was touch.

"*Käresta . . .*"

"Ahhh . . . oh yes! Yes!"

Her body arched to meet the hard invasion of his maleness. She took it into her and possessed it with the undulating rhythm and controlled fury of a familiar passion. Her awareness crested in the all-giving all-taking all-blending union of woman and man: one and together, ever and always.

≈ *two* ≈

The Testing

❦ *twelve* ❦

LYDIA GANNETT WAS crocheting varicolored squares for an afghan. Sitting on a hassock in a corner of the big oak-paneled drawing room, she was practically unnoticed by the rest of them.

At any gathering of Gannetts, that was the most comfortable way to pass the time, Lydia had always found. As a member of the family she was expected (at her mother-in-law's insistence) to sit in on their caucuses. But her opinions were never solicited; nobody ever suggested deferring to her judgment. That was fine with Lydia, who was content just to crochet and listen.

At this moment all of them were listening to Saul Peregrine as he stood at room's center, hands rammed in his hip pockets. But it was his sister Letitia who, even when seated, managed to dominate the scene without trying.

Letitia Gannett was the dowager empress of the clan, and she looked it, every inch. Rawboned and rather horse-faced as a young woman, she had been nearly forty when she'd married Dave Gannett, who was then fifty. Prosperous living and the passing years had changed her prominent features to those of an aloof matriarch. Her silver-white hair was drawn into a severe bun at the back of her head, contrasting with her dress of black satin. A gold lorgnette was attached to a long gold chain hooked to her dress above the waist. A plain hickory cane lay across her lap; her veined hands and painfully slow movements showed the ravages of arthritis. But her jet-black eyes were quick and sharp and undimmed.

There were similarities between Letitia and Lydia. Both had been the plain daughters of wealthy families. Neither had ever had a shred of illusion about why their husbands had wed them. But there, as Lydia was only too aware, the resemblance ended. Everything she'd heard of her mother-in-law's behavior as a younger woman indicated that Letitia's iron will was not an accretion of her old age. She'd always possessed it.

"All right, now. Let's get down to brass tacks."

Saul Peregrine spoke in his mild and disarming, yet abrupt, way that commanded the focus of a family gathering as much as it did that of magistrates and juries before which he had argued cases. White-haired and dapper, a diminutive wisp of a man next to his three stalwart nephews, he looked like a courtly gnome. Almost comically so. But he made up for his lack of size with a cultivated range of tricks, not the least of which was a twinkling and roguish charm.

"First of all," he went on, "I've gone over the county records myself. There's no question but that the Ottawa dam does rest partly on that Swede's land. So does the guard shanty. At the moment he has control of both. After what happened yesterday and last night, we needn't doubt that wresting that control away will be quite a chore. Any way we go about it, we've a fight on our hands."

Beau Gannett was sitting on the sill of a recessed window, his arms folded. Impatiently he came to his feet and began stalking the floor up and down.

Lydia watched her husband from the corners of her eyes. Unlike his uncle, Beau had a built-in dynamism; he affected nothing. His gray suit was tailored to a stocky frame that was quilted with springy muscle. A magnetic force flowed out of him; he looked as hard and vibrant and determined as he was. His dark brown hair was parted in the middle and slicked back;

he had his mother's snapping black eyes and old Dave's thrusting shelf of a jaw. He was thirty years old and was often taken for being years older: his deep wild currents of temper and energy were held in check by the hard-won controls of a mature man.

"We fight, then," he said flatly.

"How, Beau?" A flick of dry acid in Saul Peregrine's tone. "Got any more ideas? That gang of tough nuts you sicced on him last night didn't seem to wear too well in a stand-up fight."

Beau swung to face him. "You call that a fight? Slipping a few 'jacks a few bottles and twenty dollars apiece and telling 'em to take that shanty back? Hell! That was a mistake, was all. That Swede is tougher than I thought. But *fight!* I haven't even started." His anger broke to the surface. "Hell's bells! You want to know what I'd like? To get my hands on the stupid bastard responsible for setting that dam and shanty on Slocum's land!"

"Here, now—" Letitia rapped a ringed finger sharply aainst her cane. "I will *not* tolerate language of that sort under this roof!"

"Sorry, Mother. Didn't mean to give you a turn."

Beau's smile was faintly sour; there wasn't a note of apology in his voice. But his reply satisfied Mrs. Gannett. She leaned back, half-lidding her snapping gaze to an alert gentility. Her damask-upholstered armchair was flanked by a pair of plain ladder-backed chairs occupied by her other two sons, one on either side of her. Their positions might have been those of honor guards, except that both Shad and Adam looked to be anything but on guard.

Shad, at least, was entirely at ease. Of him one could readily believe as much. At twenty-five he was the youngest of the brothers, the handsomest of the three, and the most flamboyant. Fair and thin, with a mass of light curly hair, he was always equally ready for a fight or a frolic. At the moment he looked worn and sleepy and faintly surly, probably as a result of too much carousing the night before. His white trousers and peppermint-striped blazer were rumpled, as if he'd slept in them.

Tall and big-shouldered Adam also seemed relaxed, hands plunged in his pockets and his long legs outstretched and crossed at the ankles. He eyed the toe of his shoe with no expression at all, but in Adam such a pose could be deceptive. He was as fair as Shad, but little like him in other ways. Quiet and drawling, Adam seldom revealed his real thoughts, but Lydia knew he was different from any of his family. So different, in fact, that it was often difficult to believe he was a Gannett. Lydia had never known Dave Gannett, but from what she'd heard, Beau must have inherited his father's roughshod nature; Shad, the old man's hellion tendencies. Both possessed his hot temper. Adam had only Dave's formidable size—and if he resembled his mother in any particular, it wasn't apparent.

Letitia's gaze shuttled back to her brother now. "Go on, Solly."

Saul Peregrine was watching his eldest nephew with a kind of benign mockery. "Yes—well. As to assigning blame for a mistakenly located dam, Beau, it's a bit difficult. The U.S. surveyors platted this part of northern Wisconsin almost sixty years ago. Time enough for witness trees and wooden section markers to be cut down or plowed up or burned off. Or simply rotted away. So when Timms, our township surveyor, staked out your dad's boundary line for some newly bought territory along the Ottawa River back in 1901, he erred on his plats, that was all. Or the original surveyors erred—who knows? Regrettable state of affairs, but hardly uncommon. In the past thirty years I've handled literally scores of cases of disputed ownership of timberlands arising from misplaced survey lines. The courts have often given precedence to the original line, even if it can be shown it's wrongly placed. And I don't believe this Holmgaard fellow's line is misplaced." A dry chuckle left him. "From *his* standpoint, it's not."

"All very well," Letitia said crisply. "But we could still take him to court and win. We built that dam, Saul. We hold the franchise. You've said as much before."

"Of course we'd win. No question of it. But it would take time. You've a drive of logs waiting in high water behind that dam. Summer's coming on. A hot dry one could bring the water level way down. Suppose Holmgaard took it in his head to open the sluice gates and leave all that timber stranded high and dry? A good siege of grub rot would ruin thousands of dollars worth of logs for you."

"We can bring the case to docket fast enough," Beau cut

in impatiently. "Hell, Judge Glover owes me a half dozen favors. We can hustle it through in a month or so."

"Not if Holmgaard got him a good lawyer." Saul was in constant motion as he spoke. It might be only a twitch of hand or foot, a shift of his slight body, but always he used motion as much as voice to hold a listener. "I don't think that Swede is stupid, Beau. Soon enough he'd realize that every lawyer in Sayer County carries all the rest of 'em in his hip pocket. And why not? It's the same everywhere. So Holmgaard would bring in his own legal beagle from out of county. A smart one would find plenty of ways to throw wrenches in the works. The dam *is* flooding Holmgaard's land. Suppose he balled us up in a suit for damages? No, sir—I think we'd be fools not to settle this affair as quickly and expeditiously as possible and"—he raised a finger to emphasize his next point—"with as little fanfare as possible."

"Okay, fine," Beau snapped. "Let me get a real crew of huskies together. We'll go in and shoot that damned place of his to pieces. He's got a family he won't want getting hurt. Make it hot enough for 'em, he'll change his tune damn fast."

"Maybe he would. But not without a real shoot-out. One that might be as disastrous for us as for Holmgaard. I just don't believe vigilante justice is the answer."

"Nonsense," Letitia said coldly. "We've handled trouble-makers before this, Solly. Not farmers, but rival lumber companies. We've given them harassment for harassment, bullet for bullet. And we made it stick."

"When Dave was alive," Saul observed gently.

"Yes!"

"Back in the eighties and nineties."

"Since then too, Solly. Not as much anymore, but it happens."

"Yes, sometimes. But Letitia, this is the twentieth century. The old-time moguls' way of settling disputes has about seen its day."

Shad smothered a yawn. "Here we go again, boys. Uncle Solly on the changing times."

Saul wheeled, stabbing a finger at him.

"And you'd do well to listen for a change. You don't understand the temper of these times worth a damn!" Saul's gaze swept the room, touching each Gannett in turn. "None of you does. You live on a little rarified peak of big business dealings. You court that handful of social and business associates who share your own views, which are rapidly becoming as obsolete as dinosaurs. Lord smite me if the average 'jack in one of your camps or one of your sawmill workers isn't more realistically aware of what's going on nowadays than any of you are!"

"What are you talking about, Uncle Solly?" Beau's tone was quietly jeering. "Knights of Labor? The I.W.W.? Pullman strikes and dockworker walkouts? We've never been troubled that way. Loggers don't unionize worth a damn. They're not taken in by all that socialist bullsh—" He cleared his throat. "Bushwah."

"You think not?"

"Man, I've worked in the woods and mills beside our men. You think I don't talk to 'em? They've got gripes and grievances, sure. Every working stiff has. Nothing like what you're talking about."

"You talk *to* your men, not *with* them. There's a difference, Beau. And it's not what I'm getting at anyway."

"Okay. What the hell are you getting at anyway?"

"An attitude. A national state of mind."

Abruptly Saul half turned again, stalking over to Lydia now. His hand shot downward, dipped into the sewing basket on the floor by her feet and came up with a book.

"Mind if I borrow this, my dear? I've a point to make of which this is an apt illustration." He swung to face the room, holding the book up in one hand. "Ever read this, any of you? Hell, have you ever *heard* of it?"

Shad yawned again, blinking at the dust jacket. *"The Octopus,* huh? What is it, a sea story? Jack London stuff?"

Saul Peregrine sent him a withering look. "Shad, sometime try reading some of London's *socialist* writings instead of his thud-and-blunder boys' stories. You wouldn't like 'em, but you might find 'em enlightening—for a change. No, this is a novel by a man named Frank Norris. Ever hear of it, Letitia?"

"Of course I've heard of it," she said crisply. "Spare us your courtroom histrionics, Solly."

"But not read it?"

"No, and I'm surprised if you have. You've always insisted

that popular romances are so much deadwood. Vitiating to the critical faculty, I believe you've put it."

"Romances!" Saul groaned histrionically. "How about you, Beau?"

Beau was eyeing Lydia now, thoughtfully. His face was expressionless, but all the same she felt a rising coldness in her stomach.

"No," he said slowly, almost absently. "I've heard that name, though. Norris."

"What about 'muckraker'?" Saul demanded. "You familiar with that term?"

"Uh-huh."

"Lincoln Steffens? Upton Sinclair? Ida Tarbell? Have you heard of them, if not their books?" Saul slapped the volume down on a parlor stand at Letitia's elbow. "Well, my friends, I have *read* their stuff. Literate people across the nation have. Those novelists have greatly popularized a long-standing American theme that may sound quite 'novel' to *you*. Namely, that the wealthy are big bad wolves. And have done it so cogently as to inspire a rash of antitrust and other anticapitalist legislation. Of course you're aware of that much?"

"Beef inspection acts," Beau said contemptuously. "Pure food laws. Sure the reformers have come down on railroaders and meatpackers and whatnot. Those damned fools were asking for it. What's that got to do with us?" A fresh anger heated his voice. "Damn it all, what right does anyone have to make our kind, the lumbermen, out to be villains? We brought a railroad into upper Wisconsin. We developed the country. We gave people work. When the logging started to play out, it was us started the paper mill to provide other employment. We used our influence in Madison to form a new county and make Winterfield the county seat. What if we did feather our own nests along the way? What in hell's name is *wrong* with any of that?"

"Maybe nothing," Saul Peregrine said quietly. "But if you're starting to get my point—and I think perhaps you are—what you or I think doesn't count for a tinker's damn. It's what the *public* thinks. And what all those muckrakers and trust-busters have got the masses thinking right now is that *we* are the snakes in the American Eden."

"What you seem to be saying, Solly," Letitia said imperturbably, "is that going after that farmer would be a mistake, no matter *how* we do it."

"Exactly. Holmgaard's not another rival firm or business, remember. He's a human being, *one man*. One of the real folks, you might say. One good American family man standing against *us*. Why, it's like a classic situation illustrative of precisely what the muckrakers have been saying all along. And summons up to the public mind every heroic image they have of the little man standing against the big nasty corporation. If you want to help promote that image, go ahead and give this fellow the works. Give it to him with guns or by due legal process—the result'll be the same. You'll swing public sentiment against you and reap yourselves a mountain of adverse publicity into the bargain."

"Does that matter so much?" Letitia asked quietly. "And if so, why?"

"It matters. Nowadays it does. Oh, I know the lumber interests still have a few friends in the state legislature. But not nearly as many as they used to. The boys down in Madison don't really give a hoot what happens this far north except when it affects their own political fortunes—and these days the political winds are blowing up a big storm of reform. Bob LaFollette used to be the only one who sharpened a knife for the lumber barons. These days 'Fighting Bob' has plenty of company. The new public temper has brought a lot of crusaders out of the closet. And speaking of LaFollette," Saul added dryly, "our particular case would be just his meat." Saul Peregrine shut his jaws with a snap of finality, as if to let his listeners chew the cud of his thoughts awhile.

Only Beau would be likely to break the silence, and he did not. His attention came back to Lydia; he was faintly scowling. Again she felt a cold flutter of her stomach. It was accompanied by a movement of her unborn infant that made her catch her underlip between her teeth, biting back pain.

What a fool she had been to leave that Norris novel carelessly thrust in her sewing bag!

Reading had always filled many an idle hour for Lydia, a plain and graceless girl; she was accustomed to reading whatever she pleased. As a teenager she had concealed certain light reading of which she'd known her father and mother would disapprove. But at least her parents had been open-minded where *ideas* were concerned. Not so the Gannetts, with their rockbound conservatism. Since coming to their household, Lydia had grown accustomed to secreting her adult reading as automatically as she'd once hidden the risqué romances of her girlhood. It wasn't hard to manage. Ordinarily the Gannetts, including her husband, paid her almost as little attention as they did any other taken-for-granted fixture of their home. The lone exception was Adam, who was at least considerate.

But as usual, Saul Peregrine had missed nothing. Not even her casual caching of books. And Lord, now what? Now that Beau knew? She would catch aitch-ee-double-ell for certain.

Lydia felt like weeping. She winced to another healthy kick from within.

Why did this have to happen when things had seemed to be going well? Her pregnancy had caused Beau to soften a little; he was looking forward to being a father. While Lydia couldn't deceive herself that his solicitude was rooted in concern for her rather than the son and heir he hoped for, she'd been grateful for that much.

It was Adam who broke the brief silence. Still gazing moodily at his shoes, he said, "Well, what's to try, then? You've got to be driving at something more than what we *can't* do, Uncle Solly."

Saul Peregrine beamed. "You can *do* anything your hearts desire, my boy. I'm merely your family lawyer and sage senior adviser. But if you want my advice, you'll try diplomacy."

"Look," Shad said with a yawn, "I'll go along with whatever the rest of you decide. But let's get it done with, okay?"

"You'll keep a respectful tongue in your head, young man," his mother said sharply. "What kind of diplomacy, Saul?"

"Why, I guess we meet Holmgaard on his terms, Letitia. Partway anyhow. We pay him so much per hundred feet on logs he lets us sluice through the dam."

Beau swung his head toward Saul; a flare of outrage lifted the edges of his nostrils. *"Buy* him off? Give in to the son of a bitch? Is *that* what you're telling us to do?"

"Beau!"

"All right, Mother; you can wash my mouth out later."

Beau's face was set like iron. "Hell! Before I'd pay that damn snorkie a cent, I'd build a narrow-gauge railroad with my own hands and run it clear up to that tract of timber."

"Well, that's a thought," Saul Peregrine said dryly. "In fact I was so sure someone would come up with a notion of toting the logs out on a narrow-gauge, I did a little computing. Laying the track up there clear from Winterfield, including the purchase of right-of-way across property we don't own, will cost you about thirty times as much, at a conservative estimate, as the cost of moving those logs down a convenient river—and I'm figuring in Holmgaard's price. But you can do that, sure. Or—well, that tract is bound to increase greatly in value if you simply leave it unlogged. Hold onto it for a number of years till a chance to sell it or else log it profitably comes along, as it will one day."

"And sacrifice the logs already boomed behind the dam. The hell with that!"

"My sentiments exactly, Beau. Just trying to cover all bases. At that, it would *still* be a shade less impractical than *your* suggestion." Saul paused on that twist of sarcasm to give his next words added weight. "Look at the sense of it, boy. You own a nice piece of pineland up the Ottawa. One of the last big virgin stands in the county. A small fortune in timber, *in addition to* the logs hung up behind the dam. Over the next year, two years, you can move that whole lot of timber down the Ottawa to your mills, easily and cheaply, just as you originally planned. And simply by coming to terms with a Swede farmer."

"That's right! I'll tell you what else we can do too! Shoot him out! Burn him off! Or tie his ass in a legal knot he'll never squeeze out of! I've heard your arguments, Solly—not one of 'em cuts a damn particle of ice with me. I don't give a good goddamn what LaFollette or the great unwashed think of our operating methods! And I don't—"

"That will do!"

The tip of Letitia's cane rapped the floor. Spots of anger burned in her cheeks. "I am still making the decisions, personal and otherwise, for this family! I intend to follow whatever course is best for us. Saul has never steered us wrong. If he feels that prudence and restraint are called for in this instance, we owe his arguments a respectful hearing."

Beau said nothing more. But his hand shook as he took out a cigar, clipped its end with a gold cutter, and snapped his teeth on it.

"Now then," Letitia said briskly. "I have made up my own mind, but I would like to hear a concensus. Adam?"

"I agree with Uncle Solly," Adam said unhesitatingly.

"Shad?"

"Sure."

"Sure what?"

Shad's insouciant grin became a touch sheepish. "What I mean, Mother, is if you and Ad go along with Unc, I will too. Sounds okay to me. Honest."

"Very well. That is a three-to-one concensus, Beau. Have you any counterarguments that are *reasoned* and *temperate?* And I would appreciate a *civil* reply, if its not asking too much."

"Guess I've nothing to say that'll make a hen's tooth of difference to any of you." Beau's voice was low and taut. "But I'll say it anyway. We're this county's leading family. Father left us a mark to live up to. Let this snorkie hold us up and get away with it, and there'll be others—from two-bitters like Holmgaard right on up—anxious to try the same. We've made a share of enemies that'll be damn glad to walk all over us. Think about it."

"Beau, I'm sorry to disagree with you. That would be slightly true, but you're grossly exaggerating the case." Saul Peregrine moved over to his nephew and laid a hand on his arm. "I know how you feel. I mean that sincerely. Yielding goes against my whole grain too. But you have to face the realities of a situation. You have to count your costs in advance, my boy. You have to weigh one price against the other. And my way, I'm convinced, is the lesser evil."

"The matter isn't concluded, Saul." Letitia's tone held a brittle warning. "I do not intend to pay an exorbitant sum for the use of my own dam. Holmgaard's fee is ridiculous. Ten cents on the hundred feet!"

The lawyer nodded his white head. "I've no argument there. Naturally we'll have to beat down that sum. No doubt the fellow named an outlandish price with exactly that in mind." He smiled faintly. "We'll horse-trade him the way our folks used to Down East—eh, Letitia? Want me to take a whirl at it?"

"No. It's not your job. Let the boys do it. Or rather," Letitia nodded gently, as with a satisfying thought, "let Adam do it. He's the diplomat of the crew. Isn't that right, son?"

Adam flushed a little. "If you say so, Mother."

Lydia felt a twinge of pity for him. Adam had as shrewd a business head as any of them, but lacked the Gannett hard-headedness that the rest took for granted. She thought him both flexible and firm, refreshingly honest in his dealings. Exactly the traits that his family was likely to deprecate. Except when they could be turned to advantage.

Letitia picked up *The Octopus* from the parlor stand.

"Well," she said musingly, "I can see where I've been wanting in self-improvement. I must amend that state of affairs. Know thy enemy, eh? May I borrow this book for a day or two, Lydia?"

Feeling Beau's icy glance again, Lydia lowered her gaze to her crocheting. She nodded her head once, up and down.

꘏ *thirteen* ꘏

TWO DAYS AND nights had passed since the raid on the guard shanty.

Axel and the boys had installed a foundation for the barn site. While they waited for the mortar-and-fieldstone bases of house and barn to cure, they felled trees and whipsawed them into planks. When the old buildings had been dismantled, some of the sheathing boards had proved to be rotten. To replace them, the men harvested several of the big scattered pines on the well-timbered ridge to the north, skidding the logs back to camp with their wagon team. They sawed the logs into planks the old-fashioned way. A crude trestle was built; logs were placed on it one at a time. One man stood in a pit underneath it, another on a platform above, while they worked a long straight blade between them. It was slow and punishing work, and each boy was glad when his turn came for guard duty by the dam.

Work moved ahead, but the quiet tensions didn't abate. All of them were keyed up for just about anything. Living on an edge put a strain on their relationships.

This morning, lost in unpleasant musings, Selma at first failed to see a horseman who was coming off the tote road out of the woods.

Then she saw that Dani had paused in her task of gathering the blankets that had been washed early this morning and hung on a line stretched between two trees. The girl stood with her arms full of blankets, a faint smile on her lips. Selma straightened from her task of feeding sticks into the fire under a kettle of water she was heating to wash the dishes. Turning to follow Dani's gaze she saw the man ride into camp.

He stepped out of his saddle and touched his wide-brimmed hat to the women. He was big and fair and handsome; he wore whipcord riding breeches and a red woodsman's shirt. Selma recognized the young man who had spoken to her daughter in town. One of the Gannetts he was, and Selma felt a quick wariness.

To Dani he said pleasantly, "Well, we meet again," and returned her smiling nod. Then his gaze shuttled to Selma. "Mrs. Holmgaard? I am Adam Gannett."

"*Ja*, I know who you are. Is it my husband you want to see? Or my girl?"

Adam Gannett's glance had moved idly back to Dani. Blood rose to his face; he smiled uncertainly. "Like to speak with Mr. Holmgaard, if I may."

"Girls, go fetch your pa," Selma told the twins. "A cup of coffee, Mr. Gannett?"

"Sure thing."

Adam ground-hitched his mount and came over to the fire, sinking down on his haunches by it. Selma got a cup and filled it from the coffeepot. As she handed it to him, nodding to his murmured thanks, she glanced at her daughter. Dani, her face quite pink, had resumed plucking the blankets from the clothesline. She was careful not to look at young Gannett, or he at her.

Julia and Erika ran all the way to the timbered ridge where the men were felling a couple more big trees, limbing them off and sawing them into logs. The sounds of chopping and sawing ceased. Axel emerged from the trees, the twins running ahead of him.

Adam rose to his feet as Axel came tramping into camp and

halted on the other side of the fire. "Afternoon, Mr. Holm-gaard."

Axel didn't reply or even look at him. He tugged a bandanna from his hip pocket, removed his slouch hat, wiped the sweat from his face and from the sweatband of his hat, taking all the time in the world. Finally he set the hat on his head and looked at Selma.

"Got some coffee for your old man, too?"

More of his little games. Behind the mild sarcasm of his words Selma felt a triumphant warmth. This time the Gannetts had not sent lawmen or some of their lumberjacks armed with guns. This time they had sent one of their own. They were ready to dicker. That was what Axel had really been waiting on.

Patiently Adam said his name and that he was representing his family and it was hoped there could be a peaceful resolution of this problem. Selma handed Axel his coffee. He drank off half the steaming brew, smacked his lips, then seemed to notice the young man for the first time.

"So. What does that mean, a peaceful resolution? You come to beat me down on my price?"

"I'm here to offer you a *fair* price, sir. Two cents on the hundred feet of *our* logs to be driven through *our* dam."

"Is that right." Axel swigged the rest of his coffee and tossed the cup into the battered dishpan. "How come you folks are singing a softer tune, sonny?"

"We want an amicable settlement, that's all."

"You didn't worry none about that when you sent them bullyboys with guns the other night."

"That wasn't my idea, Mr. Holmgaard. I wanted to pursue every legal means necessary to secure our rights—but not a course of violence. It was my opinion, even before the dam was built, that the owner of this farm should be suitably reim-bursed for any flood damage to his land. My family didn't agree."

"And who are you? Maybe you're the sissy boy of the lot?"

Adam's face pinkened again. Like many fair-skinned peo-ple, he seemed to blush easily. "I just believe in square dealing and paying my debts in honest coin. Is that hard to understand?"

Axel smiled. "You're the sister that sings soft. That's why they sent you to dicker for 'em. I understand *that*, sonny."

The young man's jaw ridged with an effort to suppress anger. "Mr. Holmgaard, unless we can resolve this matter here and now, somebody may get hurt. You have a family to think about."

"That's better. Now you took the velvet off it."

"Damn it, sir—I'm trying to point out the possible consequences of your intransigence! The sheriff could hire any number of deputies if he had to, in order to serve that warrant on you. He decided against it because he believed it would result in bloodshed that couldn't possibly be justified by what's at stake. He put it to us that way—and suggested we try to reach an agreement with you. I felt that would be sensible. Beau—he's my older brother—couldn't see it. So he sent men with guns. Someone might easily have been killed in that skirmish. Unless we can agree, there are bound to be more—and worse."

Axel turned his head and carefully spat into the fire. "That's up to you."

"Man," Adam said hotly, "I didn't want any part of this! We need that dam; I won't apologize for our installing it. I believe in a fair payment for damages, but if you reject that *and* our offer of toll payment on the logs, what can I say? Have you any notion of how much a concession my family is making by offering you *any* sort of payment? I tell you, we've never done anything of the sort before!"

"I hear you. Who convinced the others? You?"

"Our legal adviser, who happens to be my mother's brother. He has a strong voice with her. Beau got voted down. Otherwise I'd not be here. If I bring back a negative reply from you, I'm afraid Mother will take the gloves off. She'll give Beau his head. Then—God knows what."

Axel's right brow quivered upward. "So they send you with an offer of eight cents less than I ask."

"Ten cents a hundred feet is far too steep. We didn't assume you were serious. Inflexible, that is."

"No. You figure I will grab what I can get, eh? Well now, let's see. How about eight cents?"

"Four," Adam said promptly.

Axel grinned wolfishly. "Six."

"Five."

Axel threw back his head, his deep laughter booming out. "I knew it. You didn't come here to name a flat price, sonny. You got sent to *compromise!*"

"What of it?" Adam said coldly. "That's how business is done. Do we have a bargain?"

"No."

Axel let the word hang like a grease drop suspended in water.

A deep flush of confusion waved across Adam's face. "I thought..."

"You thought I was serious about letting you talk me down like you planned. You were wrong. My price is ten cents on the hundred feet. If you can afford to split differences like you was just doing, you can easy afford that. You think I don't know what lumber sells for on the market these days? What I'm asking you rich people for don't come to a spit in a rain barrel. No, sonny. You ain't beating me down a cent. Like your big bad sheriff says, I got you over a barrel. And that's where you stay till I get what I want."

This arrogant declaration was so calmly, almost pleasantly, understated that for a moment Selma wondered if she'd heard Axel correctly. Was he saying that he'd carry this miserable business still farther, in the face of all good sense? A hot objection rose to her lips, but she wouldn't voice it in front of young Gannett.

"Now you got straight where I stand, you can get figuring where you are, sonny. Your whole crowd. You tell 'em. Quicker you finish that coffee, sooner you'll be on your way."

Abruptly Axel swung around and tramped away toward the ridge.

"You take the time with your coffee, Mr. Gannett," Selma said. "Take all the time you want. Have some more?"

"No, ma'am. Thank you."

Adam raised the cup to his lips. His expression was baffled and bitter. Unconsciously, as it seemed, his gaze strayed to Dani. She was slanting brief glances at him now, biting her underlip.

He smiled self-consciously and looked down at his cup.

What did it mean when two young people were so intently aware of each other and trying hard to cover it up and not succeeding? Selma felt the edge of a fresh worry pressing the other ones.

⚄ fourteen ⚄

BY THE END of the week they were laying joists across the foundation of the new house and getting a floor in place. Meantime the boys were showing signs of weary rebellion at laboring from dawn to dusk every day. It was time to allow them another holiday, and Axel readily granted it. He was eager to get in a little hunting, as were his sons.

By now spring was unfolding fully across the northern woods. Gray willow catkins were bursting their brown sheaths; hepatica and arbutus tinted the forest floor with pastel splashes. The hills were full of grouse and snipe, the river bottoms with ducks and geese. A crackle of rifle fire echoed back and forth through the woods all that Saturday morning and into the afternoon.

About mid-afternoon both Elof and Rudy left off hunting and returned to camp, where they announced their intention of taking the rest of this day off in town.

"Does your pa know you're going?" Selma demanded.

"C'mon, Ma," Elof grinned. "A fellow don't need to ask the old man every time he blows his nose. Anyway I'm of age and the Scientist here, he is coming up fast."

Selma nodded resignedly. "Just see you stay out of trouble."

"Why, Ma, what a suggestion." Elof gave her a solemn wink. "Don't worry none. I'll keep ol' Scientist right in line."

"It's not Rudolf I worry about, *dumskalle*. As if you got to be told."

After digging out a change of clothes apiece, the two boys went down by the dam, where Lennart was standing watch, sunning himself on the riverbank. A wistful look stole over his face as he watched his brothers strip down and ease into the chill water along the shore. Elof, standing waist deep and vigorously soaping his chest, called, "Hey, Len! Want to come along?"

Lennart grinned and shook his head.

"C'mon, boy. Firewater and femmes is a-waiting. High time you got your cherry busted."

Lennart reddened and ducked his face.

"Let him be," Rudy said with a grin. "Someone's got to bear the virtue of this family."

Elof splashed water at him. "You do a pretty fair job of that yourself, Scientist. Jesus, boy, when you going to latch onto a skirt? Times I'd swear you ain't a brother o' mine at all!"

"You'd never believe it, but sometimes I feel the same way. Anyhow, what has skirt-chasing ever got you but trouble?"

Elof smiled and laid a finger alongside his nose. "Fun," he said in a stage whisper.

Rudy shook his head.

Fun! Like taking on jealous boyfriends in knock-down brawls. Elof's tomcatting had barreled him into that kind of "fun" too often. Once he'd even been knocked cockeyed by an angry husband.

That had occurred only two winters ago, when Elof had been tussling in bed with a strawberry blonde and her bruiser of a spouse had burst in on them. In her surprise, the wife had bitten Elof in a highly vulnerable spot. To add injury to injury, the husband had belted Elof silly, then opened a window and pitched him out into a snowdrift. Conspicuously bleeding as he'd staggered jaybird-naked down the wintry street, Elof was frozen blue by the time he'd reached the sanctuary of a friend's home. The incident had rapidly gone the local rounds, and Elof had been a long time living it down. Ma, of course, had been properly mortified—and had packed all Elof's bedclothes out to the barn, where he was compelled to "sleep with the animals, since you got to act like one!" It had been nearly two months before Selma had relented and forgiven. Axel too had been mad at first, but later, in one of his coarsely jocular moods, had kidded Elof about "damn near getting your lifeline cut off."

They climbed out of the water and dried themselves on frayed strips of sacking, then got into their fresh clothes. They shaved and rubbed grease in their hair, and Elof combed and trimmed his silky mustache. Rudy carefully scissored the edges of the downy misplaced eyebrow he'd cultivated on his own upper lip, drawing a guffaw from Elof, who suggested that he "just let Otto lick it off."

The two of them set off on foot down the old tote road, swinging along with the easy strength of youth. The thoughts of both boys were running ahead of them, although the town held a different allure for each.

Rudy wanted a close look at the sawmills and even to wangle a tour of one if he could manage it. Behind that lay a wisp of hope that he might see Rachel Merrick again, if only from a distance. He doubted he could conquer his shyness enough to actually call on her.

Elof whistled cheerfully as they tramped along.

Rudy was sure of the approximate range of his brother's thoughts. They'd revolve around the pretty half-breed or, if she weren't available, any other girl that Elof thought passable. That was all right. Once they reached town, each would go his own way.

They parted near the outskirts of Winterfield, Elof saying with a ribald smirk, "So long, kid. See you later. Don't blow your whole wad in one cathouse, now."

Rudy paused a moment to watch Elof tramp up to a house along the way—the same place where the half-breed girl had been sitting on the porch peeling potatoes—and rap boldly at the door.

With a mental shrug, Rudy walked on. That girl would be lucky if Elof's brashness didn't land them both in hot water. Any normal guy was bound to envy the prowess and sheer gall of a born cocksman like Elof, but in the long run it didn't seem worth the wear and tear.

It was late afternoon as Rudy entered town. All the stores were open for business; a swirl of people thronged the sidewalks. Buggies and spring wagons and saddle horses and a dozen or so automobiles lined the curbs. There were as many farmers and woodsmen in evidence as there were townspeople, for Saturday was market day.

The town was particularly crowded on this weekend because of the crowds of lumberjacks fresh out of winter camp. They tramped the walks their calked boots had mutilated, or lounged around in groups. Most of them were bearded and gamey-looking. After collecting their pay at the First National Bank, they'd hit the barbershops and then the saloons. Many would be too avid for whiskey to bother with the luxury of baths, shaves, and haircuts. But some were sober family men who'd hired out to the camps for the winter and would return to their homes and farms with their winter's pay intact.

Rudy loitered among them for a while, idling in and out of the stores, taking in scraps of gossip.

There was a strangeness in being exposed to these sights and sounds after being confined for so long to his family circle. The change was as bracing as wine; his spirits rose and his senses sharpened. He was in no hurry to quit the pleasant hurly-burly. Rudy hardly minded that he had nothing in his pocket but small change and had to content himself with just looking over the store wares. Curious and observant, he enjoyed just strolling and watching. He absorbed the look of people, their laughter and talk; he amused himself by drawing surmises about their lives and occupations.

He lost track of time. As the milling of people thinned out, many taking their way homeward, he noticed it was sunset and then realized how hungry he was. He took supper at a small but clean cafe, where fifteen cents bought him a chunk of roast beef, a mound of mashed potatoes and gravy, a wedge of apple pie, and all the coffee he could drink. The droning thunder of sawmills reached even inside the cafe, for the mills ran three shifts for twenty-four hours every day. But probably things would be a bit slack on the night shift, and he'd stand his best chance of getting inside one of the plants now or a little later.

By the time Rudy left the cafe, twilight had settled and lights were coming on over the town. He started out toward the cluster of sawmills on the city's north side, but found himself turning up the side street where Rachel Merrick's rooming house was.

As he'd more or less expected, his courage failed him before he reached her front gate. He spent several minutes walking idly up and down the other side of the street, sneaking glances at the house. Suddenly he saw a twitch of movement, the stir of a curtain, behind the front window. Someone had parted the curtain to peer out at him. Face burning, he continued up the street, walking fast.

At the west end of the street, where it ended at a cut-over flat, Rudy swung up a cross street toward the sawmills. Between the mills and the main business district lay a dilapidated section of town known as Thirsty Hollow. From what Axel had said, this was a pleasure point to which all the lumberjacks and other roughs gravitated. The center of its activities was Joyner Street, where every other building was a saloon and the ones between them just as uniformly whorehouses. Two of them bore signs designating them as rooming places—Nettleton's Room and Board and Harriet's Boarding Academy, whose proprietresses were better known as "Nasty Nettie" and "Hard Ass Hattie"—but generally they were discreetly unmarked.

Rudy tramped slowly up Joyner Street, keeping an interested eye peeled, but staying to the middle of the mud-rutted avenue. This proved to be a sound precaution. A roar of revelry poured out of every saloon. A racket of boozy good cheer, but under it lay a pulse of violence.

Suddenly the swing doors of a saloon burst open. A drunken lumberjack was forcibly ejected; he skidded facedown in the gutter and lay there groaning. From another saloon, just moments later, a pair of tussling 'jacks rolled out beneath the doors onto the boardwalk, where they sprawled gouging and biting, battering one another with boots and fists, to an accompaniment of jeers and cheers from a crowd of their fellows.

It was all pretty high for Rudy's taste. He didn't linger in Thirsty Hollow.

Heading north a few more blocks, he came to the broad shimmer of Log Lake, a broad man-made flowage that fixed the town's northern boundary. Thirty years ago, the dam that spanned the Paradise River at Winterfield had created the lake by backing water into a wide flat basin which was then a stretch of swampy lowland. Here, for years, the lumbermen driving logs from upriver had corraled their winter's harvest, confining the logs with great boom chains that were maneuvered by steam tugs. Later, when narrow-gauge railroads had been constructed to tap the timber stands less accessible to the river, trestles had been built into the lake from which the flatcars could unload, tipping their cargoes into the water.

Winterfield's two big sawmills were situated along the lakeshore. This close to them, the din of the giant rotary saws was deafening. Rudy felt a ferocious exultance in the drone of harnessed power, in the tang of fresh sawdust and burning wood. Each mill was equipped with a tepee-shaped burner from which billows of smoke erupted as sawdust and tailings were fed into it.

He was so occupied in absorbing the scene that a man's sharp "Hey, you!" just a few yards away made him jump.

A stocky fellow in rough clothes strode up to him. "You work here, kid?"

"No, I just—"

"*What?*"

Rudy raised his voice against the mill roar. "No, I don't!"

"Then what the hell you hanging around for?"

Rudy's cheeks grew hot. "Nothing. I just wondered, uh . . ."

"What did you wonder, kid?"

"If I could, you know, go inside and kind of look around."

The man looked him over, then spat at the ground. "We ain't offering no guided tours, bud. There's a lot of dangerous machinery in there. Guys get their fingers and whatnot cut off. Happens all the time. Say, what you want to go in for?"

"Well . . . I—I was just curious."

"That so." The man puffed his cigar to a glowing eye; he dropped it and scuffed it out. "A real bright-eyed boy, ain't you? Maybe fixing to throw a wrench in the works. Start a burnout that would put us out of business."

"No," Rudy said bewilderedly.

"There was a bright-eyed boy tried that last year. Turned out he was working for a rival outfit." The man gave Rudy's chest a jarring thud with the heel of his palm, shoving him backward. "I tell you what, Bright Eyes. You haul ass off mill property, and that damn quick. I ever catch you poking around here again, you'll get your head broke. G'wan!"

Rudy braced himself, fisting his hands. Then he saw the quick shift of the man's weight in the dusk, a dull gleam of something in his right hand held flat against his thigh. A flicking glance showed Rudy what it was: a leather-covered blackjack. This fellow must be a watchman.

Rudy backed off a few more steps, then turned and walked away. The man's trailing chuckle was baleful in his ears.

He continued walking fast and straight toward the lights of Joyner Street. A red flare of temper rose in his brain. It made him feel as one with the spill of raucous noise that issued from the saloons. He turned unhesitatingly into the first one he came to, slamming through the swing doors and tramping across the sawdust-covered floor to the bar.

A glare of lamps hardly relieved the damp gloom of the long room. The stink of raw whiskey and men's unwashed bodies was as tangible as the reek of smoke from cigars and Durham "roll-your-owns." You could be sure that no "pimp-sticks," tailor-made cigarettes, were in evidence here. Men were bellied against the fifty-foot bar. They ganged around the tables, making a hubbub as ferocious as the mill noise.

A harassed-looking bartender growled at Rudy, "Yours?"

"Whiskey."

"Heh? Speak up!"

"Whiskey!"

"How old are you, kid?"

Rudy said promptly, "Twenty-one," his temper making the lie come easily.

"You said it, I didn't," grunted the bartender. "Two bits."

He pointedly waited till Rudy dug out a quarter, then set a shotglass before him and filled it to the brim. Rudy was irritated by the bartender's wisely sardonic stare. Something Pa had once said crossed his mind: "Girls sip. A man takes it right down."

He tossed the drink down and smiled at the bartender. "How 'bout another?"

The man slapped a palm on the bar. Rudy laid out his money, feeling the liquor flood his belly and brain. Both beer and wine had always been sparingly served at meals in the Holmgaard household; he was accustomed to them. But this was a new glowing experience.

He took his second drink as quickly and casually as the first.

"Hey. The little Swede it is. *Bon jour!*"

The soft voice at his back cut through the noise and Rudy's golden feeling. Startled, he turned around. The man stood only a yard from him, yet it took him a fuddled moment to recognize Canuck John LeBoeuf.

"Hey-hey! *Mon ami*, but look who is here!" LeBoeuf glanced toward a table some distance away. "The little Swede who help his daddy take the dam from us, *n'est-ce pas?* Come—*vous pouvez constater!*"

In the diffused dimness of the room, Rudy could hardly make out the man to whom the remark was directed. Then a face turned. He saw the gleaming dome and elongated jaw of Bear Roback. The giant pushed away from the table and came slowly to his feet. His hand engulfed the tumbler of whiskey in it; he never took his eyes off Rudy.

Talk died in the room. When this brutish slab of a man took a stance such as he was taking now, it was enough to wash out every other presence for twenty feet around him. Roback's hairless head nearly brushed a beam of the ceiling. Rudy stood rooted to the spot, confused almost as much by two belts of liquor as by this menacing apparition.

Canuck John LeBoeuf said pleasantly, "He remembers, m'sieu. So do we both. Ho! That big bad daddy of yours make the great fools of us. *Un brave homme*, eh? But not so nice as you."

Almost casually he brought up his hand, took a pinch of Rudy's cheek between thumb and forefinger and gave a sudden, vicious twist.

The pain broke Rudy's paralysis. He lunged at LeBoeuf, wildly swinging. LeBoeuf stepped away from the blow and seized Rudy's arm. He twisted the boy around in a violent arc, then flung him away with a laugh. "Eh—now! *Qu'est-ce que vous allez prendre!*"

Rudy went kiting halfway across the room. Frantically back-pedaling for balance, he plunged into Roback's outstretched arm. Roback's hands clamped on both his arms, then swung him off his feet.

Rudy screamed as the iron grip sent agony spurting along his muscle strands. A moment later he was hurled to the floor, skidding on his belly and face across a splintery carpet of wood chips. Half stunned when he came to a stop, he tried to move. Succeeded only in flopping on his back.

Almost detachedly he saw Roback looming above him. Mercifully he was too numb to be very aware of what was done to him next. And then he knew nothing at all.

࿊ *fifteen* ࿊

THE DAY WAS so unseasonably warm that Rachel Merrick opened all the windows in her boardinghouse to let every room air out. Taking advantage of the fine weather, she and Lotte Hoffenmeier spent the whole day at a spring-cleaning chore that had to be done outdoors. They carried out all the rugs in the house, from heavy parlor carpets to rag scatter rugs, to the backyard and draped them over the clothesline. Each got a thorough beating. Several of the rugs were so bulky, even when rolled up, that it had been all that the two women could do to wrestle one out the door and back inside again.

The daylong job was as dirty as it was exhausting. Of all that fell to her lot as mistress of a boardinghouse, it was the job that Rachel hated most. Even more than having to put up with the taint of tobacco smoke her male lodgers contributed to nearly every room in the house. It clung acridly to every curtain and cushion; it permeated the walls and woodwork. And like the occasional spill of ashes or char mark on furniture, it was accepted without a murmur. None of her guests was deliberately careless or inconsiderate. They were just . . .

bachelors. Rachel took pride in the reputation of her rooming house as being the best in town. She saw religiously to the comfort of her guests, to the quality of everything from spotless sheets to the wine served with meals. She never questioned their comings or goings, insisting only on a modicum of propriety.

Rachel Merrick owned a high degree of respect in Winterfield, among women as well as men. Since she hadn't been born to it, since achieving it had taken years of perseverance, it meant a good deal to her. The work and dedication she poured into the excellent upkeep and high standards of her rooming place was a small price to pay for that respect. Not that it was her sole compensation. The rates she charged for room and board were steep enough that if she weren't commensurately generous with the money as well as time she donated to worthy causes in the community, public gossip might have branded her as penurious.

The day's warmth held into the early evening, but as the dusk thickened, a chill entered with the breezes coasting through the house. Rachel went through the upstairs rooms, closing and locking windows. Not one of her ten boarders was at home this evening. All of them were bachelors, all were professional men, all were fairly young. Most of them had left town for the weekend, on fishing trips or to visit friends and relatives. Several were seeking diversions of one sort or another here in Winterfield. Each had notified her that he wouldn't be taking meals at the boardinghouse today.

Thank goodness for that, Rachel thought as she descended the staircase to the parlor. The day's work had been taxing enough without having to prepare meals, too. By now it was well after the supper hour, and Rachel hadn't had a bite to eat since early morning. Too tired to feel very hungry, she went to the kitchen, made a cold beef sandwich, and took it and a glass of milk out to the back stoop. She sat on the bottom step and enjoyed the evening coolness as she ate.

It was nearly full dark. A boisterous bedlam of mirth and rage drifted quite clearly from Thirsty Hollow, only two blocks away. Most of the loggers from camps for miles around would be in town tonight and for several nights to come, living it up at bar and brothel for as long as their winter's pay held out.

At least a few heads would be broken tonight—and scores of them would be aching tomorrow. The city's small police force would be busy most of the night; by morning the jail would be filled to overflowing.

Rachel could hear Lotte moving through the first-story rooms, securing windows. Once that was done, they could relax for the night. Tomorrow they would get to the washing of drapes and curtains. Just now it was pleasant to think of nothing but a hot bath to cleanse away the sweat and grit. Then a glass of sherry . . . a pleasant hour or so with the new Tarkington novel . . . a clean bed and a good night's sleep.

Such a few creature comforts to be grateful for, Rachel thought with only mild irony. Most of the time it seemed to be enough—along with housekeeping chores and community activities. At least it kept a body properly busy. And almost anything—she thought with a flick of bitterness—was preferable to taking the risk of being hurt, the chance of being burned. . . .

Musing in the dusk, she paid only a slight attention to the sound, muffled by intervening rooms, of someone rapping at the front door. Lotte would answer it.

A moment later she heard the girl call, *"Fräulein*, you better come here. Come quick!"

Lotte's tone held an urgent note that brought Rachel quickly to her feet. She hurried through the house to the front parlor.

Lotte was on her knees beside a man. He lay belly down on the carpet just inside the threshold. His head was turned sideways toward Rachel and his face was a shocking sight, bloody and battered. For the space of several heartbeats she could not tell who he was. Then she knew: the young fellow who had carried her packages home.

What was his name? Yes . . . Holmgaard. Rudy.

"Oh Lord," Rachel said softly. "What happened to him?"

"I do not know. There is the knocking, and the door I open. In he comes and falls to the floor. Should I get the doctor?"

Rachel felt queasy as she stared at the unconscious youth. His clothes were covered with mud as if he had repeatedly stumbled and fallen. Or else had dragged himself a long way, literally crawling. But his face. God! His lips were mashed and swollen, his nose a broken bleeding pulp, his face and clothing caked with blood. Worst of all, a triangular flap of skin hung from an inch-wide gash in his right cheek.

"Fräulein?" Lotte said sharply.

"Yes. Yes, of course. The doctor. But we can't just let him lie—"

"Ja, I think so. Suppose something busted is?"

"That's so. We won't move him yet." Rachel recovered her crisp efficiency. "Telephone Dr. Hammerstein, Lotte. Hopefully, at this hour he'll be home. Meantime I'll make up the bed in the spare room."

Dr. Jacob Hammerstein, a smallish, capable man in his forties, arrived within fifteen minutes. He made a quick examination.

"Three ribs broken," he said. "That's the worst I can tell at the moment. Miss Hoffenmeier mentioned a spare bed you have. Help me get him to it."

They carried Rudy to a small bedroom under the stairs and carefully laid him on the narrow bed. After making it up, Rachel had covered it with an old rug. The doctor pulled Rudy's boots off, then gave the women a dry glance. "You ladies want to make yourselves useful, you might boil some water and tear up something for bandages."

"Maybe the *fräulein* will do that," Lotte said grimly. "I help you. I have five brothers, doctor."

Hammerstein chuckled. "So you know how a man looks, eh? Good. I can use the help."

Rachel went to the kitchen to lay a fire in the range and put some water on to heat. She sat in a chair at the table and clenched her hands together in her lap, angry at her own qualms. Lord! She'd grown up in Winterfield at a time when it was still a raw boomtown, far wilder than it was now. Men and their rough ways were no novelty to her. Neither was the coarse side of life. Maybe that was the answer. She had been through too much. She had put that time well behind her and had no stomach for more of it.

With effort Rachel thrust her queasy revulsions out of mind, rose, and walked to the ragbag that hung on the wall beside the icebox. She dug out the remains of an old petticoat and ripped the garment into long strips. By the time she was finished, the water had come to a boil. She carried the kettle of water and the improvised bandages to the bedroom.

She halted in the doorway, feeling a wrench of genuine sickness. The boy was stripped and covered to the waist with a blanket. His bare torso was literally a mass of livid and purplish bruises, shoulders and chest and sides. In places the skin was broken, the flesh mangled to a red pulp.

"Here, *Fräulein*," said Lotte, more gently than was her habit. "I will take the water."

She lifted the precariously tilting kettle from Rachel's nerveless hand and set it on the marble-topped washstand. Dr. Hammerstein was sitting by the bed, carefully probing his fingers along Rudy's short ribs. He glanced sharply at Rachel. "You all right? Want some smelling salts?"

"Quite all right . . . thank you." Rachel drew herself erect and came to the bedside, trying not to avert her eyes from the boy. "Doctor, what could have happened to him?"

"Well, he's collected a sight more than the usual case of lumberjack's smallpox, that's sure. Matter of fact, I don't think he was stomped at all. Someone worked him over with the boots by just kicking hell out of him, is my guess. You have any idea why, Miss Merrick?"

Rachel swallowed and shook her head. "None. I barely know him. All I know about him is that he's the son of that Swedish farmer over on the Ottawa."

"Fellow who's held up a Gannett log drive? Well, well." The doctor nodded judiciously. "Maybe that's it. A retaliation."

"Doctor, I can't believe that. Whatever the Gannetts may be, they're not . . . not savages. Or butchers!"

"Uh-huh," Hammerstein said in a neutral voice. "Well, this was more than just the result of an ordinary saloon set-to. They did a job on him. Whoever. Maybe when he comes to, the lad can shed a bit of light on who."

"How—just how badly is he hurt?"

"Hard to say, ma'am. He looks a mess for sure, but I can't make out anything worse than those busted ribs. Can't tell if there's been any internal injury . . . have to wait and find out."

He began to sponge congealed blood from the youth's macerated flesh. Suddenly Rudy groaned aloud; his whole body jerked in a raw convulsion. "Coming to," the doctor muttered. "May have to give him something to quiet him down."

The boy's eyes flew open, wild with pain. "Elof!" he cried. "Elof..." He began to thrash furiously, throwing the doctor's hands away.

Hammerstein reached for his black bag. He produced a hypodermic syringe and filled it from a bottle. "Morphine. Hold his arm steady, Miss Hoffenmeier...."

Rudy quieted almost as soon as the needle was inserted, the plunger depressed.

"Rotten stuff," Hammerstein said. "Addictive. But for that much pain—it's three quarters of a grain of this or something worse, like heroin. Well, he'll sleep now, and we'll get him cleaned up. He's young and healthy. If he can sleep off the worst of it, he can bear the rest while he gets healing. And if those ribs *are* the worst of it."

Rachel said, "Elof. Was that the name he said?"

"His brother it is," Lotte said matter-of-factly.

"How would you know that?"

Lotte's wide mouth turned up at the corners. "Always people talk, *Fräulein*. If you want to learn, you listen."

"I'm afraid I haven't much ear for backyard washerwoman talk, Lotte."

"*Nein,* I think you don't. My brother Hans who works at the livery stable has a girl friend who knows the girl friend this Elof has, Swan O'Dea."

"Oh, that trapper's daughter."

"*Ja.* This Swan is a flirt and tells all to her friend. She meets with this Elof sometimes. This Rudy, maybe he come to town with his brother."

"Well—" Rachel kneaded her underlip between her teeth. "I suppose we should try to find the brother, then. But I don't know...."

Briskly, Lotte removed her apron. "To find Hans I go. He will look for the brother."

❧ sixteen ❧

DAWN BROUGHT A high wind out of the west. Mare's tails of rain gusted off and on through the morning, slashing against the tent walls. The Holmgaards stayed under shelter today, all of them in their own tents. All but Lennart, who was on duty at the dam. Claps of thunder broke the intermittent bursts of wind that tugged at the tent flaps, which were closed and secured.

Selma sat cross-legged on the groundsheet and darned socks while Axel lay on the blankets with his arms folded behind his head, staring at the wet tent roof through which a dim light filtered. He was in a sour frame of mind because the erratic weather compelled a day off from work on the buildings. And, though he wouldn't admit as much, because neither Rudy nor Elof had returned from Winterfield.

Selma had been worried since early this morning, when she'd found that Rudy wasn't back. Elof would go to town solely to carouse; he might not return for a couple of days, and it did no good to worry about him, though she always did. But for Rudy to stay out the whole night was not at all like him. Now it was close to noon, and no sign of either one.

"Axel," she said quietly.

He grunted.

"I think soon, if they're not back, you should go to town and find them."

"Hell's bells, woman. They're grown up now. When they get an itch for a fling, they will have it, like it or not. Let 'em."

Selma's lips tightened as she slipped her darning egg inside another sock. "Rudolf is a boy. Not a wild boy, either."

"No, not a boy either. He's your baby, ain't he? Your chick you cluck over."

A chuckle stirred Axel's chest. His boots were off, his sock feet crossed at the ankles, as he reclined at ease. Selma's eyes snapped at him. She swung the sock with the wooden egg in it and caught him on the toe. He let out a yowl of pain and anger, and raised on his elbows. For a moment they glared at one another, and then, almost at the same time, they began to grin a little.

"Give it a little longer, old woman. Even your little Rudy has got to get his green rubbed off sometime. Maybe that's what he went and done. If he did, he could have a head so big he won't be able to stand up today."

"But he could be hurt," Selma said severely. "Or out on the wet ground somewhere."

"Nah. With Elof, ain't he? Elof's been through it all before. He'd see to it him and his brother had a dry place to sleep it off. He's got *that* much sense, anyway."

A fresh whisk of rain rattled against the tent canvas. Selma went on darning, unable to still the growth of worry. Likely Axel was right. Maybe she didn't want to admit that Rudy, her best and brightest, could take it in his craw to raise a rumpus. All the same, if he did not come back soon . . .

"Hello the camp!" a voice called from outside.

It was a stranger. Startled, caught entirely off guard, Axel scrambled to a sitting position. He tugged on his boots and then reached for his revolver, holding it at his side as he pushed out the tent flaps. Selma followed him outside. Arvid had also come out of the boys' tent, rifle in hand.

The newcomer looked soberly at Axel and then Arvid, and back at Axel. "Mr. Holmgaard?"

"*Ja.*"

"My name is Hans Hoffenmeier. I come with news for you."

"What is it?" Selma cried before Axel could reply.

"Your son Rudy it is. He's hurt bad. He is alive, Frau Holmgaard, but he is pretty bad hurt."

Hans Hoffenmeier spoke in the labored English of one recently come to this country. He was a tall lath of a fellow, maybe twenty years old. He was muffled in a yellow slicker and rubber boots and a felt hat that was so water-soaked the brim drooped limply above his somber brown eyes.

It wasn't easy to get coherent replies out of him. Hans had a slow and deliberate way of framing his thoughts; he was slightly confused by the way Axel rapped questions, fierce and strident. But as he gave his sturdy careful answers, the story became clear enough.

For a couple of hours last night Hans had combed the streets and saloons, asking after Elof Holmgaard, but had finally quit and gone to bed. When he'd reported his lack of success to Lotte this morning she had suggested that Hans should take the news of Rudy to his family. It being Sunday and his day off, Hans Hoffenmeier had agreed.

Axel stalked slowly up and down. He was bareheaded, his red hair bushing wildly. His big hands flexed open and shut as he clipped questions at the visitor.

The first grip of Selma's fear somewhat unclenched with Hans's assurance that her son's injuries were severe, but not dangerously so. Watching her husband's face, she felt the direction of her concern veer uneasily. Axel's jaw shelved out like a ridge; his eyes held a burn of volcanic rage. He was containing himself with an effort.

"So," he murmured. "The police, they do nothing. Eh?"

Hans explained that although he'd informed the city police of what had happened to Rudy, there was little they could do as yet. Last night Chief Baird and his three-man force had been occupied the night long with keeping a semblance of order in Winterfield, the town being crowded with lumberjacks and a fresh free-for-all breaking out every few minutes. It would be almost impossible to trace back through all those melees exactly

132

what had happened to one beaten-up youth. Only Rudy could say for sure, and he was deep in a drugged sleep. Or had been when Hans had departed Winterfield a couple of hours ago.

"I'll go to Winterfield with you," Axel told him. "You show me where this Merrick woman lives."

"I will come too," Selma put in.

Axel's hot blue stare sprang to her. "You will not."

"Gud bevara! My boy is hurt and you—"

"Tomorrow," Axel said very quietly. "Then I'll take you there myself. But now I go alone."

She did not have to ask why. She knew. And she knew it wouldn't do a jot of good to object. When Axel's mind was set, you might as well try to shout down the wind. She'd defied him on more than one occasion—within limits. But this time Selma knew that Axel would not be crossed.

Never, in all their years together, had she felt such an intense fury in him.

Axel ducked back into the tent. Dani and the twins had opened the flaps of their tent so they could watch and listen, but they didn't venture outside. Shivering against another rainy gust, Selma drew her shawl around her shoulders and talked to Hans Hoffenmeier, plying him with more questions, trying to draw straws of assurance from his plodding replies. Then she heard Arvid say softly, "Ma. Elof's coming."

So he was.

He was coming off the forest road, and now he called, "Hi, Ma! What's doing?" Swinging along with that jaunty go-to-hell swagger of his that sometimes amused but nearly always infuriated her. Selma felt a rise of anger. She was about to let it out when Axel emerged from the tent. He was wearing his mackinaw and slouch hat and carrying his rifle. At the sight of Elof tramping into camp, he pulled up stock-still.

Temper blazed across his face. He started toward Elof.

Selma moved quickly after him. A moment ago she had been ready to tongue-flay Elof; now she thought only of interceding before Axel got to him.

But Axel had control of himself. He halted a dozen feet from his son and whispered the question, "Where you been?"

The grin faded from Elof's lips. His gaze swept across them, lingering puzzledly on Hans Hoffenmeier. It was obvious that something was amiss—and that his father was in no mood for trifling.

"In town," he said defiantly. "Hell, you know where I been. What—"

"Where was you when your brother got the shit beat out of him?"

Elof's expression made it plain that he was dumbfounded. Selma came up to him and laid a hand on his arm. "Rudy has been hurt," she said in a low voice. "We want to know how it happened. Do you know?"

Plainly he didn't, but mostly she'd moved just to place herself protectively between her husband and her son. She quickly explained the news that Hoffenmeier had brought.

Elof was shaking his head before she finished, a sickness of shock in his face. "Ma. I had no idea, honest to God. Rudy and me went our own ways when we got to town. After that—"

"Where the hell were you!" The words left Axel in a roar. "Off drinking someplace? Or was it screwing? Where were you when they was beating him up?"

"Now just hold on, Pa. I got no duty to look after him or anyone. And you got no damn call to—"

"You had no damn business going off and leaving that boy alone!"

Elof's face hardened. "Is that right? I need to be my brother's keeper, huh? Well, that's what you say. I don't hold myself to account—"

"I goddamn well do!" The big vein was swelling in Axel's temple. "This boy here, Hoffenmeier, he was looking for you all over town. He couldn't find a lousy sign of you! Just what the hell was you doing all night long?"

Elof's fists clenched at his sides. "None of your damn business, Pa."

Axel said an inarticulate word. He started forward again.

Selma's fingers bit into Elof's arm. "Be still," she told him fiercely. "Be still now!" And swung around to face her husband.

"No!" she shouted at him. "You do nothing! You hear me? *Nothing!*"

Axel came to a stop. His clenched teeth showed through his beard.

"He did no wrong, Axel," she said quietly then. "You are mad. So am I mad. That we can't help. But we're the wrong ones. You think, if he knew Rudy was in trouble, he wouldn't be there to help as quick as you or me would?"

Axel shut his jaw. He pulled his weight back on his heels and looked at Hans Hoffenmeier.

"Now," he said in a normal voice, "we go to town."

Looking embarrassed and more than a little bewildered, Hans nodded.

Without another word, without a glance at any of them, Axel tramped away toward the road. Young Hoffenmeier followed him, loping a little to keep up with Axel's long driving strides.

ๆ *seventeen* ๆ

"COME ON NOW, son," Chief of Police Baird said brusquely. "Who did this to you? Talk up!"

Hard-eyed and trap-jawed, Baird stood with his fists on his hips and glared down at Rudy Holmgaard. The chief's patience was thinning away. It was the third time he had put the question and had drawn no reply. Rudy lay with his pulpy lips pressed shut and stared at the ceiling and said nothing.

Rachel couldn't understand why. Certain that the youth would want to prefer charges, she herself had telephoned Tom Baird as soon as Rudy had showed signs of reviving. His refusal to name the man or men who had assaulted him vexed her as much as it surprised her.

"Rudy," she said gently. His eyes in their nests of darkly bruised flesh moved enough to fix on her. "Rudy, if you don't know the names of the parties, at least you might give Chief Baird their descriptions. Surely you want to help apprehend them... identify them?"

Rudy's head moved on the pillow, side to side. He looked back at the ceiling.

Rachel bit her lip in exasperation. She wanted to give him a good shaking. At the same time she felt a warmth of feeling that made her want to touch his rumpled hair, his hot brow, to say words of comfort. The feeling surprised and disturbed her. Of course she felt sympathy—who wouldn't? His face was mangled and swollen, stitched in places and crisscrossed with bandages. She knew he was in pain that he kept fighting back. Dr. Hammerstein had refused to administer any more narcotic, for whose addictive properties he had a healthy distrust.

But there was more to the way he touched her feelings. It was his brooding and sensitive youth that she had liked from the first, that was somehow enhanced by the stubborn little-boy silence with which he met Baird's questions.

Rachel almost smiled. She felt maternal and indulgent toward this boy. That was all of it.

Baird's face turned a deeper red under his thinning saddle of reddish hair. He lifted a fist from his hip and pointed the first finger at Rudy, shaking it. "What do you think you're up to?" he said harshly. "Planning to wait and tell that family of yours so you can all plan some kind of private vendetta against the guys who beat you up? That it?"

"Tom," Rachel said reprovingly.

"Damn it—darn it, Rachel, I'm sorry, but from what Joe Pleasants has told me about that business with the dam, it's just the kind of thing this bunch would cook up. I'd just hate like hell—like heck to see that happen. When I was a kid growing up in Kentucky, I saw family feuds kick up all over the place. Believe you me, they're something to avoid. And pretty damned—darned inevitable when your ordinary citizen refuses to cooperate with the law!"

"Perhaps he has another reason, Tom."

"Yeah? What might that be?"

Rachel smiled at the boy. "Rudy . . . won't you tell us that much?"

"No, ma'am," he said quietly. "My reason doesn't matter."

"Agh," Baird said disgustedly, and clamped on his uniform cap. At the disapproval in Rachel's glance, he yanked it off, muttering, and turned toward the doorway.

Rachel preceded him out to the parlor, saying over her shoulder, "Really, Tom, I don't understand it."

"He's a smart punk, that's what he is. Kids his age generally are."

"No," she said sharply. "He's not that sort. I am surprised you'd think so, Tom. I should think you would read people a bit more shrewdly. He's as nice and polite a young man as I've ever met, and you can be sure he's aware of his responsibilities as a citizen. If he won't talk, you can be sure—"

"Won't talk, eh?"

Andrew Fordyce was reclining on the leather sofa in the parlor, feet crossed and a notebook spread open on his chest.

He swung to his feet and came over to them. A slight, brisk, peppery man, he was in his late thirties. His sharp features were pale and freckled, green eyes as alert as a ferret's, his teeth bared in a quizzical grin.

"What's the story, Chief?" Fordyce tapped a pencil against his open notebook. "I need a lead feature for this week's paper. This has the smell of one. How about it?"

"She can tell you as much as I know," Baird said sourly. "Rachel, if he changes his mind, if you should get him to talk, whatever, get in touch."

"Of course, Tom."

She saw Baird to the door and shut it behind him, then looked coolly at Fordyce. "I think I've mentioned, Andrew, that I've no objection to anyone's lying on the sofa *if* he takes his shoes off first."

Fordyce made a slight, ironic bow. "Of course. Any favor for the fair. My apologies. Now, what's the lowdown on this kid getting beat up?"

"How did you hear about it? But that's a silly question, isn't it? There's so little you miss."

One thing Fordyce didn't miss was the tart edge on her tone. He grinned.

Rachel liked men on a non-intimate basis. She liked their company and their talk and, when it wasn't salted with vulgarity, their wit. But she had never liked Andrew Fordyce. He never attempted to flirt with her, seriously or banteringly, as most of her other lodgers did. It was easy to fend them off with polite, friendly humor, and neither she nor they ever took offense. In a lumber town, men of all stations respected decency in a woman and behaved accordingly.

Rachel couldn't justify the repugnance that Fordyce inspired in her on any rational ground. He observed the outward proprieties she demanded of her roomers. His habits were passable enough for a bachelor newsman's. He was something of a night owl, but his conduct was discreet. He did court the dregs of Winterfield's society as well as that of its well-placed members, but Rachel had realistically concluded that as editor of the town's only weekly paper he couldn't do otherwise and report the local news in a balanced and conscientious way.

And Andrew Fordyce *was* conscientious.

He was the town's maverick gadfly, its self-appointed resident Socrates. Some targets of his savage and sarcastic editorializing might howl to the heavens, but none of them could fault him on accuracy. There was something like an unnatural ardor in his pursuit of the facts—and his delight in flaying even the petty transgressions of citizens who had it coming, no matter who they might be.

Perhaps it was that which put her off, Rachel thought. If Fordyce had any need of a woman, it wasn't as a life's companion. He was married to his life's mission.

He answered her comment genially enough. "Right you are. And you're aware that a good newspaperman never divulges his sources."

"All very well," Rachel said coolly. "But if you know anything about what happened to Rudy Holmgaard, it's your duty to tell Tom Baird."

"Rudy—so that's his first name." Fordyce scribbled in his notebook. "Truth to tell, my dear, I don't know a blamed thing about it outside of what the winds of saloon gossip have told me, which is precious little and mostly unreliable. The Winterfield daily will have the story in today's issue, and about half their facts will be wrong. My version won't be out till tomorrow, but it will be straight goods. One advantage of running a weekly. Gives you time to dig around. Now—you'd prefer to see the story reported *accurately*, wouldn't you? How about an assist with the facts as you know them?"

Rachel smiled wryly. "I don't know much, and *that's* a fact."

They sat in Rachel's back parlor while she told him the little she did know. As she was finishing up, someone began knocking loudly at the front door. Rachel was about to tell Lotte to answer it, then remembered that this was her day off and Lotte was visiting her sister and brother-in-law. Excusing herself, Rachel went out to the front parlor. Before she reached the door, the caller had increased his knocking to impatient, thunderous blows.

Good Lord! What was it?

She opened the door. A big rawboned red-bearded man stood there. The jagged look in his blue eyes was enough to frost a body's marrow.

"Yes?"

"I am Axel Holmgaard. My son is here?"

"Yes. Please come in."

He scuffed his muddy boots on the doormat and stepped across the threshold, pulling off his hat. Rachel asked if she might take his coat; he shook his head once. She looked pointedly at the rifle he carried, but he didn't offer to relinquish it.

Rachel smiled resignedly. "If you'll come this way, Mr. Holmgaard . . ."

Andrew Fordyce was standing in the entrance to the back parlor, wearing an avidly curious look. Axel Holmgaard's chill and forbidding manner decided Rachel not to delay by introducing them. She led Holmgaard directly to the little room under the stairs, opened the door for him, and stepped aside. He ducked his shaggy head beneath the low lintel as he entered, halting a few feet from the bed.

"Pa . . ." Rudy's puffy lips barely formed the word.

Holmgaard watched his son's face for a full ten seconds. Finally he said in a strained voice, "Who did it, boy?"

Rudy's gaze slid past his father to fix accusingly on Rachel. "Ma'am . . . you shouldn't have had him fetched here."

"I didn't," said Rachel. "I sent a man to tell your family what had happened. Wouldn't you want them to know?"

Rudy didn't answer. He looked back at his father.

"Talk up, boy," Holmgaard said impatiently. "I asked you who done it."

"No," Rudy said almost inaudibly.

"What!"

"Mr. Holmgaard, I must ask you not to shout," Rachel said quietly. "He would not tell the police either. I don't think he'll tell you, unless it suits him to. So shouting won't really help, will it?"

Axel Holmgaard stared at his son. "So. You don't talk to the police."

"That's right, Pa."

"Me neither. Eh?"

"No." Rudy moistened his lips. "You brought us enough trouble as it is."

"Here now! What kind of a way is that to talk?"

"It's true. That whole business with the dam. It's got all of us worried sick. Now you want to make it worse."

"I swear to *Gud*, boy, I don't know what you mean."

"You know what. You want to find out who beat me up so you can go after 'em on your own. That's just the sort of thing you'd do."

"Now, I swear. Why would I want to do that?" Holmgaard's rumble turned almost gentle. "Rudolf, you try to understand a man too fast. That's a bad habit you got."

"You don't fool me, Pa." Rudy said the words through set teeth. "Damn it. I'll stick by you when there's trouble. But I won't help you make more. I am not going to tell you who did it so you can go out and kill someone or get killed yourself. Now. That's all there is to it. You hear me?"

The flinty resolution in his voice and face startled Rachel. There was little or no actual physical resemblance between these two. Yet the iron of the father's character was stamped as plain as day on the son's face.

If Axel Holmgaard saw it too, he gave no sign. Only reached out and touched the boy's hair with his big hand. A gesture that was half rough, half awkward. And held a tenderness that Rachel wouldn't have believed in this man.

"Crazy boy." Holmgaard's lips did not smile, but his voice did. "You crazy boy."

Without another word, he tramped past Rachel out of the room and went across the front parlor and out the door. The way it slammed behind him canceled his flicker of gentleness.

⚉ *eighteen* ⚉

LEAVING RACHEL MERRICK'S house, Axel swung north along the street. Before he'd reached the end of the block, he heard a man call after him, "Hey. Wait up there!"

Axel threw a glance backward, but didn't slacken his pace. He'd taken passing notice of the man in the Merrick woman's parlor and had decided he didn't rate a second glance. Nor did he concede him any further notice now, as the man overtook him and fell into step beside him.

"Name's Fordyce. I publish the *Winterfield Weekly Clarion*. Listen, Mr. Holmgaard. . . ." He had to break into a trot every few steps to match Axel's stride. "Listen to me, damn it! Maybe I can give you a hand."

Not slowing or looking at him, Axel said with a cold disdain, "Can you?"

"Yes, damn it! If you'll listen!"

Axel halted and swung to face him. "Why the hell would you help me?"

"News. You're news. Practically a walking headline. Christ, man, that's reason enough."

"All right. Talk. What do you know?"

"Enough," Fordyce said gently. "The man who beat up your son was Bear Roback. After Jean LeBoeuf egged him into it. At least that's how the grapevine has it. But I guess they'd have reason, eh? Or think they did."

Axel studied Fordyce's narrow face. "So. You didn't see it. Then how you know?"

A smile jerked the edge of Fordyce's mouth. "Sources. I have sources. And I keep my eyes and ears open. I put things together. It happened in a crowded saloon, Mr. Holmgaard. A lot of men saw it happen."

"They let it happen."

"That's how a lumberjack brawl goes. Nobody buys in. A pair of fellows get in a tangle, the others let 'em go to it."

"That?" Axel murmured. "Roback beating up my boy? You call that a tangle?"

Fordyce had a hand on his companion's arm. Now he let the hand drop and took a step backward. "Not at all," he said carefully. "I call it a slaughter. Let's just say nobody wants to cross up Roback. The way I got the story is, he dragged your son out in an alley and worked him over and then left him. A couple of the boys went out a little later to have a look, but your son wasn't around. I reckon he had just enough left to stagger or crawl to the boardinghouse."

A twinge of pain in Axel's hand made him relax his hold on the rifle. Loosening the muscles that much took a conscious effort. "Okay." The word sounded oddly distant in his own ears. "Okay, Mr. Fordyce. Maybe we'll talk a little bit, eh?"

There was little more that Fordyce could tell him, except the talk had it that the fracas had taken place in and outside of Red Morgan's saloon. Whether LeBoeuf and Roback usually hung out there, he couldn't say. When the lumberjacks came off the spring drive for their town fling, they were generally a footloose lot that drifted from one watering place to the next. But they would live it up, every man of them, for several days or until their money was gone; meantime the saloons would operate all day and all night. There were no curfews and no Sunday shutdowns in Thirsty Hollow at this time of year; the police knew better than to attempt enforcing any. They did their best to keep an order of sorts, and let it go at that.

"Where is Morgan's?" Axel asked.

"First place to your right this end of Joyner Street. That's one block over." Fordyce pointed with his thumb. "Mind if I tag along?"

"They say it's a free country."

They swung up Joyner Street's muddy trace. Axel tramped onto the porch of Morgan's and paused, peering over the swing doors. The place was going full blast, all right. No lamps were lighted, for it was still daylight, but the place was dim with tobacco smoke. At another time, Axel might have felt at home with the out-roll of men's coarse badinage and laughter.

Just now he felt only the hot coil of rage. He was scarcely aware of Fordyce stepping onto the porch behind him, then pausing.

It took a few moments to pick out LeBoeuf, bellied up to the bar with other drinkers. Axel's gaze quested the room, the long bar itself, and then one table at a time, till he made out the hulking shoulders and hairless head of Bear Roback at a table in a dark corner.

Axel thrust open the doors and walked in. His right hand gripped his rifle by the stock; his left one closed around the barrel. He came up behind Canuck John LeBoeuf and said mildly, "Hey."

The soft word cut through the hubbub as clearly as a slap. Canuck John came wheeling around in a blank-faced surprise.

Axel brought the clubbed rifle up from his hip in a savage sweep. The butt of the stock smashed LeBoeuf's jaw with a sound of breaking bone. LeBoeuf didn't utter a sound. His knees buckled and he folded to the floor.

Axel backed unhurriedly off from the unconscious Canuck, halting in the middle of the floor well away from anybody, before they knew what had happened. He waited for the wave of realization to spread through the room, washing it into silence before he moved again.

Bear Roback was motionless and watching him, a kind of still caution in his grotesque face. Axel deliberately jacked the shells out of his 15-shot Winchester. They rattled to the floor in a brassy cascade till the magazine was empty.

"Now we are even," Axel said into the stillness. "Now do you stand up, Mr. Roback, and come get it? Or do I got to come over where you sit and wrap it around your big dumb skull?"

A sound rumbled out of Roback's throat. He stood up, his height stretching toward the ceiling. The other two men at his table hastily evacuated it now. Roback's hand dipped and struck the table's edge. Little more than a gesture, the blow sent the table crashing on its side. Bottles and glasses shattered; an oily gurgle of liquor trickled into the silence.

Roback picked up the wooden armchair he had vacated, lifting it in one hand by its back. It was a heavy hand-carved piece that an ordinary man would raise in a two-handed grip. Roback hefted it like a feather.

Axel rolled his shoulders against his mackinaw and stepped forward, light and fast. He feinted at Roback's shoulder with the rifle barrel. Feinted again at the other shoulder. Then gave the giant a hurtful jab in the arm. Wicked lights smoldered in Roback's little eyes.

Suddenly, with an unbelievable quickness, he swung the chair overhead and then downward.

Axel was ready. He moved sidelong and away as the piece came down, missing him by a clear foot. The force of the swing shattered legs and rungs to splinters against the floor.

For an instant Roback was wide open and slightly off balance. Axel had already shifted his double-handed grip to the rifle's barrel. With no time to pick his target carefully, he took a chopping swing at Roback's head. The weapon's stock caught him glancingly above the right ear. Roback staggered backward a step. But he didn't go down. He shook his head, spraying drops of blood left and right. The gun stock had ripped a red track down the side of his face; his right ear was torn. Blood coursed down his neck and dyed his red shirt a deeper red.

Axel began moving slowly around the giant, holding his body in a crouch as he circled him. Roback kept turning to always face him. Roback's teeth were bared, his spatulate hands half-raised, ready to grasp or pummel at the first chance.

Axel continued to shift around the giant, lifting each foot and setting it down with care. Above all he mustn't get inside that terrible reach, those crushing hands. It left him only one option. As he had before, he must let Roback make the first move. Or goad him into it. And somehow counter that move

145

and use the opening it gave him to take the initiative. Gain the victory in one stroke.

But Roback wasn't to be opened up so easily again. His eyes under their shelving brows were watchful and weighing. Maybe he was not very bright, but he wasn't altogether stupid.

Axel shifted the grip of his aching hands on the rifle. He was barely aware of the men pulled back along the bar and wall, silent and just watching. When these men tangled, they fought to let off steam. But never with Bear Roback. Nobody challenged Roback. Except maybe a crazy dead-serious Swede who did not fight for fun. Who went straight for the throat, wolflike, without preliminary.

"Come on," Axel muttered between his teeth. "Come on, you big dumb *oxe*."

Maybe the taunt did it. Roback made a lumbering rush at his opponent. Axel stood his ground till that split instant in which he saw Roback's massive fist pull back. It gave him the briefest of openings. Enough to let him drive the rifle butt into Roback's unprotected belly with all his strength.

It was like hitting a board wall.

Axel wrenched his head backward and sideways, not quite in time. Roback's blow landed in the same moment his own did. But not with the full impact that might have broken Axel's neck like a rotten branch. The knot of bone and sinew that was Roback's fist swiped the side of his skull at an angle.

It was enough to send Axel plunging away, backpedaling for balance. The wall brought him up with a crash.

For a moment he hung blindly against the wall, fighting to keep his legs from giving way. Silver lights popped in his eyes. He shook his head and shook it again, trying to clear his spinning senses. At any moment he might feel the smash or grasp of those terrible hands.

Suddenly his vision was clearing, his eyes focusing. And unexpectedly, Roback wasn't anywhere near him. The giant had crumpled to the floor on his knees and one hand, his back arched with pain. The other hand was holding his belly. Rasping sounds wheezed out of him.

Axel took a shaky step away from the wall, then another. Pain rocked his head; the rage still sang in his veins. He halted beside Roback and planted his feet apart, raising the rifle in both hands to club it down on his skull. Then he hesitated. What had that Hoffenmeier told him?

That three of Rudy's ribs were broken.

Unhesitatingly now, Axel drove his heavy work boot into Roback's ribs. His great bulk hardly budged from the blow, but a high wordless grunt of agony exploded from him.

Axel drew his boot back again, then let it settle to the floor. He shook his head with a growl of angry disgust, letting out a last simmer of wrath. Suddenly it was all gone and he felt hollow and weary.

Nobody tried to stop him as he tramped to the swingdoors and walked out.

Another gust of rain had started up. Axel put his face to it and let its cold wetness clear his throbbing head. Then somebody touched his arm and he wheeled quickly.

Andrew Fordyce backed off, raising his hands with palms out. "Easy there. Man, that was a thing to see." His sharp nose twitched. "I'd hate to have you take offense at *me*. So I'll very considerately ask you—would it bother you a hell of a lot if I wrote this scrap up in my best purple style and sent it out to the wire services?"

"Do what you want with it."

Axel swing off Joyner Street at a rapid walk, heading back for the boardinghouse. Fordyce hurried to keep up with him.

"Hope you got my meaning, Mr. Holmgaard. I meant this story could get picked up by newspapers all over the country, given all the things that've led up to it."

"Damn it, yes! I got your meaning. Now get off my back, eh?"

Fordyce made an amiable little shrug with his eyebrows. He continued to walk beside Axel, sometimes running to keep up.

Till now Axel's thoughts had revolved around meting punishment to the men who had hurt his son. Now his mind turned to Rudy and his injuries. The boy might not be fit to be up and around for weeks. Damn! Probably he'd have to be boarded at the Merrick woman's. That would cost money. So would the doctor bills.

Thinking about it ruffled up his temper again. The side of his face where Roback's fist had connected was starting to pulse like a vast toothache. Likely by tomorrow it would be swollen all to hell and hurt even worse.

He said abruptly to Fordyce, "These Gannetts. Whereabouts do they live? Eh?"

Fordyce came to a stop. "What?"

Axel stopped too. "I said—"

"Yeah. I heard you." Fordyce tipped back his derby, then plunged his hands deep in the pockets of his ulster. "You want to know where the Gannetts live. Guess that earns *me* another question too. Why?

"I want to talk to 'em."

A smile of disbelief touched Fordyce's mouth. "Really? What about?"

"Look, you want a story," Axel said impatiently. "All right. I want to talk with these Gannetts. After, I'll tell you what I told them. Then, by God, mister, you'll have yourself a story!"

Fordyce's smile broadened. "And you, mister, have made yourself a deal."

☙ *nineteen* ☙

FOLLOWING THE PUBLISHER'S directions, Axel walked across town to the east side. By the time he reached the big hill where Winterfield's wealthy had their homes, it was getting dark. The sporadic rain had turned to a steady downpour. He was drenched to the skin, his socks squishing in his boots. His mood was as foul as the weather.

Like other pioneer moguls of his time, Dave Gannett had built his mansion on that height of land which formed his town's tallest eminence. In Winterfield, this height was a tall glacial-drift ridge that ran east to west across the town's northeast limit on its original plat. The Gannett home had been the first of a dozen mansions to be built along the ridge top; it was still the biggest. As Fordyce had said, you couldn't miss it. A square and boxy-looking structure, painted yellow with white trim, it was heavily gabled and dormered in the old New England style. A broad-roofed veranda ran the length of each side, entirely surrounding the house.

As he turned up the macadamized walk that led to the front veranda, the full drag of his tiredness hit Axel. He was a forty-six-year-old man who'd tramped ten miles through the woods and beat up on a giant and now was walking around in an icy soaking rain. His body was starting to betray him as it wouldn't have a few years ago. If he met any trouble tonight, was he in shape to handle it?

Axel shook himself angrily. He had come this far. Let these rich people learn what a man was made of.

He tramped onto the veranda with his shoulders back, his head up. He noticed the electric doorbell but ignored it, instead raising his fist to hammer at the door, beating his clenched hand against it as hard as he could.

Axel kept it up till he heard the latch click. The heavy oak-paneled door swung open a cautious foot. A girl in a maid's frilly apron and cap peered at him, wide-eyed. Her mouth formed a dainty *oh*.

"Yes, m'sieu?"

"I want to see Mr. Gannett."

"Qui est-ce, m'sieu! There are three of them. All are at dinner now."

Setting his spread palm against the door, Axel applied pressure that made the girl step back.

"M'sieu, you cannot—!"

He stepped across the threshold and found himself in a dimly lighted foyer with a stairway leading off it in one direction and a hallway in the other. From an archway at the hall's end came voices and a clink of dishware.

Axel pointed at the archway with his rifle.

"In there?" he growled.

The maid nodded, pressing a hand to her bosom. Her eyes were round and scared.

Axel tramped through the hall and halted by the archway's beaded portieres. He saw a long table with five people seated around it. Three men and two women. He recognized Adam Gannett. He'd never seen any of the other Gannetts, but what he'd been told about the family enabled him to quickly identify each one.

Axel thrust aside the portieres and stepped into the dining room. At the rattle of beads, the five people stopped talking and eating. One of the men crumpled his napkin on his plate and came swiftly to his feet.

"Who the devil are you?"

He was a hard-faced fellow of thirty or so, with a hard athletic frame that wasn't in the least diminished by his fancy dinner attire. *Helvete!* So—people who were rich *did* dress up for dinner in their own homes, and not just on holidays. The men wore suits of tailored broadcloth. The gowns of the two women, the old one and the young one, were costly and obviously made just for them.

Axel looked at the hard-faced man. He had to be the tough one. "So. You are Beau Gannett."

"I am. And I asked who the hell you are!"

"Beau, it's Holmgaard," Adam Gannett said in a low voice. "Axel Holmgaard."

There was a stir of reaction around the table.

All of them stared at Axel's face, his rifle, his face again. He could guess how he looked to these people: fierce and disreputable and uncouth, a man not to be trifled with. They would damned well be right, too.

The elderly woman at the head of the table cleared her throat in a genteel way. "But of course. Shouldn't we have known?"

The maid slipped into the room past Axel, her face pale and distraught. "Madam Gannett!" She wrung her hands. "This—this person forced himself by me! I could not stop him."

"Quite all right, Emilie," Mrs. Gannett murmured. "Take Mr. Holmgaard's coat, please, and set an extra place. You *will* take supper with us, won't you, sir?"

"Mother!" Beau said in a voice that was flat and hard and faintly shocked.

Mrs. Gannett ignored him, her long old face serene and smiling. "Well, Mr. Holmgaard?"

Axel recognized the note of quiet mockery. This woman was gracious and unruffled and had a look like needles. He felt instinctively that she knew men, knew the temper and weakness of any man as well as she knew her own.

It was hard for Axel Holmgaard not to be uneasy and overawed as he let his glance circle the room now, taking in the heavy oaken woodwork and fancy wallpaper and the velour curtains that embellished the tall windows. The table was heavy and oaken too, spread with snowy damask and bone china and gleaming silver. A chandelier of many-prismed pieces that might well be crystal shed a glow of electric light to every corner of the room.

As he stood dripping on the grass-green carpet, Axel again felt as chill and wet and weary as he was. He tightened his will against letting a shred of the feeling show.

"I don't think so, Mrs. Gannett," he said. "You are the old she-bear of the den, eh?"

The dandified-looking youth who was as slim as a whip rose halfway out of his chair, clenching a fist. "Why, damn you, damn your gall anyway! You can't talk—"

"Be quiet, Shad." The old woman spoke mildly, but a steely flick in her voice cut her son off at once. "I'm the aforementioned old she-bear, Mr. Holmgaard, yes."

"Well then, I guess my news is for you. You'll hear it anyway, but I thought I would bring it."

Mrs. Gannett's right eyebrow rose a quarter inch. Her smiling look implied a touch of respect. She wasn't disconcerted, only conceding that her challenge had failed and willing, for the moment, to play Axel's game.

"Oh, and what might that be?"

"You folks got a man, LeBoeuf. I just now busted his jaw for him. He's got a big dumb buddy, name of Roback. I cleaned that fella's clock for him, too."

From the tail of his eye, Axel saw Beau Gannett's square hard face break a little. *That scored on him all right!* Axel thought. But he watched only Mrs. Gannett, not expecting her to turn a hair. She didn't.

"Indeed?" she murmured. "With that rifle, Mr. Holmgaard?"

"*Ja,* that's right." Axel let his teeth show through his beard, enjoyably taking his time. "I didn't shoot Roback. All I done was hit him a couple times with my gun. He don't feel too good, though. I thought you would like to know."

The shock in Beau Gannett's face gave way to a flush of anger. "Just what the hell do you think you're about, Holmgaard! First the dam, you drive those two men off it, and now you...! Jesus! Are you crazy or what?"

"Maybe. About the dam, no. There, I am just holding you up for money. Nothing crazy about that."

"Well." Mrs. Gannett tipped back her head, that frosty smile lingering on her lips. "You may be a jackleg crook, but *that's* honest, at least. Don't sugarcoat your motives, do you?"

"No, missus. There's something else I don't put any sugar on. You set them two guys on my boy Rudy. He's over at the Merrick boarding place, all beat up. You been told about that, eh? All right. I fixed them two for it. Now I tell you this."

Axel raised a finger and waggled it slowly. "You leave my boy alone. He's got no part in what I done. He helped me some because I'm his pa and have the say-so. That's all. You ever hurt him again, him or any of mine, and you people are going to be sorry. I'll make you sorry."

"I believe you would try," Mrs. Gannett said calmly. "Would *you* believe, Mr. Holmgaard, that I knew nothing whatever about your son being set on by a pair of our men?"

"*Ja*, is that right?"

"Quite. Not until you just mentioned it." Her gaze tipped to her eldest son. "What about you, Beau? Did you know of it?"

Beau nodded reluctantly. "It's been talked up some. I heard about it this morning."

"Did you order it done?"

"Good God, no. If I want to cut a man to size, I damn well do it myself. You know that."

"Yes, I know what a sweet roughneck you can be. Well," Mrs. Gannett said crisply, "there you are, Mr. Holmgaard. Do you care to believe us? Or not?"

Axel nodded. "It sounds good enough. All the same, I meant what I said."

"I'm sure you did. As to the matter of the dam, might we not discuss it here and now?"

"*Ja*. But my price stands. That's no good talking about."

"M'm." Mrs. Gannett gave a slow nod, as if deliberating. "Well, I am bound to say that we *were* somewhat at fault at the outset. We did flood a portion of your land, however inadvertently. And talk has it that the farmer from whom you bought it misled you. Really, you had no idea what you were getting into. Neither did we, I fear, when we thought you would back down or scare off."

The woman's tone and smile were relaxed and half humorous now. Axel wondered if she had taken a fresh measurement of him—or if this was a trick of some kind.

"What about my toll on them logs?" he asked bluntly.

"Let it stand. We'll meet your price."

"Mother!" Beau's voice was thick with anger. "Damn it, you can't do this. You said yourself it's too damn much to pay! And Uncle Solly—"

"—is not giving orders for the family," Letitia Gannett cut in. "Nor are you, except at my word. And it is my prerogative to change my mind. Perhaps, as you might surmise, because I am a woman. But more likely it's simply because I am in the position of giving orders and being assured they'll be obeyed. The real boss, after all, makes his or her own prerogatives. Wouldn't you agree, Mr. Holmgaard?"

⚜ *twenty* ⚜

IT WAS A long wait for Selma, lying alone in the tent. She dozed on and off, always jerking awake with a start. What a way for a family woman to spend a night—alone in the dark, listening to a dismal patter of rain on wet canvas. She turned restlessly on her pallet of blankets spread above a mattress of springy pine boughs.

Gud, men were a trial! They did exactly as they pleased. If they happened to feel like telling you what they were up to, fine. If not, you were supposed to blindly accept it.

In all her years with Axel, Selma hadn't spent a night like this. She knew very well what he would try to do. How easily he might be hurt or killed. *Or kill someone else!*

Sometime after midnight, the rain slacked away.

Selma's sensitized nerves began to prickle at odd sounds. Finally she wrapped her heavy shawl around her shoulders and left the tent to walk up and down. Presently Dani joined her. It was a comfort to have her daughter close, walking beside her and softly talking.

Dani exclaimed suddenly, "Look, Mama!"

Selma saw the beams of an electric torch waver among the trees. Then a man's dark form came tramping out of the woods. She'd sworn to herself that she would greet his return coolly. Yet she couldn't help calling out in a voice that cracked with anxiety, *"Axel?"*

"Sure, sure. It's me."

In a moment he was folding her in his big arms, rubbing his wet beard against her face. Then the kids were rousing out of their tents, all of them gathering around and plying Axel with questions.

"Pipe down!" he roared. "One at a time. Rudy will be all right, he'll be fine. But that ain't the big news. We won, by God!"

Selma peered at his face in the near-darkness. She couldn't make out his expression, but the jubilation in his voice was unmistakable.

"Damn it, I'm saying we *won!* The old Gannett lady gave in. I had a talk with her and she'll meet my price." Axel laughed, giving Elof a slap on the shoulder. "Hell, the way things worked out, I ain't even mad at this lunkhead anymore!"

Selma said slowly, "But why? What did you do or say to change her mind? It must have been something."

Axel gave an impatient shrug. "Who knows? Maybe because I gave her two bullyboys that hurt Rudy a good licking."

"Did you, Pa?" Erika said eagerly.

"Sure. I found out who they were and cleaned their clocks good. Don't matter why the old woman changed her mind, long as she did. We worked things out. Day after tomorrow, a river crew will be here to start moving them logs through the dam."

Arvid said dubiously, "Pa, you sure them Gannetts ain't got some'at up their sleeve? Some kind of trick?"

"Helvete! Who's sure of anything?" Suddenly Axel sounded drained and weary. "But we'll be on hand to keep a tally on logs they sluice through. Nothing they can do if we keep our guard up."

Selma was not overly reassured. It was a relief to have the tense waiting done with. What bothered her was that Axel still seemed so *ready* for trouble.

Tomorrow, Axel said, they would go to town and visit

Rudy. Just now all he wanted was to sleep. No, nothing to eat—he was too damned tired. Selma couldn't remember when Axel had been too tired to eat. But she insisted that he strip off his wet clothes and let her give him a good rubdown. Meantime she had Dani heat some rocks in the fire and wrap them in gunnysacks. After getting Axel snugly rolled in his blankets, Selma left the tent to fetch the heated rocks.

She was gone only a few moments. Yet by the time she returned Axel was dead to the world, snoring soundly. Carefully she tucked the sack-wrapped rocks close to his feet.

It was late the next morning before Axel roused from sleep. He was groggy and irritable, chagrined because he'd overslept. Selma noticed that his left temple was discolored and swollen, but didn't ask him about it. She waited till his mood was softened by a big breakfast and several cups of hot coffee, then reminded him of his promise to take her to Winterfield.

Axel grunted an assent and hitched up the wagon. As this was wash day, Dani and the twins would have to remain in camp to take care of the laundering, and none of the boys cared to visit town.

Selma and Axel arrived in Winterfield by early afternoon. They drove directly to the Merrick boardinghouse.

Meeting Rachel Merrick for the first time, Selma saw at once that Dani hadn't exaggerated the woman's beauty. Rachel was gracious, even warm in her greeting, but a quiet aloofness clung to her. She was not a kind of person who would easily give much of herself.

Rachel took them to the little room where Rudy was.

He was awake, and there was a good color to his face where it wasn't bandaged or marked by bruises. He was quick to assure his mother that he looked a lot worse than he felt. Selma thought he might be a touch embarrassed, especially after he said, "I'm sorry I got into this fix, *Mor*. It's sure made a pile of trouble."

"Get well," Selma told him. "Think about that only, Rudolf." She turned to Rachel Merrick. "We'll pay you whatever his board comes to, miss."

Rachel smiled. "You needn't worry about that. I owe Rudy

a favor. He did me one. He's welcome to stay till he's quite well."

Selma protested, but her mind wasn't really on her words.

Again, as Rudy looked at Rachel Merrick, he was wearing that moonstruck look. Maybe his high color came from blushing. That disturbed Selma a little, but she knew this was the normal jealousy a mother felt at seeing a favorite son lost to the growing pains of maturity.

She felt both sad and amused, thinking, *This one isn't for you, my son!* Quite probably, Rachel Merrick wasn't for any man.

Selma and Miss Merrick came to a compromise. The Holmgaards would pay the full doctor's fee and a quarter of the customary boarder's rate. Rachel was generous and agreeable, Selma had to admit. Privately, she wished that Rudy could do his convalescing somewhere else.

While they were chatting, a slight, freckled man barged into the room, brandishing a folded newspaper. Rachel introduced him as Mr. Fordyce, publisher of the *Winterfield Weekly Clarion*.

With a flourish, he unfolded the paper and held it under Axel's nose. "What do you think of that, Mr. Holmgaard? You're featured!"

Peering over Axel's shoulder, Selma saw a four-column headline: FARMER BESTS BULLIES WHO MAUL HIS SON.

Axel took the newspaper from Fordyce's hands, his brows arching in disbelief. "All this is about *me?*"

"You bet," Fordyce said jovially. "I spent half the night setting up the story. Had the forms locked and the press in operation by six this morning. Makes a powerful piece of writing, if I do say so. I soft-pedaled the stuff about your feud with the Gannetts and how you finally settled it last night. Might blow up any arrangement you made with 'em if I made it sound like you were crowing."

"*Ja*, that's good," Selma said tartly.

Fordyce gave her a raffish wink. "Never you fear, ma'am. I'll save the full story for a future issue. Meantime I've sent this one out to the wire services. Your husband is going to be *heard of*, I promise you."

Axel was paying no attention to either of them. The paper crackled in his hands as he devoured every line of the two-column story. He was nodding slowly to himself as he read.

There was a faint smile on his lips.

⚘ twenty-one ⚘

BY LATE AFTERNOON Dani had finished the washing and hung it up to dry. She poured out the wash water, rinsed out the copper tubs, and turned them upside down. Then she delicately stretched her arms and legs, glancing around the camp.

It drowsed in the afternoon quiet. The twins were taking their nap; Arvid and Lennart had hiked downriver to do a little fishing; Elof was on guard by the dam. The scene had a feel of peaceful desertion, broken only by a pair of excited chipmunks chasing each other up and down a pine trunk.

Dani watched them for a few minutes, but she was restless. She decided to go for a walk up the old tote road used by the logging crews.

The day was beautiful. The May warmth had caused spring to burgeon through the forest like a green explosion. Trailing arbutus mantled the ground in pink and white clusters. Dogwood osiers flamed along the riverbank. Chickadees gave out the soft and plaintive calls of mating, while somewhere in the near distance a partridge drummed his wings in a slow muffled beat.

Dani could never get enough of nature. Walking along the woods-flanked road, she lost herself in sensual pleasure. Her nostrils were teased by a rise of earth odors, of which the strongest was a resin smell that baked out of the pines. She had gone nearly a mile uptrail before she remembered Pa's injunction that she was never to go far from camp by herself.

She started back along the road at a leisurely saunter. Then she heard, from up ahead, something that was out of place against the forest noises. Any farm-bred girl would identify that sound at once: a team of horses hauling a wheeled conveyance of some kind along a bumpy road whose spring mire hadn't yet dried up.

Pa had said that this tote road, after swinging past their own place, followed the river north to a logging camp owned by the Gannett Logging and Boom Company. Whoever was coming must be driving up to that camp. Dani had an impulse to slip into the woods bordering the trail, but discarded it. She wasn't a girl to shrink from any sort of encounter.

She continued walking.

Presently the team, a pair of sturdy draft horses, came into sight. It was pulling a heavily loaded spring wagon. On the seat was a big young man, handsome and blond, whom she recognized at once. A smile of pleasure flashed across her face before she could stop it.

He pulled up the team, shouting, "Whoa!"

"Hello," said Dani.

Adam Gannett thumbed back his wide-brimmed hat, smiling down at her. "Well, hello. I was disappointed not to find you in camp."

"Were you? I mean, were you at our camp?"

"Uh-huh. Stopped by to talk with your father. Discuss a few more details of our agreement. And of course," he added frankly, "I'd hoped to see you again. Your sisters told me your dad and mother had gone to town and they didn't know where you'd gone off to."

There was a moment's silence. Dani didn't know what to say. Not a forward girl, she'd never been a shy one, either. Yet she felt tongue-tied. Adam's smiling look had a funny effect on her. All of a sudden she felt so warm that she wondered if she were blushing all over.

"I'm heading up to our camp on the Ottawa," Adam said. "Taking 'em a load of grub supplies. And I'm the walking boss, too. So I get to kill two birds with one stone."

"Oh." Dani nodded, not really knowing what he meant. "Yes."

He smiled. "A walking boss is a superintendent, you might say. I'm the super for all our logging camps."

"Oh."

"Say, listen." Adam leaned forward a little, elbows on his knees. "How about taking a little spin? This isn't a surrey, and these boys aren't a pair of pacers, so I guess spin isn't the word. But why not ride with me to the camp? Give us a chance to talk a little."

Dani smiled and shook her head. "I don't think so."

"Well now, why not? The tomahawk's in the ground. Your father and my mother have buried it. No reason we can't see each other socially, is there? Unless you'd prefer—"

"Oh no! It's not that."

"Oh? Well, we're not exactly strangers any more. A little ride would hardly amount to a cosmic upset of the proprieties, now would it?"

His tone was half humorous, but he was not laughing at her. He seemed sure of himself without being offensive.

"No, I don't think so. I mean," she laughed, "that I *will* ride with you."

"That's great."

Adam dropped easily to the ground, catlike for a man of his size. "Dani," he said musingly as he gave her a hand up to the high seat. "Pretty name. It suits you."

"It's short for Danielle."

"Oh? Thought that was French."

"Everyone says that."

She arranged herself primly on the seat, tucked her skirt around her ankles, and folded her hands on her lap. Adam stepped up beside her, took up the reins, and hoorawed the horses into motion.

He was right. The spring wagon was no surrey, and the choppy muck of this old logging road was no highway. Dani held onto the seat with both hands, letting her body roll to the team's gait and the wagon's shuddering jolts. Now and then her shoulder brushed Adam's.

Finally the road climbed to higher ground and attained a fairly even stretch. Adam gave the horses their heads and relaxed, pointing out and naming various woodland herbs and flowers for her. That was a game Dani knew well; she easily kept up with him and was often ahead of him. Wryly grinning, Adam switched to identifying trees along the way, and here his knowledge far surpassed hers.

The road still paralleled the river course, following the summit of a glacial-drift ridge. Adam pointed to an elderly tree that grew in solitary splendor close to one bank.

"That one is a yellow birch."

"I don't think I've seen one before," Dani admitted. "Just white birches. You see those everywhere."

"No white birches in North America, ma'am. You're referring to the common paper or canoe birch. Your true white birch is native to northern Europe."

"Really? How do you know so much about it?"

"From growing up with the subject. Trees and lumber. If the Gannetts have a Bible, it's a lumberman's journal."

Dani was intensely aware of him without looking directly at him. She knew—without knowing how she knew—that Adam's interest in her was just as strong and no different in kind.

For lack of anything better to say, she said, "You *do* believe in God, don't you?"

"Oh sure. I guess all of us do, one way or the other. But we've never made much to-do about religion. None of we Gannetts do. Not even Mother, and she was raised an Episcopalian back in Boston. High church, too. Your folks being Scandinavian, I suppose you're Lutheran."

"Yes." Dani laughed. "But we don't make much to-do about it either."

They grinned at each other. In the glances they exchanged Dani felt a rush of perfect understanding. The conviction of feeling so powerfully *right* with this man burst along her nerves like an electric shock.

It was Adam's turn to feel consternation. A flush grew out

163

of his collar; the grin on his lips faded. Afterward he looked straight ahead as he drove, his face almost comically wooden.

Dani smiled to herself.

She was glad that Selma had taken the time and trouble to acquaint her so frankly and thoroughly with all facets of what it meant to be a woman. A quiet knowledge fed the swell of her confidence.

This is my man, she thought. I wonder if he knows it yet. He feels it, sure enough. But does he know?

Dani thought of her father—and of Adam's family. Some of the glory drained from her moment. But not all of it. She couldn't believe, no matter what might happen, that anyone could feel as she did (and as she was sure Adam did) and not find a way to overcome any obstacle.

Those obstacles would be very real ones. She couldn't deceive herself on that score.

"Would you tell me," she said casually, "what really happened last night? When my pa came into your house the way he did?"

"Didn't he tell you?"

Dani smiled. "Not very much. He never does. But you were there, weren't you?"

"Uh-huh. Well, I'm not sure myself. My brother Beau was dead set against any sort of accommodation. I think Mother would have been too, if Uncle Saul hadn't advised her to reach a compromise of some sort with your father. Then, well, the way your dad came barging in last night . . ."

"It's all right to say. I know how he can be."

"Well, he was pretty belligerent. Ordinarily that would be enough to set Mother's hackles a-rising. So what happened next really rocked us back on our heels, all of us. Mother giving in and handing over the whole hog! Unbelievable. Pa must be spinning in his grave."

"But why?" she persisted. "Why do you think . . .?"

"Can't say for sure. But I did some thinking on it. Our dad was a tough old bird. He was a deal like your father in a lot of ways. Especially when it came to knocking heads together. Mother . . ." He hesitated. "I might as well say it. Mother was an old maid, a genuine New England spinster out of a nineteenth-century novel, when they met. But her family had money.

Dad was desperate for money to invest in Wisconsin timberlands, and he urged Mother's father to provide a loan. To make a long story short, he got the loan. But on condition of taking the spinster daughter in marriage."

"Lordy!"

Adam chuckled. "It wasn't a union made in heaven—guess you'd say it was forged in purgatory. But it turned out well. Mother was wild about Dad from the moment she set eyes on him. After they were wed she went out of her way to make herself into exactly the kind of wife a man like him would appreciate. Properly yielding, but always keeping a mind of her own—along with a superbly run household. In time Dad grew to have a mighty affection for the wife he'd taken unwillingly. Anyway—I wanted to say that I think Mother, whether she realized it or not, saw more of old Dave in your dad than in any other chap who's ever come down the pike. What he did last night was *just* what Dad would do."

"So that's why?"

"My guess, is all. Partly it may have been a mere whim on Mother's part. Being born to wealth and growing old with it makes one indulgent, if not wholly spoiled. And given to eccentric whims. Mother has her moments. But I think she really couldn't help accommodating a fellow like your dad."

Adam shook his head, grinning. "He has quite a way about him, all right. This morning we got word of those two lads he buffaloed. Roback has a couple broken ribs and a mighty sore belly. LeBoeuf's on his feet, but he's going around with his jaw wired up. Can only take nourishment in liquid form and can talk only in a mumble. Doc Hammerstein assured me, not without a dash of satisfaction, that this is standard treatment for a busted jaw and incidentally is quite painful. You slip a wire around the base of the patient's teeth and it has to be very tight in order to hold the bones in place."

Dani made a small grimace. "How much farther to your camp?"

"We're practically on top of it. Just over that hill ahead."

The area around the logging camp was covered with old stumpage. It bore all the characteristics of land that had been cut over some time ago. Stunted and gnarled jack pines mingled with small straight poplars; heaps of rotted slashings had provided a rich mulch for blackberry brambles and woodland shrubs. Adam explained that the current cutting was going on in the virgin timber to the west of here.

"The last good-sized stand of original white pine in this country," he added. "When it's gone, there'll be the end of an era."

Dani said, "I don't see why the lumber companies take only the pines."

"Pinewood floats. Hardwoods don't. Pine logs can be moved down driving streams—and white pine is the best kind of wood for all building purposes. Nowadays, of course, we've narrow-gauge railroads running back in the woods to tap the remote stands. Hardwoods can be brought out too. We've a veneering plant in Winterfield that manufactures plywood packing cases, for which oak and maple and other hardwoods are ideal."

"Does your family own that, too?"

Adam laughed. "We have an interest in it. But we're not even majority stockholders, I suspect you'll be astonished to learn."

They crossed the low hill and came into the camp. Its main building consisted of two long one-story structures built of massive logs and connected end-to-end by a single roof that formed a covered alleyway between them. Adam told her that this was a combination bunkhouse-cookshack and that they were constructed separately for sanitary reasons.

He drove up to the door of the cookshack, halted the team, and stepped to the ground. Dani held out her hand, but he circled her waist with his big hands and swung her down.

Adam beat his fist on the door and yelled, "Cookee! Send out the cookee! Grub's here!"

The door swung open and a gangling youth in a soiled apron came out. He gawked at Dani. Adam jerked his thumb at the load of supplies, said, "Take 'em inside, Howie," and then took Dani's arm. "Cook's assistant. He'll unload the wagon. Let's walk over to the river. I want to show you our 'decking' area."

He was very used to giving orders, she thought as they crossed the trampled compound toward the riverbank. And very used to having things done for him. Dani wasn't sure she liked this side of him—but of course he had been born to his position and then raised in it.

Still, it disturbed her.

About a hundred yards from the camp they came to a high bank that overlooked the river. Adam explained that the logs now marooned behind the dam a couple of miles downriver had been skidded out of the deep woods and loaded on sleds that were team-drawn along icy roads to this spot. Here the logs had been stacked, or "decked" as he termed it, in huge piles at the top of the bank. When the ice went out of the river in the spring, the piles were knocked loose and the logs went tumbling into the river. Then the river drivers took over.

"Take a good look," Adam told her. "This method of getting logs out of the woods on a large scale is becoming old hat. In another few years it'll be a memory. Then it'll all be done by narrow-gauge railroad—and not long afterward, all the big pine in the upper Middle West will be gone. The end of a way of life."

"Won't that put a lot of men out of work?" Dani asked.

"Hopefully not. In Sayer County we've done all we can to encourage new industry. Enough, we hope, to absorb the slack as the big-tree logging plays out. We'll still have crews of men in the woods, to harvest pulpwood to supply the paper mill. A lot of our lumberjacks already spend their summers doing just that. And we're planning an expansion of our paper-making facilities that will make our plant the biggest of its kind in the world. That is, in the manufacture of grease-proof papers for wrapping food."

Adam pulled off his hat and wiped a bandanna over his forehead. His skin had a ruddy glow; sunlight sprinkled the golden hairs of his wrist.

Dani toed at a pine chip on the ground, turning it over with her shoe. "You care about that, don't you? You care about the people who work for you."

"Sure I do." Adam clamped his hat on his head. "I care about growth and industry because . . . well, I guess that's why. I care about people. About doing for people. That's part of it, anyway."

"Is that how all rich men feel? I read a novel called *The Iron Heel* . . ."

167

Again his quiet chuckle.

"I can't answer for *all* rich men. Some feel my way. Others are about as bad as Jack London made 'em out in that book. Which I read just recently, at my Uncle Saul's behest. There are extremes like that. Point is, we're *people* like everyone else. Take your plain everyday folks. Wouldn't a lot of 'em behave on a par with the worst of the capitalist barons if they were given that kind of power?"

"I guess they would."

Adam took her arm again and they walked slowly along a cleared trail that followed the riverbank. "Well . . . I suppose most of the big lumbermen are bad enough. They don't even bother to assume the posture that *my* family does."

"What's that?"

They were walking into a sun-spattered grove, cut off entirely from view of the camp. Dani became more conscious of the pressure of Adam's hand, the bulking closeness of him. Somehow she could *feel* the play of muscle under his woodsman's shirt. His head was leonine, with a cap of golden curls; his profile was as imperial as the bust of a Roman emperor.

Dani moistened her lips with her tongue tip and looked at the ground as they walked.

"I guess it's a modified kind of feudalism," Adam said. "A benevolent overlordship of the vassals. All of us feel a genuine *duty* to the men who work in our mills and camps, and to their families. My brothers and I learned that lesson at our daddy's knee. You treat your workers at least as well as you would your favorite hunting dog or as the best Southern massas used to treat their darkies. You deal with them in a kindly way not just so you can get better performance out of them—although that's part of it—but because, as a Christian gentleman, you recognize a duty to faithful dog Trey, the dumb brute who's toiled in your vineyard so long and loyally."

Dani came to a stop. She pulled her arm from his hand and swung a stare on his face. "But that's *terrible!*"

"Sure. I think so too. Seems the only reasonable attitude to take. Yet my whole family regards it as radical. I'm their resident radical."

Dani laughed, turning her eyes down again. "I'm sorry. I must have sounded like a fishwife."

"You couldn't sound like a fishwife if you tried."

She folded her hands in front of her, then thought, No—I don't want to look prim and demure and all that. It's just silly! She unfolded her hands and straightened her mouth. "I really should be going back now."

"If you think so. I'll give you a ride."

But neither of them moved. Dani lifted her eyes to his. Her pulse made a ragged beat in her ears. I don't know, she thought wildly. What do I do?

She'd thought she could manage anything that might develop between them. But with soft-wild lights kindling in his eyes, the masculine bigness of him inches away, the smell of leather and tobacco engulfing her senses, she was suddenly unsure. Then his sinewy hands, strong and yet gentle, were on her arms and pulling her close.

The kiss lasted for a long time.

Dani's consciousness spun away on a timeless wind of sensation. Her young blood flamed with awakened love. It was as nothing she had ever known.

When they drew a little apart, Adam whispered, "Dani," and kissed her again. This time she answered his demanding arms and lips with a fierceness of her own.

A drug of desire possessed her. She was hardly aware that his insistent weight was bearing her back and downward with a quickening urgency. Her hips met the needle-carpeted earth. Somehow that broke the spell.

She began to struggle. "No, Adam—no—"

For a moment Dani knew the fright of utter helplessness. He was too strong for her; he made her strength like a child's. Even in that moment of knowledge, there was a shocking cry in her mind: I want him. I want him to!

But Adam's grasp was easing. He released her and pulled back on his haunches.

"Good God." His face was red, shame battling with passion. "Dani . . . forgive me, please. I'm not that kind of a man. Believe me, I—I don't know what—"

"It's all right." She rocked up onto her heels and hitched away from him a little, not trusting herself. She managed a shaky smile. "I'm the one who's supposed to say that, aren't I?"

"Say what?"

"That I'm not that kind of a girl."

"I know you're not." He shook his head tightly. "Oh damn!"

"Don't look so miserable, Adam." She brushed her fingers across his hand. "I'm not angry. You are. I'd almost think you never . . . well . . ."

"Made love to a girl?"

A tide of blood rolled back to his face.

All at once Dani felt older and wiser than he. Adam Gannett was handsome and smart and polished—but had preserved an attitude toward women that was essentially innocent. He'd spoken sardonically of "Christian gentlemen." Yet he was that oddity—a genuine one.

"I bet you have," she said placidly. "Haven't you?"

"Oh well, I guess, uh, sure, a few." He scowled at the ground. "But listen—don't think I'm just another playboy or a lounge lizard."

"A what?"

"Don't ask me what a lounge lizard is. A big-city girl my brother Shad was romancing called him that."

"It sounds dreadful." Dani's fingertips played over the back of his hand. "I suppose it's just hard to believe a fellow as nice-looking as you doesn't have a lot of girl friends."

"Guess I'm not much of a hand at light loves. I don't know, maybe I take things too seriously. But it seems to me that if a chap really cares for a girl—or even if he doesn't—he has no right to . . . well. I let myself get carried away. That's all."

"Is it?" Her fingers continued to stroke his hand.

"Dani, are you laughing at me?"

"Of course. You're right, you are too serious. Can you kiss me and do it nicely . . . now?"

❦ *twenty-two* ❦

A KIND OF suppressed excitement gripped the family this morning. The log drive would resume today, and they were looking forward to watching the logs run through the dam. It should be quite a spectacle.

While Selma and Dani were preparing breakfast, Tom O'Dea came knocking at the door. He presented them with a dozen fresh eggs and a crock of goat's milk. Selma thanked him for the gifts and invited him to stay for breakfast. Axel was in a pretty good mood this morning, waiting for the river drivers to show up. He was even civil to O'Dea, which pleased her.

As they all gathered by the dam, Adam Gannett came riding up on his big bay horse.

He gave them a pleasant good morning and said that the "river pigs" should be along shortly. As the drive was getting under way again after a lengthy delay, it had taken a day to round up the necessary men to fill out a crew. Most of the Gannett loggers, after collecting their winter's pay, had pulled out for other parts or other work. Mustering a gang of experienced men this late in the season was no easy matter.

In a little while the crew of lumberjacks made its appearance, headed up by Pat Delaney. The drive boss hadn't forgotten his humiliation. His manner was more insulting than humorous as he elaborately bowed to Axel and asked "your lordship's permission" to open the sluice gates.

Axel only chuckled. When he didn't have any personal ax to grind, he was right at home in the rough exchanges of a man's world. "Sure, Irish. You think you can do it all by yourself, go ahead."

The gates were opened and the 'jacks began to sluice the logs through. Axel stood off to one side, keeping an eagle eye on the operation and jotting down a rapid tally of the logs in a small notebook. Arvid was stationed on the other side of the river, making a similar tally to check against his father's. Delaney kept still a third reckoning in the interests of the Gannett Logging and Boom Company.

Selma and Tom O'Dea stood on a knoll a little west of the dam and watched.

"Well then," commented O'Dea. "Your man has made his score. He has won his great gamble."

"I suppose he has," Selma answered half absently. "If that's all there is to it."

"What else might there be? He's played out his hand to a fare-thee-well. Stuck to his guns till the old she-augur gave in."

"Who?"

"I'm referring to Madam Gannett, darlin.'"

Selma folded her arms under her bosom and looked away from him. "It was nice of you to bring us the eggs and milk, Mr. O'Dea. . . ."

"Tush. It's the neighborly thing, mavournin. Think nothing."

"I was going to say, I don't think it gives you a license to call a married woman such things as darling and what else you just said. Maybe it's only what you call a touch of the blarney, eh? But it could get you kicked in the river."

"My saints!" O'Dea lifted his hands in mock dismay. "Would you be doing that all by yourself, darlin'?"

"Mr. O'Dea. I have a husband who won't need any help if he should hear you say that. Or if I tell him."

O'Dea threw back his head with a full-throated laugh that was loud enough to make Axel, standing some distance off, send him an irritable look. "Well, *that* would get us a shindy for fair! But he's such a charming soul, that lad o' yours, I would purely hate to stir up his ire over nothing. You're quite right, a touch of blarney it was, a joke between friends, and no harm intended."

Selma thought that was about half true, but the matter didn't seem worth pursuing. Just now something else demanded her attention.

Dani and Adam Gannett were standing off together, a short distance away, idly talking as they watched the log-driving. It looked innocent enough, but Selma wasn't so sure.

Dani had readily admitted going for a ride with young Gannett yesterday, had told her parents of it so frankly and disarmingly that even Axel hadn't responded with anything worse than a scowling grunt. To him all ways of womanhood were a foolery that was beneath a man's notice. Or should be. He left strictly to Selma the handling of anything that affected Dani and the twins. Last night he'd mumbled something about not being keen on Dani getting chummy with "some damn rich boy" and Selma ought to have a talk with her.

Selma herself wasn't sure how to deal with the situation. Adam Gannett seemed a decent young man. If he'd been a well-to-do farmer or an ordinary merchant of some kind, she would have encouraged his suit. But all that Gannett wealth! It made for a bad matching—that was all there was to it. The gap between them, all that social business, was too wide to be bridged.

"Why now," O'Dea said idly, "that might be a worry all right."

Selma gave a little start. "What?"

"Why, the thing that's still troubling you. That's it, ain't it? The daughter and Mr. Fancypants there."

"You have such a lot of gifts, Mr. O'Dea," Selma said frostily. "I should have known you read minds."

"Minds be damned. It's signs I read, and I've a woodsman's eye. It never ceases to peep and pry."

"Who would have guessed it!"

"If I was you, Mrs. Axel Holmgaard, I'd fret less and count

my blessings more. Why, you might be giving folks the notion you're not such a contented wife and mother after all."

"Is that so," she said tartly. "And you have a daughter you never worry about, eh?"

O'Dea grimaced. "In the case of my Swan, best if a man just gives over worrying. And humbles his spirit with prayer and contrition. Which, unluckily, would be foreign to me nature."

"You don't say."

"Indeed." His grin held a sour twist. "Well, you've had sufficient of the O'Dea for this day, it's plain. I'll be on my way. Hope ye enjoyed the eggs and milk."

"It has been a nice change," Selma said politely. "Goodbye, Mr. O'Dea."

She watched O'Dea move off south along the riverbank at his free woodsman's stride and vanish in the woods.

He was a forward Irisher, but he had a disarming twinkle about him. And he was an attractive man in the magnetism he seemed to radiate. A woman liked to feel womanly. Tom O'Dea understood that. And he was warm and amusing nearly all the time, in contrast to her brooding husband. Still, that probing, curious way of O'Dea's could be annoying. And she felt a little uncomfortable with him—a fact that O'Dea seemed to realize and tried to humorously aggravate.

Some of the loggers were clowning around on the mass of logs. They were making a game of riding the bigger ones through the sluiceway and down the stretch of whitewater below the dam. Some of the men tumbled into the whipping spray; others kept their footing on the turning cylinders with apparent ease.

Selma walked nearer to the dam in order to have a better sight of what was going on. It was a perilous kind of play, that was certain.

Pat Delaney, standing by with his tally sheet, winked at her. "Some fun, missus, eh?"

"Yes, Mr. Delaney. Some fun. Couldn't someone get killed having such fun?"

"It's happened. Takes balance and know-how and a lot o' practice. The older boys, they know enough to ride out such a turn. They take a long log with its butt end behind so it won't upend on 'em in the rapids." Delaney chuckled. "Takes the young fellows a spell to catch on."

"And meantime one could get killed," Selma observed.

"Ah well, it happens rarely. Ye take your chances on the river and in the woods. That's how it is."

Spoken like a true man. But she knew that men were funny that way. A man might put his own life in jeopardy to save another's, but in the name of "fun" the same man was like as not to encourage the other to take a senseless risk in some foolish stunt.

Yet it was fascinating to watch the loggers cat-foot it through the rushing water on their precarious perches. All the Holmgaards watched from the bank for a long while, and Elof got excited enough to want to try it himself. Axel growled that if he was such a damn fool as to try it without calked boots, to go ahead and break his damn-fool neck.

Elof decided against it, sardonically declaring that he didn't feel like giving Pa that much satisfaction.

Julia and Erika were the first to lose interest in watching the sport. They raced off toward the woods with Otto. Selma watched the log-running a little longer and then turned away, starting to walk back to camp.

It was only then that she noticed Dani and Adam Gannett were no longer standing on the bank. The realization made her come to a stop. She swept a quick glance around the expanse of cleared land this side of the river. There was no sign of them anywhere.

❧ twenty-three ❧

DANI AND ADAM strolled into the woods bordering the cleared fields, quietly talking. They were a few dozen yards into the trees when she stopped and caught hold of his hand.

"I don't think we should go any farther. Let's go back now."

Smiling, he gave her hand a light squeeze. "Worried?"

"I just don't want to get my folks upset."

"Why should they be? You told them about being with me yesterday. And you said neither of them objected."

"Yes, but..." Dani pulled her hand away and turned to face him. "It isn't that simple. Adam—"

"It's this simple," he murmured, his big hands coming up to cup her shoulders. "Come here."

"No." She laid her palms against his chest. "Please, we must talk about this. You never said you love me, Adam. If it's not too soon to say..."

"I do love you." His face sobered. "You love me, don't you, Dani?"

"Yes. Of course!"

"That's all that needs to be said...now. I don't want to

rush it with us, darling. We'll have a lot of time for everything to work out."

"But we must talk about it now. Adam, we can't pretend my pa and mother are going to be happy about it. They're not. And your family certainly won't be."

Adam hesitated, then nodded resignedly. "I guess I wanted to put off thinking about it. No putting it off, is there?"

Dani took his arm and they walked slowly back through the woods.

"I don't know what we can do," she said. "I've thought so much about it."

"Look, dear. I still think it's simple. All we can do is go it very slowly. We'll go places together. Be seen together. Give our families time to get used to the idea." He shook his head with a short, bitter laugh. "What a damn pestilence it is! Class. That's all it comes down to. And class is the phoniest thing under the sun. It's a perspective that says a man or a woman is to be judged by their wealth or by their ancestors—instead of by their own worth. Christ, I hate it! I always have."

"But it's just about as bad with my folks, Adam. Oh, Ma would come around after a while. She just needs what you said—time to get used to something. But Pa! I don't think he'd ever understand." Dani hesitated. "Do you think your mother would?"

"No," he said slowly. "But she can be made to accept it. If I stand up to her. *That's* the hard part."

She pressed his arm, saying gently, "It isn't so simple after all, is it?"

"I guess . . . not with anything that's truly important. And this is." He drew her to a halt. Again his hands clasped her shoulders, swinging her almost roughly to face him. "Dani. Have you had any beaux—ever?"

"Nothing serious—ever. Not till now."

"Damn it. What are we walking and talking for? I want to kiss you."

She laughed softly. "You *do* have a few things to learn about girls. Don't ask. *Ever!*"

"Never? You objected a minute ago."

"That was a minute ago."

Last night Dani had lain awake for hours, restless with

memories of his kisses and touchings a few hours before, thinking of the next day, when he would be on hand to oversee the log drive, and finding the waiting almost unbearable. She'd thought of him often enough in the days since they had met. But those thoughts had been nothing to the intensity of feeling that had devoured her since his first caresses.

Yet she wasn't prepared for the flame of desire that consumed her now, taking the hunger of his kiss and the clasp of his arms.

She'd always been puzzled by reading of romantic heroines who were lifted to "transports of rapture" by a lover's kiss. A boy kissed you and you kissed him back. So what? Sometimes it was a pleasing sensation, sometimes a modestly exciting one. But what was so transporting and rapturous about it?

After yesterday she hadn't had to wonder; she had found that a lover's touch could set her on fire. But she hadn't realized till this moment how completely it might blaze out of control, burning away her slender restraints, consuming her with a need for the wholeness of a man's love.

Just as he had yesterday, he was bearing her backward to a couch of warm pine-needled earth. But this time she had no power to fight back, no will to resist.

Dani was writhing in the same fever of love that possessed her lover. Her hands were wandering wildly over him, clutching and tugging, seeking all of him. Her throat was moaning and murmurous as it arched to the shower of his kisses trailing across her face and neck, even as her body arched and twisted to his searching hands.

Her fingers aided his as they undid the collar of her dress, parting the wash-softened calico away from the ivory flesh of shoulders and upper bosom, bearing them—and only moments afterward the smooth little cones and rosy tautened nipples of her breasts—to the hot fierce seeking of his mouth. . . .

Then a sound outside of her seemed to echo, distantly, the pulse of her own blood hammering in her ears. In the churning drug of her truant lust, Dani heard it and yet did not hear it. Then it grew louder, an insistent beat that cut like jagged ice through the opiate of love.

Otto. He was barking with that steady mindless yap of his. And she could hear the childish voices of the twins, the strike of their running feet through the ground, as they came into the woods.

They were coming straight this way. Along the same game trail she and Adam had taken.

"Adam—Adam . . ."

She was struggling against him now. Fighting his ardor with the same fervor with which she'd embraced it only seconds before. He didn't pull back at once. Dani beat wildly with her fists against his arms and shoulders.

"Adam!"

He raised only his face. It was hot and flushed, full of angry resentment. Then his own awareness sharpened to the nearing sounds. But too late.

Otto came racing into the clearing. He launched himself at them with a joyous yelp, landing square in the middle of Adam's back and flattening him atop Dani. The pup scampered over the pair of them, leaping and licking, making it impossible for them to scramble apart, much less to adjust their disarranged clothing.

A moment later the little girls burst into the glade.

They saw their big sister sprawled on the ground, dress and underclothes stripped from her upper body and twisted around her waist, and a large man partly on top of her. The twins came to a stop, their eyes turning huge and solemn.

Julia's pause lasted the space of a heartbeat. She turned and ran from the clearing with a shrill cry of "Mama! Mama!" Erika stood her ground for a moment longer, her mouth pouting to an *O* that held a mingling of amazement and curiosity.

Then, taking the contagion of Julia's example, Erika turned and ran after her sister. Otto followed them, noising it up happily.

Adam scrambled to his feet, hastily putting his clothes in order. His face was white. "My God, what will . . ."

Dani pushed herself up to her knees.

"Adam! He will kill you!"

Her own words sounded unreal in her ears. Everything seemed suddenly unreal, tatters of a nightmare that had somehow materialized.

Adam's jaw fell. He looked at her. "Kill . . . ?"

179

"Pa. He will kill you. Oh God, Adam, get away from here! Get away now!"

Selma had started walking back to the camp in order to prepare the midday meal. She was still worrying about Dani.

The girl had a high-school education, and Selma had hoped she might make something of herself—perhaps become a teacher. A couple of years' training at the local normal school would get her a teaching certificate, and she could also tutor her young sisters—since the Holmgaards' new home was situated prohibitively far even from a country school. But maybe, Selma thought, that had been her own dream more than it had been Dani's.

The real trouble was that in some ways Dani was clever beyond her years. It obscured the fact that in other ways she was still a child. As she wished to see only the good things, that was what she saw. Selma had done her best to correct this by speaking frankly to the girl on every subject, but she'd never been sure how much of it had taken.

Not very much, evidently. This growing affair with a man out of her class . . .

Selma was walking through the jackpine grove between the dam and the camp. Abruptly she stopped in her tracks, hearing one of the twins screaming, "Mama! Mama!" at the top of her voice.

Selma turned and hurried back toward the dam.

Coming out of the jackpines, she saw Julia—her dress was red, Erika's blue—running and stumbling across the uneven cut-over ground between the woods and the river. Axel had heard her and was walking swiftly to meet her. Julia promptly changed her cry to "Papa! Papa!"

Not far behind her now came Erika, followed by the crazily barking Otto.

Axel caught Julia up in his arms. Selma was too far away to make out what was said, but knew Julia was spilling out a wild sobbing explanation. Catching up her skirts, Selma ran toward them as fast as she could.

Axel set the child down and took a dozen long steps to reach the stump against which his rifle was leaning. He snatched it up and whirled toward the woods. Though she was still many yards away from him, Selma could see the killing rage in his face.

Gud! What had happened?

In the same moment she saw something else. Adam Gannett coming out of the woods, heading straight for his horse, which he'd left tied to a tree at the north edge of the jackpine stand. Axel pulled to a halt and levered the Winchester, bringing it to his shoulder.

Selma screamed, *"Axel!"*

He sent off a shot. Blind with rage, he made a clean miss. Adam was already going for his mount in a zigzag run.

Axel dropped to one knee and steadied his rifle by bracing his elbow on the other knee. This time he took careful aim.

Selma summoned all her strength for a burst of speed that covered the last yards between herself and Axel. She reached him. Struck blindly downward with the heel of her hand. Slapped the rifle barrel groundward as the weapon went off.

The shot blasted up a clod of earth close to Gannett's feet.

Then Adam was in his saddle, slamming his heels against the horse's flanks, sending it into the jackpines. Selma heard the swish and crack of boughs as he plunged through the trees that momentarily hid him. A drumming of hooves as he broke free of the grove on its opposite side. Still out of sight, he would be crossing their camp now, heading for the tote road and escape.

Axel rose slowly off his knee. His face was bloodless. He looked at Selma as if he didn't see her. He said one hoarse word: *"Dani!"*

"She's coming. She's all right." Selma caught his arm and pointed at the edge of the woods. "See? There she is."

Axel stood dumbly for a moment. The berserk look ebbed from his face.

Then he walked swiftly to meet his daughter. Selma hurried after him. Anxiety made a chill pinch around her heart. She didn't know what Julia had told Axel, but it was probably exaggerated. Dani, walking out of the woods to meet them, looked undamaged. It was the unpredictable turn of Axel's temper that worried Selma.

As they came up to Dani, she looked a little rumpled—like a girl who had hastily put her dress and hair in order. That was all. There wasn't a mark on her, and she was trying to look very composed.

Axel grasped her by the arm and shook her. "You all right? Are you?"

"Yes—yes. Nothing happened, Papa, I—"

"Nothing!" Axel roared. "Your little sister seen you on the ground with your clothes off and that bastard all over you! You telling me that ain't so?"

"Well, there was—I mean, he didn't—"

"You swear that? He didn't get to do it? You swear it?"

"Yes! Listen, I—"

"Thank *Gud* for that!"

"Axel," Selma said sharply. "Give her a chance to speak, won't you?"

"Helvete! That bastard tried to rape our girl! What else is to say?"

Axel's face was congested with blood; he was so red that Selma feared he would burst a blood vessel. Maybe she'd better not say anything more.

"Take Dani back to camp," he said abruptly. Then he spun on his heel and tramped back toward the dam.

"Mama," Dani said in a frenzied whisper, "he's wrong! He's terribly wrong! It wasn't that way at all!"

"I never thought so," Selma said wearily.

"But Papa is wrong about Adam! He wasn't trying to—I mean, good God, Mama! What the girls saw, it...it was as much my fault as Adam's! I've got to tell Papa...."

And Dani started after him.

Selma turned on the twins, who were standing not far away, close together and round-eyed with awe. "You," she told them sternly, "get back to camp and stay there. And"—she pointed at the capering pup—"take that *vildhund* with you!"

The edge on her tone made them obey quickly.

Selma moved firmly after Dani and overtook her. Seized her daughter's arm with a violence that almost pulled her off balance.

"No. You don't tell him anything. Nothing!"

"Mama—!"

"Nothing!"

"But God, Mama, don't you see? He's put all the blame on Adam—"

"I see. If that's what he thinks, you leave him think it."

Dani shook her head bewilderedly. "*I* just don't see at all. . . ."

"Dani. We've got to leave it this way. *Forsta?* Because *Gud* knows what he'll do if you say the truth. But I tell you this. It will be all the worse."

"I *still* don't—"

"If you were a man with a daughter, you would. I don't know why sometimes fathers feel so. But they do." Selma hesitated; this was hard to say. "A man thinks his daughter is, I don't know, too precious and pure for this world. He is jealous a little of the boyfriend, maybe. You let Papa think what he wants to. That's best."

"But what . . . what would he do?"

"I don't know. Give you a good hiding maybe. Or order you to leave home. Whatever it would be, it might break our family up. I won't let that happen. *Forsta* . . . understand?"

Axel slogged down the slope of the riverbank to where Pat Delaney was standing. He gave the drive boss a savage jab in the arm with his rifle muzzle.

Delaney wheeled on him, bristling. "Here now! What was that about?"

"Clear out," Axel told him.

"What? What's this now?"

"You heard me. Get out. You and all the rest. Clear off my land and off this dam."

Delaney stared in disbelief. "Man, what the divil is it with you? We've a deal on. Have you forgot?"

"The deal is off. All deals with any goddamn Gannetts is off."

"What, are ye daft?" Delaney swept a hand toward the big float of logs, where the riverjacks were pausing in their work, turning a puzzled attention on the two men. "We ain't driven through a fifth o' the logs—"

A grunt exploded from the drive boss as Axel rammed the

rifle against his belly. He took a step backward, sputtering with anger.

"The deal is off," Axel repeated. "Now you get out, you and your pack of timber dogs. Out! Or by God, I start shooting!"

❧ *three* ❧

The Passions

⁂ twenty-four ⁂

FROM ELOF, WHO paid him a visit the day after it happened, Rudy learned about the blow-up between his father and the Gannetts. Naturally Elof offered his own sardonic slant about what had occurred.

"Girls is girls, Scientist," he observed. "Even our little sister."

Rudy angrily asked him exactly what he meant by that. Elof merely grinned and shook his head.

On the same day, the Gannetts took the matter of the blocked dam to court. Beau Gannett was quoted in Winterfield's daily paper as saying that he "expected a ruling in our favor very shortly." When pressed by a reporter about what steps might be taken by the Gannett Logging and Boom Company in the event of a favorable ruling, Gannett merely replied that "you'll know about that when everyone else does."

Damn Pa anyway, Rudy thought dismally. There had to be a better way than this. Almost anything would be better than putting the family in jeopardy all over again.

Over the next few weeks his ribs knit quickly and cleanly.

Dr. Hammerstein recommended some light exertion. On his first day out of bed, Rudy confined his pacing to his own room—and on the next day, to the first story of the boarding-house. On the day after that, he extended his range of exercise outside.

He walked slowly around the backyard, stretching the twinges out of his muscles, enjoying the warmth of a late-spring day. Strolling up and down between Rachel Merrick's flower beds and lilac bushes, his only difficulty was getting the feel of moving around on open ground. He wasn't so wobbly from inactivity as he was from having gotten his first legs back on a level floor. Anyway, no use overdoing it.

Rudy's idle circuit of the yard took him back to the rear porch. He sat down on the bottom step to rest. Behind him, Lotte Hoffenmeier opened the door, carrying several small rugs over her arm. Briskly she began to shake them, snapping off puffs of dust and grit.

Rudy got to his feet and stepped back, shielding his face with one hand. He glared at the girl. She paused, saying crossly, "If you don't like it, don't stand around like a *dummkopf*. What's the matter with you?"

"You might give a guy a word of warning."

"Ho!" Lotte planted a fist on her hip. "I think we done enough to make life soft for you, boy. All the day around you lay and do nothing. Who ask you to dump yourself on our step?"

His face warmed with resentment. "Where else could I go? I didn't know anyone in this town."

"Ach, so. If into saloons you don't go and get busted up, you don't need to camp with other people. If you want to come in, around to the front door you go. Go!"

Rudy tramped away around the house, his ears burning. God, what a crosspatch! She'd done as much as Miss Merrick in seeing to his comfort during his convalescence, but he was fed up with her acid sarcasm. However, he'd become friendly with her brother Hans, a frequent visitor at the boardinghouse.

Despite a lifelong closeness to his family, he'd been a little surprised to find he didn't miss them very much. But then he'd never had very much in common with any of them, even including his mother and Dani. Affectionate the Holmgaard world might be, but it was also bounded and narrow. This sojourn away from his family had quickened a wish to see more of the world outside.

Also, it was nice just to lie around and have nothing to do for a change.

Nothing, that is, but read. For the first time Rudy had been able to satisfy his appetite for reading. Rachel Merrick's own collection of books was small but well chosen; she had brought him other books from the public library. Sometimes in the late evenings they would discuss what he read. And a lot of other things, too.

Rudy had been surprised to learn that Rachel's background was even humbler than his, and that she was largely self-educated. By now his admiration for her was on a par with his infatuation. Still, he had enough wry objectivity to compare himself to one of the love-struck swains that populated the several volumes of Georgian pastoral poetry he'd found among Rachel's books. He was fully aware that being in love with Rachel Merrick was a hopeless thing—for an eighteen-year-old with no prospects. It was a bitter lemon on which to bite, but he bit it. Besides, his feeling for her was diluted with too much worshipful awe to get out of control.

When he reached the front porch, Rudy found himself undecided whether he wanted to go inside or not. He'd taken enough exercise, and the doctor had warned him not to over-exert. Yet there was nothing to do inside but read; for the time he'd had his fill of reading. The day was sunny but not hot. A perfume of lilac and locust coasting on the warm breeze spurred a restlessness in him. An urge compounded of youth, leafed-out spring, exalted thoughts of a beloved woman. And of being just plain tired of lying or sitting around on his duff.

He set off slowly down the block, feeling his stride firm up with the swing of his legs. He turned onto Main Street and idled down the sidewalk. Winterfield had a drowsy look at this season. The spring whoop-up was over; only the dull roar of the sawmills relieved the town's placid currents of life.

Rudy's eye was taken by a big touring car as it cruised up the street. He halted, eyeing it with mild amusement. It was built so high off the ground that it was equipped with two levels of running boards. He'd heard of Shad Gannett's new Olds-

189

mobile Limited. It was said to have a six-cylinder engine and huge forty-two-inch wheels that would clear the bumpiest of backwoods roads.

So the young fellow behind the steering wheel must be Shad. And Rudy recognized the darkly attractive girl in the seat beside him. She was the one who had taken Elof's fancy—Tom O'Dea's daughter. She was wearing a pretty flowered dress; her companion was immaculate in white flannels.

They made a handsome, carefree-seeming pair.

Oh brother, Rudy thought with a shake of his head. Seemed as if Holmgaards and Gannetts were bound to have common interests at every turn. Except that common differences would be a more apt phrase.

"Sizing up the competition?"

Rudy turned his head toward the speaker. Andrew Fordyce, in his shirtsleeves and wearing an ink-stained apron, was lounging in the doorway of his newspaper shop a few doors away. He grinned around the thin cigar he was smoking.

Rudy said, "Hello, Mr. Fordyce. I'm not in competition with anyone—I hope!"

Fordyce nodded idly toward the Gannett auto. "Well, one of your brothers is. So the grapevine has it."

Rudy laughed. "If you want the story on that, you'll have to try somewhere else. I'm not talking."

Fordyce gave him an approving wink. "Sound policy. One that any newspaperman is bound to applaud—when it's in his interest." He eyed Rudy critically. "You're looking pretty smart. First day up and around, is it?"

"More or less. But don't kid me, Mr. Fordyce. I looked in the mirror this morning."

"Well, you still carry a few traces of your annihilation. But the last of the bruises are fading out. Doesn't appear as if that pretty puss of yours will bear any scars. You'd do well to take it sort of easy for a while, though . . . just being back on your feet."

"That's what Doc Hammerstein said."

Fordyce fingered ash off his cigar. "Step inside a minute, son, and take a load off. I've been meaning to have a talk with you. Now's as good a time as any."

Curious, Rudy followed the publisher into his shop. The

town's weekly tabloid was housed in a narrow frame building wedged between two larger ones. The lower half of its big front window was painted white to stress the black block wording: WINTERFIELD WEEKLY CLARION. JOB PRINTING. A. FORDYCE, ED. AND PROP.

The long room was something of a shock on first sight. It was a monument to hopeless clutter. Boxes and cartons and stacks of yellowing newspapers were piled along the side walls. To the left of the doorway stood an iron safe and a clothes commode, to the right a swivel chair and a desk heaped with papers and proofs. The room was divided midway by a wooden railing; Fordyce led Rudy through its swing gate and circled a tall cabinet that formed a kind of rear alcove containing a stone-topped table and two metal cases set on a sloping frame.

Seating himself on a tall stool, Fordyce said, "Don't mind if I set type while we talk. Working against a deadline. As usual."

He picked up a metal stick and held it in his left hand as he selected type from the two cases and slapped it into the stick. Working with speed and deftness, Fordyce's right hand was almost a blur as he worked.

"Say, that's really something!"

"Compositing?" Fordyce grinned crookedly around his cigar. "A veritable snap, once you've mastered the knack. Takes time and patience. And a kind of strong slender hand that's best for this work. Piano paws like mine. Or"—he nodded at Rudy's hand resting on the cabinet—"yours."

"You do everything by yourself?"

"Just about. Except for cleaning up the place, which, as is painfully obvious, don't get done. And delivering the papers, which I hire a kid to do." Fordyce went on casually blurring type into sticks as he talked. "Good compositors—aside from a generic tendency of the breed to get thoroughly soused at times inconvenient to deadlines—are hard to come by nowadays. And they cost money. Which is no small consideration for a small weekly sheet. Not being equipped—for a similar reason—with such advanced amenities of the trade as the linotype or even, Gawd save me, with as standard a device as a treadle press, I am thrown back on my own resources and then some. Even to typesetting in the time-honored fashion. You behold one of the final practitioners of a dying art, my boy."

"It's sure something to see," said Rudy, fascinated. "What do you do—just make up a sentence as you go along?"

"For brief items—announcements and fillers and that sort of thing. No great trick to rely on memory or a few notes. Naturally I write up copy of a more elaborate sort in advance." Fordyce paused in his work now, flicking a small wicked leer. "And I lavish a genuine care and attention on one of my snotty but justly celebrated editorials."

"They're awfully good. Well written, I mean. I don't think I know enough about the issues hereabouts to judge your opinions."

Fordyce laughed. "Well, you must have some opinions on your pa's activities, anyway. They've provided some pretty trenchant themes for my recent editorial blurts."

Rudy made a wry face.

Fordyce said in a kindly way, "I know you don't approve of a lot of what your pa's done. Our pulchritudinous landlady has mentioned as much to me."

"I guess not, Mr. Fordyce. It's like kicking a polecat. What's the sense of it?"

"A man's pride," Fordyce said smilingly. "How's that?"

Rudy only shook his head.

"Then a gutsy stand taken by the little man against the abuses of wealth and privilege. That ought to be a good and sufficient reason."

"Maybe it is. But it's not Pa's reason."

"It's mine, though, Rudy. It's why I've taken up cudgels on your pa's behalf in print, and why I'll continue to. I reckon your opinion has been that I've only aggravated a bad situation."

"Well . . ."

"Don't hedge on declaring your honest views, boy. That's what a free press is all about. I know it's been hard on you, being put on the spot over an issue you can't see. But I believe, I *have* to believe, that there's more at stake in this affair than any one man's motives. Follow me?"

"Sure."

"But you don't agree. Well, fine. Could be that's what I

need around here. Someone who runs enough against my own grain to keep me on my toes. Think you could get interested enough in this business to take a hand in it?"

"You bet!"

"Okay, you're on. Five dollars a week and rooms. Not much to start with, but maybe..."

"Wait a minute, sir. Are you offering me a job?"

"That's right. It's not a spur-of-the-moment thought, Rudy. Been thinking about it for some time." Fordyce slid off the stool and gave him a hearty slap on the shoulder. "I need an assistant. Someone who can handle the shop well enough to free me for more news-hounding. Fellow I can rely on, smart and hardworking, no bad habits. Also"—he grinned unabashedly—"one that I can hire as cheaply as possible. Can't afford an experienced man."

Taken completely by surprise, Rudy smiled uncertainly. "I don't know anything about the newspaper business."

"Well now, nobody does at the outset, do they? You learn my doing. And I'm a hell of a good teacher. Call it an apprenticeship. Even if you don't want to make it your life's work, it's a damned handy trade to know—compositing is. Good compositor can find a job anywhere, anytime. Unless the damned machines take over everything."

Rudy was already shaking his head. "I don't think so, Mr. Fordyce. But thanks."

"Why not, for hell's sake?" snapped Fordyce. "I must be slipping. I had you pegged as a bright guy who'd want to widen his horizons. You won't find much opportunity stuck on a backwoods farm. Thought you'd leap at a chance like this."

"It's not that, sir. I can't just up and leave my family. I mean, not yet. They need me."

"The devil they do! You've three grown brothers living at home, haven't you? How much free help does your pa need to work the place? He ought to be gratified that at least one of his kids wants to strike out on his own. Try for something better in life. And that's where this job could lead, in time. Look on it as a stepping-stone. Besides—living and working in Winterfield, you'll still be close to your folks. Come on, lad. What about it?"

Rudy pulled gently on his lower lip. "Well, I don't know.

I think it would be great to learn the work. But Pa just won't go for the notion. I'd hate to clash with him about it."

"All right." Fordyce stabbed a peremptory thumb against Rudy's chest. "You let me handle your pa. Next time your family comes to town, I'll talk to him. Meanwhile, now you're recovering, you have plenty of time on your hands. Nothing to prevent your learning the ropes. You can come in for a little while every day . . . whenever I'm in the shop. Okay?"

"Sure, okay. I mean, it sounds fine."

"Right. You take it easy for a few more days and then we'll get started. Want to see the upstairs?"

Fordyce led the way up a back stairway to the building's second story. It consisted of two good-sized rooms that had a musty closed-in smell. They contained a cot and some rickety furniture, as well as a sink, an iron stove, and other facilities for light housekeeping. An entire wall of the bedroom was devoted to a set of homemade bookshelves that were literally packed with books.

Just some of the titles—*Das Kapital, Anti-Dühring, Fabian Essays*—made Rudy stare in openmouthed fascination. He had *heard* of these books, but they weren't to be found in any ordinary libraries, public or private.

Fordyce explained that the upper-floor rooms had served as his own quarters for several years. "Then," he added, "my stomach went bad from my own cooking. And I couldn't stand living in my own hogsty any longer. That's when I took up lodging at Miss Rachel's, despite the obvious strain on my budget. I am not, left to my own devices, a person of tidy habits. Are you?"

"Guess I'm passable," said Rudy.

"Good. You can move in here whenever you're ready. You'll have to spoil your own meals, but at least you can save some on grub money by not eating out. Say—"

Fordyce walked over to the shelves and pulled out three of the books. "While you're recuperating, you might like to glance through these. . . ."

☙ twenty-five ☙

THE TIME OF day to which Rachel Merrick most looked.
forward was the hour or so before she retired for the night. A
hot bath, dressing in gown and wrapper and slippers, retreating
to the solitude and quiet of her first-story room, relaxing in
armchair or bed while she sipped sherry and read till drowsiness
took her and she was ready for sleep.

Tonight, however, Rachel was restless and a little distraught. A second and then a third glass of sherry didn't help
to quell the feeling. If anything, they heightened it. She was
accustomed to such times as these; they came and went with
the female tides of her body. But they were fed as much by
vague frustrations of a private nature as by any fleshly rhythms.

Three glasses of brandied wine calmed Rachel's nerves, but
not the trend of her mood. She felt excitable and uneasy; she
paced her room for a while, sipping a fourth glass of sherry.
Then she left the bedroom and walked back and forth between
the kitchen and back parlor. All of her lodgers were abed, and
so was Lotte; the house was quiet except for the creaks and

ticks that any building gave out in the silences of night. The stillness and sharp noises did nothing to abate her restlessness.

Shortly she thought of Rudy Holmgaard, and went to the front hallway, where she could see the door to his room beneath the stairs. A straw of light showed under his door.

She knocked at it gently. "Rudy?"

He answered readily, "Yes'm. I'm awake."

Rachel opened the door, left it several inches ajar, and crossed the room to his bedside. He was sitting up in his nightshirt, reading by the bed-table lamp. She could tell from his polite attempt to iron out a pucker of concentration that he'd been deeply absorbed in his reading.

Rachel took the book from his hands and read its title aloud. *"Das Kapital—*by Karl Marx. Volume One. Literal English translation." She laughed. "Goodness. That's much too steep for me. Where in the world did you find it? Not in my little library."

"Mr. Fordyce loaned it to me."

"M'm. I might have known."

Rachel handed back the book. She pulled a ladder-backed chair over beside the bed and sat in it, tucking her wrapper around her slippered feet. She felt a little tipsy and only faintly self-conscious.

She had spent a number of evenings in this room, sitting and talking with the boy. Eventually their nightly visits had come to seem so natural a thing that she'd finally gotten in the habit of preparing for bed first and then (properly gowned and robed) joining him. She'd ceased that pleasant practice several nights ago, after Rudy's first time out of bed. It was well within propriety's bounds to see to an invalid's comfort before retiring herself, but now that he was almost fully recovered, the pastime should be discontinued.

Even if he was, really, only a boy.

Only a boy.

Her eyes followed the solemn lines of his young face. Rudy was a nice boy. Kind and attentive, sensitive to others. Deep in his own thoughts so much of the time, but always ready to abandon them in favor of another's attention. Yet he possessed a quiet intensity. Once he found his life's direction, not much of anything was likely to deter him. He'd do whatever he wanted to do, and he would go far.

Rachel touched the book in his hands. "You're determined to better yourself, aren't you? In every way possible."

"Yes'm. I think the job with Mr. Fordyce will show me a few more things. I hope so."

Rachel smiled. He and Fordyce had discussed Rudy's employment at the supper table this evening.

"Oh yes," she said musingly, "it will be an education of its own sort, I've no doubt. And you can learn from Andrew. He's quite . . . worldly. But you're bigger than Andrew Fordyce's little clutch of ideas, Rudy. Don't let him influence you too much."

"I won't," Rudy said evenly. "I always do my own thinking."

"I know you do."

Rachel put out her hand, unthinkingly. Then she drew it back, a little too quickly. She had felt like ruffling up his hair.

"Well—" She took another sip of sherry. "Perhaps you'd rather read than talk. I could tell how absorbed you were."

"No, ma'am." Smiling, he closed the book and laid it aside.

That smile of his! He couldn't have any idea of what effect it might have on feminine emotions. But he was bound to find out before too long. Rachel was well aware that he was infatuated with her. It no longer amused her, as it had at first. Nor did she feel inclined to pity him. Rudy did not inspire pity. He was a young man with his feet solidly under him. He might be infatuated, but he was also completely self-possessed.

I must tell him, she thought suddenly.

Was she allowing the wine to affect her judgment? Rachel didn't know. She thought: I must tell him, that's all. And did not think about it anymore. She said with a self-conscious smile, "Rudy, um . . . something I've been meaning to speak to you about. It's a difficult matter to bring up, but I feel it should be said frankly."

"Anything you want to tell me, ma'am. It'll be kept in strict confidence."

"I know that. You're a friend. We've become . . . rather close friends, haven't we?"

"I sure hope so."

"That's why I feel there's something about me you must know. Simply because it's *not* confidential at all. Not so many years ago, as a matter of fact, it was the talk of the town. You've not been out and around Winterfield enough to have heard it. Not yet. But you would, sooner or later. The small-town grapevine never dies ... and it never forgets."

Rudy's face held a puzzled curiosity, but he said only, "Boy, that's the truth. I grew up near a Minnesota town like that."

"So then, you know what I mean." Rachel lowered her gaze to her glass. "I'd rather you hear the story from me—even if it makes you think less of me—than pick up a secondhand and distorted version from someone else."

"Miss Rachel, there's not really any need ..." He paused, embarrassed. "What I mean, I'd never believe anything about you without you told me yourself."

She smiled wryly. "But that's why I must tell you myself. I value your friendship, you see. There was a man ... perhaps I should say, there was a boy, first of all. We grew up together. By that, I mean we attended the same public schools in Winterfield. There was nothing else in our lives that could have drawn any sort of association at all between us. I was from the wrong side of the tracks. The Gannetts didn't even *notice* my sort of people, much less speak to them."

Rudy's look turned sharp and questioning.

She nodded. "The man—the boy—was Beau Gannett. We were in love from grade school on. I'm not really sure why to this day. We never had all that much in common even as *people*. But that was just how it was—something neither of us could help. As for the social aspect ... what have I told you about my folks?"

"You've said they were poor."

"Yes. That was the least of it. My father was a lot of things. Hopeless drunks don't hold any job for very long. Luckily he was never home very much, because he was never sober very much when he *was* home. My mother died when I was four, and I grew up living with her sister. My father also lived with her ... when he happened to be around."

Rachel spoke matter-of-factly, but she was closely watching Rudy's face. "Does this shock you very much? Would you rather I didn't go on?"

"It surprises me is all," he said slowly. "Guess it takes a lot more than that to shock any small-towner. I'm proud of your confidence, Miss Rachel. But if it distresses you any way at all . . ."

"Remembering does . . . sometimes. Just talking doesn't. All that I'm telling you is over and done with. I had to come to terms with it long ago. Nor would I have reason to tell you now, if other people would only forget. Anyway—Beau's mother loathed our relation. Beau's dad, old Dave, found it amusing. Boy had to sow his oats, you know. Long as there was no question of wedding the wench. Well—we went together, more or less openly, through high school. Of course the girl friend never got brought home to meet Dad and Mom. But then she never expected to be. It was enough that we attended all the usual school affairs together. And . . . we were intimate."

She looked at Rudy again. His dark eyes were somber; there was no condemnation in his face. Didn't you know there wouldn't be? she asked herself.

Of course she'd known. Rachel felt a nudge of shame, but also a sense of relief. Almost of cleansing. She'd needed so much, for so long, to talk about it to somebody. She had known that young Rudy Holmgaard would listen intelligently and not condemn. He would be understanding, and, God!—she needed that from someone.

"I guess—I was just too much in love to think about it ever ending. And the day came. Beau graduated from high school. We had a final summer together. Then Beau was packed off to the University of Wisconsin to get the education his papa never had. It had to be that way, of course. He was the oldest son. He would shoulder most of the responsibility for *his* generation of Gannetts."

Rudy said hesitantly, "But he didn't give you up . . . just like that, did he?"

"Oh, he did. Beau loved me very much. But he loved all that went with being a Gannett far more than he could ever care for a woman. Any woman. It was a painful decision for him—but there was never any doubt of what his choice would be."

"But it must have been a lot harder on you."

"Oh, I think so. If a woman loses, society doesn't leave her much to fall back on. Her whole life is supposed to be her family—if she gets to have a family. I hadn't even a pair of loving parents to turn to." Rachel smiled. She put the wineglass to her teeth. "But you know? There's nothing like hitting every bump in the road to make a body find out what they're really made of. Nobody *wants* to find out, of course. You'd be mad to go out and *try* to experience that much pain. Since I had no choice, it's not to my credit that I pulled myself together. The only other thing I could do was fall utterly apart.

"Well . . . I'd been hired out working for my keep since I was twelve. By that time, Aunt Belle was no longer working, and my pittance of earnings as a hired girl was all that kept her body and soul together. Her mind was degenerated from alcoholism. My father died about that time, and the only legacy he left my aunt was his drinking habit. By the time I was sixteen, she had to be committed to an asylum. After that, I began saving what money I could. After Beau . . . ended our relationship, I did nothing but work. At first, all I wanted was to lose myself in work. Finally, when I began to come back to life again, I realized I wanted more than a lifetime as a 'workbeast.'

"So—I enrolled at the county normal school. I attended classes and continued to hire out for my keep, and of course the county contributed to my tuition. After graduating, I taught for three years in a country school. I was still saving and scrimping. Finally, with the help of installment payments and a small loan from a sympathetic banker, I was able to buy this house."

"Did you, uh . . ."

"Did I see Beau again?"

Rudy nodded, averting his eyes.

"At least occasionally. Wouldn't it be pretty hard to avoid in a town of this size?"

"Yes'm."

Rachel smiled. "I saw him one more time to really *talk* to. He asked for the meeting. That was when he returned from his first year at the university, for summer vacation. He had changed. . . ." Memory tightened her lips. "He hadn't turned hard yet, not as he did later on. But the signs were there. I had to flatly tell him our relation was ended. That it had been as of the moment he had told me our *understanding* was ended. I made clear to him that I would not be any man's kept woman. He respected *my* decision. After that our meetings were confined to polite hellos on the street."

The break of relief in Rudy's face made her smile. Again, suddenly, she wanted to ruffle his hair. This time she nearly gave way to the impulse. Now it made her feel more amused than uneasy.

"Um, what was I about to say? Oh yes—having become a respectable landlady, I set out to work my way into society's good graces. No easy thing, but I had an unexpected ally on my side. Whoever do you think it was?"

"I couldn't guess, ma'am."

"Mrs. Gannett!" With a little flourish of triumph, Rachel drained her glass and set it on the bedside table. "Given her position in the community, she could have made it impossible for me. But she didn't. For a time, apparently, she simply watched and waited. Once she was certain that everything was over between her son and me, she set out to make amends for her old animus toward me. Not directly, of course. Not a word ever passed between us. But she became . . . I guess you'd say my silent sponsor. Dropping a word here, a word there, in the circles where it would do me the most good."

"That's sure strange," said Rudy.

"Not if you think on it. Mrs. Gannett has a code all her own. She hews to it religiously. She can be a generous friend. Or a deadly enemy."

"All the same," Rudy said slowly, "you showed a lot of courage on your own."

"I did?"

"Well, sure. Staying on in Winterfield like you did. For someone who hurts as deep as you, it would have been a lot easier for you to pack up and leave. Start a new life somewhere else."

"Rudy, I gave it more than a passing thought. Making a clean break with the past. And the place. It would have been the sensible thing." She shook her head, quickly and vehemently. "But I couldn't. It would have been like running away. I *couldn't* do that!"

"I don't think you could," he said. "I don't think you'd do that for anyone, no matter what."

The quiet heat in his voice brushed her with a tender impact.

"But you must understand, Rudy . . ." She shifted a little on the chair. "Eventually I intend to leave Winterfield. I've saved a good deal of money, and much of it is soundly invested. I suppose a large city will be most to my taste. Winterfield simply holds too many sour memories. Too many to let me live as fully as I believe I can. I think . . ." She hesitated. "Having said so much, I may as well be frank. It's hard for me to trust a man, *any* man, any longer. It's a stupid way to feel. I want to rid myself of it. I think I'll have my best chance in another place."

"I don't blame you for feeling that way." A scowl clouded Rudy's face, giving it a brooding, saturnine cast. "When I think what that Gannett louse did to you . . ."

"Swedes!" Rachel laughed. She put a finger under his chin and playfully tipped up his face. "I've never met a Swede that couldn't turn out a Gloomy Gus in a second flat. Do all of you have dark places in you?"

Rudy swallowed and forced a small grin. "My mother says so. Says that's one way we're all alike." He hesitated, then added abruptly, "Miss Rachel, now that I've got my legs under me again, I think it's time I moved out. You know Mr. Fordyce is turning his old quarters at the newspaper building over to me. . . ."

"That's fine. But you needn't feel hurried about leaving here."

"I just think it's best if I do. I'm very grateful for your hospitality and all—"

"Rudy, it has been a pleasure." She laid a hand on his where it rested on the coverlet. "You must do as you think best. But try not to overexert. Don't let Andrew work you too hard at first."

"No, ma'am."

"Ma'am," she chided him gently. "Aren't we still friends?"

"More than ever."

"And how many times have I told you I have a name?"

"Miss Rachel."

"Just Rachel."

"Rachel."

"There. Is that really so hard to say?"

"No'm," he said dubiously.

Rachel's answering laughter had an immoderate note in her own ears. She held his hand tightly, aware now of the undercurrent rising in her pulse. Suddenly she leaned forward, both hands moving to his face, the tips of her fingers racing his brow and cheeks.

"Oh Rudy," she whispered. "Rudy . . ."

"Yes'm—Rachel."

She bent quickly to his mouth, meaning the kiss to be brief. But her lips trembled and clung, and she did not want to stop.

She felt his hands come hesitantly to her shoulders, and his touch broke the spell. Rachel pulled away, staring at him wildly. A wave of blood filled his face; his brows frowned, questioning her.

Her lips parted. Suddenly her mouth was paper-dry. No words came out.

She rose blindly and whirled, starting toward the open door. Stopped with her hand on the doorknob. What now? Run from the room? Run to escape? Escape from what? Her mind was a maelstrom of indecision.

Abruptly she closed the door and shot its bolt into place. Swiftly and lightly, she came back to the bed. He opened his mouth to speak.

"Don't," said Rachel.

She moistened her lips; her pulse filled her ears with soft thunder. Again she bent to his lips, her mouth stirring and parting.

She drew back, feeling a momentary pang. "Oh Lord," she murmured. "You're so young. So . . ."

With a little moan she let her mouth sink fully into the kiss, closing her eyes as her weight settled onto the bed. At the first hesitating touch of his fingers on her garments, she did not open her eyes, but at once assisted his awkward gropings, twisting and turning, slipping free of robe and gown and slippers. Her hands turned almost rough as they helped him shed his nightshirt.

Not once did she open her eyes.

Rachel felt his hands reach for her breasts. Hands that were confident now, and eager.

"*Yes!*" she whispered. "Oh yes. . . ."

She drew his head to the swelling mounds and their pink-aureoled nubs. Her legs twisted up and down, sleeking against one another in a frenzy as his mouth hungrily sought and found the two hard-soft points of her passion.

She felt wet warmth and the spreading delirium of pleasure in her loins. An animal whimper rose from her throat.

When with a quick movement she rolled to her back and he came atop her, both their bodies were tautly ready, explosive with expectancy. A soft scream of joy escaped Rachel Merrick as her boy lover plunged into her. And the fierce and tender grapplings of love began, flowing into an ecstasy of now and forever.

✷ twenty-six ✷

SELMA HAD BEEN bawling Elof out for the better part of five minutes when Axel broke into her tirade, irritably.

"Always you're at the boy because he fools around a little," he growled. *"Helvete!* A man is only young once. Let him have his fun."

"Fun!" Selma swung to face her husband, one fist braced on her hip. "Sure, let him have all the fun he wants. Let him break all the commandments, that's a fine thing, very manly, eh? But if his tomcatting keeps him from work, from helping you, that's something else. Then you don't like it so much anymore!"

Axel muttered something inarticulate and continued eating his breakfast. Elof sat cross-legged on the ground, unconcernedly finishing his own breakfast, the trace of a grin on his lips. Selma glared at him. How she would love to slap that smart grin off his mouth! But it wouldn't change anything. Even as a child Elof could never be whipped into line for very long.

Selma began to gather up dirty dishes, clattering them into

a pan. It was her husband and not her son against whom the real brunt of her temper was directed. But he was just as impervious to her indignation as Elof was.

The tension had grown since Axel's lunatic decision to break his agreement with the Gannett Logging and Boom Company. She'd wondered if he had gone completely crazy. What did the business with Dani and the Gannett son have to do with the other? But no use to talk. As long as what went on in Axel Holmgaard's head made sense to *him*, the rest of the world could go hang.

This time Selma had been unforgiving. Once such an agreement was ruptured, it would take a miracle to patch it. She and Axel had quarreled violently that night, and just about every night or day since then.

Today they were to journey to Winterfield, to do some shopping and to see Rudy. Elof had blandly declared his intention of going with them, as he had "some business to take care of" in town. That was when Selma, her nerves badly frayed, had lit into him about his carryings-on with that O'Dea brat and other cheap girls. Currents of gossip were conveying scraps of Elof's doings, as they had back in Minnesota. While shopping in Winterfield, Selma had been mortified to overhear a pair of woman discussing her son's new wave of exploits.

Still seething, she bustled about the camp tasks while her sons and daughters, sitting around the fire, kept a discreet silence as they finished their breakfasts. Only Lennart was absent, installed again in his familiar post of guarding the dam and not minding it at all. Lennart had a great fondness for that solitary duty. However, the guard shanty was beginning to resemble a boar's nest, and Selma remembered that she'd planned on giving it a thorough cleaning today.

This would be a good time. She needed to work off her tension and anger. The accumulated dirt and disorder of that shack should provide a worthy challenge.

Selma got out a broom and a mop, a bucket, a bar of strong yellow soap and a knife, and an armload of clean bedding. Then she called Dani to help her carry the things over to the shanty. It would give the two of them a chance to talk, and Selma felt it was past time for a good talk with her girl.

Axel came tramping over to her, scowling. "What's all this?"

"I'm going to clean up that shack," she said curtly. "It's a mess."

"Okay, it's a mess. But we're going to town. Clean it when you get back."

Selma straightened up, saying between her teeth, "I will clean it *now!* It won't hurt you to wait on me once, Axel Holmgaard!"

She waited, braced for an outburst. But Axel only glowered and tugged at his beard, then turned and strode away, roaring at Arvid and Elof to come work on the house with him. By now the building was roofed and framed and enclosed, and they were at work on the interior walls and floors. The barn was already completed, and the house would be ready for occupancy soon.

Selma and Dani set off through the jack-pine grove toward the dam. Now that they were free to talk, Selma wasn't really sure what she wanted to say. What was to be said or done about Dani's problem? The girl was in love. She was so gentle and obedient as a rule that one tended to forget that like every other Holmgaard, she had a mind of her own. Dani was no more easily swayed or changed than the rest of them.

"About the young Gannett," Selma began tentatively.

"Ma—" Dani's gaze was straight ahead. "I don't want to talk about it. It's just no good."

"You have changed one way," Selma observed quietly. "It's not a good way, Dani. You were a happy girl, before. No matter how bad things were, you were always up. Now you're most always down. It's no good for you—it's not natural to you."

"I'm sorry, Ma. Nothing can change how I feel."

"You hate your pa now? Is that it?"

"No—" Her voice trembled. "Oh, I don't know! It's just so wrong! We're not the wrong ones—Adam or me. You know what he said? That the whole thing about 'class' is so silly—so *phony*. It doesn't even *exist* except in people's minds!"

"Maybe not. Maybe if you get everyone else to think so, then you have no problem. Can you do that, Dani?"

"Ma, what are you saying?"

"That the world's what it is and you can't make it different."
Selma shook her head. "Dani, you think if you want a thing
hard enough, it will be. The world is not that way. It will never
be."

Dani had gone white around the lips. "You're telling me to
give up Adam. That it won't ever work out. Is that right?"

"Girl, I don't tell you what to do. Your good sense will tell
you that, if you use it. I know if you want to see the Gannett
bad enough, nothing will stop you."

Dani firmed her lips and set her eyes straight front. By this
Selma guessed that Dani had more than toyed with the notion.
Possibly she and Adam Gannett were already contriving, somehow, to meet in secret. But what more could a mother say or
do?

Reaching the shanty, they found Lennart sprawled on the
cot, reading a dime novel. He was taken by surprise as his
mother and sister came through the propped-open door. Lennart
scrambled to his feet, grabbing for his rifle. Then he relaxed
with a sheepish grin.

"Go on," Selma told him brusquely. "I'm going to clean
up here. Go on to camp and get some breakfast."

"But Pa said—"

"Oh for *Gud*'s sake, leave your gun here! I'll shoot anyone
who comes around! Go!"

She also dismissed Dani.

When the two of them were gone, Selma rolled up her
sleeves and attacked the job of setting the shanty to rights. She
doubted that the Gannett watchmen had ever bothered even to
sweep it out, and knowing her sons' talents as housekeepers,
it seemed a good bet they had added to the litter. First she
carried the dirty bedclothes outside, then gave the place a good
sweeping. Afterward she fetched a bucket of water from the
river, pared shavings of soap into it, and worked up a lively
suds with the mop. She gave the floorboards a furious scrubbing, and was nearly finished before her temper simmered back
enough to let her pause and consider things more coolly.

She was sick of the way it was.

Sick of the coarsening arrogance that had begun to sit her
husband like a heavy fist. How much of it was a woman expected to take? How far did a marriage vow extend?

I can leave him, Selma thought. I can leave him and take the girls with me.

She was standing in the middle of the floor, leaning on the mop, as the thought sprang through her mind. And her mind recoiled from it, appalled. Such a thing was not done, had never been done, by any woman of her family. How could she even think such a thing...?

An oblong of sunlight fell across the floor from the open doorway. Suddenly a man's form filled it. Selma's eyes were turned downward, and she saw his shadow first. She lifted her gaze with a start.

"A good morning to you, mistress," said Tom O'Dea, stepping into the room.

Selma muttered something and hastily resumed her scrubbing, wielding the mop with a fresh violence. She felt devastated by embarrassment. O'Dea could hardly read her thoughts, but curiosity burned in his look; she could feel it without even glancing at him.

"Is something ailing ye?"

"No."

"Well, then. Look at a man, will you?"

Selma dropped the mop into the bucket, but kept a hold on its handle as she straightened up, eyeing him almost balefully. "You're just passing by, I suppose?"

"So I am, and thought I'd look in on young Lennie."

"Oh, you did. The way you come up on a body, I would think you were spying on me."

Selma gave the words a half-angry ring of challenge. O'Dea chuckled unabashedly. "Well, and who's to say I ain't been?"

She thought it wasn't unlikely. He had a knack for catching her alone and at unguarded moments. It both infuriated and fascinated her, and she knew O'Dea was aware that it did. The ardent magnetism of the man had an unsettling effect on her that had strengthened, and he knew that too.

O'Dea smiled at her, stroking his beard with one hand. "You're in a pretty pet this morning. A little shindy with the mister?"

"None of your business!" Selma snapped.

"Ah, oh. Touchy, we are. So touchy I'd give wager that's

it, exactly. Well, he's put his tail in a crack for fair, and why should you stand by while he pulls down the roof on you?"

"What do you mean?"

"Pack up and go off, darlin'. That's what. What d'ye think? Don't tell me the thought ain't even crossed your mind."

Selma said coldly, "I never thought anything of the sort," but knew her cheeks were flaming. "That is nothing to joke about!"

"And who's joking?"

O'Dea moved forward, lightly and quickly. She let go the mop and stepped back just as quickly. He'd taken perhaps three steps, she only one. Now they were less than a foot apart.

"Sure, and it's not me joking," he said softly. "Nor you, I think. What's that banner of scarlet you've lofted, then?"

He raised his hand and brushed a finger across the hotness of her cheek. The finger moved on and touched the lobe of her ear, stroking a free tendril of her hair back into place behind it.

Selma's tongue touched her lips. The run of her blood felt so sluggish that she could count every separate beat of her heart. "You must not. I have a husband...."

Words that whispered from a dry throat.

"Well enough. And does that husband know how to treat a beautiful woman as she should be treated?"

A short step brought him nearer, his hand tipping up her chin. "I give a tug to ye, don't I now?" he murmured.

His hands slipped down to her bare arms, clasping them above the elbows. They were standing so close that the tips of her deep breasts touched his chest.

"Ah," he whispered, "so ripe and robust, that fine woman's body o' yours. It's like an Amazon you are, mistress."

She knew she should try to move away. Back from the touch of his hands, the compelling warmth of his voice, the blue heat of his stare. And from the lips that tipped down and brushed a lingering kiss to her own. But Selma did not move. His brief and touching kisses continued, teasing the moist pout of her lips till they stirred and parted, shaping themselves to his kisses. She tried to resist the scalding rise of passion in her loins, but resistance flickered away as her mouth turned avid for his.

Feminine passion and masculine hunger met with a deepening fire. Even as the mouths shaped one to the other, so the yielding curves of a woman's body blended to the assertive muscle of a man's. The firm softness of two mature breasts flattened against the hardness of a muscular chest. Loins and legs molded in the surge of a common desire. Arms locked around straining bodies. Tongue answered tongue in the savage ardor of a lover's kiss. . . .

"Hey, Ma! I'm back!"

Lennart's shout from outside the shanty slashed ice-sharp across the roar of blood in her ears. It shattered the moment like a rock breaking glass. She and O'Dea were already well apart, Selma pushing the mop vigorously around the floor once more, as Lennart came through the doorway.

❧ twenty-seven ❧

THE WAGON HIT a bump that jolted Elof awake. He had been catching forty winks in the wagon bed, taking advantage of a stretch of smooth road and that chill silence that held between Axel and Selma. Now Elof sat up and yawned and looked around. They were almost to the farmhouse where Swan lived.

"I'll hop off here, Pa," he said cheerfully. "Thanks all to hell for the ride."

Axel pulled the team to a halt. Elof stepped onto the side-board and dropped lightly to the ground. He gave his mother an impudent salute.

"So long, Ma!"

Selma, on the high seat beside Axel, did not speak. She did not even glance at her son. Despite the day's warmth, she had a heavy shawl drawn tightly around her shoulders. And she hadn't said a word during the entire drive.

Axel hoorawed the team into motion again. Elof stood gaz-ing after them, an unconscious scowl knitting his brow. Pa and Ma had always scrapped now and then, and sometimes it had gotten hot and heavy. But it had always seemed part of a pattern, the Holmgaard way of doing things, and nobody in the family ever took it very seriously. The icy silences to which Axel and Selma had been treating each other of late were different.

However, Elof never stayed down very long, and the prospect of an afternoon with Swan picked his spirits up quickly.

He strode up the gravel lane to the farmhouse and rapped at the front door. His knock was answered by Mrs. Coyne, the jolly and round-faced widow who owned the farm. At sight of him, she put on a mock frown.

"Oh, it's himself, is it?"

Elof grinned. "Sure, and it's *your*self that's looking really great today, Mrs. C. Positively ravishing."

"G'wan with ye! If it's your soulmate you've come to see, she's out back. But you better be warned, my bucko."

Elof widened his eyes. "Saints preserve us. And what for?"

"She's all togged out to greet her *real* boyfriend, who'll be along directly. They'll be going for a ride." Mrs. Coyne eyed him sternly. "Hadn't ye better be on your way before he arrives? So far, you've gone out of your way to avoid him, and I applaud your good sense."

"That's 'cause I'm scared as all get-out of him," Elof said soberly. He tipped back his hat and leered at her. "But what makes you think I'm here to call on Swan? I mean, with a lovely colleen like you available ...."

"Oh, go along with you!"

He tramped around the house and headed for the apple orchard back of the truck garden. He and Swan had spent a number of pleasant hours on a bench in the shade of those trees. She was sitting on the bench now, thumbing through a magazine, and she looked up in surprise.

"Elof...."

"Hi, kid. Waiting for your young man?"

Swan flushed as she laid down the magazine and came to her feet. She was wearing a peppermint-striped frock that rustled crisply. The high color in her cheeks was becoming to the gold velvet of her skin.

"Yes," she said nervously.

"Okay," Elof said carelessly. "I won't be long. Just dropped by to see how things were."

"Fine. Everything's fine." She smiled, a little tremulously. "Do I look all right?"

"Like a million bucks. How do you feel?"

"Oh . . . kind of jittery. Elof, I think he might propose today!"

Elof had heard that one before. "Oh, yeah?" He managed to keep a sardonic note out of his voice. "Well, good luck."

There was a dew of perspiration on her upper lip. He smoothed it off with his finger, saying softly, "Hey."

Swan's lips parted to his touch. She ran her tongue over them and turned her eyes downward. "What?" she whispered.

"This—" He tipped up her chin and kissed her gently.

"Don't."

"Why not? Won't be any more of it in a while. And you've liked it plenty. A lot more, too."

"Yes, but I don't think . . ."

He took her face between his hands and held it, dropping his mouth over hers. She made a murmur of protest, but it died in the avidness of her response. She rose on tiptoe to meet his kiss, her arms going tight around his neck.

When they drew apart, her eyes were slumbrous and half-lidded.

She said huskily, "You!" with a half-accusing smile. "You devil. But that was the last time."

Elof grinned and was about to say, "We'll see," when he heard the sound of an approaching car on the road.

"Oh, that must be Shad!" Swan's voice held a hint of panic. "Go on now! You can go back through the woods."

"Nothing doing," he said lazily. "I'm not hiding from this gink."

"Please!" She kneaded her fingers together, agitatedly. "I don't want him to see you here!"

Elof scowled. "Look, there are no flies on my conscience. I ain't looking for trouble. Came to pay a sociable call, that's all. Now I'll leave. But I'll go by the front way. Just take it easy, all right?"

Swan stood biting her lip, saying no more.

Elof swung away from her, irritation quickening his steps

as he skirted the house. Shad Gannett's big Oldsmobile was pulling up in the gravel lane. He brought it to a stop, switched off the engine, and got out.

He stared at Elof. "Say, buddy. Are you the guy who's been hanging around my girl?"

Elof was nearly to the car. He halted and gave Shad an amused stare of his own. "I wouldn't be surprised."

"All right, now." Shad moved forward and stopped in front of Elof, setting his fists on his hips. "I'll tell you what. I've been hearing talk about you and Swan. It makes out that I'm being made a sap of, and I don't like it."

Elof felt tempted to say he didn't see how anyone could improve on nature. But he only raised an eyebrow and said politely, "That right? Well, you might ask her about it."

"I have. She told me she wasn't seeing any more of you."

"That's about it." Elof yawned. "I called on her just now, not the other way around."

"Yeah? Now get this." Shad began tapping a forefinger against Elof's chest to emphasize his words. "You've called on her for the last time. I catch you around here again, I'll take your ass apart."

"Don't get sore," Elof advised mildly.

"You've a smart way about you I don't like!" Shad said in a flare of temper. "I've a mind to trim it out of you!"

Elof shrugged. "Well, you can always try."

Swan came running up the lane with a starchy rustle of skirts.

She caught at Shad's arm. "Honey, please. It's nothing to fight about. He was just—"

"Sniffing around like a hound in rut's what he's been doing," Shad said between his teeth. He took a step backward and slipped his arms out of his blazer, then tossed it into the car. "Swan, you just stand back now. Stay out of the way."

He set a foot forward and raised his cocked fists. He looked like one of the classic poses on the Jim Jeffries and Bob Fitzsimmons prizefight cards that Elof remembered collecting when he was a kid. Elof still felt more amused than annoyed, and didn't bother to conceal it.

"Come on!" Shad yelled, giving him a hard jab on the arm. "Fight!"

"Oh, hell," Elof said wearily.

He wasn't really in a mood to fight, but he supposed the guy's cocky arrogance would have to be chastised sooner or later. It might as well be now. He put up his hands. Promptly Shad beat through his guard and landed a hard right on his chin. Elof went flat on his back. Momentarily his eyes darkened. They cleared quickly and he sat up, rubbing his jaw.

"You know," he murmured, "you're commencing to rile me, chum."

"Get up!" Shad was smiling as he began to weave and shuffle around, jabbing at the air. "You're going to learn what a real fight is like, bud. I boxed in college."

Elof got slowly to his feet, now guarding himself warily. He managed to keep Shad from landing another punch solid enough to knock him down. But Shad kept up a hard fast drubbing of his arms and shoulders, and got in two more stiff licks that rocked Elof's head.

Quite calmly and deliberately, without a flicker of warning, Elof swung his foot up in a short savage arc. The square toe of his heavy work shoe took Shad Gannett squarely in the crotch.

Shad wilted to the ground, his face twisted and pasty with anguish. He lay writhing and holding himself, making noises like a sick hen.

With a little cry, Swan fell on her knees beside him. "Oh, Shad! Oh, darling!" She looked at Elof in a cold fury. "You go on, you—you— Get out!"

Elof wiped a thumb across his mouth. He eyed the two of them with a deep annoyance, feeling damned well put upon. Also his lip was bleeding. He rolled his shoulders in an irritable shrug, muttering, "You two have really made my day."

He plunged his hands in his pockets and sauntered down the road toward town.

❧ twenty-eight ❧

SELMA AND AXEL continued to ignore one another as they drove into town. Not until Axel pulled the wagon up at a curb near a dry-goods store did Selma break silence, saying icily, "I would like to see Rudy before we do the shopping."

Axel's assent was a mere grunt.

Her thoughts were still in a turmoil as they set off down the sidewalk toward the newspaper office.

This morning's interlude with O'Dea, the passionate embrace they had shared, had left Selma shaken and bewildered. And a little frightened. Not merely because of the guilt she felt, although that was part of it. She'd never reacted so intensely to any man except Axel.

O'Dea had caught her at a moment when she was alone and vulnerable, beset by troubles and full of angry indecision. Selma knew her own strengths. She was too strong to be taken like that again. Yet the full implications of the hot awareness that burned between O'Dea and her was worrisome.

How much did it mean?

The incident had diverted her enough to prevent her from

coming to grips with the idea that had crossed her mind just before O'Dea's intrusion. *To leave Axel.*

Could she do that? Selma shook her head, almost imperceptibly. No . . . yes. She could go live with her oldest sister, Hedvig, the sister to whom she had always been closest. Hedvig and her husband Soren, who lived on a farm in Ohio and whom she had not seen in many years, would welcome a long visit by Selma and the girls. It would give her a space to make up her mind as to her future course. Perhaps, too, a temporary desertion by his womenfolk would snap Axel out of his stupid obsession.

The trouble was, Selma didn't believe it would. She knew her husband too well.

She glanced from the tail of her eye at Axel, striding big and stony-faced at her side. *Gud,* but he was strong! The strongest man she had ever known. Strength emanated from Axel Holmgaard like a tangible force. Bullheaded and foolish he might be, but there was a kind of seductive *purity* in a strength that was never diluted by doubt or hesitancy. *Wait,* she counseled herself. Axel might change his attitude. He had done as much before; he might do so again. But with a man like him, change could only come as a solid conviction from within.

They entered the newspaper office.

Selma's gaze only briefly registered, with a housewife's flicker of disapproval, the clutter of the long narrow room. Her attention moved at once to Rudy, whom she'd last seen as a bandaged invalid. Elof, having seen him on a visit to town a few days ago, had assured her that "Ol' Scientist was looking great." All the same she was relieved to see for herself that the beating had left little mark on his face other than a few fading scars.

Rudy was seated at a desk, wearing a scowl of concentration as he hunched over a heavily scrawled piece of paper, pencil in one hand, the other combing through his mussed hair. Then he looked up, his face turning blank with surprise.

"*Mor* . . . Pa. or Pete's sake!"

He came out of his chair and around the desk to them. Selma gave him a brief strong hug. Instantly her spirits rose. How she had missed him! Rudy had his own brand of strength, sensitive and concerned. He had always been supportive of her in a way that Axel was rarely inclined to be.

She held him at arm's length, smiling. *"Gud bevara!* But you look so well!"

"I am well, *Mor.* All healed up."

"Ja, I see you are."

Rudy grinned. "Well, I guess Elof has told you about the job. . . . Mr. Fordyce has me doing a little of everything. From learning to set type to sweeping floors."

Selma nodded, her glance circling the room. "So. This place could still use a good housecleaning."

"Oh, Mr. Fordyce doesn't want any of this stuff moved around. Says he'd never be able to find anything." Rudy looked a trifle embarrassed as he motioned at the desk. "Right now he's got me writing society notes. You know, like, 'Miss Philomena Jones, the beautiful and accomplished daughter of Dr. and Mrs. Jones of this city, is visiting relatives in Milwaukee.' Mr. Fordyce says it's the best way to learn to put a strong sentence together."

"That's just fine." Axel's tone was heavy with disapproval. "So now you're up and around, when you planning to come home?"

"Ah, well. . . ." Rudy ran a hand through his hair. "Look, come out back and say hello to Mr. Fordyce, why don't you? I know he'll want to see you both."

Without waiting for a reply, he turned and headed for the back of the room, almost loping in his haste. What was this? Selma wondered. She followed after him, and Axel fell in behind her, muttering. They passed through a swing-gated railing and skirted a big cabinet that formed a sort of cubbyhole at the rear.

Andrew Fordyce was standing by a stone-topped table, setting sticks of type into a page form. He wiped his hands on his ink-stained apron, then pumped Axel's hand effusively. "Mr. Holmgaard. Good to see you, sir. I've something to show you."

He turned to a shelf and rummaged through a stack of papers, bringing down several news clippings which he put into Axel's hands. "There you go, Mr. Holmgaard. All about you. What do you think of that?"

Axel thumbed through the clippings, his beard parting in astonishment. "All about me?"

"Every word. Editorials I've printed on your disagreement with our ruling family since I last saw you. They're yours. Take 'em along and read 'em at your leisure."

"Do you mind—?" Selma took one of the clippings from Axel's hands and scanned it. "Think of that," she said gravely. "All these years I have been married to 'a crusader for the people' and 'a champion from their own ranks.' And I never once guessed."

Axel slid her a raking glance, then stuffed the clippings in his coat pocket. "Thanks," he said gruffly. "It's a nice thing you done, letting my boy work for you, but . . ."

"I wanted to talk to you about that, sir." Fordyce folded his arms and put on a serious little frown. "I would like to keep Rudy on here for a while. . . ."

He went on in that vein, describing his need for an able apprentice, praising Rudy's aptness and quickness at whatever task he was set, telling Axel and Selma how proud they must be of him and what a wealth of worthwhile experience he was acquiring.

Axel scowled and rubbed a hand over his beard as Fordyce talked, but he didn't offer to interrupt. By this Selma knew the publisher's words were sinking in and being weighed seriously. Fordyce was heaping fuel on a fire.

Weeks ago he had won Axel over with that glowing write-up of his barroom fight. Now, again, he was massaging Axel's pride, telling him this was only the beginning: He meant to drum up sympathy for Axel's cause across the state and into the legislative halls of Madison. It would be fitting if Axel's own flesh and blood were to assist him in this undertaking.

Irritated as she was, Selma felt a flick of envy at Fordyce's skill with words.

Yet she'd long realized that Rudy's way would not take him into a career of farming, as Axel took for granted with his sons. Rudy must make his own life. That was right. She just wished that it wasn't Andrew Fordyce who was fixing his direction.

By now Axel was thinking about it.

As always, of course, he took a tack of self-persuasion,

observing in a grumbling tone that, well, he supposed it wouldn't do any harm. For a while, anyway. It would mean one less mouth to feed, and if Fordyce thought Rudy would be any damn value to him in this campaign, that's if Fordyce really meant to go ahead with it, the kid might be a hell of a lot more use right here than at home. . . .

After the excitement of the loggers' spring exodus from their camps had subsided, the affairs of Winterfield settled into a drowsy routine. The town council would invariably lay off three of its four-man police force by early summer. Only Chief Tom Baird held his post year-round, and he had little to do but make his twice-a-day tour of the business establishments and another in the late evening to make sure all stores were securely locked.

Since it was Saturday, the town was reasonably astir this afternoon. But Baird paid no attention to the bustle on the street outside his city hall office. Ordinarily he would spend Saturday strolling up and down the sidewalk, his presence a pointed warning to all and sundry that this was a law-abiding community.

Today, however, he was so bored that he remained in his office, slacked back in his swivel chair with his feet propped on the desk, wistfully toying with his fly rod. Damn! To be out on a trout stream somewhere was the only proper way to spend a day as fine as this one. That's what everyone from hizzoner the mayor down to the local j.p. was doing. But the town fathers insisted that on Saturday, of all days, the chief of police must keep himself available. Hell! A saloon brawl or two might liven up the evening, but nothing that required his attention was likely to occur before then.

The building was deserted except for Baird, and so he turned his head with a mild interest as footsteps sounded in the hall outside. His office door opened abruptly, and Monty Harp strode in.

"Hey Tom," Harp drawled. "Get your ass in gear, boy. There's big game afoot."

"What's up?"

The sheriff's deputy wore an exultant grin. "That Holm-

221

gaard guy is in town. Drove in a little while ago, bold as brass. And me with a crisp new warrant for his arrest in my pocket!"

Baird nodded sourly. He had heard about the warrant.

The Gannett Logging and Boom Company had had its day in court and had obtained a new writ of injunction against Axel Holmgaard. The new judgment had teeth in it. Holmgaard could be arrested on sight—and face a year or more in prison. Even if that didn't happen, Beau Gannett was already planning other steps to take. Talk had it that he was petitioning powerful friends in Madison.

"Yeah, I know about the warrant. Judge Glover mentioned it to me just before he took off fishing. Guess this would be a good time to serve that paper, huh?"

"Never a better," said Harp. "We'd have a hell of a time taking him at his place—with his whole damn family around him. But he only brought his wife with him. I saw 'em come out of the *Clarion* office, where their kid is working, and then they went over to Sam Overland's Merchandise. They ought to be a while buying up supplies."

Baird nodded again, yawning. "Well, that's fine. You shouldn't have no trouble taking him."

"He's packing a sidearm, Tom. I think the son of a bitch is hotheaded enough to go for it if I throw down on him."

Baird dropped his feet abruptly to the floor, pointing a finger at Harp. "Then you be damn careful how you arrest him, hear? This is market day. There's a lot of innocent people around could catch a stray bullet."

"Right," Harp said patiently. "That's why I need your help. We got to take him by surprise, then. If we can catch him inside the store, two of us could manage it."

"Yeah. . . ." Baird tugged his lower lip. "Be better than out on the street. That's if there's hardly nobody in the store."

"You can bet there ain't, except for old Sam himself. Most all the people done their food shopping this morning. How about it, Tom?"

"Sure. It's all right by me. Go ahead."

"Hell, man. I meant, will you lend me a hand?"

"I can't do that," Baird said irritably. "My jurisdiction ends at the town limits. Holmgaard ain't committed any crime in

Winterfield. Nothing anyone's got out a warrant on him for. Where's Joe Pleasants, anyway?"

"Oh, the sheriff, he left on a fishing trip upstate a couple days ago."

"I might've known."

"Look, Tom. I'm in charge of the sheriff's office while he's gone. I can make you a special deputy. How about it, now? Otherwise I'll have to handle it myself. You don't want nobody getting hurt. All right, you and me together, we can take him without firing a shot."

Baird spread a freckled hand on his desk top, staring at it. "How you plan on doing it?"

Harp planted his fists on the desk, leaning forward. "One man in front of him. And one in back. That's how. Get him between us, he'll think twice about going for his gun. . . ."

Selma was reading off the last items on her shopping list to the owner of Overland's General Merchandise Store when a voice spoke loudly in her ear, nearly startling the wits out of her.

"Hi, Ma! Want some help?"

Elof had come into the store and sauntered up behind her unnoticed.

"Don't you ever do that again, *dumskalle!* . . . Well, what brings you away from your important 'business' so soon? Did your 'friend' tell you to go take a jump in the lake? Is that it?"

"Kind of," he admitted with an unabashed grin. "Ain't my day, that's for sure."

Selma eyed his cut lip. "So I see," she observed with a touch of satisfaction. "You got so smart she gave you a punch in the mouth, eh?"

"You betcha." Elof's grin was lopsided; his yeasty aura of beer indicated that he'd stopped at a saloon or two on the way here. "Whaddaya say? Want some help?"

"Augh! You smell like a whole brewery by yourself. Yes, go on and help your pa."

Axel was wrestling a barrel of flour out of the storeroom at the rear. Elof joined him, and they lifted the barrel between them and carried it toward the front door. Selma turned back to the storekeeper. "Now, Mr. Overland, I want eight pounds of coffee and three pounds of tea. . . ."

"That's far enough, Holmgaard," said a voice. "You don't move another step."

Selma whirled around.

She saw Monty Harp, the deputy sheriff, standing in the open doorway with a Luger pistol in his hand. Both Axel and Elof were caught flat-footed, their arms straining around the heavy barrel. They came to a halt a few feet short of the door.

Harp advanced slowly into the room, halting a couple of yards from the two. "Now you boys you set that barrel down. You both do it nice and slow and then you put your hands up." He raised his voice abruptly. "Hey, Baird! Where the hell are you?"

"Right here." A stocky balding man in a police uniform came out of the storeroom, holding a big Colt revolver.

"What the hell held you up?"

"Couldn't come in by the back door while Holmgaard was in the storeroom," Baird explained. "I seen him through the storeroom window. I thought you said there was only him and his woman."

"My mistake. This here's one of his kids. He wasn't with 'em when they come into town." Harp's drawl turned harsh. "Now I told you two boys to set down that barrel. You do it. *Slow.*"

The first surprise in Axel's face had changed to a baffled and mulish fury. Now a recklessness sharpened Elof's lean face. Selma felt a rush of apprehension. Elof might attempt something foolish and not even need a reason for it. And he, like his father, was packing a pistol.

Slowly, almost delicately, they eased the barrel to the floor.

"Listen, Monty," the aged storekeeper said acerbically. "You and Baird just back out o' here. Both o' you, hear me? You want to roust anyone, you do it outside o' my store. You got no damn business rousting my customers."

"We ain't rousting nobody, Sam," snapped Harp. "This guy busted the law and I'm putting him under arrest. Damn it, Holmgaard, you put up your hands now!"

Axel stood with his feet apart and his hands forming loose fists. His teeth were slightly bared, and his blue eyes had that volcanic tinge. Selma wanted to shout at him, anything that might shock him to his senses.

She was facing toward the front of the store with its broad plate-glass window. A movement in the street beyond caught her eye.

Rudy?

Yes, it was him. Quartering across the street from the newspaper office at a half run, coming straight for Overland's store. He must have seen Harp enter the store—and was coming to his family's defense.

No! Selma thought wildly. *Stay back!*

She willed the words at him with a fierce concentration.

"Get those hands up!" yelled Harp. "I'm telling you guys for the last time!"

Slowly Axel's arms lifted. Neither he nor the man in uniform, both of them facing toward the front, appeared to be aware of Rudy's approach. Elof was half turned toward the policemen, who kept a wary attention on him.

"You too, young fellow," he told Elof. "Get 'em up there."

Rudy's running feet hit the porch with a clatter.

Harp had taken a step toward Axel, reaching for the gun holstered at Axel's side. Now he pivoted wildly around as Rudy came charging through the doorway at his back. The instant his eyes left Axel, the latter's right hand, raised above his head, made a fist that fell hammerlike and caught Harp at the base of his skull.

The force of the blow knocked the deputy sideways and downward. He crashed to the floor.

The rest of it happened almost too swiftly for Selma to follow. The uniformed man voiced a yell of warning, and in the same instant Elof's hand dived to the butt of his pistol. The policeman fired his Colt into the floor—a warning shot. It was a mistake on his part. When his Colt rose to counter the upswing of Elof's gun, it was too late.

The revolver in Elof's fist made thunder in the narrow room. The policeman spun to the bullet's impact. He went skewing off balance against the back wall. Let out a broken cry as he slid to the floor, clutching his hip.

Axel had leaped on the fallen Harp. His own pistol was in

his hand now; he swung it up and down in three chopping arcs, pistol-whipping the deputy.

"Pa, don't!" Rudy shouted.

He grabbed Axel's arm as it came up for another blow. Axel tried to shake him loose, but Rudy held on. Axel swung to his feet and wheeled on his son, drawing back his other fist.

"No!" Selma almost screamed.

Axel's face turned partly toward her. The madness boiled in it unabated, but something stayed his hand. Slowly he lowered the fist. Only then did the craziness seep out of his face.

Harp lay on his back, out cold. His mouth hung open; blood streaked his face. Selma pushed away from the counter, her legs trembling. Making her voice firm and quiet, she said, "Mr. Overland, you had better get the doctor."

The policeman, Baird, was sitting as he had fallen, back to the wall and one leg straight out before him, the other doubled beneath him. He looked peculiarly and terrifyingly helpless in that position. His face was a drawn mask of pain; his teeth were clenched.

Elof stood where he was, loosely covering the policeman with his pistol. Selma turned on him in a chill fury. "Put that away. Do you hear me, Elof? *Now!*"

Baird's gun had fallen to the floor and lay well out of his reach. With a cool shrug, Elof holstered his own gun. As Selma started toward the policeman, Elof commented, "Careful of him, Ma."

"You shut up!" Selma said over her shoulder.

She knelt by the wounded man. A dark wetness stained the whole side of his dark blue coat and trousers.

"How . . . how bad are you hurt?"

His eyes turned on her without seeming to see her. "Feels like my hipbone is busted . . . busted all to hell, feels like."

His voice was an agonized husking, his skin a bloodless gray. His eyes stared glassily, the whites showing all around the irises, as his gaze slid past Selma and fixed on Elof.

"You . . . !"

Baird spat out each word, spaced and barbed and careful, from between his clenched teeth. "Get out of Winterfield. Don't ever show yourself here again. Or I'll kill you on sight. I'll shoot you like a goddamn dog. I swear to Christ I will!"

❧ *four* ❧

The Choices

↻ *twenty-nine* ↻

AT LAST THE new house was finished. It still needed a lot of refinements, but it was ready to be lived in. On their first night of occupancy, after moving their belongings into it and spreading their blankets on bare floorboards, the whole family could feel—in the midst of its troubles—a measure of security that came of having walls on all sides and a ceiling overhead. Already they had sent for the crated furnishings they had left with a neighbor in Minnesota.

Within a week after they occupied the house, the crates arrived by railway express at Winterfield. Notified by the baggage master that the Holmgaards' goods were waiting at the depot, Andrew Fordyce rented several wagons and rounded up a couple of unemployed lumberjacks to help Rudy and him load up the wagons and drive them out to the Holmgaard farm. Even then, the house was not fully furnished. Only their best pieces of furniture as well as family heirlooms and smaller articles that could easily be packed, such as kitchen utensils, had made the journey from Minnesota. The rest, with their old farm machinery, had been sold at public auction. New household pieces could be purchased as time went along; there was no hurry. Arvid, the skilled wood-carver of the family, would while away the winter evenings fashioning chairs and stools and wooden bedsteads.

Meantime Selma continued to prepare their meals outside. Much as she welcomed the arrival of cherished things, she looked forward most of all to the coming of a new Monarch stove, which had been ordered from the factory at Beaver Dam, Wisconsin. For years she had dreamed of owning one of these stoves, reputed to be the finest wood-burning ranges manufactured. She had patiently harangued Axel in exactly the way he sometimes badgered her, in getting him to agree to the purchase.

On the midsummer day that the stove arrived, brought from Winterfield by Rudy and Fordyce in a sturdy dray they had hired, Selma could hardly contain her excitement. She gave the men brisk directions for carrying it into the kitchen, affixing unattached parts, connecting it to the stovepipes that were waiting to be assembled and mounted. When at last the stove was in place, set on stone flags between the copper sink and the woodbox, she felt a glow of fulfillment that brought tears to her eyes. She stood and gazed at the Monarch's gleaming black hulk and polished fixtures. She lifted the perfectly fitted stove lids and set them back in place. Time after time she swung open and closed the ornate warming ovens. She could not stop running her hands over all the shining surfaces.

Members of her family made the right sounds of approbation, then withdrew from the room, leaving Selma alone with her new possession.

For the first time in her life, she was surrounded by a balance of old and new that felt completely *right*. Until the arrival of the stove, familiar things of her existence, utensils and decorative objects, had seemed in a state of incompleteness. Selma was fond of every separate piece. Each one, outside of heirlooms, had been chosen over the years with an eye to her own wants and needs. The money to buy them had been saved up penny by carefully hoarded penny.

Her thoughts ranged with equal contentment through the whole house: roomy parlor and dining room, master bedrooms on the lower floor, upstairs divided into other rooms for sleeping and storage. Both roomier and better-constructed than any dwelling she had known from girlhood in Sweden through married life in Minnesota, it was the only one that had been designed and built according to her wishes. Each room was planned exactly as she wanted it. Its dimensions, relation to adjoining rooms, location of its doors and windows, had been figured out with an eye to convenience and the placement of furnishings. She had been at pains to point out to Axel that it was she who'd have the duty of keeping this big-family house in order.

For nearly a quarter century she'd lived in a farmhouse that had been planned and built by her father and husband: a home in which she, a nervous and unsure bride of sixteen, had been given no say whatever. The necessity of building a new house on their new acres had presented Selma with a golden opportunity. She had argued Axel into giving in by grudging degrees to her demands, one after another. Provoking all the expected bellows of anger and dismay ("For Christ's sake, woman, you want a goddamn palace or something?") and not hesitating to shout back when she had to, in order to gain a concession.

Selma was content. She stood in the center of her big kitchen, arms akimbo, and savored her moment.

From upstairs came the murmurs of the girls, no doubt exchanging more ideas on how to decorate their new bedrooms. Dani had a second-story room to herself, the twins had another, and Arvid and Elof and Lennart shared a third. (Lennart, however, had practically taken up residence at the dam shanty.)

Out in the parlor Axel was talking with Andrew Fordyce.

Awareness of their voices roused Selma to her duties as a hostess. She laid a fire in the new stove and set a pot of coffee on to boil.

It was pleasant not to have to cope anymore with uneven cooking on an open fire, dirt getting in the food, all the sharp vagaries of Wisconsin weather. In this country you either froze or you broiled. The big Monarch would ensure a cozy kitchen during winter's worst; the pot-bellied stove in the parlor, set on a stone platform in its center, would shed a good heat. The dining room, with doorways opening on both parlor and kitchen, would be warmed by both stoves.

This could be a very good place to live. *If only—*

In the parlor, Fordyce was waxing enthusiastic in his talk. Listening to it, Selma felt a slow rise of anger.

"...I don't think you have to worry about 'em trying anything, Axel. At least not for a good while. The talk has it that for all the legal fuss they've made, none of the Gannetts has really changed his or her position from what it was before you made a deal. Beau still wants to go ahead and clean you out. Old Saul Peregrine still says no. The old lady is still on the fence about it."

"I wonder if they know *why* I called off the deal?" Axel mused. "If that Adam told the rest of 'em?"

"There's just no way of telling. All I can say for sure is, there's been no public talk about Adam Gannett and your daughter. So if the other Gannetts do know, I guess they don't want it noised around. Hell, would you wanted it bruited about that someone in your family's a would-be rapist?"

"No."

"Anyway, none of that really matters," Fordyce went on. "What's important is that a month's gone by since the court ruled for their side, and the Gannetts haven't made any sort of move to implement the ruling. Could mean they're delaying in order to lull you into a false sense of security. But any delay o theirs buys time for *us*. Longer we have to plead your case in the court of public opinion, the bigger the furor we can create statewide. Even *nationally*. This is a test situation, Axel. Whatever comes of it could decide, finally, whether this country really belongs to the moguls or to the *people....*"

Selma clenched her teeth till they ached.

For a time she had hoped that Axel might persuade himself that it would be in everyone's best interest to pursue a moderate tack. His rage at the situation he'd misinterpreted between Dani and Adam Gannett had cooled. If the Gannetts were as yet unwilling to use force, negotiations might still be reopened. But with Fordyce constantly fanning the flames, that hope had thinned.

Rudy had continued his employment at the *Clarion*, no charge having been lodged against him. But it had been a month since any other Holmgaard had ventured into town. Fordyce had told them that Tom Baird, the police chief whose hip Elof's bullet had broken, had sworn out a warrant for his arrest. Nobody had attempted to serve it, but Elof, with a rare show of good judgment, was staying clear of Winterfield. Fordyce had told them not to worry; he and Rudy would fetch all the supplies the family needed.

But what kind of a way was this to live? Fordyce. She would like to strangle the man. But she must be a proper wife and a proper hostess. *As long as I can stand to be*, Selma thought grimly.

The coffee was ready. She set out her good cups and saucers on a tray and filled the cups with steaming coffee. Then she carried the tray to the parlor.

"Good day to you, mistress," Tom O'Dea said cheerily.

Selma came to a complete stop in the parlor entrance. She halted so abruptly in her surprise that one of the cups sloshed on her wrist. She bit her lip, then gave him a pleasant nod.

"Good afternoon, Mr. O'Dea."

Doing her best to hide embarrassment, Selma moved around the room, serving the men their coffee. Damn the man! He must have knocked and been admitted while she, occupied with a glow of reverie, hadn't been paying a lick of attention.

As she finished passing the tray around, he gave her an innocent and sleepy-eyed grin. "What hey, Mistress! Is the O'Dea to forego a cup of your delicious brew?"

Selma shaped her lips into a smile. "I'm sorry. I'm a cup short. If you'll be patient for just a moment, Mr. O'Dea, I'll bring you some coffee."

She went back to the kitchen.

Curse his Irisher gall! Sitting in the leather chair that had been her father's, paying amiable attention to what Axel and Fordyce were saying, or pretending to. All the while laughing at her from behind the stillness of his face and knowing that she knew he was.

Clearly he still regarded her as a challenge and was deriving great zest from the game. Since the day she'd briefly succumbed to him, he had shown up quite a few times. He'd paid more attention to Dani and the twins than he did to her— charming them with that smooth Irish wit of his.

She knew only too well what was in his mind.

Selma's hand shook as she poured the coffee. Then an inspiration came to her. She was almost smiling as she carried the cup and saucer to the parlor.

"Here you are, Mr. O'Dea . . . oh!"

In mid-step as she started to hand him the cup of coffee,

Selma managed to turn her ankle on a scatter rug. The saucer tipped in her hand; the cup rolled off. O'Dea's hand was raised to take the cup. The boiling-hot liquid drenched his hand and splashed on his pants.

A braying hiss exploded from him: an automatic effort to suppress pain. His face was ruddy with that effort as he gingerly wiped his hand on his shirt.

"Oh, I'm terribly sorry!" Selma exclaimed. *"Himmel!* Did I burn you, Mr. O'Dea?"

"Ye might say that." O'Dea twisted a tortured grin over his set teeth. He dug out a bandanna and wrapped it around his hand.

"How could I be so clumsy! Can I get you anything for it? A pan of cold water? Or some salve—there's a kind we put on horses when they have gall sores. . . ."

"No ma'am, no thank you. It'll be just fine, and no harm done."

O'Dea spoke lightly, peering at her slit-eyed from under his brows, banking a hot fury behind his face.

"Well, let me get you some more coffee."

Selma picked up the cup, glancing at Axel as she turned. He looked a shade irritated at the interruption of his conversation with Fordyce, but only a shade. Having no use for O'Dea, he never conceded him more than the barest hospitality. She felt like bursting into song as she returned to the kitchen. She rinsed the cup and saucer, poured another cup of coffee, and carried it to the parlor. When she held it out to O'Dea, he started to reach for it, then hesitated. His gaze was just a touch murderous.

Selma grinned sympathetically and set the cup on a taboret at his elbow. "There you are, Mr. O'Dea! I won't burn you again."

"Say, Mrs. Holmgaard," Fordyce said genially, "you might be interested in these clippings. Brought along the latest batch of 'em."

Selma accepted the sheaf of folded news cuttings he held out. Leafing through them, she saw that nearly all of them were from newspapers other than the *Winterfield Weekly Clarion,* and that they all said pretty much the same things. They were simply slightly changed versions of articles that had been printed in the *Clarion,* as well as several of Fordyce's own editorials that had been reprinted verbatim on the editorial pages of other papers. Most of them had been clipped from various

Wisconsin papers, but some were from out-of-state tabloids. Chicago . . . Minneapolis . . . Akron.

She glanced at Fordyce with a raised brow. "You have sent this stuff all over, Mr. Fordyce?"

"Sure. Wire services across the country have picked it up. And that's not all." He pointed at a thick manila envelope on a hassock in front of Axel's chair. "Have a look at what's in that."

Selma picked up the envelope and opened it. Inside was a bulky packet of letters, dozens of letters. She flipped briefly through them, looking at the addresses. Some were directed to Andrew Fordyce, most of them to Axel Holmgaard, sent in care of the *Clarion* or simply to "Winterfield, Wisconsin."

"The post office delivered the lot of 'em to me," Fordyce explained. "Word has gone out, I guess. You can read those at your leisure, Mrs. Holmgaard. They all contain more or less the same message, praising your husband for his stand. They come from readers all over the Middle West, ma'am—your kind of people. Little people. Folks who are elated at seeing one of their own kind standing up to the big moguls."

"So," Selma said tonelessly. "I guess I had never thought of myself as a 'little person,' Mr. Fordyce."

"Ha ha, is that right? Anyway, take it from me, they love it. They're eating it up."

Selma kneaded her underlip between her teeth as she thumbed through the letters. Axel sat slumped in his chair, hands folded across his middle, watching her expectantly. Temper rose in her. What did he expect? That she'd weep for joy at all the attention that the trouble he had caused was bringing on them?

No, Axel would not expect that. He knew her too well. What was important to him, as plain in his face as spoken words could have made it, was that Axel Holmgaard was becoming a noticed man, a person of renown.

At first it had seemed odd that he would be gratified by anything of that sort. The Axel she knew was taciturn and be-damned-to-you, not caring a whit about anyone outside of his family or their opinions. A dimension of his nature she hadn't suspected had come to the surface, thanks to Andrew Fordyce painting his pictures-in-print of Axel Holmgaard, righteous defender of the underdog. Axel, who had never cared a whoop for anything outside his own few and narrow concerns, had been entranced from the first by his own glowing notices. Fordyce had fed some unconscious craving in him as one might satisfy an alcoholic's need for liquor.

It had been appalling and even frightening to watch Axel expand to the trappings of his new role.

Fumbling through the letters to cover her thoughts, Selma found something that wiped everything else from her mind in astonishment. She extracted several wilted banknotes from one of the letters.

"Money? People have sent money?"

"Surest thing you know," Fordyce said amiably. "Quite a few of 'em did. Nothing munificent—a dollar or a few dollars apiece. Whatever they could afford to send. But it's starting to add up to a tidy sum. And unless I miss my guess, this is just the beginning. Your story is seizing the imaginations of people everywhere, Mrs. Holmgaard."

"But we can't take money!" She made no attempt to hide her shock and dismay. "It's not right to take people's money like this!"

"Why not?" Fordyce demanded. "They sent it in good faith. You folks are fighting the good fight for all of 'em. That's how they see it."

"We did not come here to fight. We came to farm." She looked at Axel, half extending a handful of letters toward him. "Is this what *you* want? To take money that a lot of honest, foolish people worked hard to earn?"

"You talk like it was stealing," he growled defensively. "It's like he said. We're in the right. We'll need money to carry on the fight. Why not take help when it's offered?"

Selma eyed him for a moment, her lips thinning. She dropped the package of letters on the hassock and turned her wrath on Fordyce: "You have got big ideas, mister. I think they've given you a big head."

"Here now!" Axel rumbled. "That's no way to talk to a guest."

"He's your guest, not mine. And I will say what I please!" Anger had carried her beyond restraint. "What will you do, Axel, if you don't like it?"

His face darkened; he glowered at her. But he said no more.

"I think Mrs. Holmgaard should have her say," Fordyce

said equably. "Why not bring it into the open? You haven't liked any of it from the start, have you, ma'am?"

Selma ignored the note of sympathy. "Let me ask you something."

"Anything at all."

"The reason you have got this . . . campaign going, is it because you really believe all you say? Or are you just doing it to sell papers?"

Fordyce flushed. "I believe in everything I say, Mrs. Holm-gaard. You might allow me that much."

"But why use *us?* Mr. Fordyce, *you* haven't broken any laws. *You* have no family to be hurt. *You* have nothing to lose. We have everything to lose."

"I have to disagree, ma'am. I don't believe you're in any danger—"

"But you don't *know!*" She gazed in fury at this slight and unprepossessing man who represented a key threat to all she held dear. "And always you're stirring it up! How can we ever work things out with those Gannetts if you keep stirring it up?"

"Ma'am, I'm sorry. My goal has been to swing public opinion to your side. To create such a feeling toward the Gannetts that they won't *dare* a move against you. And I'm succeeding. I think I *have* succeeded."

"I do *not!*" Selma swung toward the kitchen doorway, then back, pointing a finger at Fordyce. "If any of us gets hurt, any way, by what you're doing, I'll hold you to account! I will make you sorry."

As she whirled out of the room, she caught Tom O'Dea's eye. And surprised a strange look on his face. It was a complex of emotions in which she thought she detected a sober admiration. And other things at which she couldn't—or didn't dare try to—guess.

thirty

AFTER THE VISITORS departed, Axel and Elof and Arvid returned to work in the fields. They had found time during the raising of the house and outbuildings to sow the old acreage Slocum had put under cultivation with potatoes and rutabagas. There would be a good crop this year, and depending on the market prices, maybe a fair profit.

Just now Selma did not care very much. Her quarrel with Fordyce had plunged her into a black mood. In the whirl of her preparations for supper, she lost her temper with Dani and the twins, who were taking turns operating the butter churn, not very enthusiastically. Miffed, Dani went for a walk on the logging road. Meantime Erika and Julia continued to drive Selma to distraction, running in and out of the house with Otto yapping at their heels, undaunted by getting yelled at repeatedly.

The situation reached a climax when a mighty *bang* startled Selma nearly out of her wits.

Otto let out a terrified yelp. Selma was standing at the sink; she swung around to see what had happened. And stared at the smear of tarry substance that had exploded across the west wall of the kitchen.

Axel's *snus* can had blown up. Or rather had sent its top and part of its contents flying.

He liked to make his own pungent preparation of snuff. That consisted of drying a batch of black stringy smoking tobacco over a slow fire, grinding it to a powder in the coffee mill, moistening it with potash, and allowing it to ferment in a tightly closed tin can. This wasn't the first time it had been allowed to ferment too long.

"Mama?" Julia said softly. "Otto went poo-poo on the floor."

Selma looked. Yes—the pup's sudden fright had loosened his bowels.

She leaned her hips against the sink and gripped both hands tightly on its edge till her wildly pounding heart had slowed and she could trust her voice.

"Clean it up," she said. "I mean what that dog did on the floor. Then you take him and you all *get out of here!*"

She whipped up suds in a bucket and set to scrubbing down the defaced wall. The twins finished wiping up the floor and stole quietly out of the house with a chastened Otto.

Selma felt like weeping. You can still leave him, she thought. What's to stop you? Go to Hedvig's and take the girls along. . . .

A shadow fell across the floor.

Selma was on her knees, wringing out a dirty washrag in the pail. She looked up quickly. The hint of a shriek died in her throat.

Who had she thought to see? O'Dea again?

It wasn't O'Dea. The man who stood in the doorway was a stocky gnome of an Indian in white man's castoffs and a plug hat set squarely on his head. His long grease-slick braids reached nearly to his waist. He was Billy Saginaw, a Chippewa trapper who lived upriver with his family.

Selma felt limp with relief. The Saginaws and other Indians in the district often came visiting, walking into the house unannounced. Usually they wanted something to eat.

"Um, hello, Mr. Saginaw."

Billy Saginaw entered and sat down at the kitchen table, leaning his Winchester rifle against the wall. "Smell good," he announced.

"The snuff? Oh, you mean the bread."

"Unh."

The loaves she was baking ought to be ready by now. Selma got wearily to her feet and went to the stove. With rag-protected hands, she lifted out the bread pans and set them on the sink board to cool. The loaves were smoothly plump and golden brown; Selma tapped the crusts of both to see if they were done.

"Very good! Would you like a 'hot heel,' Mr. Saginaw? With fresh butter?"

"Unh."

Selma cut three thick slices of bread and set them on a plate in front of him, with a knife and a dish of butter. She also put coffee on to boil. Then she returned to her scrubbing.

"Where man?" Billy Saginaw asked around a mouthful of bread and butter.

"Axel?" she said absently. "He's out in the field."

"Sons too? They with him?"

"Yes, the boys too."

Curse this black bile of Axel's! It adhered like glue; you had to rub and rub. And it had spattered across most of the wall.

She heard a man's heavy tread on the back porch. She knew Axel's step and didn't look away from her work as he came through the door. His steps paused behind her.

"What happened to the wall?" he asked in a half-absent tone.

"Your snuff can blew up. *Again.*" Still not looking at him. "What do you want?"

"Some coffee."

"It's on the stove."

Axel moved to the stove and poured himself a cup of coffee, and only then seemed to notice Billy Saginaw. "Oh . . . hello, Billy. How you doing?"

"Good," said Billy Saginaw. "Where your sons?"

"The boys? Lennart's over by the dam. Elof and Arvid are out in the field."

"Where young one?"

"Rudy? He's working in town now."

Axel toed a chair out from the table and slumped into it. His manner was sluggish and preoccupied.

Only a little while ago, after she'd argued with Fordyce, he'd been bitterly angry with her. Selma stole a glance at him. He was staring glumly into his cup. It wasn't like him to come in from work this early, two hours short of supper, for coffee or anything else.

"Is something wrong?" she asked.

He scowled and muttered something.

"What?" Selma said with asperity. "Can't you speak up?"

"I said, maybe we ought to talk about things."

She wondered if she were hearing right. Axel condescending to talk a thing over? "Well—fine. We'll talk then. But when we're alone, eh?"

She gave a faint, meaningful nod in the Chippewa's direction.

Axel gave his boots an impatient shuffle. "All right."

Billy Saginaw finished his bread and butter and stood up, wiping his hands on his shirt. "Good bread. You got good woman, Holmgaard."

"Ja. I know."

Selma's gaze crossed her husband's; a smile tugged at her mouth. He had not looked at her in quite *that* way in . . . how long had it been? Suddenly she felt tremulous and excited. Was there a softening in Axel at last?

To cover her confusion, she rose and walked to the stove. Then she couldn't think of anything to do except pick up the big half-gallon coffeepot. "Uh, you want some coffee, Mr. Saginaw?"

"No," said Billy Saginaw. "I go."

"Axel? Some more?"

"Sure," he said gently.

Billy Saginaw wiped a hand over his mouth, then picked up his rifle and pointed it at Axel.

"Get up, Holmgaard," he said.

Selma halted halfway across the room, coffeepot in hand. She and Axel had been gazing at each other. They looked quickly at the Indian, with a kind of dazed surprise.

"What's this?" Axel demanded.

"You hear me good. Get up." Billy Saginaw motioned with the rifle. "Then you walk out door. You go ahead of me."

Axel did come to his feet, so abruptly that his chair crashed to the floor. "What the hell you think you're up to, Billy?"

"I arrest you. Take you jail. Citizen arrest, Holmgaard."

Axel's lip curled. "You dumb Injun! You ain't no citizen. You're a ward of the government. How the hell can you arrest me?"

"We see. I take you to sheriff. He arrest. You go now."

Again Billy Saginaw motioned at the door.

Axel came slowly around the table, never taking his eyes off the Indian. Selma knew that Axel would not permit himself to be taken to jail without a fight. He might bide his time, but before Billy Saginaw ever got him to town, Axel would try one thing or another.

That thought filled all her mind.

In her hand was the big coffeepot, a thick potholder wrapped around its hot metal handle. Selma snatched off the lid and flung the boiling contents at Billy Saginaw.

All he could do was throw out a hand to protect his face. Most of the burning liquid splashed across his neck and chest. With a strangled cry, Billy Saginaw staggered backward.

Axel moved fast, wrenching the rifle from the Indian's grasp and landing a savage punch that slammed him against the wall. Seizing him by the shirtfront with both hands, Axel shook him so furiously that his teeth rattled as he moaned in pain.

"Why?" Axel roared. "Why do this?"

"Money," groaned Billy Saginaw. "Big money—"

"What money?"

"Money they offer for you. Gannett people. Give plenty money for take you in."

"How much? Talk!"

"Five hundred dollar."

"Where did you hear that?"

"This morning. In town. . . ."

With a curse Axel hurled him to the floor. Billy Saginaw crawled to his knees. He held a hand over his scalded face, but made no further sound. His one exposed eye glistened with pain; he seemed dumbly to await more punishment. Axel looked ready to inflict it.

Selma clasped a hand on his wrist. "Don't."

"You heard him. *Money!* He'd eat a man's food, then take the money on his head!"

Selma gave her husband a hard cuff on the shoulder. *"What do you expect!* You who take money from strangers for no good reason? You expect this man to do better than you? Him, a poor man with the care of a big family? Anyway he's got a *reason!"*

"Helvete! If that's how you feel, why not let him take me? You didn't need to do nothing!"

Bending down, Axel dragged Billy Saginaw to his feet and over to the door. A powerful heave sent him hurtling off the porch and into the dirt of the yard, sprawling on his face. He got to his feet and staggered away.

Axel kicked the door shut and dropped into a chair, rubbing both hands over his face. Selma watched him for a moment, feeling a kind of nameless despair. She crouched down and began to mop up the spilled coffee.

"Well," she said almost offhandedly, "it seems they are done playing pat-a-cake with you. Now they've put money on your head, there'll be other men trying to collect it. Don't you think so?"

"Ja," he muttered.

"Ja," she jeered quietly. "Before, you had a lot of friends in your foolishness. All you had was a few lawmen to worry about. You could lick them, eh? Now we'll see."

"Damn it, woman! What are you trying to do?"

"Make you see what you must do. Stop this thing. Stop it before you bring some real harm on us."

"You come down on everything I do," Axel said heavily. "No matter what it is, you fight me."

"You!" In a mixture of surprise and hurt and anger. "You dare say that to me? I—we—gave up all we knew to move to this place. For *you.* I fight you when you're *wrong.* And this was wrong from the start!"

"All my wrong, was it?"

"Not all. But enough of it. I tell you, I am sick of how things are!" She dropped the mop rag in the bucket and rose off her knees. She faced him with feet apart, fists on her hips. "What's happened to you? You were always a tough man, but not so tough you forgot you had a family. *Us*, Axel. *We're* your life! Not that Fordyce and his pretty puttering of words. At first I could understand. Things had got too tame for you, *ja?* But what is it now? When did you stop caring for us?"

"I . . ." He shook his head doggedly. "You don't understand. A man needs more than food and drink, Selma. He needs more. . . ."

"More than the people who care for him? That he used to care for?"

"That ain't so!" he bellowed. "If that's how you feel, go! Go on and leave!"

Slowly, Selma shook her head.

"No. I almost did that. And I would take the girls with me if I went. But we're not just men and women . . . girls and boys. We are a family. We're *one*. I don't forget that, even if you do. *This* is my life. Where you are and where our kids are."

For a long doubtful moment he watched her. Then he began to get up, lifting his hands to her.

"Don't touch me." She raised her own hand, flat-palmed and fingers spread, to ward him off. "No more touching. Till death us do part . . . was that it, Axel? But when we touch, we have to care. *Ja*—a little, anyway. And you don't anymore."

✿ *thirty-one* ✿

RUDY SNATCHED DEXTEROUSLY at a piece of ten-point type in the typecase and got it out fast enough. But trying to slap it just as quickly into a brass typestick, he dropped it on the floor.

He muttered, "Hell's bells," as he slid off the tall stool and picked up the bit of oily metal. He had the knack of efficient typesetting down pretty smoothly by now, but every time he tried to equal Andrew Fordyce's eye-blurring speed he'd invariably drop two or three pieces before getting a stick filled. Well—Fordyce had told him it would take years to master the technique at its best.

He heard the door open at the front of the shop.

"Is anyone here?" It was Selma's voice.

Rudy wiped his hands on his ink-blotched apron, then stripped it off and walked up front. "Hello, *Mor*. I thought you were stuck on the farm."

She kissed him, then held him away from her with a little grimace. "Your hands, Rudolf. They are getting like Mr. Fordyce's."

245

"Compositor's hands." Rudy grinned and spread them open, palms up. They were black with an almost indelible blackness. "I don't know about a fellow getting printer's ink into his blood. But it sure works into the hide."

He cleared some papers off a couple of chairs, and the two of them sat down.

"I came in by myself," said Selma. "I wanted to talk to you, Rudolf. We didn't have a chance to talk the other day." She glanced about the shop. "*He* is not around, is he?"

"Andrew? He's out circulating a petition on Pa's behalf. He wants to get it in this week's issue—and mail a copy to every member of the state legislature."

"I might have known," Selma said brusquely. "He's putting a lot into his big 'campaign.' Do you like helping him with it, Rudolf?"

Rudy shifted uneasily. "I know you don't like it, *Mor*. But..."

"I think I like you helping him even less."

Rudy only shook his head. He lowered his gaze to a knothole in the floor.

"Rudolf...I do not want to say how you should live your life. You're a man now and you'll do as you will. That is right. But Fordyce—I think he is making you a..." She hesitated. "There is something called a pawn in a game. What is that game?"

"Chess, *Mor*."

"Yes. Well, that is how Fordyce is using you."

"I don't think so," Rudy said stubbornly. "I think he's sincere. And I'm not so sure as you that he's wrong."

Selma pounced on that. "But that says you are not sure he is right."

"I don't know. Look, *Mor*. I owe Andrew Fordyce a lot for giving me this opportunity. I'm not about to just quit him cold turkey."

Selma's lips thinned. "When the trouble starts up again— then we'll see."

Maybe the stubborn rejection he felt showed in his face, for Selma smiled in a kind of forced way. She reached out to pat his arm. "Nobody is saying you should quit right away, son. But I wish you would think about it."

"I've been thinking. I've been thinking about a lot of things."

"Good. You think some more. Then if you think it's right, give Mr. Andrew Fordyce your notice."

The talk turned to easier channels, how things were going at the farm, and how each member of the family was faring.

Rudy could feel the deep unhappiness behind his mother's effort at cheerful talk; he wished he could help relieve it. He knew what the family meant to her—and her fear that it was coming apart at the seams must be devastating to her.

But his life belonged to him. It was time that he became his own man. Like it or not, she must learn to accept it.

He was a little ashamed of the relief he felt when Selma took her leave. He went back to the typesetting alcove and resumed work, but he couldn't find much heart for it.

Rudy was troubled. He was going on nineteen and groping for a life's direction. Fordyce's messianic ardor for the socialist cause tugged at him. He had read the volumes that Fordyce had loaned him, books by Robert Owen and Karl Marx and Bertrand Russell. They had opened new doors in his mind, broadening its perimeters.

That was exciting. But was it right? He was still full of doubts.

While he was thinking about it, Fordyce came breezing into the shop. He flung a sheet of paper down in front of Rudy.

"There it is, m'boy—" Fordyce was whipping off his coat, donning his canvas apron and paper cuffs as he spoke. "A hundred signatures, more or less, of citizens good and true, on that damned petition of mine! Good—that'll make those ninnies in Madison sit up and take notice."

Rudy smiled. "I guess you want to set this story up yourself."

"You're damned well told I do! Is the society page set up yet?"

Rudy motioned at the page form laid out on the stone composing table. "Just about done with. I was about to write up the society notes."

"Fine. You get up front and do that. I'll finish up the editorial page, then get this petition—and that nice long list of signers—into print. And not on the editorial page, by God. On the front page—under a banner headline."

Rudy shared only a fleck of Fordyce's excitement. He felt oddly depressed today, and it didn't all stem from the disagreement with his mother or his uncertainties about his present position.

Seated at the front desk, he puttered around with the society notes, setting them down in the usual stereotyped language. But his thoughts kept drifting with a quiet misery.

Rachel!

Usually he could turn back thoughts of her as long as he could occupy himself with work or reading. It took a mighty effort, but most of the time he could manage it.

That hour of passion lingered with him like a dream. Had it happened at all? Sometimes he could hardly believe so. If flesh and fire could ever seem unreal in memory, that had been a time for it. A time as intense as it had been brief. How he *felt* about it, Rudy knew full well. But he wasn't sure of anything else—except that as far as Rachel Merrick was concerned, nothing had changed between them.

Occasionally, at her invitation, he visited the boardinghouse. They took tea together and talked of familiar things. But that was all. He was sure her beautiful, mobile face would betray any hint of something more. On Rudy's part, the passionate interlude had left him feeling like a man fit to stand beside other men. His quiet worship of Rachel wasn't dimmed by the intimacy they had known. But now his senses were fired as fully as his mind.

He felt like a man who has gazed on a room of riches and then had a door slammed in his face. . . .

The actual opening and slamming of a door gave Rudy a wild start. He looked up from his desk, staring at the man who had just come in.

It was Beau Gannett.

This was the man who had been Rachel's lover—and his intrusion on Rudy's thoughts at this moment brought a surge of heat to Rudy's face.

But Gannett's glance at him was almost impersonal. Batting at his dusty coat, he said, "Christ, some wind. Starting to blow like a son of a bitch out there."

Looking more sharply at Rudy now, he said, "Are you the

kid I heard was working for Fordyce—that kid of Holm-gaard's?"

Rudy nodded, feeling his muscles tighten. But Gannett only grunted and said, "Where's that blue-ribbon boss of yours?"

"Right here." Fordyce had stepped out of the typesetting alcove and was sauntering forward, an unlighted cigar clamped in his grin. "Well, well. What can I do for you, pal?"

"You know damned well what you can do for me," Beau said coldly. "Take a long walk off a short pier."

Fordyce laughed. "This is the first time you've conde-scended to take note of my humble fleabites to your dignity. I take it they're starting to hurt. Leastways I can always hope."

Muscle rippled in Gannett's jaw. "I won't bandy words with you. I understand you've been circulating a petition you intend to print and distribute across the state."

"Uh-huh. Was just setting it up. Stick around a while and I'll pull a proof for you."

"What do you want, Fordyce?"

"Come again?"

"What's your angle? What is all this bullshit you've been printing about us big bad moguls leading up to? I mean—just what the hell are you after?"

"What do you think?"

"Money," Beau said bluntly. "I think you want a payoff to pull in your horns. All right . . . how much?"

Fordyce took the cigar from his mouth, his grin fading.

"You better think again, shithead," he said mildly. "What I'm after is your ass. Yours and those of all the other robber-baron sons of bitches who've been mulcting and bleeding the people these many years. What I'm after is what I've said in my paper more goddamn times than you can count. If you've read it there, you got it all."

Beau just looked at him.

Fordyce gestured impatiently. "What else do you want to hear? If that says it all for you, get the hell out of here so I can fumigate the place."

Anger slid like a thin wave across Gannett's face and washed away. He laid a gloved hand on the doorknob and said tone-lessly, "So you don't want to get paid. But you'll get paid all right, inkslinger. Sure as there's a hole in your ass. I'm going to see to it."

"Good. A threat." A wolfish pleasure lighted up Fordyce's face. "You heard him, didn't you, Rudy? You're a witness."

Gannett whirled and went out, slamming the door so hard it bounced open again. A raw gust of wind swept the room, sending a rattle of blown grit across the floor before Rudy closed it.

He looked at Fordyce, who was chuckling softly as he lighted up his cigar.

"You saw it, Rudy—you heard him. I've put a bee in his butt and he can't shake it out." A fierce exultance rose in his voice. "That's what I wanted. He's put a lot of poor suckers up against the wall—he and his kind. Now he knows how it feels."

"Yes, I heard him," Rudy said uneasily. "I don't think he was kidding, Andrew. If—"

"Bombast was all." Fordyce sounded very confident. "There'll be no retaliation. Hell, he'd run me through my own press if he thought he could get away with it. But the time when that sort of thing was just blinked away is past, and he knows it. Don't let a cheap scare technique get to you, my boy."

Rudy said nothing.

Fordyce walked over to him, saying gently, "Doubts, Rudy?"

"Some. I just wish I knew how it will all end."

"Did your mother drop by?"

"How did you—?"

"Spotted her in a local store purchasing some notions." Fordyce laid a hand on his shoulder. "I can guess what she told you, Rudy. Understand how she feels, too. But listen. We can't back down now. We've got that bastard Gannett on the run. Help me keep him there."

"Did I say anything about quitting?"

Fordyce studied him a moment, then laughed and slapped his shoulder. "That's telling me! Now, why don't you take off and get some sustenance in your belly? We've still a long day's work ahead of us—and I don't want you dropping out from weakness."

A glance at the clock told Rudy it was now well past noon.

He was hungry enough to want a hot meal, but not of his own cooking. He stretched the cramps out of his shoulders, shrugged into his coat, and went out.

The strong wind was skirling up plumes of dust along Main Street. Rudy turned up his collar and ducked his head, then started up the street toward the Star Cafe. Sulphide fumes from the paper factory mingled with the pummeling grit. He had to keep his eyes squinted nearly shut as he slogged into the wind.

The weather was a match for his mood.

Head bent as he pushed against the wind, Rudy almost collided with a man coming along the sidewalk. He muttered an apology and tried to sidestep him. The man moved with him, blocking his way. Big and wide-shouldered, he did it with a formidable ease.

Rudy recognized him then.

"Mr. Holmgaard? I'm Adam Gannett."

Rudy took a step back. "I know who you are," he said guardedly.

"Can we talk a moment? Here, in the alley."

Adam stepped into the areaway between the shoe shop and a drugstore. Rudy hesitated, then swung in behind him. It took them out of the wind and effectively cut them off from the street.

"I don't know how to say this," Adam said slowly, "except just to say it. I have to get a message to your sister . . . to Dani. Will you deliver it?"

Rudy felt a rush of anger. "My God—you've got your gall!"

"I know what you've heard. About Dani and me. But you heard wrong. If you don't believe it, ask Dani herself. She'll tell you."

"I don't get it." Rudy eyed him with an undiminished hostility. "Why tell me this? Why the hell would I believe you anyway?"

"You'd believe Dani, wouldn't you?"

"Yes. But, well . . ."

"That's what she told me. She's closer to you than to anyone in her family. You've no secrets from one another . . . or hardly any." Adam smiled a little. "Will you take her a message?"

Rudy's flare of suspicion had partly relaxed.

He'd had little opportunity to talk with Dani during his few visits with the family. Then he'd been disturbed by her somber manner. Something had killed her happiness, and he'd suspected it might be tied in with Adam Gannett.

"Depends what the message is," he said cautiously.

"You can read it yourself." Adam fumbled in his coat pocket, then thrust a folded paper in Rudy's hand. "I want to meet her. She'll tell you a place, and you'll tell me."

Rudy did not even look at the paper. He studied Adam Gannett's broad, handsome face. It was calm, and his voice was steady. Yet Rudy felt an intensity behind it: the plea of one man to another.

"All right. I'll give it to her."

❧ *thirty-two* ❧

DANI'S NERVES TINGLED as she glanced for the hundredth time at the clock on the parlor wall. Its big hand was edging toward ten o'clock. In a few minutes she would be able to slip out of the house without the risk of arousing anyone.

Rudy had brought Adam's note yesterday afternoon. He had slipped it into her hand unobtrusively and without a word; no words were needed once she'd scanned the message. Rudy was on her side, and that was all she needed to know. Before he'd left, she had given him a note for Adam. It told Adam they would have to meet after dark, and at some distance from the house. Otherwise his presence might be picked up by Otto, who was nightly chained in the yard. The pup never barked at any member of the family, but a whiff of a stranger would set him off at once.

By ten o'clock the whole family would be in bed and sound asleep. However, Dani herself would stay up on the pretext of finishing a shawl she was knitting.

Since she would have to show her mother a completed shawl tomorrow, she concentrated on her work, only now and then looking at the clock. Her stomach was full of flutters. How long was it since she'd felt anything that approached pleasure? She knew very well. Since the last time she'd been with Adam, weeks ago.

Ordinarily Dani was the most obedient of daughters. But she was also young. The idea of giving in (for once) to an act of reckless defiance made her feel more pleased with herself than guilty.

Earlier, she hadn't felt so ebullient.

The household had been in an uproar most of the evening. That was nothing unusual with the Holmgaards. Their tempers were often on short fuse over one thing or another. But of late, family clashes had been more sharp and frequent than at any time in Dani's memory. Tonight had witnessed two intense outbursts in a row.

While they were eating supper Ma had lit into Pa about his drinking. Axel was accustomed to making his own wine, but had always strictly rationed his intake of it. Lately he had been getting half drunk nearly every evening, starting in about an hour before supper and keeping it up for an hour afterward. Tonight, just to show what he thought of Selma's heated objection, he had drunk so much that Arvid and Elof had had to help him upstairs to bed.

Next had come a shouting match between Elof and Selma. It was the first time Elof had ever shed his facade of good-humored raillery and yelled back at his mother. He was, he'd declared, up to here with being stuck on this goddamn farm day after day. Unaccustomed to such curbs on his carousing, he was getting edgy as hell. So he was going into town. Rudy had mentioned there'd be a dance at the Odd Fellows Hall tonight, and Elof by God was going to attend it.

"Are you crazy?" Selma had cried. "You know what that police chief said! He will shoot you on sight!"

But Elof was determined to go. And he went.

Elof did not want to grow up, Dani reflected. She and Rudy and Arvid could accept the inevitable and sometimes bitter facts of coming to adulthood. Elof couldn't or wouldn't. He *acted* like a man, cool and amused and self-possessed, but there was a perennial adolescence about him.

It was nearly a minute to eleven. Dani's hands fairly flew. In less than a minute she took the last stitch in her shawl.

She stowed the knitting needles and remnants away in her sewing bag. Then she turned the big parlor lamp down to a dim glow and stood listening for a moment. No sound but the faint drift of her father's snores from upstairs. Dani flung the shawl around her shoulders and went to the front door. Softly she raised the latch and stepped out on tiptoe, crossing the broad veranda and descending the steps.

As she came out of shadow into full moonlight, Otto rose off his belly and whined softly. His tail whipped back and forth at her approach. The pup was growing fast; sturdy and well-muscled, he would make a formidable watchdog before long. Already he could raise a racket that was like to wake the dead. But he did not bark now, only wagged his tail happily as Dani patted his head and spoke to him. He sent a plaintive whine after her as she crossed the yard to the deep shadow of the barn.

Drenched in the light of a full moon, the landscape was almost as bright as day. Dani passed along the west edge of the long rutabaga field to its far corner.

She ascended a pine-covered height. Beneath the tall trees it was almost clean of brush. Her feet made hardly any sound on needle-carpeted ground which held the moonlight vividly. Dani had a strong memory of the afternoon when she and Adam had stood, and sat, on sun-warm ground under pines like these.

As she neared the top of the hill, a man's form glided out of pine shadow. He materialized in front of her so suddenly that though she recognized him at once, she closed her teeth on the edge of a scream.

"Dani. . . ."

The embrace was long and fierce. There was a kind of frantic urgency in the way they clung to one another, bodies taut and straining. Dani felt a dynamic flow of energy from her lover to herself. He was so strong and so gentle. Lately she had hungered for both these qualities of his: the strength and the gentleness.

"It's been a long time," Adam said huskily. "Sometimes I've thought I'd go crazy."

"Didn't you think before of asking Rudy to help?"

"Sure. But I guessed it'd be better to wait a while. I hoped things would simmer down—and they haven't. To the contrary." His hands tightened on her arms. "This is risky for you, isn't it? But I had to see you."

Dani gave a shaky laugh. "Not as risky as you might think. I just waited till the folks were abed. Once they are, they're dead to the world. At least Pa is, tonight. He had too much to drink."

"All the same, I hate meeting you like this." His tone was grim. "It shouldn't have to be, Dani. My God! We're a pair of ordinary people in love. We didn't make this trouble. Neither of us wants any part of it. Yet we have to prowl the damned woods in order to be together. I had a bad start tonight."

"What was that?"

"Coming along the wagon trail to get here, I nearly ran into your brother Elof. Luckily I heard him first and ducked off the trail. Luckily too, it wasn't quite dark then and I didn't have my electric torch on. He'd have spotted me sure. I watched him from the trees as he went by. Carefree sort of a chap, isn't he? But he looked madder than the devil."

Dani explained about Elof's quarrel with his mother.

". . . but he was bound and determined to go to town anyway. Talk about being crazy! Sometimes I believe Elof is as crazy as anyone can get."

"In a way all his own, it sounds like," Adam said. "Anyway, Tom Baird is still on his back in bed with a broken hip. He'll not be on hand to keep any promise he made Elof. Not too likely your brother will run into trouble unless he starts it."

"Trouble!" Dani buried her face against his chest, her voice muffled by his shirt. "Lord, I'm sick of thinking about trouble."

"Don't think about it. Not here. Not tonight."

His hand tipped up her face. Again their lips fused in the tension of a lovers' kiss.

"I need you, Dani. . . ." Whispering against her ear. "Not for just now. Not just for tonight. For always. You understand?"

"Yes—yes!"

"Then why can't we clear out of this mess? Both of us. We could go away."

Dani pulled back a little in his arms. "Where?"

"I've thought about it. The West's our likeliest bet. Oregon or Washington. Montana—"

"And just leave everything we have. Is that what you mean?"

"What do we *have* but trouble?" His voice was vibrant with anger. "None of it is our making! We don't owe them any-thing—my family or yours. What do we need of them and theirs? We can start with a clean slate."

Adam's words sparked an excitement in her. His closeness was like a drug rioting in her veins. Gently she pressed herself away from him, out of his arms.

"Adam, that's not... I mean, how in the world would we live? What kind of a life would we have? Running from pillar to post—"

"It wouldn't be like that." He sounded a little hurt. "I've money of my own. Some, I mean, that's not tied up in the family's capital investments. Enough to start us out. Dani, lumbering is a business I know inside and out. And that western country, the Pacific Northwest, has opened up to lumbering. It's America's last great timber frontier. Fortunes will be made and lost there. I can *make* ours!" His hands reached and caught both of hers. "We could leave tonight. Tomorrow night. A week from now, if you like. I can make all the arrangements."

"What you're saying," Dani said slowly, "is we don't have any responsibilities here. With our people. Is that it?"

"Damn it, I'm saying I love you! I want you to be my wife."

"I know that. I asked—"

"All right. I don't see any responsibility of ours in this mess. Are you saying you do?"

Adam dropped his hands, waiting. Dani lowered her face. The cry of a screech owl coasted through the woods and died in the silence.

"I guess I'm saying that. Yes. I can't talk for you, Adam. Just myself. I don't know if I can make any sense of it. Only, it's *because* of the trouble I can't... just up and elope. If only there weren't any trouble, or if it were to end tomorrow...."

Dani's voice trailed away. How to explain what it meant to be a Holmgaard? To be counted with a family that was more shredded by its own differences than by its conflicts with any outsiders? A family torn against itself and yet unshakably *one* in all its troubles?

She couldn't explain. Because it made no sense.

"Then you'd say yes?" Adam prompted.

"Yes yes yes!" She moved forward and into his arms, blindly. "Oh God, Adam! I can't turn my back on them. Not now. Don't ask me to do that!"

"Hush. Dani, don't. Please don't cry, darling." Adam's tone held a note of defeat. His big hands smoothed her hair; his lips found her wet cheeks. "It's all right. We'll wait as long as we have to. God help us, we'll wait."

❧ *thirty-three* ❧

ELOF ARRIVED IN Winterfield a little after dark. He had
no idea where the Odd Fellows Hall was, but finding it was
no problem. A few quick drinks at a saloon, a casual question to the bartender, and he was pointed in the general direction
of the hall. Then it was just a matter of following the flow of
traffic toward the west side of town, for the regular Saturday-
night dance at the Odd Fellows was the social event of any
week.

The hall was a two-story brick building located at the end
of a block adjacent to one of the city parks. It was easy to spot
from the lights in every window, the outspill of waltz music,
the autos and wagons parked outside, and a steady movement
of people into and out of the place. But Elof decided he wasn't
ready to go in just yet. Halfway down the block was a saloon
that was doing a lively business tonight. A lot of men who'd
squired their ladies to the dance, along with a host of guys
who'd come stag, would be going in and out of the saloon all
evening.

Three quick ones had left Elof feeling so good that he decided to have a few more. He swung into the saloon and elbowed his way to the bar, liking the racket of masculine talk and laughter, the smells of liquor and beer and tobacco. After signaling the bartender for whiskey, Elof set his back to the bar and hooked his elbows on it, idly surveying the patrons. Nearly all were in their spanking-best duds, exuding sweat and bay rum and bibulous cheer. He didn't recognize any of them, and apparently none recognized him.

That was dandy with Elof. Tonight he didn't feel like inviting trouble. The squabble with Ma had left him with a sour belly, now soothed by whiskey. He was minded to booze for a spell and later pick up a skirt if he could manage it—but that was all.

A burst of manly mirth pulled his glance toward the swing doors.

Three young men strode in, arms flung over each other's shoulders. They were weaving so violently they could hardly stand without one another's support. And the guy in the middle was Shad Gannett.

Elof straightened up, feeling his belly tighten. The three moved past him so close that one of them brushed him. Shad's gaze touched his, but Shad's eyes were bleary, not a glint of recognition in them. He and his companions bellied up to the far end of the bar and yelled for whiskey.

Somebody tapped Elof on the shoulder. He balled one hand to a fist as he wheeled around.

"Easy there!" Rudy exclaimed. "Don't hit me—I'm just your friendly neighborhood newshound."

Elof's grin was a little sheepish. "Hi, kid. Want a shot of something wet and ring-tailed?"

"Huh-uh. I'm underage. Also working. Shouldn't even be in here. I'm supposed to cover the dance for the *Clarion*. But I took a peek through the door and saw you. What brings you to town, for Pete's sake?"

"The call of the wild, I reckon. Wildcat liquor and wild women."

"I don't know why I bothered to ask." Rudy glanced across to where Shad and his pals were noising it up. "You must be looking for a lot more. Mr. Gannett there has publicly vowed to nail up your hide. I'm surprised he and his buddies haven't climbed all over you."

"Me—look for those bums? They came in here after I did. Anyhow, the shape they're in, they couldn't tell one end of me from the other."

"You know, I have that trouble sometimes."

Elof gave him a fond cuff on the arm and said, "How's the career in journalism? Fordyce keep you hopping?"

"Sure. But I like it. I'm learning every side of the work, as he promised. The pay stinks, but nobody could just hand you a million bucks' worth of the kind of experience I'm getting."

Elof took his second drink in a swallow, then suggested that he and Rudy go over to the dance.

Leaving the saloon, they idled along the block toward the Odd Fellows Hall, chatting. Rudy wanted to know how things were going at home. Elof gave him answers that put a good face on everything. In fact, things were lousy all around, but why unload it on the Scientist?

Just before they reached the Odd Fellows Hall, Rudy halted and said soberly, "Say, listen. You got a gun on you?"

"Sure as shootin'." Elof patted the left underarm side of his coat, where a pocket sewn to its inner lining contained a .32 Colt. "You reckon I'd come to this damn town without one?"

"Well, I wouldn't go inside with it. The constable is touchy about guns in public places. Any guys packing 'em are required to check 'em at the door."

"Hell," Elof laughed. "He can't tell I got one without he frisks me. What constable, by the way? Baird ain't up and around yet, is he?"

"Not yet. A bird named McCrary is the city copper in Baird's absence. McCrary usually serves with the sheriff's department, as constable of an outlying township. But look, Elof—there's still a town warrant out for your arrest, and if McCrary spots you—"

"How the hell can he? I ain't met him and he ain't met me."

"A few other folks around Winterfield have. You could get pointed out." Rudy shook his head, slowly and wryly. "Suppose it's no use to suggest you stay away from the dance tonight. But if you *have* to live it up, why not go over to Thirsty Hollow? The crowd that hangs out there will be on *your* side."

261

"Uh-uh." Elof was already shaking his head impatiently. "Nothing like that, Scientist. I am honing to trip the fantastic with a pretty girl or two. Damned if I'll settle for one of them beasts that hang around the Hollow."

Rudy shrugged. "Your funeral. I mean, I hope it's *not*."

"Me too. Christ, don't be an ornery long-faced Swede! I ain't looking to mix it up with anybody. Let's go in and have a time. Maybe I can round up a gal for you, too."

They entered the hall. Just inside the foyer, Constable McCrary, a dumpy character with old-time handlebar mustaches, was demanding hardware from any man who was packing it. He had already collected a small arsenal of revolvers and automatics, laid out on a table at his back. Between a fourth and a fifth of the guys in this part of the northwoods, Elof thought, must think they were Wild Bill Hickok or somebody.

The constable gave the two Holmgaards a fishy look. "Either of you fellows packing a sidearm?"

"Nope." Elof flipped back the skirt of his coat to show he was weaponless.

McCrary curtly motioned them to go inside.

The hall was a single big and barren room with a high ceiling spanned by iron beams. Bits of colored bunting lent a festive touch to the sallow plastered walls. On a platform in one corner, an orchestra of one accordion, one fiddle, and one harmonica was rendering a not-too-off-key polka. About a dozen couples were on the floor.

Elof was eyeing the trim ankles of a red-haired girl who was dancing up a storm and enjoying every moment of it, and thinking he might cut in on her partner, when he spotted a familiar face on the other side of the room.

"Gonna circulate a little on my own," he told Rudy. "If I come up with more than one young thing that's sweet and randy, I will give you the high sign."

"Don't bother. If you want to do me a favor, stay out of trouble."

"Scientist, you are just bound not to get your weenie roasted. Well. . . ."

Elof crossed the room, weaving through the dancing couples. Swan O'Dea had caught his eye, but was pretending not to notice him. She was standing by the refreshment table, toying with a glass of punch and chatting with a skinny buck-toothed girl about her own age.

"How's things with you, kid?" Elof asked.

"Oh! Hi. I didn't see you." Swan indicated her companion. "This is Agnes Johnson. Agnes, this is Elof Holmgaard."

Elof said, "Hi, Aggie," with the slow grin that made the plainest girl feel she was something special. Agnes giggled toothily.

Swan gave a nervous laugh. "We were just hoping a couple big handsome Swedes would ask us to dance. Ain't that your brother you came in with?"

She was wearing a bright red dress that contrived to defy convention and the world, as though she were out for a high old time and nothing else. But something strange and stricken lay in her eyes. They seemed to implore him, dumbly.

Puzzled, Elof nodded. "That's my little brother." He motioned to Rudy.

Obligingly Rudy came over and was introduced to the girls. Knowing what Elof expected of him, he said, "May I have the pleasure of the next dance, Miss Johnson?"

"Ain't he mannerly, though?" Elof winked at Agnes. "I'd take him up on it, Aggie. Regret it all your life if you don't. He's too pretty to turn down."

Rudy stepped out on the floor with an enraptured Agnes, as the orchestra struck up a varsoviana.

"How about you?" Elof said to Swan. "Want to trip the fantastic a few measures?"

"No. I . . . Can't we go somewhere and talk?" She clasped her hands around his arm. "Please, Elof."

"We can talk, sure. Long as you ain't still feeling testy about me booting old Shad in his center of activity."

"I wish you'd kicked him ten times as hard," Swan said bitterly. "Can we step outside?"

Elof nodded. They skirted the floor to the rear of the hall, where a pair of big double doors were propped open to admit a cooling breeze. In back of the hall was a small city park. Its clumps of trees and thickets were well groomed; paths paved with macadamized stone threaded between them. Benches were scattered here and there on the grass, whose fresh-cut smell was sharp in the warm night. Most of the benches were occupied by couples, and others were strolling about in the dim throw of light from the hall.

Elof and Swan took a path that swerved off into the near-total dark where the west end of the park bordered the Paradise River.

"I don't know what to say," Swan said low-voiced. "Except you were right about Shad."

"Well, I'm not one to rub it in, kid."

"I know you're not. I can *talk* to you . . . so easy." She was silent a moment as they walked. "He was pretty drunk tonight."

"I saw him."

"And he told me he wasn't going to marry me, ever. That he'd never meant to. I tried to tell myself it wasn't true, he didn't mean it, it was the booze talking. But I knew it wasn't. I went home and changed to this dress. I made it for myself a while back. But Mrs. Coyne told me no decent girl would wear a thing like that. So I never wore it. I don't *want* to be a tramp. I . . ."

They came to a bank overlooking the river. The current glimmered like ink under a wash of moonlight. Swan came to a stop, her face bent. Elof thought she was crying, but suddenly she flung her head back. Her eyes held a shine of pure anger.

"I put on the dress and went back to the dance and flirted with a lot of boys. I wanted to make Shad jealous. But he saw and he didn't care! He just laughed. He couldn't have cared less."

"That's okay," Elof said gently. "He's better off without you. Don't you know that?"

"What?" Swan planted her fists on her hips, glaring up at him. Then she collapsed in laughter. "Say, don't you ever stop kidding?"

"Living is for laughs, kid. Get long-faced over it and you end up getting kicked in the teeth. You did."

"I guess." Her face sobered wistfully. "I guess . . . I never cared for Shad as much as I wanted to. I keep telling myself how much it hurts. But we been talking, you and me, and now it doesn't hurt all that much. Just the same—"

"What?"

"Wish *you'd* be serious for once, Elof."

264

"That's not gonna occur, punkins. Anytime you're looking for laughs, I'm your boy. But that's it."

"Yeah, I know. Elof, I feel like such a fool."

"Well, we ought to be doing something about that."

He pulled her into his arms, and she came willingly, putting all her young intensity into a long kiss.

When it ended at last, she said huskily, "Let's get away from here."

"Feel better?"

"Yes. Let's go somewhere else, okay?"

"Huh-uh." He grinned and kissed the tip of her nose. "Maybe another time. But not tonight."

"Why not?"

"Because you and me are going back to the dance. We're gonna show that whole bunch of stuffed shirts what fun is. Kick up our heels and knock their eyes out. How about it?"

Swan clapped her hands together. "Yeah! I'd like that."

"Then may I have the next dance, Miss O'Dea?"

He crooked his arm with mock gallantry. She laughed and took it, bouncing a little on her toes as they walked back to the hall.

They were almost to the back entrance when a man lurched out through the open doors. He was silhouetted so darkly against the light that Elof couldn't make out his face. It was the man's slurred voice that gave away his identity.

"So there y'are," said Shad Gannett. "Goddamn li'l hoor! My back ain' turn five minutes and y' off in the brush with some yahoo. Who'n hell's that with ya?"

Elof halted, feeling Swan's hand tighten on his arm. Shad looked even drunker than he'd been in the saloon. He was holding to the doorframe with one hand; he was hatless and his pale hair was mussed.

"Shadrach," Elof said amusedly, "you do look like hell."

"Wha'?" Shad pushed away from the doorframe and took a couple of wobbling steps, squinting at them. "Who'n hell is that?"

"Give you a hint," said Elof. "You could collect another sore crotch finding out."

"Oh . . . yeah." Shad came to a stop, legs braced apart. "Well, you got your goddamn gall. Tol' you what happens you come sniffing around my girl again."

"Don't you call me your girl!" Swan said angrily. "Not after what you went and told me!"

"You sure hell are, Swan baby." Shad's face looked bloated; his eyes held a wild glitter. "You b'long t' ol' Shad. I can jew you or screw you or tattoo you if I want, and ain' nobody gonna say diff'rent."

"Just suppose," Elof said cheerfully, "I say different. Then what?"

"You." Swaying, Shad pointed a finger at Elof. "You think I don' know I'm too drunk to fight? You fucking ay I know. But I got frien's, ridge runner. Got lotsa friends in this burg. I give a whistle, you get your ass tar' an' feathered. Now you get away from my girl."

Elof shook his head. "You want her, you got to go through me. You better whistle."

Shad's face glistened sweatily. He was still a dozen feet away. His hand fumbled under his coat and back to his hip pocket. Something glinted in his upswinging fist.

Swan let out a thin scream.

Elof heard the click of a pistol cocking. For an instant he clearly saw the weapon in Shad's hand. His hand dived inside his coat and came out with the .32. He fired point-blank.

Shad did not make a sound. He took a broken step backward. His knees folded and he fell heavily.

A horror sharp as acid filled Elof's brain. He had shot and killed game. He knew a shot's accuracy by how a shot animal went down. You took the feel of a killing shot through your body like an electric thrill.

A man came running out of the hall, so quickly that he must have been expecting trouble.

He said tonelessly, "Shad?" And dropped down on his knees by the body. Then he looked at the gun in Elof's hand, and the light hit his face. It was Beau Gannett.

Other men came hurrying out. One of them was Constable McCrary, who demanded to know what was going on.

Beau Gannett stood up, fists knotted at his sides. His face was like stone. "That fellow killed my brother," he said evenly. "It was murder. Plain damn cold-blooded murder."

Elof stared at him. "The hell it was! He pulled a gun on me."

"What gun?" said McCrary. "Where?"

"The one in his hand, damn it! Anyhow it was there when he went down."

McCrary swung on the gathering crowd of onlookers. "All right!" he barked. "Stand back, all of you. Don't anyone go near the corpse."

He knelt on the grass by Shad Gannett and made a quick inspection. Then he rose, shaking his head. "No gun that I can see."

Elof felt his heart lock in his chest. It was true. There was no pistol in the dead man's hand. None on the ground anywhere near his body.

"But he had a gun!" Swan burst out. "I saw it!"

"That's right," said Elof.

McCrary eyed him narrowly. "Now why should I believe you, my lad? You're a proven liar. You smuggled in a gun you told me you didn't have." He held out his hand. "I'll take it now."

Elof slid a quick glance to Beau Gannett.

Christ! Where else could it have gone? When briefly kneeling by the body, shielding it from sight with his own, Gannett must have . . .

Beau Gannett raised his arm and pointed it at Elof. "Arrest him," he said in a coldly quiet voice.

But Elof's brain was working with a wolfish quickness of its own. Before a man of them could move, he whirled around and charged straight at a groomed hedge of thickets a few feet away. Holding his crossed arms in front of his face, he crashed through the hedge and broke free of it.

"Halt!" yelled McCrary. "Halt or I'll shoot!"

Elof ducked his head and bent his body, making himself smaller as he raced full-tilt across a moon-washed stretch of lawn.

No gunshot came.

Ahead of him was a grove of tall pines, and he plunged into it. It was dark under the trees, but free of brush; a mottling of moonlight showed enough of the ground for him to move fast between the pine boles. On the other side of this grove was the river. If he could get across, he could easily lose himself in the dense woods that began on its far bank.

But he'd have to swim like hell. The sounds of pursuit were lifting behind him. If they reached the near bank before he achieved the opposite one, any man with a gun could pick him off in the water.

Weaving swiftly through the trees, Elof tried to quicken his run. He saw a gleam of water ahead. It was almost near enough to spit in. . . .

His running feet struck uneven ground. Thrown suddenly off balance, he veered to one side, churning his arms to keep from falling. His head crashed against a pine trunk.

The next thing he knew was that he was sprawled facedown, his cheek against the pine-needled earth. Sparks flailed in front of his eyes. His head ballooned with pain. Voices. Even through the roaring in his ears, he could make them out plainly. They were a lot closer now.

Gathering all his strength, he climbed to his knees. Tried to get his feet under him and failed, falling back to his knees. By now the voices were in the grove. They would be on him in seconds. Dizzy and vomitous, Elof surged back to his feet. He took one step and then another.

He put every atom of his will into getting through the few remaining yards of pinewoods. Then he was out of it, coming onto the bank above the river. The moon-shot water pinwheeled; he was falling again.

He rolled down the bank. The inky water closed over his head and shocked him back to a sputtering awareness. The river wasn't five feet deep this close to the bank. Getting his feet under him, Elof crouched down till his nose was just above water. He flattened himself against a steep tilt of bank where the river had undercut it.

Men reached the bank. They halted a few feet above where he hugged against it. Electric torches flashed across the water.

"He musta swum t'other side," a man said.

Beau Gannett spoke up with a hot intensity, urging them to fan out through the park, to search up and down the riverbank. His brother's killer might still be anywhere among the goddamn trees or bushes.

Elof clung to his precarious hiding place. A mass of blueberry bushes that overhung the water helped to partly screen his head. But if any of them actually thought to enter the water and take up the search, he thought muddily, he was a goner sure.

For the next half hour he stayed where he was. He wasn't sure how badly his head was injured. The skin of his forehead was mashed and bleeding. A painful slugging filled his skull; he feared that he might pass out anytime. Maybe he would have, if not for the icy current whose chill ate clear into his bones.

After a time, Elof was numb even to that.

He waited half conscious through what seemed an eternity, till the flashlights ceased to play across the water and the men's voices drifted away. . . .

❧ *thirty-four* ❧

AFTER BREAKFAST THIS morning, Axel and Arvid went out to work in the scrub timber north of the fields. For a couple of days they had been cutting and trimming maple trees, bucking them into ten-foot lengths, loading them on the post wagon, and hauling them to the woodshed for cutting and splitting into stove-length pieces. As the supply of wood was low, it wasn't too early to be laying in the stacks of cordwood that would fuel both kitchen and parlor stoves through a long northern fall and winter.

Selma made up a tray of food and told the twins to take it to Lennart at the guard shanty. Afterward she and Dani cleared the table and washed the dishes, exchanging few words as they did so. There was no particular hostility in their lack of communication. So much ill will had pervaded the household of late that when they weren't at odds over one thing or another, the Holmgaards seemed drained of any feeling at all.

Just now most of what Selma felt was a kind of dreary indifference. Elof still hadn't returned from last night's outing. That was nothing unusual; if he felt like going on a tear, it might last for two days and nights. But the streak of temper he'd shown when she'd objected to his going was something else. Not at all like Elof, it had left her so uneasy that she'd gotten very little sleep last night.

This morning she was feeling too sluggish even to give Dani "Hail Columbia" for sneaking out of the house last night. As she'd lain awake upstairs, Selma's ears had been attuned to the least awry sound. She had heard the parlor door softly open and close. From the bedroom window, she'd seen her daughter cross the moonlit yard.

To meet Adam Gannett? No other way to account for it.

Selma hadn't been surprised, having suspected before that they might be meeting. Now, however, she believed that last night had been the first time. For this morning, Dani's old serenity had returned. Outwardly she seemed neither particularly happy nor unhappy. Yet she was calm once more, exuding the contentment of a girl who was harboring a pleasant secret.

Well, let her harbor it, if it made her happy. There was little enough happiness in this household anymore. If Dani had found strength and solace with her lover, why shouldn't she have it? Only days ago Selma would have recoiled from such a notion. Fretting that Dani might be getting herself "in trouble," she'd have put her foot down flatly. But *Gud!* What bigger trouble could any of them be in?

Don't ask, Selma told herself humorlessly; you might find out.

Maybe she ought to worry more about Dani. No doubt she would, except for a conviction that the girl was no longer as vulnerable as she had been. The fanciful innocence of her nature had always been a worry to Selma. The crushing of Dani's first deep love affair by Axel's misfocused rage had hurt and sobered her bright spirit, but hadn't broken it. She was tough and resilient; in accepting what had happened, even if bitterly, she'd taken a step toward womanhood.

Even if she was meeting her lover in secret (and Selma wondered if Rudy hadn't played a hand in that arrangement), she hadn't run off with him. Selma had no fear that she would; Dani's family sense was as firm as her own. And she felt in some sure and intuitive way that Dani would no longer easily be swayed by Adam Gannett. She loved him; that was past argument. But it seemed to matter less than it had.

For Selma was now sure that in the middle of travail, Dani had become her own woman. Thinking about it put her in a better humor.

She smiled at her daughter. "Do you mind finishing up the dishes? I think I'll go chop a little wood."

Dani gave her a look that was surprised and a bit guarded. "Of course I don't mind," she murmured.

But Selma's temper revived before she got to the woodshed.

Damn Axel! Damn him for what he was doing! But damn him most of all for what he would not do.

Despite her resolution, Selma could feel her rage refueling itself every day. Axel had made it very hard for her to hold back a tide of feeling that might easily burst all restraints. And that would mean the end of the Holmgaards as a family. I have got to hold on, she told herself doggedly. She'd given herself that rote command so often that she was beyond asking herself whether it any longer made a lick of sense.

Selma had one outlet. Lately she had used it often. Maple trunks the men had hauled from the woods lay stacked beside the woodshed. Many were cut to stove-fitting length; they only needed splitting. The double-bitted ax was where she had left it yesterday, sunk in the chopping block.

Selma wrenched it free, set a maple piece on the block, and split it with a strong blow. It was green wood and did not split easily, but she welcomed its resistance. She felt like striking hard and strongly.

If she imagined that each chunk was Axel's thick skull, it wasn't difficult to get up the necessary force.

She worked steadily for a half hour, piling up a heap of split wood, while a pleasant ache worked into her shoulders and arms. She was sweating a little, and that felt good too. Selma was no stranger to wood-splitting; she'd done it since girlhood, and it always made her feel better, physically and mentally.

Quite a lot of her temper was gone. It was time to quit. Likely she'd do the same thing all over tomorrow. She drove the ax bit into the chopping block, then bent to gather up an armload of wood to carry into the house.

"Fine morning, mistress, ain't it?" Tom O'Dea said amiably.

Holding a chunk of wood in her hand, Selma straightened up and whirled around. O'Dea stood by the corner of the woodshed, leaning a shoulder against it.

"How long . . ." She swallowed. "How long have you been standing there?"

"Ah, it wouldn't be polite to tell that. Long enough, suffice it to say, for you to finish up your choppin'. Otherwise I'd feel obliged to offer me help, and I'm thinking you need the exercise more than me."

"Oh, *ja?* and why?"

"To let off all that ire. You'll not be denying you were all steamed up."

Selma pursed her lips, determined not to let him disconcert her. Yet he hadn't shown his face around here since the day she'd dumped hot coffee in his lap—and she took courage from that fact.

"So were you, last time you were about," she observed coolly. "In more ways than one, I'd say."

O'Dea pushed away from the woodshed and sauntered forward a few steps. He tucked his thumbs in his belt and eyed her, grinning kind of lewdly. "Well, that's so. A cute trick it was, mistress. But it only beggared the question."

"What question?"

"The one you'd be asking yourself, lady. Why a woods-loafin' shamrock like the O'Dea gets you so warm and labored. Don't be telling me I never made you feel so."

His bluntness put a warmth in Selma's cheeks. "That kind of feeling, Mr. O'Dea, is what men and women were put in this world to rise above."

"The divil they were!" The humor ran out of his tone. "What we had, you and me—even if for a moment or so—went deeper than a pair o' children playing at hanky-panky."

"You are fooling yourself. You had me a little confused before, Mr. O'Dea. I'm not confused anymore."

O'Dea said, "Hum," and stroked his beard. He looked a little nonplussed. "You been shy about not letting me catch you alone, though. Ain't you?"

"Yes," Selma said honestly. "That was before, too."

"Was it, then?" O'Dea had been edging forward as he talked. "Ah now," he said quietly, and reached for her.

Selma twisted away as his hand brushed her shoulder. In the same moment she took a two-handed grip on the stick of cordwood and swung it at his arm. He jerked the arm away, but the splinter-edged piece slammed him across the knuckles. O'Dea swore and dropped back a step, nursing his skinned and bleeding hand against his chest.

"Agh," he murmured. "Damn ye, mistress. You led me on all this time."

"I never did!"

"I think so. A woman has a free way with her . . . with her looks and manner when she likes a man. Agh, I can believe you never knew it. It's all in a woman's nature. But ye did it all the same."

"You liar!" Hot-faced and mortified, Selma waved the chunk of wood at him. "Go on, you liar! Get out of here or I'll hit you again!"

❧ *thirty-five* ❧

SELMA DECIDED TO do the week's dirty wash this morning, a day earlier than usual. Laundering was the most disagreeable task she knew, and it always helped to tackle it in a spirit of violence. After the encounter with O'Dea, she had no trouble getting into that frame of mind.

She wondered uneasily if there had been a mote of truth in his accusation. Could she have led him on without knowing it? She could not believe it. He had unsettled her now and then, and no doubt she had shown it. He had placed a wrong-headed interpretation on the matter, that was all.

In any case, this would surely be the end of her problem with Tom O'Dea. He would not be around again to annoy her, to spotlight her flecks of weakness, to poke fun at her. She'd had quite enough of that. Yet a tinge of regret mingled with her relief, and it annoyed her all over again. Did she really dislike him that much?

I suppose I did like him some, Selma angrily conceded to herself. But she was glad she had finally put him off for good.

She and Dani had hardly started to sort out the wash when

they had an unexpected caller. The back door swung open; Rudy came tramping into the kitchen.

He said without preliminary, *"Mor,* did Elof come home?"

Selma was on her knees, fumbling through a pile of dirty clothes she'd dumped on the floor for sorting. She got slowly to her feet, watching her son's face. It was pale and agitated.

"What is it, Rudolf?"

"Is he here, *Mor?"*

"No. What is it?"

Rudy took off his cloth cap and dropped into a chair, passing a hand through his thick black hair. He looked as if he hadn't gotten a wink of sleep all night. Slowly and stumblingly, he began to talk.

Listening, Selma felt as if her blood had gone to ice. Elof . . . shooting a man down in cold blood? Shad Gannett? And over that hussy daughter of O'Dea's?

In a horror of disbelief she moved unsteadily to a chair and collapsed into it. Dani came up beside her mother and stood there, gripping the back of another chair. Both of them stared at Rudy seated across the table from them, trying to collect their wits.

In all the trouble she had anticipated might occur, Selma had never thought of anything like this. Elof had put a bullet in Tom Baird, the policeman, coolly enough. But that, in its way, had been self-defense. And he had not killed Baird.

"Rudolf . . ." She forced herself to speak slowly. "Are you sure of this? That Shad Gannett is dead?"

"Yes, *Mor.* I came on the scene right after. He was as dead as a man can be."

Selma nodded, moistening her lips. "And Elof got clean away. This you said."

"Yes'm. A whole crowd of 'em went after him. They looked for hours, but couldn't find him. They figured he got away across the river. Gangs of 'em were out searching for him all night, and after it turned light they spread out in the woods across the river. They were still looking for him when I left town a few hours ago. I waited till daylight to come tell you, because I wasn't sure what might develop. But they still hadn't found him."

"And he hasn't come home," Dani whispered. "Oh, Ma!"

276

"Could he have got hurt?" Selma asked. "Could that be it, Rudolf?"

"It's hard to say, He got away before anyone could get off a shot at him. But he might have hurt himself some way . . . I just don't know. Maybe he just panicked and kept running, to get out of the country. But that wouldn't be like Elof."

"I think not," said Selma. "Elof would keep his wits about him. Still, he didn't come back home. But . . . this would be the first place they'd look, wouldn't it?"

"Well," Rudy said slowly, "that's a funny thing."

"What is?"

"Well, the town is pretty much up in arms over Shad Gannett getting killed. A lot of men were talking about coming out to the farm and collaring Elof. And it was Beau Gannett who talked 'em out of it."

"Him? What could he mean by that?"

Rudy shrugged. "I suppose to let the law handle it. But that hasn't been any worry of Beau Gannett's up till now. And the law sure hasn't had much luck when it's come to collaring Pa."

"But now there is a charge of murder," Selma said quietly. "That's another thing, isn't it?" Briskly, she rose from the table. "Come along. We have to tell your pa."

She and Rudy and Dani left the house and walked back to a clearing on the farm's well-timbered northwest forty. Here, Axel and Arvid were engaged in sawing up a number of maples they had felled, teaming up on either end of a crosscut saw. They were surprised to see Rudy, and only a little more surprised—so it seemed to Selma—at the news he'd brought. Arvid glowered and shook his head and muttered an expletive, as if this were only what he'd expect of a prodigal brother.

Axel took it less casually, though he stayed surprisingly calm. He questioned Rudy carefully and intently, never raising his voice. But his eyes held a wolfish glitter. Pondering what Rudy told him, Axel seated himself on a stump, opened his *snus* can, and tucked a pinch of its contents in his jaw.

"Elof," he murmured, "claimed this Shad pulled a gun on him? That right?"

"That's what he said, Pa. At least that's what they say he said. I didn't get on the scene right away."

"But Beau Gannett was there?"

277

"Yes. I tried to get as much of the story as I could from people who were on the spot. From what they said, Beau was the first one to get out there."

"So. That's interesting. And whereabouts was he? Just standing there or what? Did they say?"

"Why, kneeling next to the body . . ." Rudy paused. "Pa, are you saying . . . ?"

"He might of grabbed up the evidence." Axel lifted his shoulders and let them fall. "It's a thought. Maybe it don't matter much."

"Doesn't *matter?*" Selma said hotly. "How can you say that! Maybe your son is not a murderer, and it doesn't *matter?*"

Axel flicked her an irritated glance. "What I mean, if we can't produce the gun, it ain't evidence. If there was a gun and Beau Gannett sneaked it away, likely it's at the bottom of the river now."

"I am concerned with whether or not our son killed a man in cold blood! *That's* what concerns me! If he did, he's a murderer. There's no way of getting around that, evidence or not."

Axel rose to his feet. "All right," he said coldly, "that's what concerns you. Fine. What concerns me is if he gets caught or not. Tell me this, woman. Would you turn him over to the law?"

Selma opened her mouth, then closed it. She gave a tight shake of her head. "I don't know. How can I answer a thing like that? I would . . . 2I would have to think."

A sardonic smile curled Axel's mouth. "So. At last. One thing you're not sure of. You're so damn sure about every other damn thing, I would think—"

"Pa," Dani broke in hastily. "What if they catch him? What will happen to him?"

"In Wisconsin? For first-degree murder, life imprisonment. They ain't had a death penalty in this state for fifty or sixty years." He paused grimly. "That's if they don't shoot him on sight or hang him on the spot. That could happen too."

"What are *we* going to do, Pa?" Rudy asked. "I guess we'll all go along with what you say. Whatever."

Axel turned and walked over to a tree where his rifle was

leaning. He picked up the weapon and checked the action as he talked.

What they had to do was try to find Elof before anyone else did. It stood to reason that he'd make his way through the woods in this direction from town, staying off the beaten trails. He might have gotten himself lost. Or he might have got nearly home and then, fearing his pursuers might have got ahead of him and laid up for him close to the farm, had hesitated to come in. Or a man fleeing through the woods, over rocks and roots and swamp holes, could get himself hurt in a lot of ways. Especially trying to cover ground in the dark. Anything that got broke or sprained could slow a man all to hell. It might be that Elof was out in the woods somewhere, not far off but pretty near helpless.

So what the three of them would do—Arvid and Rudy and him—was take rifles and fan out through the woods, working in the general direction of Winterfield. Every once in a while they would fire off a shot and yell Elof's name as loud as they could. That way, if Elof was lying low for fear of discovery, he'd know their voices and give answer.

It wasn't too much of an idea, Axel admitted. But he couldn't think of one that was any better. Glancing at his wife as he spoke, he added with a sardonic courtesy, "But maybe *you* can?"

Tight-lipped with misery, Selma only shook her head. She refused to look at him.

Selma knew the best anodyne for worry. It was work. Do what you had to, and meantime try not to think about the way things were.

She and Dani worked furiously, scrubbing and rinsing and wringing out the clothes, carrying them outside in baskets and pinning them to the clothesline. Now and then, distantly, they heard the crack of a shot as Axel or one of the boys fired off his rifle. They were working away through the woods slowly, taking their time, for that stretch of forest was dense and tangled. A man would be forced to traverse it slowly unless he were on a trail. If Elof had been hurt in some way, he might have little voice for answering their shouts. So Axel had ordered his sons to take the search slowly.

By noon, the two women had done about half the washing. As they were pinning a fresh batch of wet wash on the lines, Dani said, "Mama, should I fix us something to eat?"

"*Ja*, do that. I'll finish up here."

"For Pa and the boys, too? He didn't say whether they'd be back for lunch."

"There's that leftover roast from yesterday," Selma said absently. She was half listening for another gunshot. "Make some sandwiches. Enough for us and them, too. That way, they can eat whenever they get back here."

She cut off her speech as a roll of gunfire drifted from the distance.

Suddenly she was intent, straining her ears. Previous shots had been spaced one at a time, with long intervals between. The last burst had been a sustained rattle of fire, each shot following hard on the heels of the one before, then cutting off abruptly.

Silence now. No more shots came.

"Mama, what is it?" Dani murmured.

"Did you hear that?"

"Yes. It wasn't like the other shooting. What do you think?"

"I guess," Selma said slowly, "that all we can do is wait. Be ready for anything, eh? Go on, fix the sandwiches."

Dani went into the house. Selma continued to hang up the wash, but working very slowly now. Often she glanced toward the woods. A wire of worry tightened around her stomach.

In about fifteen minutes, waiting was done.

Axel and Rudy and Arvid came out of the woods, walking abreast. Arvid had been hurt—she saw that at once. His right sleeve had been torn away; the arm was streaked with blood. The sleeve was knotted around his bicep, and it was soaked through from his bleeding.

A cry rustled in Selma's throat. She suppressed it and held her face composed as the three men came tramping into the yard.

"What is it?" she said. "What is it now?"

"Later on," Axel growled, "you ask all the questions you want. Right now we got to get him cleaned up. He's been shot."

"Elof—?"

"Nothing. Not a damn thing. Get to it, woman!"

Dani had come to the kitchen doorway, her blue eyes wide with surprise and shock. They entered the kitchen and Arvid dropped wearily into a chair. Selma went to the stove and poked up the live coals inside. They would need hot water and something for bandages. The wound should be treated with bluestone and sweet oil—did they have any on hand?

For a moment Selma couldn't recall; her mind seemed a blank. *Move!* she goaded herself, and opened a cupboard to rummage in it for the wanted items.

After stripping the bloody knot of bandage from Arvid's arm, Selma found the wound wasn't as bad as she'd feared. Bone and major vessels had escaped damage. The bullet had gone cleanly through the loose outer flesh of the bicep. The front opening was a livid-lipped hole; the one where the shot had emerged looked worse, a clot of mangled flesh.

As she treated the hurt, Selma remembered an occasion when her father, after a hunting accident, had cleaned a gunshot wound in his own leg. He'd soaked a rag in whiskey and had run it clear through the wound with a wire. But she didn't think any such heroic measure was called for in this case. Arvid's wound had bled cleanly.

Rudy told her what had happened in the woods. He and Pa and Arvid had spread out among the trees, out of sight of one another, as they searched. Axel had encountered a couple of armed strangers, who had hailed him amiably. At first he'd been on his guard, eyeing them with suspicion. But in addition to pistols the two men were carrying surveyors' equipment, including an expensive transit. He'd had no reason to doubt their explanation that they were checking survey lines for the county. It was then, with his guard relaxed, that the men had drawn guns on Axel and disarmed him.

Arvid, working back through the trees toward his father, had surprised the pair as they were starting Pa in the direction of Winterfield. The exchange of shots that followed had brought Rudy on the run too. By the time he'd reached the scene, the two strangers were in full retreat and Arvid was nursing a hit arm.

"I guess," Rudy said, "they were just more guys looking to collect that reward."

Selma's mouth tightened as she bound up Arvid's arm in strips torn from an old sheet. First Billy Saginaw. Now a pair of surveyors, or men pretending to be. Who would try for the money next? What kind of subterfuge would they attempt? Who would be the next one to get hurt? Or killed?

Worse: Elof, too, was now a fugitive from the law. And the charge was murder. What had happened to Elof? Where was he?

She finished tying the bandage, then laid a hand on Arvid's brow. As she'd thought, he had a touch of fever. "Son, you go up to bed now. You hear me?"

Arvid nodded. He rose from the table and left the kitchen. His tread was heavy, going up the stairs.

Dani began cleaning up the litter on the table, a pan of dirty water and rag ends of torn sheets. Rudy was seated at the table, lightly and nervously drumming his fingers on it. The twins, who had come in from playing by the river, sat side by side on a wall bench, hushed and solemn.

All of them were carefully watching, or trying not to watch, their father and mother. Arvid's wounding had generated a tension that was obvious to everyone.

Selma gave Axel a long, hard stare. If he had anything to say, now was the time.

Axel was sitting in a chair pulled out from the table. Sullen and heavy-browed, he appeared to be brooding on one thing or another. Selma wasn't impressed. She continued to stare at him till he raised his eyes to meet hers. His gaze was bleak and disinterested, and after a moment he looked away.

So did Selma. They had nothing to say to each other.

⚛ *five* ⚛

The Crisis

———————————————————————

~ *thirty-six* ~

ON THE MORNING that Shadrach Gannett was buried, the sky promised rain. But it did not rain. The sun flickered on and off through banks of clouds during the brief graveside ceremony.

Lydia Gannett had always tried to resist letting the state of weather influence her moods, yet often they did. She didn't feel particularly sad, just tired and depressed. The shuttling effect of sun and shadow had a jittery effect. The droned words of the minister's eulogy were lost on her. She only wanted it to be over. To return to the cool quiet of her bedchamber.

Lydia's eyes watered as her baby gave a healthy kick within.

Her time was very near. She dreaded it and was glad of it. But glad only in knowing that soon it would be over. She wasn't built for childbearing. Her physician hadn't spelled out his fears, but his worry had shown through his cheery discussion of a Caesarean.

The eulogy ended.

For a minute the mourners stood in silence, heads bowed. Shad's funeral wasn't a heavily attended affair. His two brothers, his sister-in-law, his uncle Saul. A few of his old comrades in carousing, looking ridiculously sober. A handful of Winterfield's leading citizens and their wives, in attendance purely for social reasons.

Beau Gannett picked up a handful of earth and dropped it in the open grave. Adam Gannett and Saul Peregrine followed his example, solemnly. Lydia felt vaguely nauseated by the sound of clods striking the casket lid. She turned away from the grave.

Saul took her arm, saying, "Come along, my dear," as people began dispersing toward their cars and buggies.

The Gannetts' big family auto, a Studebaker 40, was parked by the road outside the cemetery's iron-picket fence. The chauffeur was slacked carelessly in the open front seat, smoking a cigarette that he hastily discarded as he saw Lydia and Saul approaching.

The two of them climbed into the closed rear compartment of the car, Lydia arranging herself as comfortably as possible. The heat was stifling. Lydia's slight body and limbs felt anchored in the hotbox of a heavy black dress and many petticoats. She threw back her veil and fumbled for a handkerchief. Saul Peregrine handed her his own. As she dabbed at her sweat-beaded face, he patted her hand, saying, "You'll be home soon, my dear." His concern for her distress sounded genuine.

Lydia half believed it; she gave him a wan smile. Beau had paused to speak with Adam, who was heading for his own car. Climbing into the Studebaker on Lydia's other side, Beau spoke into the speaking tube in the glass pane beside the chauffeur's head: "Take us home, Daniels."

The car started back toward town.

The chauffeur drove carefully, mindful of Lydia's condition. The gravel road to the cemetery was poorly graded. A car ahead of them churned up billows of July dust that flew back into Daniels' goggled face and grayed his dark uniform.

"Well, nephew," Saul Peregrine said dryly, "can we get down to business now?"

"Business?"

"You're not so fond of old Uncle Solly that you invited him to ride in your car as a gesture of family solidarity. I know you better than that, Beau. What's on your mind?"

Beau took out his cigar case and extracted a cigar. He clipped the end and stuck the cigar in his mouth, but did not light it. "The business with Axel Holmgaard. I'm going to squash that fellow like a bug. No diplomacy this time around, Solly. No payoffs to that damned crook." He slid a deliberate glance past Lydia, at his uncle. "That was a mistake."

"Oh, I don't know. If Ad hadn't gotten amorous with the Swede's daughter—"

"We shouldn't have tried buying Holmgaard off in the first place," Beau cut in roughly. "*That* was the big mistake, Solly."

"Ah?" Saul lifted a white brow with a hint of his fine irony. "And how so?"

"Because it was as good as admitting the son of a bitch had a strong case."

"And that was my mistake, eh? Well, as things happened to turn out, you were right. It certainly hasn't helped our case with the public."

"That's it. But you were right too, Solly—about the power of the press, and the effect of public opinion. I've learned that the hard way. We've important friends in Madison, and a hell of a lot of good it's done us. Public sympathy for Holmgaard has 'em in such a sweat they've dragged their heels whenever we've petitioned 'em for help."

Saul nodded his white head gravely. "Mr. Fordyce has done his work well. Even unto the halls of the state legislature."

"Sure," Beau said softly. "But they'll not drag their heels anymore. Not after what happened night before last. A Holmgaard murdered Shad. Shot him down like a defenseless dog. Overnight, the whole picture's been reversed. The locals are in a lynching mood, and it's Elof Holmgaard's neck they want to stretch. Word's gone out on the wire services, too. So we're going to strike while the iron's hot. Now the funeral obsequies are done with, I'm going to shake up those Madison pals of ours."

"Exactly what do you have in mind?"

"The works. I've been in touch with the Pinkerton Detective Agency. A dozen of their operatives will arrive by train in a couple days. Today I'm wiring the governor's office requesting that state police be sent to root out that Holmgaard gang of crooks and murderers. *This* time, they'll damned well listen.

By the time the Pinks and the state men have arrived, I'll have gotten a passel of the locals sworn in as deputy sheriffs by Joe Pleasants. With feeling running as high as it is, we should collect quite a crew by that means alone. We'll have pulled a damned army together, Solly. It'll march right over that nest of nits."

Saul Peregrine nodded his head up and down, smiling.

"Ah, I've wondered why you've bided your time. Even to talking that lynch-minded crew of stalwart citizens out of tackling the job right away, the other night. That's it, eh? You're taking no chances."

"That's it," Beau echoed with satisfaction. "I want to know one thing, Solly. Are you with me or against me?"

"That's hardly the question. I'll go with what the family decides."

"You mean, you'll go with what Mother decides. But you have the most voice with her. Solly, I want this to be unanimous. I want the family in back of me. None opposed, no halfways. Damn it, I want to know where you stand!"

"Well, if it's important to you . . . I think public sentiment's on our side for the nonce. That's been all that's concerned me."

"Good enough." Beau let his weight settle back against the seat cushions, tapping nonexistent ash from his cigar. "Will you tell Mother that?"

"Certainly. When she's in a condition to discuss the matter."

Momentarily Beau frowned. But he nodded. "That ought to be in a day or two. Shouldn't be any problem. I'm sure Mother would go along anyway . . . after Shad. Jesus, that really threw her."

All of them had been stunned by Letitia Gannett's sudden collapse.

On learning of Shad's death she'd risen painfully out of her chair, then had fallen, striking her head on a table. The physical blow had not been serious. But she had been in a trancelike shock for hours afterward and was still confined to her bed.

"Letitia's not what she used to be, Beau," Saul Peregrine said quietly. "I'm sixty-two and she is nine years older than me, almost to the day. She bore you three fellows late in life, and after Shad was born her health was never the best. Even crippled up as she is, one tends to forget that. But I'm worried

288

about her. That collapse could be a prelude to ... anything. So be careful what you tell her and how you do it."

"Yeah." Beau brooded out the window for a moment. "I just want to be sure we're all of one mind where that goddamned Swede is concerned."

Saul Peregrine gave his nephew a slanting look. "You know, my boy, that's become quite an obsession with you."

"What has?"

"Getting Axel Holmgaard. You don't just care, anymore, about getting logs through a dam. Or even forcing Holmgaard off his land. You want to wipe the man out—literally. You want to destroy him."

Lydia wasn't surprised that Saul Peregrine had glimpsed the dark places in her husband's nature. Yet she tensed for a burst of Beau's ready temper.

But he only nodded calmly. "One way or another, yes. I reckon that's about it. Do you care?"

"Not a whit. As long as there's no danger of it backfiring on all of us." Saul paused. "Have you discussed any of this with Adam yet?"

"I'm about to. Told him I want to talk to him as soon as we get home. But hell, he'll go along. What else can he do? His brother's been murdered. Even old Candy Ass will want to see that crowd brought to justice, now his brother's been murdered by one of 'em."

"But not the one he's softheaded about," Saul observed dryly. "That's the girl."

"Put on your thinking cap, Solly," Beau said irritably. "He was trying to get into her drawers was all. And got caught at it."

Saul gave a shrug of supreme irony; he said no more.

Lydia, swaying sickly to the car's lurching progress, thought dully: He doesn't know his own brother any better than ... than he does his wife. Oh God, I'm going to throw up if we don't get off this!

But the worst of the journey was behind them. The automobile had left the rough cemetery road and was on the graded highway that led into Winterfield. In fifteen minutes it swung into the alley back of the Gannetts' big house. Daniels guided it into one of the wide stalls of the Gannetts' old carriage shed, now renovated for a garage. Adam had already arrived home; his battered old Model A Ford was parked in the next stall.

Adam was waiting in the house. He and Beau and Saul Peregrine repaired to the big den for their conference.

From the tight-lipped look on Adam's face, Lydia guessed it would be a stormy session. She was grateful she wouldn't be required to sit in on it. Letitia had always insisted on her presence at family caucuses . . . but Letitia would be out of this one.

Moving heavily to the foot of the stairs, Lydia mustered her strength for the ascent to the second floor. One of the maids was standing at the top landing, polishing the balustrade. At sight of Lydia, her petite, lovely face shaded with concern.

"Madam would like help on the stairs?"

"No . . . no. That's all right, Emilie. Go on with your work."

Slowly climbing the rises, Lydia automatically ran her hand along the balustrade, inspecting for traces of dust. Again feeling Emilie's glance, she dropped her hand. Lydia knew it was merely her own fussiness cropping out again. Yet she'd never been fussy before she'd become pregnant. Since then, she'd been edgy about the littlest things.

At the top of the stairs she paused to rest, then went down the hallway, past her mother-in-law's closed door, to her own room adjoining Beau's.

Inside, Lydia discarded her hat and veil and bathed her face with cold water. She peeled off her layers of clothing and gave herself a sponge bath. She donned a light silk kimono and stretched out on her bed. Somewhat cooled and refreshed, she found herself able to relax with little effort. A slight breeze through the open window, a rustle of elm leaves, twitter of birdsong, mild stridulation of crickets—all combined to lull her toward sleep.

The pleasant drowsiness was wiped out by a lift of angry voices from the den, which was just below her own room. Adam and Beau were quarreling.

Lydia sat up, nerves quivering. She grimaced and pressed a hand over a surge of pain in her belly.

Soon. Please—let it happen soon!

No longer drowsy, she rose and bathed her face again, aware that the muffled exchange from below was becoming louder and sharper. Now they were shouting at one another. Lydia shivered. She was accustomed to Beau's shoutings, but had rarely ever heard Adam raise his voice.

Lydia could guess at what had happened. Beau must have let drop some off-color remark about the Holmgaard girl.

She wondered how Beau could be so foolishly blind as to what was under his nose? Adam was in love with that girl. Admittedly he'd never mentioned her except in strictly impersonal terms. That included his admission of blame for her family's having caught them in a compromising situation, thus wiping out the Gannett-Holmgaard agreement. Such honesty was typical of Adam, whose flaming idealism wouldn't permit him to avoid responsibility for a blunder, no matter what it might cost him.

Someone tapped softly on the bedroom door; Lydia went to open it. Emilie stood there, kneading a dustcloth in her hands. "Oh, madam! Can you not do something? They are yelling so loud, your 'osband an' his brother. Madam Gannett is having the nap, I fear they will wake her an' opset her—"

Lydia made a helpless gesture. But she said, "I'll try," and left her room to hurry to the head of the stairs. Even as she reached it, the door of the study was flung open; she saw Adam stalk across the foyer to the front door.

"Go on, you candy-assed son of a bitch!" Beau roared after him. "Get your bleeding-heart ass the hell out of here!"

The front door slammed behind Adam. Beau closed the study door with equal violence. He resumed talking, now to Saul Peregrine alone, his voice still angry but low-pitched.

Feeling a flood of relief, Lydia returned to her room. Emilie was moving around the chamber, whisking her dustcloth over sills and bedposts and marble commode tops that were already immaculate. Lydia's legs felt weak; she eased herself into an armchair. She smiled at Emilie's timorous glance.

"It's all right. Mr. Adam has taken his departure. That should quiet things down. For a spell, anyway. If you have to dust, why not do Mr. Beau's room? It certainly could use a good cleaning."

"I . . . I do not want to be there if he comes in, madam. He's in ver' bad humor."

"Well, I fancy he and Mr. Peregrine will be occupied for

291

a while. His room's a mess, and I suppose he'll never notice if it's cleaned or not . . . but why don't we do it? I'll help."

"Madam should rest," Emilie said reprovingly. "It's time for your nap."

Lydia gave a shaky laugh. "Afraid I couldn't do much sleeping now. My nerves are all a-rattle." She got slowly to her feet. "Come along. We'll do it."

There was a connecting door between Beau's chamber and her own. Opening it and surveying his room, Lydia shook her head with wry despair.

Only a week ago she had "picked it up," setting everything in its place. Already, with his knack of never putting anything back where it belonged, Beau had things in disorder. If he wanted a fresh tie, he'd grab a handful from his tie rack, select one, and drop the rest on the closet floor. Letitia, who had tried since Beau's infancy to mend his careless habits, had once told Lydia dryly, "Don't try to reform him, child. Best clean up after him and let it go."

Lydia moved slowly around the room, picking up scattered articles of clothing. "Madam should not be on her feet," Emilie scolded her. "Sit, and tell me what to do."

Lydia did not object. Even stooping down was an effort. She sat on the edge of the bed and watched Emilie move briskly about, putting things in order. Lydia could not resist running a finger down the grooved column of one ornately carved bedpost. Her mouth puckered with distaste. Dust! Everywhere she looked, threads of dust in the seams of furniture and woodwork. She was aware that her aversion to dust verged on a nervous disorder. Her physician had assured her that such aversions were common in women who were expecting. But all the same . . . !

"I think you might change the bedding while you're about it," she told Emilie. "But we'll dust first. Yes, there I go again"—she returned Emilie's faint, chiding smile—"but *this* room really needs a cleaning."

It did. Especially some of the fixtures and woodwork that were out of easy reach, such as the molding where walls and ceiling met. Set in the center of the ceiling was a large glass globe of a lamp painted in thickly opaque red and yellow squares. It had been installed in place of an old gas-jet fixture when the house had been wired for electricity several years ago. Screwed into a brass collar, the globe housed an electric light. But now, when Lydia went to the wall switch and touched it, the light failed to go on.

"Burned out. I'll get a fresh bulb, Emilie. I have one in my dresser. Meantime you stand on a chair and unscrew that globe. It's an awful dust-catcher; we'll clean it before we put it back."

When Lydia returned with the bulb, Emilie had pulled a chair beneath the painted lamp and, by standing on the chair and stretching her diminutive height on tiptoe, was able to unscrew the globe from its brass fitting. "Oh . . . !" She almost lost her grasp as it came free. Then she gazed inside it; her eyes grew round.

"Why . . . look, madam."

Lydia walked over and took the glass orb from the maid's hands. She was startled to see a small blue-steel automatic pistol nestled inside. "What in the world? I know he likes to keep guns about. But what a strange place to have one!"

"Madam—" Emilie hesitated. "This gon, I think—"

"What?"

"I think . . . it is one belong' to Mr. Shad."

"I really wouldn't know. Guns look quite alike to me." Lydia smiled. "Are you an expert?"

"*Non*. This gon I know." Emilie touched a fingertip to a deep nick on the pistol's squared butt. "I 'ave seen Mr. Shad clean it. He say once it is an, um, an *Anglais* . . . English pistol. See? It is the same blue color an' so small a gon. But this scratch, that is 'ow I know for sure it's his . . ."

Gooseflesh rippled the back of Lydia's neck. *Shad's gun?*

Slowly, against an uneasy stir of revulsion, she took the gun out of the globe. But *why*, she wondered. What reason would Beau have for . . . ?

Footsteps sounded outside the hallway door. They touched Lydia's taut nerves like a live wire: She let the gun fall from nerveless fingers.

A moment later Beau opened the door and strode into the room, his brows knit in a scowl. That was no surprise. Once aroused, his temper was slow to simmer away. Seeing the two women, one standing on a chair and one beside it, he came to a halt, his face blank with surprise.

Pinpoints of flame touched his eyes.

"What—the—hell—are—you—two—*doing?*" Spacing out each word between set teeth.

Lydia did not reply. Both she and the maid were frozen in place.

Beau's glare pounced to the pistol on the rug. His lips shaped a soundless word.

Suddenly he was gripping Lydia by the arm, shaking her. He was livid with anger. Paralyzed with fright, she rocked bonelessly in his grasp. He shouted, "What the hell do you mean by . . . ? *Goddamn!*"

Some thread of restraint snapped in his mind.

His free hand swung up and landed a savage slap. Even as he struck her, he let go of her arm. Lydia stumbled backward and fell heavily to the floor. Dazed and confused, she groped to her feet. Stood swaying uncertainly, a hand pressed to her throbbing cheek.

Later she might remember with compassion and regret the shock in Beau's face as he realized what he'd done. Even recall an impression of seeing his hand half lifting toward her— imploringly. But now there was only a pall of terror and rejection that filled all her mind.

Lydia slipped past him, past his outstretched hand, and out the door into the hall.

She ran blindly, a pain deeper than any physical one tearing at her. And coming to the head of the stairs, pulled herself up with a kind of despairing instinct. But one of her slippered feet caught on a raveled loop at the fringe of the carpet.

Momentum tripped her. In a wild try for footing, she stabbed her other foot at the brink of the landing. Her ankle turned.

She plunged forward and down, arms outflung. Her unwieldy body crashed against the balustrade. Her own scream piercing her ears trailed endlessly into darkness. . . .

♻ thirty-seven ♻

RUDY WAS RELUCTANT to return to Winterfield. He felt his place was at the farm, in case of a surprise attack by a posse of inflamed locals. It might still happen. But Selma fiercely insisted that he go back to town and send a doctor to attend Arvid.

To her surprise, Axel growlingly agreed with her, though for a different reason. Rudy could be of more use to them by remaining in Winterfield, where he would be their eyes and ears. Also, he would be able to pick up any word of Elof. Axel had come to the discouraged conclusion that it would be futile to continue aimlessly scouring the woods for a missing son when they had no real idea of what had happened to him. Further, Axel was leery of any more bounty hunters who might be prowling about.

So Rudy headed back for Winterfield. The family settled down in the house to wait out a dreary day. Nobody ventured outside except to do the necessary chores and to take Lennart's meals to the shanty.

Before nightfall, Selma knew she had been mistaken about

the seriousness of Arvid's injury. By late afternoon he was burning up with fever. The doctor had not come. But allowing for the time it would take Rudy to reach town and the doctor to get out here, they shouldn't expect to see him before tomorrow, even if he consented to make so distant a house call.

Beset by a torment of worry, Selma spent another near-sleepless night. One son missing . . . dead for all they knew . . . and a hunted murderer. Another son tossing in the throes of fever from a gunshot wound. She had clung to an insensate determination to keep the family together, no matter what. Now the cost was suddenly too high. Blood had been drawn. Even Axel was shaken. His confidence had sharply sagged.

Before the night was spent, Selma reached a decision. The girls must be sent away. Dani and Julia and Erika must go. She, Selma, would remain with Axel and her sons. That she might depart with the girls was a consideration which barely skimmed her mind. Her place was here—it couldn't be otherwise.

But by morning, Arvid's condition drove every other thought from her head. His arm was infected. It had bloated to twice its normal size, the flesh hot and taut and reddened. Fiery streaks of blood poisoning showed beneath the skin. The gland underneath his arm was hard and swollen. Selma did what could be done in the way of some remedies. She made Arvid stay flat on his back and set pillows under his arm to elevate it. She applied fomentations of hot water and Epsom salts.

Arvid's fever mounted; by noon he was in a babbling delirium.

Dr. Hammerstein arrived at mid-afternoon. He wasn't very encouraging. He told Selma that her treatment was about as efficacious as any other for holding the blood poisoning in check. He administered quinine to the patient, left a supply of it for him, and told them to keep him as quiet as possible. Then he took his departure, with no assurance of when he'd be able to pay another call. Town patients had first claim on his services.

After the doctor had left, and Arvid had fallen into a fitful sleep, Selma let her mind budge tiredly to her decision regarding the girls. She couldn't avoid discussing it with Axel. He hadn't spoken to her since his caustic remarks of yesterday morning. Wearily, she supposed that if silence were to be broken, she would have to break it.

She found Axel in the parlor. He was slumped on the horsehair sofa; his face held the surly mask it often wore of late. Just now, though, the mask seemed more worn and haggard than anything. For the moment he and she were alone. Maybe he would listen.

Selma sat on the hassock by his knees and laced her fingers together, elbows resting on her knees. "Look," she said quietly. "Let's say it out plain. It was bad enough before, now it will be ten times as bad."

His eyes flickered with a kind of tired scorn; he said nothing.

"I want Dani and the twins out of here. They can go to my sister's place in Ohio."

"I been thinking the same," Axel said heavily.

"You . . . you have?"

"*Ja*. This is no place for girls or women. You go too."

Caught entirely off guard, Selma was speechless for a moment. She searched the lines of his face for some hint that he'd repented of his madness. She found none. His eyes looked straight into hers, hard and unblinking. Unrelenting, too, tinged with the acid of a scorn that was almost indifferent, as though he expected nothing of her. And wanted less.

Selma flared out in the hot flush of her anger: "I will not! My place is here. I told you so!"

"All right. Stay. It's going to get a lot nastier, woman. You said so yourself."

Too furious even to retort, Selma rose and wheeled, stalking from the room. The stairway shook to the hard, angry strike of her heels as she ascended to the second floor. She entered the boys' bedroom.

Dani was sitting up with her brother. She was curled up in an armchair drawn up by the bed.

Selma moved to the bedside and gazed down at Arvid. He had sunk into a hot, twitching sleep. His face had the red and puffy look it always took on when he was sick with anything.

"Dani, you can get your things packed," Selma murmured. "Pa and me have talked it over. We are sending you and the kids to your Aunt Hedvig's in Ohio. Lennart will take you all to the railroad station in the wagon."

Dani didn't reply, and Selma looked at her.

"I can't," Dani said quietly. "Not while Arvid is like this. I have got to wait till I know he is better."

The family feeling again. Or was it a reluctance to go so far from Adam Gannett? Selma did not know, but she nodded her understanding.

"All right," she said gently. "All right, Dani."

A delay of two or three days shouldn't make any difference. As long as the girls were away from here before too long.

The afternoon passed and waned into early twilight. The mood of the household was much the same as yesterday: an uneasy silence overhung by a sense of dread. Worry and nerves. That was all there was to it. But it wasn't a thing you could either shake off or do anything about.

So you waited.

The supper hour came and went. Selma and Dani were clearing the table when Otto, tied out in the yard, started to bark wildly. Axel was sitting at the table, scowling into his coffee cup. He gave a start, dropping a hand to the butt of the revolver he now wore holstered at his side all the time. Then he rose and went to a window, peering out.

"That damn mick," he said softly, contemptuously.

Selma nearly dropped the dishes she was gathering up.

A moment later there was a heavy knock on the door. "It's me," O'Dea said loudly. "Tom O'Dea. If ye'll open the door, I've something to tell you."

Axel raised the latch and opened the door a crack. "What is it?"

"Would you mind a hell of a lot if I step in the house?" O'Dea's tone was cross and tired and sarcastic.

Axel made his distrust pointedly clear by drawing his pistol and covering O'Dea as he came through the door. O'Dea halted and looked at each of them, his gaze not lingering on Selma. His look was as unfriendly as Axel's, and Selma could not remember when she'd seen the Irisher appear surly. But that was how he looked now.

"Your son is at my place," he said without preliminary. "The one called Elof. He was too sick to make it home. So I come to tell you."

Axel continued to eye him with suspicion. "What's the matter with him?"

"Enough. From what he said, he hurt his head and then got himself lost in the woods. Been out there a couple days and nights getting et up by mosquitoes. It's in bad shape he is, but I reckon he'll live."

O'Dea's voice conveyed indifference as to whether Elof's condition took a turn one way or the other. But a few questions elicited from him a fuller account of what had happened.

O'Dea had paid a visit to town earlier today. From his daughter Swan he had learned in detail what had happened back of the Odd Fellows Hall two nights ago. When he had returned to his cabin, O'Dea had found Elof crumpled across his doorstep, nearly unconscious. When he was somewhat revived, Elof had told his version of how the shooting had occurred.

After eluding his pursuers, Elof had continued, he'd remained all night in the river. In the early dawn, when the search had drifted away from his vicinity, he had crossed the river and entered the woods. His intention had been to return to his father's farm by cutting through dense woods, avoiding all trails which might be watched. But dizzy and sick from a blow on the head, he'd soon lost himself. He had alternately rested and wandered for two days, trying to find his way out of the woods, never sure in his confusion whether he was on a straight line or going in circles. Chance had brought him back to the tote road along the Ottawa River, and he'd managed to follow it as far as O'Dea's cabin before he collapsed.

"That's all there is to it," O'Dea told them. "He is resting in me own bed now, and I've seen to his hurts as well as I'm able. I'm thinking he has what a sawbones would call a mild concussion. Bit o' rest an' care should fix him up."

Selma said quietly, "We owe you quite a lot, Mr. O'Dea."

He nodded coldly. "Enough, I'd say. But I count it as no debt. The lad is innocent, that's clear. His account o' the shooting is like Swan's, to a detail. It's my duty as a human bein' to give him help. And letting that crowd o' scuts in Winterfield get their hands on him would be no help."

Axel had put his gun away. When he spoke to O'Dea again,

his face and voice had changed. "Would you keep him at your place?"

"That I would. He's a bit sick to be moved here. And mine's the last place any lawdog would look for him. He'll be safe enough there."

O'Dea had relaxed a little too. His manner was still gruff, but touched by a glint of satisfaction. Obviously he relished the idea of helping cheat a misguided "justice" of its victim. He'd enjoy defying restrictions of any kind.

Selma said, "Mr. O'Dea?"

"Aye, mistress."

"Whatever your reason was for helping us...thank you. Thank you."

≋ *thirty-eight* ≋

THIS HAD BEEN another of the gray and muggy days touched by a threat of rain that it seemed would never materialize. As she went from one store to the next on her rounds of Saturday shopping, Rachel Merrick looked up at the sky often. But she never had to open the umbrella she carried. Gusts of wind began to kick up as she walked back to her house, laden with packages.

Less than a minute after she was inside, rain started to fall. The sky broke like a shattered melon and drowned the earth. Peals of thunder shook the house. Rachel hurried through it, downstairs and upstairs, securing the windows as sheets of rain slashed through them. Windows on the lee side she left open to catch cool drafts that would sweep a pall of dead heat from the halls and rooms.

She celebrated the end of sticky humidity with a bath and a change of clothes. Her boarders—after days of sometimes profane complaints about the weather—would have been equally grateful, had any been around. But none were. All had escaped into the countryside for the weekend, on one diversion or an-

301

other. Lotte Hoffenmeier was away too, spending a few days on the farm of a married sister. Rachel had the house to herself.

She had looked forward to a break in the usual routine: planning meals for no one but herself, sewing and reading, enjoying a little solitude. But Rachel wasn't used to solitude. Her typical day was an active and sociable one: less from the desire to be gregarious than to fill up the hours of her life.

It hadn't always been that way. When she was a girl, she had often spent hours by herself. Hours filled by the sort of diversions in which inward-looking people could find contentment. Happy hours untroubled by any sense of loneliness. But now . . . often she thought that all her frenetic sociability was aimed at filling an emptiness, not an altruistic need.

Then she would think defiantly, *All right—suppose it is?*

She had no intention of deviating from the goal she'd set for herself: She would save a good deal of money, sell this place, move to a southern city, and begin a new life. She'd never quite dared to ask herself what kind of a life—sometimes feeling that the real problem resided in her own nature, not in the place she lived. To that she'd always give herself the same reply: *How can you know till you try?* And so thrust the nagging needle of doubt out of mind.

But today, a few hours of solitude and silence had preyed on her nerves to such an extent that after she'd eaten her lonely lunch and had gone downtown to shop, she had dropped by the newspaper office in hopes that Rudy Holmgaard would be in. She'd found him holding down the place alone, for Andrew Fordyce was taking a rare holiday in the country. After chatting with Rudy a while, she had invited him to supper.

Perhaps it would cheer up both of them.

He'd told Rachel about the wounding of his brother Arvid. And his brother Elof was still missing, or had been two days ago when Rudy had visited the farm. Rachel took a dim view of Fordyce's campaign, and she suspected from a remark or two Rudy had let drop that he was having uneasy misgivings about his own part in it. But that was none of her business; Rudy must work it out for himself.

What struck closer to home was Rudy Holmgaard's infatuation with her. It hadn't troubled her much before that single time they had bedded together. Since then she'd had frequent and bitter twinges of guilt. She had no idea of how to deal with a love-struck boy. For more than a decade she'd shunned any romantic involvement. If she were his own age, it might be comparatively easy to put him off. (Then, in fact, she might not want to!) The age difference troubled her more than anything. The gulf between eighteen and twenty-nine seemed overwhelming. In some respects, it was true, Rudy was maturing quickly. But he still had a long way to go.

As she set about preparing supper, Rachel did some hard thinking.

She had to make Rudy understand how impossible the whole situation was. Make an adroit appeal to the good sense in which he surely wasn't lacking. The only trouble was, she wryly knew, men and women could be extremely stable in their heads and still be God's fools in affairs of the heart.

Suddenly a white and dazzling glare filled the kitchen. Then an ear-splitting crash of thunder yanked Rachel out of her gray musing. It startled her so badly that she dropped a pan.

Her heart was pounding, her hand trembling, as she bent to pick it up. In the same instant she heard a crackle of tearing wood. She rushed to a window in time to see the old oak at the corner of her backyard plunge to the ground. Lightning-struck, its trunk was jaggedly split and smoking.

Thank God it had fallen away from the house!

Then she heard the terrified whicker of a horse. Turning her gaze to the woodshed beyond her flower beds, Rachel saw through the blur of rain a mounted rider. His big black was rearing and pawing. The man was fighting for control; he muscled the frightened beast to a standstill. Then he climbed to the ground. He would have fallen, but for his grasp on the horn of his western stock saddle.

Rachel threw on her coat and hurried outside. She reached the man and caught at his sleeve, raising her voice above the rattle of pounding rain on the woodshed's corrugated metal roof.

"Sir . . . are you hurt?"

The man's face was bowed against the horse's neck. Almost painfully he turned his head.

With a heart-stopping shock, she recognized Beau Gannett. His face had a grayish pallor; his eyes wore a sickly glaze. He

303

was bareheaded, his dark hair straggling over his forehead in dripping strands.

"'Lo there . . . Rache." Mumbling the words almost unintelligibly.

"Beau, what in the world are you doing?"

"Wha'sit look like. Takin' li'l ride in the rain. Great stuff."

"Well, good heavens! You can't just stand here in the wet. Come in!"

Rachel seized the reins of the black horse and tugged him forward till he was beneath the shelter of the wide woodshed eaves. "Will he be all right here?" she asked.

Beau was swaying on his feet, hardly able to stand alone. His eyes glared like dull coals.

"Beau!"

"Wha'?" His gaze rolled to dim focus on her. "Oh. Yeah. He be okay. Sure."

Rachel caught hold of Beau's arm and slung it over her shoulders. Awkwardly supporting him, she floundered to her back porch. The kitchen door stood open; she half dragged him inside and let him collapse into a chair near the stove. He was drenched to the skin and shivering. She'd already laid the supper fire, and the big Monarch radiated a rich warmth.

Rachel shed her coat. She said, "You stay right there," and swept out of the room. In a minute she returned, carrying a towel, a pair of men's slippers, and a man's thick woolen dressing gown. Both slippers and gown had been left by a former boarder who had departed a year ago, leaving no forwarding address.

"Here." Rachel thrust the towel and clothing at him. "There's a little bathroom at the end of the west hall. Go in there and dry off and put these on."

Beau's chin was sunk against his chest. Slowly he raised his face. Some of the slack-jawed vagueness had left it, but his eyes held a sick misery that shocked her all over again.

"Rache," he said helplessly. "I . . ."

"Go on," she said gently. "You can say it afterward. Go on, now. Do you want to catch your death?"

He muttered something so faintly that she barely caught the words: "That would be a mercy."

He got to his feet and plodded out of the kitchen, trailing

runnels of water along the floor. Rachel wondered how much of his condition was caused by liquor. And how much by whatever emotional blow had fallen on him. She couldn't believe that even the death of a brother would account for this much grief in the Beau Gannett she'd known.

His sudden intrusion into her life after all these years left her mind in a turmoil. She hardly knew what she was doing as she spooned coffee into a pot, added water, and set it on the range.

Presently Beau returned to the kitchen, carrying his wet clothes rolled in a bundle. He looked a little better. He had combed his damp hair; his face had regained some color. The long robe muffled him from neck to feet. His step was steadier as he crossed the kitchen and dropped into the chair by the stove.

"What a damn fool." He scrubbed a hand over his face. "Jesus. What a pluperfect damn fool."

"You needn't look for any contradiction from me," Rachel said coolly. "I'd offer you a drink, but it's clear you've had considerably more than enough."

"I have," he muttered. "Christ. I've never been a drinker, Rache. You know that."

Rachel dropped his clothes in the sink and began to wring them out, one garment at a time.

It was true. Not only had Beau never been a drinker, he'd never troubled to hide his contempt for people who used liquor as a crutch, either steadily or occasionally. Even as a child, he'd been rather priggish on the subject. It had been one of the many differences that had strained their youthful relations. If she, as the daughter and niece of drunkards, could feel charity toward them, why couldn't he?

She'd often wished for a certain answer to that question, whether it was for good or bad. But some things died hard. Not the love they had known. That, she firmly believed, was as dead as old ashes. But memories stayed banked and flickering, like ripe coals in a closet of the mind. Burned once, Rachel had refused for years to seek the vital living that would have replaced those memories with—better ones?

Different ones, in any case.

"I, ah, really shouldn't be here," he said to her back. "Not like this, I mean." His voice was still a little slurred with drink, but the words were consciously careful.

"You're quite well illuminated and it's raining like sixty out there," Rachel observed matter-of-factly. "At least stay till the rain lets up a little. And you needn't worry about embarrassing me. I run a men's rooming house, remember? What in the world were you doing out by my woodshed?"

Beau didn't reply. She glanced over her shoulder at him, sickling one eyebrow upward. He shifted uncomfortably on the chair. "Well, I . . . had it in my head I wanted to call on you."

"By the back door?"

"Damn it, I'd been drinking!"

"No. Really?"

"Don't laugh at me, Rache! Hell, I don't know what I had in mind. I think . . . just to see you and talk with you. But I'd changed my mind and was pulling my nag around. Then that lightning hit the tree. And you came running out. Is that my fault?"

Rachel wrung the moisture out of his coat and shook it out. Sight of the black armband on its sleeve brought a wave of remorse. She bit her lip and did not look around as she said, "Beau, I am sorry about Shad. I did think about coming to the funeral, but . . ."

"Oh—that. A lot of people didn't come. It's no matter. Nobody'd expect you to attend the obsequies for any Gannett. Or blame you, either."

So whatever had gotten him into this state had nothing to do with Shad's death. Unwilling to put the question to him point-blank, she finished wringing out the clothes and got out her clothes-hanging rack. She unfolded and set it up by the stove, and draped his garments over it.

"Rache . . ." Beau lowered his eyes as he spoke. "How has it been for you . . . these years?"

She opened the oven door and propped his wet boots in front of it. "As an ordinary citizen? Not too badly. Thanks largely to your mother. In her discreet way, she opened a number of doors for me. Pity I've never had the opportunity to thank her in person."

"Mother thinks highly of you. She has said as much."

"Really? Too bad she didn't feel that way 'back when.'"

"She didn't realize your mettle in those days. I guess... none of us did. As to her not calling on you or inviting you to tea, I think you'd have to agree it wouldn't be comfortable for either of you. Mother has made amends, or tried to, as best she can."

"And I appreciate it." Rachel dried her hands and turned to face him, folding her arms under her bosom, her manner neutral. "You may tell her so. And give her my best regards."

Beau lifted his gaze, a wry quirk on his lips. "She may need more. Even your prayers, Rache."

"What do you mean?"

"When word of Shad's death came, Mother had a... nervous collapse. Serious enough to confine her to bed and keep her there."

"Oh, Beau. I *am* sorry. It is Shad and your mother too."

A quizzical frown knit his brows. "I don't understand."

"I mean your reason for... drinking. First Shad, and now your mother—"

"No—" Beau was shaking his head before half her words were out. "It's a lot worse than that." He spoke with difficulty, as if dredging up each word from a bed of pain. "Well, not to dwell on it, I... I got mad at Lydia. I hit her. It's the only time I ever did anything like that, Rache—I swear it. And she ran from me—she fell down the stairs. Did you know she was about to have a baby?"

"Beau. Oh Lord."

"She lost the baby. That damned temper of mine." His hand formed a fist on his knee. "That goddamned evil temper of mine did it!"

"But she... will she be all right?"

"Yes, thank God. I mean, she won't die, at least. She is in the hospital..." His voice trailed away. He fingered his unshaved jaw. "That was yesterday. I've been in a daze ever since. Can't remember half of what I've done. Been drinking the whole time. Might as well be drinking water. Didn't feel any different from all of it. Christ! I *know* I'm loaded, but I don't *feel* it inside. You understand?"

"I... I think so."

The words left her as a husky whisper. She felt unnerved and shaken, as she couldn't remember feeling in her life. Not from what he had told her, for which she felt only a kind of horrified pity.

It was seeing Beau Gannett as she had never seen him—with his armor of capable and ruthless strength chinked, his defenses breached, the man beneath bared and hurting. To see him this way struck her with a terrible and poignant force. It stoked up all the memories of a time she had thought done with. Unforgotten, yes, but lacking any power.

Their eyes met and locked. And the years melted away.

For both of them—she knew suddenly and painfully—the past still lived. It was as though the vital part of her had been immured for twelve long years, as if the clock of young love had ticked to a stop in the summer of 1898 and was frozen in time. In a chill corner of her being she could feel it thawing, wrenching alive with an immediacy that was hungry and throbbing.

She pressed a hand to the pounding pulse in her throat, her eyes holding his in the grip of a common hypnosis. Beau got slowly to his feet and came to her, halting inches away. Memory and remorse worked a strange ferment in his dark face.

"Oh Rache," he whispered. "I never stopped loving you."

Rachel shut her eyes to his face. "Not enough, Beau. Never enough."

"Then God forgive me for being what I am." His hand touched the side of her face, cool against the hotness of her cheek. "Open your eyes. There. You know I loved you as much as I could ever love any woman. And I never loved any other. You know that ... don't you, Rache?"

"Yes."

Her lips formed the word soundlessly and stayed parted to his mouth as it came down to hers.

Desire spread like a fever through her body. She moaned in her throat, a sound compounded of despair and longing. A hunger that had held itself in abeyance for a dozen years.

When the kiss ended at last, he whispered a question; she murmured an answer. Still holding each other, they moved through the house, through rooms dimmed by the lowering daylight, reverberating to the muffled impact of thunder. Outside, the storm was dying away. But the storm within had only begun.

308

She opened the door of the small bedroom under the stairway. He entered, moving toward the lamp on the commode. Then she closed the door behind them, and they stood in pitch blackness.

"Rache . . . the lamp. I want to see you."

"Not till I'm ready. Please."

She undressed quickly, dropping her clothes on a chair. The glide and whisper of cloth on flesh tantalized her own senses; she could hear his stirrings, too. Then she stood naked to the dark and to her lover. Tinglings of anticipation shot to every nerve-end of her body. Her brain reeled to the drug of lust.

Yet she delayed, loosening the heavy coils of her hair, letting them tumble over her shoulders and down her back.

"Over here," she said softly.

Rachel heard him grope to her side, felt the warmth of him loom in back of her, then the heats and hardnesses of flesh on flesh, he as naked as she was, his arms circling her from behind and tightening. Then his hands moved, exploring and discovering, learning again the body that had been a slim girl's, the hips and thighs and buttocks that were as firm and satiny as he had known them, but ripened into those of a woman. His hands cupped the swelling globes of the mature breasts, his thumbs massaging the nipples in gentle teasing circles till the nubs stood out like rubbery buttons. Caressings that continued downward over dip and curve of belly to the triangular mat of her maturity.

Rachel pressed back against the growing tension of him, crying out softly in the agony of her need.

"The lamp," he said hoarsely. And moved away to light it.

When its saffron rays filtered through the room, she was lying on the bed. Her limbs were loose and wanton, her body goldened by lamplight and pinkened by a fiery flush of blood, all of it pulsing for one man.

She whispered his name.

Beau's eyes roved with a caress of their own over every detail of the lovely body his hands had fondled moments before. "My God," he whispered.

Again the thrill of a man's muscular body pressing hers length to length. For a time the kisses were tender and full of pauses murmurous with husky, broken words. Then the kisses

309

turned deep and fierce, and there was no room for speech, only the wild eloquence that tongues could find without language.

His mouth left hers to trail downward over the pulsing throat, over the sculptured beauty of the shoulders and the coral-crested breasts. The rasp of his whiskers only heightened Rachel's fierce joy in his masculinity. His tongue circled the pink-red aurolae of her nipples; he kissed and suckled the swollen teats till she gave out little mewling sounds of animal ecstasy.

Oh . . . oh God! The boy had done these things to her and it had not been the same. She wanted to be possessed by a *man*. This man. Him and him only.

Legs tangled and clasped, bodies thrashed and grappled, in the mounting fury of their lust. . . .

❧ thirty-nine ❧

AT SIX O'CLOCK Rudy locked the front door of the *Clarion* office and headed up the street to keep his supper engagement with Rachel.

His anticipation of seeing her was less intense than usual. He was too worried about his family's situation. Andrew Fordyce's arguments as to the value of his newspaper campaign seemed less and less cogent. Only his parents' insistence that he stay in town, coupled with Fordyce's own urgings, was holding him in Winterfield. If any real force were brought against his family, he was determined to join them.

At present it was hard to be sure exactly what was developing. There was a rumor abroad to the effect that the Gannetts had sent for a force of state troopers. It might well be true. By making his brother's killing appear to be murder in the first degree, Beau Gannett had gained the leverage necessary to summon all the official help he would need to subdue the Holmgaards.

The rain had ceased an hour ago, but there was a damp chill in the air. Chuckholes in the streets were full of murky puddles.

Rudy's shoes were caked with mud as he went up the flagstone path to Rachel's porch and knocked at the door.

When there was no response, he rapped again, louder. Once more he waited and knocked. A fourth attempt failed to bring Rachel, and he began to feel a dismal annoyance. Could she have forgotten she'd invited him? It occurred to him that she would be alone in the house; she might have suffered an accident.

He tried the doorknob, but found it locked. As he stood there, undecided as to whether he should try to force the lock or perhaps a window, the latch clicked free. The door opened several inches.

Rachel peered at him from around its edge, giving him a warm smile. She was wearing a gray wrapper which she held closed at the neck with one hand. Her hair was tousled, her beautiful face flushed and drowsy-eyed, as if she'd been aroused from sleep.

"I'm terribly sorry, Rudy. I took sick quite suddenly a little while ago. My stomach. I seem to have picked up some kind of summer influenza bug. Would you mind awfully if we postpone the dinner? Perhaps till next week?"

"No, of course not." He hesitated. "Is there anything I can do—anything I can get for you?"

"I don't think so. Rest and quiet are what I need. I've gotten a little sleep and I'll try to get some more."

"I woke you up. I'm sorry."

"Oh, that's nothing. I was just dozing off and on. Next week, then. I'll let you know. Good-bye, Rudy."

"Good-bye."

The door closed. He stood gazing at its blank panels for a moment. Biting his lip in disappointment, he went down the steps and skirted around the house. He was hungry and in no mood for preparing a meal in his drab quarters. Might as well take supper at the Star Cafe, and he could spare himself some puddle-hopping by cutting through the alley in back of Rachel's.

In the backyard Rudy came to a surprised halt. A large black horse, saddled and bridled, stood under the eaves of Rachel's woodshed, its reins ground-hitched. Funny place for anyone to leave his mount. He walked over to the animal. The black gave an irritated snort and swung its head away from his outstretched hand.

Rudy frowned. Something about this nag was familiar . . . and he had seen that finely tooled saddle somewhere. His gaze found the initials worked into the leather of the saddle skirt: BG.

And he knew. This was Beau Gannett's personal mount, Caesar. But what in the devil was he doing here?

A flare of suspicion made his brain reel. Shocked, he discarded the notion at once. And it promptly seeded itself again. Feeling a hollowness in his belly, Rudy looked around at Rachel's house. All the windows were dark; there wasn't a sign of life in any of them.

No. He would not believe it. Once, she and Gannett had been lovers. But that had been long ago. Rachel wouldn't lie about a thing like that . . . would she? And why ask him to dinner if she were planning a rendezvous with Gannett?

Unless it had been unplanned.

The thought stuck in his brain and burned like a ripe coal. He walked blindly past the woodshed and swung up the alley at a hasty, jerky stride.

Rachel . . . Rachel! Would she do that?

In the agony of doubt and jealousy, he didn't know what else to think. A hurting pulse of misery settled in his stomach. Hardly aware of what he was doing, Rudy slogged down a cross street and stopped at the first saloon in Thirsty Hollow. It was the one where he'd taken a beating at Bear Roback's hands, but the fact barely registered. He walked in and wedged himself between two drinkers at the crowded bar, saying hoarsely, "Whiskey."

A half hour later, after five times as much liquor as he'd ever taken at one time, the pain in his belly had deadened. But even thickheaded from drink, he felt no lessening of the burning jealousy, the tearing sense of loss. No . . . he hadn't lost Rachel Merrick; she hadn't been his to lose. But all the same—God!

Rudy thought muddily, *Suppose it's a mistake?* He had to find out. He had to be sure beyond any shred of doubt.

After a few fumbling moments, he dredged enough change out of his pockets to purchase a pint bottle of whiskey. Then he made his weaving, stumbling way back to the alley, back to Rachel's woodshed.

The black horse was still there.

The woodshed door, facing the rear of Rachel's house, stood partly open. Rudy entered the shed with its mingled odors of raw wood and damp earth. After dragging the heavy chopping block close to the door, he sat down on it, pulled the bottle's cork, and took a long swig. From here he could watch the back door of the house. If Beau Gannett came out, then Rachel had lied. Obviously. Simple.

Rudy lost track of time, sitting in the damp semidarkness and taking a pull at the bottle now and then. He had a dim realization of just how drunk he was when he found himself groping for whatever the hell reason he had for being here like this. And to consider the question for a few dumbly panicked seconds before it came back to him.

His stomach felt queasy. Suddenly the taste of liquor revolted him. He threw the bottle into a corner of the woodshed and sat rocking back and forth, holding his crossed arms over his middle. God, this was no time to be sick. But he was sick all the same, dropping onto his hands and knees and throwing up violently. He continued to feebly retch till his belly was empty. At last, slowly and weakly, he dragged himself to his feet.

The back door of Rachel's house opened. A man stepped out, pausing to sweep the adjoining houses and yards with a cautious glance.

Then he started across the yard toward the black horse. The day was graying toward twilight; the man's wide-brimmed hat put his face in shadow. But his stocky frame and impatient stride told his identity. It was Beau Gannett.

A spark of fury ignited Rudy's trampled emotions. He reeled out of the shed and lurched across Gannett's path, bringing him to a stop.

"Bastard," Rudy said in a sickly voice.

"What the hell?" Beau said blankly. "Get out of my way!"

Rudy muttered, "Fight. C'mon, fight," and drove the heel of his palm against the older man's chest, shoving him backward a step. *"Fight!"*

Beau's face hardened. He caught Rudy by the arms and

tried to whirl him out of the way. Rudy fell into a clinch. Gannett wrenched himself free of it, muttering, "God*damn!*" And hit Rudy in the pit of the stomach.

Rudy doubled over, gagging.

Gannett started to push past him. But the chaos of Rudy's brain was almost impervious to pain. Out of the dregs of rage and sorrow he found strength to hurl himself into Gannett and grapple him again.

This time Beau's fist exploded on the point of his jaw.

Rudy had a sharp salty taste of blood as his teeth met in his tongue. And he had a sense of falling. But he never knew when he hit the ground.

Rachel had let Beau out by her back door. Looking through a rear window of her darkened kitchen, she watched him cross the yard. Her thoughts were a bitter mingling of shame and sated pleasure. But all of it was wiped from her mind as she saw a man stumble out of her woodshed and lurch toward Beau. Rudy!

What happened next, the brief, furious scuffle and Rudy dropping to the ground, was over before she could move from the spot. Then she flung open the door and ran across the yard.

Beau looked shaken; stains of anger burned in his cheeks. "Who the hell is this drunk?" He pointed at Rudy. "He was hiding in your woodshed and he came at me like— Say, is he that Holmgaard whelp?"

Rachel didn't reply. She dropped to her knees on the wet grass and lifted Rudy's head. A reek of vomit and raw whiskey rose from his clothes.

"Oh God," she whispered. "Oh God, no."

What had led to it was clear as crystal. Rudy had short-cut across her backyard and had seen Beau's horse.

She felt a clammy sickness of her own. And drove it from her mind. "Help me get him in the house," she said crisply. "You get on his other side."

"What? Are you crazy, Rache? Leave this damn drunken pup where he is! Just who the hell does he think he—"

"Do as I say!" Rachel cut in coldly. "You're responsible for this, Beau. So am I."

"What do you mean?"

"Never mind, now. *Help me with him!*"

Beau growled something inarticulate. He stooped down and took hold of Rudy and hauled him up, Rachel lending what support she could on the boy's other side. Rudy was limp as a rag, his chin bouncing on his chest, as they maneuvered him inside and through the house, to the door of the small room under the stairs.

Beau said uncomfortably, "You want him here?"

"Why not? You don't feel *guilty* about anything, do you, Beau? Yes, in here. Set him in this chair." They eased the unconscious youth into an upholstered armchair. "Take off his coat and shirt and shoes. I'll get some warm water and we'll clean him up."

"And put him to bed, I suppose?" Beau asked sardonically.

"Yes, that too." Rachel looked him straight in the eye. "This is our doing. Not so much yours as mine. But we're both to blame. I think it best if you have no illusions about it."

"What the hell *are* you talking about?"

Rachel told him everything, briefly and matter-of-factly. As she spoke, she watched his expression change from shock to disbelief to acceptance. And finally, inevitably, to a savage and bitter disgust.

"You *invited* this kid to make love to you? Jesus!"

"Once," she said calmly. "It was a very special occasion, Beau. The breaking of a long, long fast, as it were. Some people bruise rather deeply, you ought to know by now. People like me. Like Lydia. Like this boy. You've had a hand in all those bruisings. You and I, one might say, did a collaboration on Rudy Holmgaard."

Beau stared at her as if he were no longer listening. His face shaded from repugnance to a scowling resignation. He looked like a little boy caught with his hand in the cookie jar, covering guilt with defiance.

"All right, Rache," he said heavily. "All right. I suppose you have reason, from *your* way of looking at it. Even a reason to think I ruined your life."

"I wouldn't put it quite that severely," Rachel said dryly. "But it's been no picnic, I warrant you. Will you take care of him as I asked? I'll fetch the water."

Rudy let out a few groans as he was being cleaned up, but

didn't really regain consciousness. It was just as well, Rachel thought dismally. She didn't want to confront whatever she would see in his face. Not right away. Tonight he would sleep it off and tomorrow she would talk to him. Try to make him understand.

But understand what?

She couldn't find an excuse that rang true even to her own mind. It wasn't loving Beau Gannett or making love with him that made her feel ashamed. It was the betrayal of a vow she had made to herself long ago.

Still, that wasn't the worst of it. When they had put Rudy to bed and she stood gazing down on him, the long lashes of his shut eyes dark and curling on his pale cheeks, his face incredibly boyish, she felt a pang of regret as sharp as any she'd known. What had she represented to his young mind? No doubt a feminine ideal that no ordinary woman could live up to. And she had destroyed it. She had broken something that could never be mended.

For all her good intentions, she had led Rudy Holmgaard on. Without really thinking about it, she had done coquettish little things to encourage a sensitive youth's infatuation. And had done so out of pure vanity, the hunger for tribute to her charms. It was one thing to take pleasure in the boy's company and even his adoration. Going to bed with him—just once— had been a spontaneous act. But offering little, demure enticements now and then because it amused her to do so had been playing with fire. Now, unwittingly or not, she had brought a shattering disillusion to the boy's emotional commitment that she had fed and nurtured. For her vanity's sake.

She closed the door of the small room and walked back to the kitchen. Beau followed her in silence.

He paused at the kitchen door, turning his hat between his hands. Rachel couldn't make out his expression in the half darkness; she supposed he was scowling. Beau usually scowled when he didn't know what to say.

"Rache . . . I'm sorry for this. Sorry it happened as it did, I mean. But not that you and I could give each other what we did."

"Neither am I," Rachel murmured. "Even if it was for one last time."

Beau's head lifted sharply; his voice was husky with disbelief. "You can't mean that. Not after what we had together just now! My God, it was like nothing I'd ever known!"

"I know. It was all of that for me, too. All I ever dreamed of knowing...with you. But it was the last time ever, Beau. Understand that."

His quick temper flared. "Are you denying how you feel about me, then? Go on—deny it!"

"I can't," she said calmly. "I did that for twelve years. I guess you're an incurable malaise with me. I can't lie to myself any longer. That's as may be. Years ago, I told you something...something I know you remember, because you always did, till today: I will not be any man's kept woman."

"Ah?" A confident fury stoked his angry tone. "Are you so sure? Suppose, just suppose, that I were to come tapping on your door another time. Say you were alone and lonely. As you were today. Are you so damned sure you could deny me? Be honest. What would you do?"

"If I were dead sure it was you," Rachel said quietly, "I would shoot you through the door."

"Rache. Good God!"

"I am sorry. I have to make you understand how much I mean it. I have my father's Colt pistol, Beau. I keep it loaded and ready, in case of prowlers. And I know how to use it. I would shoot you if I had to, and pray God I would only wound you. And I would swear that you tried to attack me. That is how much I mean it. Please believe me."

⚜ *forty* ⚜

ON THE MORNING after O'Dea's visit, Axel and Selma went to the woodsman's cabin to see how Elof was faring. They found him weak as a kitten, but chipper enough and not lacking in his usual irreverence. Obviously he was going to be all right.

O'Dea had summoned his daughter Swan from town to tend the invalid; she wasn't at all averse. Selma wondered if she'd been wrong about what she had put down as the girl's wanton manner. Swan appeared to be subdued, almost shy, in the presence of Elof's parents. She seemed completely devoted to Elof, doing little things to make him comfortable. Her feeling for him shone out of her dark eyes.

Elof might do worse. He'd managed to do worse through most of his young life. This Swan did not seem a bad girl so much as a foolish one. Her behavior had helped lead to Elof's being accused of murder, but once Selma had the full story from Elof of how everything had happened, she found it hard to condemn the girl.

On the evening of the third day after the onset of Arvid's infection, his fever broke. By the next morning the swelling

319

in his arm had gone down, and he was able to take a dish of broth for breakfast. Now that he was on the road to recovery, Selma felt free to remind Dani of her promise to go to Ohio with the twins.

Within a couple of hours, the girls' belongings were packed and stowed in the bed of the spring wagon. The team was hitched up; all the Holmgaards except Arvid gathered in the yard for the leave-taking.

The twins did a little sniffling, but not very much; they were too excited about "going on a trip." Dani was pale but calm. She gave her father a good-bye kiss, then embraced her mother with more warmth than she'd shown in some time.

"Take good care of yourself and the girls," Selma told her. "By now your Aunt Hedvig has the letter I sent her some time back, saying we might come for a visit. She won't know when to expect you, but you'll be welcome. When you get to Zanderville, Ohio, you can hire someone to drive you and your stuff to Uncle Soren's farm. Take care, Dani!"

Dani's smile had no heart in it. She was departing as an obedient daughter, not a willing one. "I will, Ma. I just wish you were coming too."

Selma gave a tight shake of her head, not trusting herself to speak.

Dani climbed to the wagon's high seat, taking her place beside Lennart. He sat hunched forward with the reins loose in his hands, looking glum; he hated towns. The twins scrambled into the wagon bed among the trunks and bags.

Lennart hoorawed the team into motion. Selma and Axel stood side by side as the wagon rolled away across the clearing toward the tote road. Both lifted their hands to the girls' waves just before the wagon disappeared into the forest.

Once it was out of sight, Axel turned on his heel and stalked away. Selma continued to gaze at the wall of greenery that had swallowed her children. She should be relieved, knowing they'd be removed from danger. But she wasn't. Something like an uneasy stir of premonition prickled her scalp.

She could not put a name to the feeling. She was a worrier, given to nervous forebodings. A lot of times her worries came to nothing at all.

* * *

After yesterday's heavy rain, a cool freshness clung to the forest along the road to Winterfield. Moisture sparkled on leaves and darkened the trunks of trees; the verdant greens of a July morning were washed to a sunny sheen.

But the sylvan beauties around her touched only the edge of Dani's consciousness. Sadness filled her thoughts.

Though never given to open displays of affection, Axel and Selma had always provided between them the adhesive that bound a family together: an unspoken feeling for one another that there had been no cause to doubt even when they had a shouting match.

That feeling was gone, vanished as if it had never been.

Even if all the problems were resolved, things would never be as they had been. How could the clock be turned back, bitter words be unsaid, angry deeds be undone? If people could really start over anew, it would be different. But everything that passed between them left a residue of change, like an indelible stain.

Dani was too gentle for strong angers; she felt more sadness than resentment. Every time she tried to assign blame, she only became confused. Nothing was as simple as it used to seem.

To blame Pa would be somewhat like blaming an elemental force—a force of nature which acted as it did because it couldn't do otherwise. As a child, she had worshipped him. Not because he was lovable or understanding. He'd never been either, and she had never expected such things of him. A good deal of that childish awe still threaded Dani's feeling for her father. She could never change toward him or Selma as they had changed toward each other. Not even Axel's blundering breakup of her relation with Adam could make a difference.

Adam.

If only she had some way of getting to Adam, of seeing him before they boarded the train today.

Of course he would find out from Rudy where she was, and nothing would prevent them from exchanging letters. Adam might even be able to visit her in Ohio. Perhaps they could arrange it. God willing, they might not be too long apart.

The wagon pitched and jolted over the badly rutted trail, causing the girls to clutch at the seat. The spring mire that had clogged the old tote road had dried to a stonelike consistency that even a heavy rain couldn't soften. The churned-up clay of the April thaw had hardened into ruts and ridges that threatened to shake the wagon apart.

Lennart's frame of mind didn't help matters. Like any immature boy assigned to a job he found onerous, he acted brattishly. He pushed the team, heedless of the girls' comfort. The wheels banged and bucked over every irregularity.

Finally Dani said, "For heaven's sake, Lennie! Slow down, will you *please!*"

"You got a train to catch," Lennart said sulkily.

"I know we have a train to catch, but we'll make it in good time. It's a milk run that won't stop in Winterfield till late this afternoon."

Lennart grumbled something and pulled the horses back to a reasonable pace.

They passed the pine-covered hill where Tom O'Dea's cabin stood. Dani thought of telling Lennart to stop so they could drop in on Elof. But they knew that he was rapidly improving and should be up and about in no time.

Maybe we are luckier than we should be, Dani thought.

Beyond O'Dea's, the tote road was less rugged and they made better time. By now Julia and Erika had decided this whole business was an adventure. The two of them began to get rambunctious in the back of the wagon, tussling back and forth among the bags.

Dani twisted around on the seat to speak sharply to them.

At that moment a man's voice called sharply, "Hold up there! Throw up your hands!"

There were at least four of them. They came jumping out from behind the cover of brush and deadfalls on either side of the trail. They were all men and maybe they all had guns, and Dani thought there were four of them. It happened so quickly she could hardly be sure of anything.

Lennart let out a yell and jerked at the reins so hard that the horses were thrown in panic. Then he grabbed under the seat for the rifle he had cached there.

Shots. At least two shots.

Dani would remember two shots being fired. Maybe there were more. She felt a hard blow, a terrific punch of a blow,

322

in the middle of her body. And she was aware of Lennart spinning sideways off the seat.

Dani saw him fall to the ground. He fell as loosely as a rag doll. She thought to herself that Lennart had been killed. Somehow knowing it from the way his body hit the rutted earth. She realized that Lennart was dead even before a gush of blood over her shirtwaist and skirt made her think dumbly, *I've been shot!*

Then Dani was toppling sideways too. She had a shadowy sense of falling into oblivion. The cries of her sisters made only fading echoes along the thread of her consciousness. . . .

🔁 *forty-one* 🔁

SELMA WENT ABOUT her morning's chores in a mechanical way. At noon she prepared a meal for Axel and herself. They never exchanged a word as they ate, and she hardly noticed that, either.

Selma couldn't remember when any home of hers had ever been quiet for more than minutes at a time, during any day. She had been born into a lively and raucous family, and the one she and Axel had raised was no different. The clock on a kitchen shelf ticked with a lifeless monotony; a rasp of cricket song drifted through an open window. Ordinarily unnoticed, these noises seemed aggravatingly loud.

A house with no life in it was oppressive to her. After washing the few dishes, then looking in on the sleeping Arvid, she decided to go for a walk.

Her stroll took her along the river's edge. From here she had a clear view of the fields to the north, where Axel was working along the rows of 'bagas, hoeing out weeds.

On her right side as she walked, the river was filled with a jumble of logs from bank to bank. At the butt ends of logs and in places where bark was scraped off, sun-bleach had begun to gray the bare wood. Weeks ago Axel had raised the dam's sluice gates enough to let some of the backwater, already shrinking in the summer heat, flow out, leaving much of the mass of logs high and dry. Already grub rot was starting to attack them. Axel had taken a grim defiance in his action.

By now Selma was past the point of being appalled by anything he might do. It could be, ran her speculation, that he was just plain crazy. There had been something quite insensible about a lot of his behavior right from the start, where this dam was concerned.

Now, Axel had gone beyond her reach. There was no longer a touching. When that was gone and you couldn't even care—what sort of caring was there any more?

She felt weary with a tiredness deeper than any that physical work might cause. The morning's after-storm coolness was gone, swallowed in another spasm of humid warmth. It increased her drowsiness. She walked back to the yard and climbed into the hammock stretched between a pair of shady oaks. Crickets stridulated; a breeze swept the leaves. Flecks of sun and shadow danced on her face, flicking points of light between the half-shut lids of her eyes.

Selma's thoughts went lazily awash. She dozed.

Otto's barking brought her suddenly awake.

Hours had passed. The sunlight was slatting almost horizontally through the leaves, and shadows were long. She rubbed a hand over her eyes, feeling a rush of chagrin at having slept so long.

One late-afternoon shadow lay across the hammock. Suddenly that shadow moved. Selma turned her head in quick alarm.

Tom O'Dea was standing not six feet away. His face was set like brown stone. Still confused by a fog of sleep, a little flustered too, she swung herself out of the hammock, adjusting her disarranged skirt.

"Uh, Mr. O'Dea—?"

"Mistress, ye'd better take a strong hold on yourself. I've bad news for you."

Selma blinked at him, unspeaking.

O'Dea began to talk.

The sunny world darkened in her eyes. She swayed; she would have fallen but for O'Dea. His big arm went around her shoulders, and he guided her over to the porch. Selma slumped onto the bottom step. A pall of horror had locked around her brain, freezing the core of thought.

Then she was aware of Axel coming across the yard at a lope. Otto's barking must have fetched him. He was coming fast, yet in the dark shimmer of her vision his movements seemed as sluggish as those of a swimmer moving against a current. The omnipresent rifle was swinging in his fist.

"What is this?" He hurled the words at O'Dea with a half snarl.

Tom O'Dea told it all again, and now in more detail. Selma still felt numb, but his words registered with terrible, indelible clarity.

This noon O'Dea had been returning from town when he heard several shots up the forest-flanked road ahead of him, and at no great distance. Very quickly he'd come on the scene. The Holmgaard wagon and team of horses were standing in the trail. The two little girls were in such a pitch of hysteria that they could tell him little that was coherent or that made any sense. But the bloody evidence at hand had told its own story. Lennart Holmgaard had been killed instantly by a bullet through the head. Dani was sprawled on the ground beside him, her clothes covered with blood. For a moment O'Dea had believed her to be dead as well. But her pulse had still carried a thread of life; he had done his best to staunch the flow of blood.

Since they were closer to Winterfield than to his cabin, O'Dea had decided to take the lot of them, the dead boy and the wounded girl and the twins, to the hospital in town. Driving the wagon as fast as he'd dared, he had arrived at St. Mary's Hospital within the hour. Leaving the girls there, he had hurried back on foot to give Axel and Selma the grim news.

"Who were they?" Axel spoke with difficulty, his voice labored and disbelieving. "Who did it?"

O'Dea shook his head. "That'd be anyone's guess. They was gone by the time I come on the scene. Took to the woods . . . I guess scared to death by what they'd done. My guess, they was a passel of local yokels who threw in together and came trying for that money that's on your head."

"Then what's the sense to what they done?" Axel roared painfully. "Why? *Why shoot at my kids?*"

"That needs to be another guess. Mine, for what it may be worth, is they heard the wagon coming and laid up by the trail. When they saw it was just the young'uns, they thought to take 'em anyway. Maybe use 'em as hostages to force your surrender. Who knows? But it's possible that young Lennie went after that rifle o' his. There was one laid by next to hand, underneath the seat. Well, if he did—"

"Gud in himmel!" Axel shook a closed fist above his head. "If I find those men . . . !"

"I wouldn't bank on that coming about, Mr. Holmgaard," O'Dea said gravely. "They could of been any lot of spalpeens from around these parts. Don't seem too likely your daughter or the kids may be in a case to identify 'em. But that remains to be seen. Anyway, whoever they was, I don't reckon they was part o' that crowd from Madison."

Axel's gaze flickered with banked flame. "What? What crowd? From where?"

"Well then, ye've had no word. There's talk in Winterfield to the effect that the Gannetts have summoned up a whole gang of Pinkertons, state police, and whatnot, and are deputizing a mess of locals into the bargain. Then they will all come and take you in your shoes. That's the word I got, rumor or no."

Selma listened to it all with thoughts that pulled against one another and made no sense. She heard her own voice sound calm and low: "I have to go to Dani. I have to go to her."

"Aye," O'Dea said soberly. "Your girl's in a serious way, and I can't deceive you there. I will go with you to town, if you want."

Selma rose to her feet and looked at her husband. "Axel? Now do we go to Winterfield?"

Axel's glittering stare made a long swing across his house, his outbuildings, his fields. His eyes came back to her, but she had the feeling he did not see her at all.

"The place," he muttered. "They will not take the place. Not while there's a man to hold it."

Selma wondered if she'd heard him correctly. "What? What did you say?"

"There's me. There's Arvid. We can hold it. They will need to send a goddamn army to take us."

O'Dea said mildly, "Well, if the tale's true, they'll have exactly that."

"Then let 'em come, damn 'em. Let 'em come!"

It was hard for Selma to say anything at all without being sick on the spot. But she made herself say it. "Our boy is dead. Maybe our girl will die too. Do you care about this?"

"*Ja*, damn it! But what do I do? I can't change what's done. I can't do anything for Dani. But, by *Gud*"—he thumped his chest with a balled fist—"I can fight for what I got! Right here!"

Selma stared at him. She felt herself start to tremble all over.

"*What* have you got, Axel? Tell me! What have you got here?"

"What . . . ?"

"You got nothing!" she blazed at him. "Not a damn thing! We had it all—all that any two people could want! And you have thrown it away, piece by piece! Well, by *Gud*, I will not stand by and see you throw away all the rest. Do you hear? *I will not!*"

Axel looked disconcerted; his eyes wavered. "What are you saying now?"

"I say this is *the end!* There will be no more of it for me. I am leaving!"

"*Helvete*, that's what I told you to do."

"You don't see it." She braced her fists on her hips and lashed out at him. "You don't see anything, do you? Not even when it's too late! I tell you that I am leaving you for good. Do you understand? For *good*, Axel!"

His face reddened and swelled. "Leave then!" he roared. "*Leave*, goddamn it!"

Selma, more shaken by her own vehemence than by his, turned her back on him. "Now, Mr. O'Dea—we will go, eh?"

❧ six ❧

The Siege

❧ *forty-two* ❧

SOMETIME IN THE early morning hours, Rudy awakened from a deep sleep to find himself in Rachel Merrick's house, in the familiar room under the stairs. Still half drunk and not too impossibly sick as yet, he felt a fierce determination to get out and away from there. A determination fueled by shame and disgust. Somehow he pulled on his clothes and made his way out of the house and back to his own quarters above the newspaper shop.

Fully dressed, he collapsed across his cot and into another deep sleep. When he next opened his eyes, around noon, a blaze of sunlight from the north window cut against his eyeballs like fire, making him cry out and burrow under the bedclothes. For hours he dozed on and off, feeling only a little better each time he awakened. At one point during the afternoon, someone came pounding loudly at the door of the newspaper shop. Rudy refused to answer it, and finally whoever it was went away.

By early evening he was slept out.

He lay on his back, blinking at the dim ceiling. It had been a hell of a bat for someone unused to much drinking. After more than twenty-four hours, he still felt sick as a cat. He was sore in more places than he cared to think about. Mostly in his head, where a drumroll of pain still slugged at its back and a knife-edge of pain sliced at his eyeballs. His stomach wasn't too queasy any longer, but it ached from repeated retchings. His tongue felt like a raw pulp where he had bitten it through when Beau Gannett hit him the second time.

I must have been crazy, he thought.

He had a vague memory of confronting Beau and getting knocked down by him. After that, only a patchwork of painful impressions.

To hell with all of it. What did any of it matter?

Rudy stared at the ceiling with baffled bitterness. If it really mattered to Rachel, why would she jeopardize that precious and hard-won reputation of hers by taking up with the likes of Beau Gannett once again? For that matter, had she ever really quit him? Or had she lied about that, too? For hours, through nasty scraps of wakefulness, Rudy had tormented himself with speculations that had chased each other in his mind like mice running in a circle.

Now he just felt sick of the whole mess.

He should try to get up, he supposed. Even if he felt as though if he raised his head, it might roll off his shoulders.

Rudy rolled out of his coat, lighted a lamp against the growing darkness, and shuffled over to the washstand. He gazed at himself in the cracked mirror above it. He looked exactly as scruffy and seedy as he felt. Maybe he'd feel better if he cleaned up a little.

He stripped off his clothes, gave himself a sponge bath, shaved off his downy smudge of beard, and put on a fresh change of clothes. Ravenously hungry by now, he went out to the kitchen area, boiled up a pot of coffee, and made himself a couple of cold beef sandwiches. He wolfed down only one before a warning quiver in his stomach told him not to overdo it.

He did feel a little better.

Rudy was pouring himself a third cup of coffee when he heard someone knock loudly at the outside door of the newspaper office.

Rudy got up and went to one of the windows facing the

street. He wrestled it open, stuck his head out, and called to the man below, "Hey! What is it?"

The man stepped back from the door and looked up. His face had a pallid saffron hue in the glow from a street lamp. It was Hans Hoffenmeier.

"Rudy?"

"What's up, Hans?"

"It's about your brother," Hans said soberly. "Your brother and—"

"What? *What* brother?"

"The one that is called Lennart. Just now the news I heard, and I come to tell you."

"Damn it, *what?* What about Lennie?"

"He shot to death is. And your sister, she is called Dani? She is shot too."

Selma and O'Dea had come to town on foot, arriving about sunset. They went directly to the hospital on Winterfield's south side. A grave, rather shy young doctor named Mueller told them of Dani's chances for recovery, which he estimated were "just about fifty-fifty."

The bullet had entered her side at the waistline, angled through a kidney, and had somehow lodged against her back-bone close to the spine. It lay so near the surface of the back that the flesh in the region was swollen purple. Removal, as such, would be easy to accomplish. The danger lay in the lead slug's proximity to the spinal cord, so that any operation would be a definite risk. If the bullet were left to encyst, a chance movement of the patient might cause it to shift position.

That, Dr. Mueller told Selma with all the deadly gravity of his youth, could result in paralysis from the waist down.

What all the discussion boiled down to was that Dr. Mueller and his older colleague, Dr. Hammerstein, had concurred that to operate or not to operate was like a choice between the frying pan and the fire. While Mueller didn't quite say as much, Selma sensed he was leaving the decision up to her.

She made it quickly: Dani must not be made to live with such a thing. The bullet must be removed.

So Dani went into surgery. Selma watched as she was wheeled into the operating room. There had been no opportunity to

333

speak with her. Dani had been heavily dosed with morphine after O'Dea had brought her in. As her daughter was taken from her sight, Selma thought, If she dies on the operating table, it will be my fault. And there will be no good-byes.

Selma and O'Dea and the twins returned to the waiting room. To wait...

Selma's belly was sour with worry, her nerves wrung dry with nervous exhaustion. What a depressing place this was. If a person had to keep a life-or-death watch, almost anyplace would be better than a hospital.

St. Mary's of Winterfield—established in 1895 by the order of German nuns who still maintained it—was a big frame box of a building; it was as drably utilitarian on the inside as it was on the outside. The rooms were like boxes within a box, Selma thought: the walls uniformly plastered and whitewashed, unadorned except for isolated pictures and plaster figures (mostly of the Crucifixion, featuring a bethorned and bleeding Christ) that she thought ugly and tasteless. The strong odors of sweetish ether and sour antiseptic that pervaded every corner of the place turned her stomach. Heavily cowled nuns, soft-voiced and soft-stepping, seemed to be everywhere. She found that unsettling too. It was a place of sterility; it held more of non-life than of real living.

Selma was ashamed of the thought. These sisters had goodness in them; they were dedicated and hardworking. It was just that so much in this place seemed alien to her Protestant eyes. Sensing her discomfort, O'Dea gently kidded her about it. For him, he declared, setting foot in a Catholic hospital was almost like coming home: Two aunts of his, and one sister, had become nuns.

Thank *Gud* for the kids and O'Dea. Having them beside her in this place, at this time, was an anchor of sorts. They demanded her attention; the twins complained and O'Dea talked, trying to divert her and succeeding a little.

She wished Rudy were here to share the waiting, to lend her the strength he always did. Fearing that if she left the hospital she might miss some crucial word from the operating room, Selma asked O'Dea to find Rudy and tell him what happened. Very shortly, O'Dea returned with the news that he couldn't locate her son. All his banging at the door of the newspaper shop had brought no response. Supposing that the boy must be out and around somewhere, O'Dea asked around town. But nobody had an idea of Rudy's immediate whereabouts.

O'Dea popped in and out of the hospital a few more times in an effort to find Rudy. (So he claimed. Selma suspected that actually he found the sights and smells of the place as unsettling as she did.)

It had been a hard day for the children. But much of the waiting, if perhaps not the absolute worst, was over and done with. The twins began to get fretful and whiney, disturbing the hospital hush. Several times Selma fiercely shushed them. But she did it halfheartedly, knowing that in some respects they felt more miserable than she. Time passed so slowly for a child. Also the girls had missed their supper.

"We're not leaving here till word of your sister comes," she told them sharply. "So be still!"

"Why now," Tom O'Dea said gravely, "it's no small thing for a small stomach, this missing a meal. Tell ye what. I'll take this saucy pair of wenches to supper. You carry on, mistress. We'll fetch you back a sandwich or something."

"Don't, please. I couldn't eat. And you shouldn't trouble yourself so, Mr. O'Dea. You've done enough already . . . for all of us."

"Trouble! Thought you knew me better, mistress. Trouble is the last thing an easy-livin' scut like me would court. Why no, indeed—this is my pleasure." He winked at the children. "What about it? Do I get to squire the two prettiest girls in town to a local beanery?"

Erika said seriously, "Do we get something to eat?"

"That's what I'm telling ye, darlin'. Let's be on our way, eh?"

With a twin on either side, his big paws engulfing their small hands, O'Dea marched out of the waiting room and out through the foyer.

A smile flickered on Selma's lips. She was coming to lean on the burly Irisher in ways that went beyond any physical attraction. Of course O'Dea himself had brashly declared as much, that time she'd whopped him with a piece of wood.

What had surprised her today and now, waiting with him, was that she no longer felt inclined to deny the fact.

Maybe later it will worry me, she thought remotely. I wonder if it will.

Selma tried to make her body relax on the wooden bench, propping her back against the wall. But her shoulder blades were sore from hours of such leaning; her seat ached from the hardness of the bench; her fingers kept aimlessly fiddling with the pleats of her skirt.

Finally she got up and slowly paced the little room back and forth, as she'd done countless times.

The family. Always in her mind the unity of the family had been like a talisman: a candle held against the dark.

No more, she thought bitterly. No more!

If not for that foolishness, she would have taken Dani and the twins away long ago. Dani would not be lying under the surgeon's knife—maybe Lennart would be alive.

Lennart. A numbness filled her mind whenever it touched on Lennart. The reaction was so intense that she could feel hardly anything as yet. When they had shown her his body, it had hardly seemed real. I loved him, Selma thought, but I never did much thinking about him. None of us did.

Even now, when Lennart was dead, she could barely think of him in her concern for the still-living daughter. . . .

"Evening, Mrs. Holmgaard," Adam Gannett said.

Selma had seated herself on the bench again. Now she looked up with a jerk of surprise.

Adam was standing in front of her. He wore a pleasant, tentative smile.

The hospital's evening visitor's hours had kept a steady trickle of people coming in and out of the place. She'd taken vague notice of them, the foyer being widely visible from the waiting room, but afterward had paid them little attention. Sunk in gloom, she hadn't even noticed Adam's approach.

"Hello . . . Mr. Gannett," she said in a mild confusion. And thought, My *Gud*—he doesn't know!

Adam seated himself on the bench, twirling his hat on one big hand. "I just came from seeing my sister-in-law . . . my brother Beau's wife. She lost her first baby a few days ago."

"Oh? I'm—I'm sorry."

"All of us are. She'll be in the hospital a little longer, but she's coming along fine. What brings you here, Mrs. Holmgaard? Nothing serious in the family, I hope."

He was a nice young man—friendly and concerned. She thought wildly, How do I tell him?

Somehow, she managed to. She stumbled over the words at first, and even more as she saw him flinch and blanch, and saw the sickness that seeped into his face. He gripped the end of the bench so tightly that Selma thought he was in danger of falling.

Alarmed, she caught at his arm. "Mr. Gannett!"

"It's all right." His voice seemed to come from a distance. He straightened on the bench, giving his collar a tug. Some of the shock had ebbed from his face, but it was still deathly pale.

"Go on," he said.

Selma told him as much as she knew.

For a long time, Adam held a strained silence. Then he said in a dazed murmur, to Selma or to himself, "I didn't know. All the while I was visiting with Lydia . . . Dani was right here. Maybe dying. And I didn't even know."

Now there were two of them. The mother and the lover. Two that would not break vigil until word came to them.

Selma felt a strangeness in waiting with Dani's young man, the sweetheart outlawed from the normal courtship to which he had every right. Yet it seemed a natural thing too, this waiting. Even reassuring—behind the pall of their mutual misery.

They talked a little.

Chatted, really, about odd matters that skirted the real center of their concern. Adam sounded like a man in a trance, one whose mind was far from what he was saying. Do I sound like that? Selma wondered. It was very hard to think about and then be able to tell for sure.

In a kind of mechanical way, Adam tried to reassure her. He told her not to worry about the operation. Dick Mueller, who was a fishing buddy of his, was a really fine surgeon—a graduate of Detroit Medical College who had also studied in Heidelberg and Vienna—and you wouldn't find any better in all of northern Wisconsin. With him operating and an "old reliable" like Doc Hammerstein assisting, all the odds should be in Dani's favor.

But Selma was no longer listening. Looking out into the foyer, she saw Rudy coming through the door.

In a moment she was embracing her son, hugging him tightly. Then she held him away from her and eyed him critically. Rudy looked sickish and pale; her first thought was that he was spending too much time indoors. *"Gud bevara!* Look at you," she began to say, but he interrupted:

"Dani, *Mor*—how is she?"

"We don't know yet. They are operating on her to take out a bullet." Briefly, Selma told how it had happened. Then she said severely, "Rudolf, where have you *been?*"

"In my room."

"Ah? Were you there when Mr. Tom O'Dea come banging on your door?"

"Did he? I suppose I was." A forced grin touched his lips. "I had too much to drink last night, *Mor*. It really floored me."

Selma shook her head disappointedly. Rudy—of all people. She'd thought that he might be one Holmgaard male who would always resist the lure of whiskeyed whoop-ups. Maybe it had been too much to expect.

Selma sat beside her son and tightly held his hand. There was something beaten and withdrawn in his manner; she did not like it, and she wondered what had caused it. More than just a hangover was troubling him.

In a little while O'Dea returned with the twins.

"Mistress, I've grim news for you, I'm afraid," he said without preliminary.

"What is it?"

"Why, it seems this rumor of detectives and state men coming for your husband had some meat to it. The late train pulled into the depot as we was coming back from the restaurant. A whole lot of men piled off it, a hard-looking bunch. I caught enough of the talk to be sure why they're here."

Rudy got slowly to his feet. "They'll be going after Pa . . . and Arvid."

"Aye, directly. They and some locals are assembling at the Armory—I gather to lay their plans." O'Dea shuttled a curious glance at Adam. "This 'un's brother will be addressing 'em, so the talk is."

Adam gave a wry, bitter nod. "True. But it's no doing of mine, Mrs. Holmgaard . . . and there's nothing I can do to stop it. I have no voice in my family's affairs anymore."

"I've got to go to the farm," Rudy muttered. "Tell Pa—"

"No!" Selma caught at his sleeve. "Don't, Rudolf. He broke the law, and sooner or later this had to happen. Don't you break it too! You're not in trouble. Do you want to be?"

A frown tightened his brow. "No . . . of course not. But I can't just let Pa and Arvid take on a mob of armed men and I don't lift a finger. It's all right for you and the girls to leave, *Mor*, but a man—"

"—does not have to be a damned fool!" Selma blazed.

She was on her feet too, and she gripped his wrists with her two hands. "Rudolph . . . don't. Stay with us. Your duty is here, with me and the girls. And Dani! Will you just leave without knowing whether your sister dies or lives?"

Tom O'Dea cleared his throat gently.

"Well, mistress—I'm thinking we'll have that in a moment, the answer about your girl." He was gazing down the corridor that led off the foyer. "Here comes young Dr. Mueller now, and he has the look of a man who's done his work."

Before he even spoke, Mueller gave them the answer. His usually somber face wore a smile as he came up to them.

"Your daughter will be fine," he told Selma.

She sank back on the bench. She was starting to tremble as she had when she'd declared to Axel that she was leaving him for good. But now for a different reason.

Like her, Adam was unable to find words. All he could do was thrust out a hand toward Mueller, who gripped it tightly, still smiling. "She's a mighty pretty girl, Ad," he said. "Is it too early for me to offer congratulations?"

Rudy sat down by his mother and she held him tightly for a moment, fighting for control of herself. Then she looked at Mueller.

"Doctor, when—?"

"She is still under anesthesia, Mrs. Holmgaard. You should be able to look in on her early tomorrow."

Selma nodded. Suddenly her eyes blurred and she had to blink them clear, smiling at Rudy. Then her smile faded.

Rudy's face no longer looked sick. It was cold with purpose. "I have to, *Mor*," he said quietly. "There's nothing to hold me now. I've got to go and be with Pa and Arvid."

"Rudolf . . . you are wrong." She barely whispered the words. "What he is doing is a wicked foolishness."

"Maybe," he said. "Maybe it is. But that doesn't change anything. It's what *I've* got to do."

❧ forty-three ❧

RUDY PAUSED OUTSIDE the hospital. If the meeting at the Armory was just getting underway, he had plenty of time to get word to his father and brother. Maybe he ought to go to that meeting . . . at least long enough to get an idea of what the enemy had in mind.

That's why Pa had wanted him to stay in town. To size up the plans of the opposition. All right, then.

The Armory was a large, brick-walled building located in downtown Winterfield. Its long, well-lighted hall was starting to fill up as Rudy went in. Fierce partisanship, a yen for excitement, or plain curiosity had brought a good-sized crowd to the gathering. They were all men, and they were standing around or sitting on benches along the walls. There was a wooden dais up front with a speaker's stand and some empty chairs.

As Rudy stepped inside, Andrew Fordyce hailed him: "Hey! Over here."

Fordyce was seated on a bench at the rear of the hall, close to the door. He had a notebook spread open on his knee, and was rapidly scrawling in it.

"Sit down," he invited, moving over to make room on the bench. "Say, where the hell were you a little while ago? After the train brought me in, I dropped in at the office. You were nowhere about—upstairs or downstairs."

"I was at the hospital," Rudy said quietly.

"Oh. Yeah, I heard about your brother and sister." Fordyce shook his head soberly. "Sorry about that. Too bad it had to happen. How's your sister doing?"

"She'll live."

"That's swell." Fordyce said it half absently; he was busy jotting down more notes.

Rudy eyed him narrowly. Was that all the man had to say? He bore a full measure of responsibility for what had happened to Lennart and Dani. And all he had to say was "sorry" and "swell."

But you helped him, Rudy reminded himself. You thought maybe he was right. Wasn't that what you told Ma?

To cover his thoughts he said, "Where'd you hear about Dani and Lennart?"

"In Tomahawk. It's a stop on the railroad line, and the telegraph office there had received word from Winterfield."

Rudy nodded. Fordyce had taken the train to Madison a couple of days ago, hoping either to substantiate or discredit rumors that Governor J. O. Davidson would send a force of state troopers to Winterfield.

Fordyce grinned. "Seems the governor turned a cool ear to the urgings of the Gannetts and their bigwig friends. Instead of dispatching state troopers, he's sent along two personal emissaries. His attorney general, Frank B. Gilbert, and a Colonel O. G. Munson, who—so they say—is the governor's personal secretary."

Rudy felt a small lift of hope. "Does that mean the governor wants to find a peaceable solution?"

"Sure he does," Fordyce said carelessly. "Keeping the peace is always good politics, unless the electorate's fired up agin something. Right now it's mostly fired up on your pa's side. Davidson knows that."

"But I thought the Gannetts had imported a lot of toughs."

"Paid for out of their pocket. Some Pinkerton dicks, the talk has it. But no agents sent by the state." Fordyce chuckled. "Beau must be mad as the devil over that kind of weak spot in his legal aegis. Of late, he's been trying like hell to put a respectable face on things. It's the same old lumber-baron horse-shit—screw the people in the ass any way that'll work, just so the boys on top get theirs. But it looks good in print. Hell, you must have read what our sterling rival sheet had to say about it in their yesterday's ish."

"Well, um, no," Rudy said sheepishly. "I was about four sheets to the wind last evening."

"You? Why, Rudy! For shame. Here."

Grinning, Fordyce handed him a crumpled copy of the *Winterfield Daily News*. It contained a first-page announcement of tonight's meeting, ostensibly to provide a public forum for discussion of the Holmgaard stalemate. Transparently, it was an effort by the Gannetts to rally public support behind their position. The killing of Shad Gannett had given his family a better handle on things, and they meant to strike while the iron was hot. The Armory meeting was scheduled to coincide with the arrival of the state agents.

"I just now found that copy lying on the bench," Fordyce commented around his well-chewed cigar as he continued to write notes. "Christ! My last few days have been spent traveling on lousy milk-run trains, hanging around the state capitol, and logging one night's sleep in a shitty Madison hotel room. But it's been worth it. Came back on the same train that brought the Gannetts' hired toughs, so I picked up an earful all the way."

Fordyce's appearance bore out his itinerary. His clothes were dirty and rumpled; a reddish growth of several days' whiskers burred his jaws. His eyes were blinking and bloodshot from lack of sleep, and they held a kind of feverish intensity.

A party of four men entered the hall, pushing their way to the platform up front. They shed their overcoats and seated themselves on the four empty chairs. Rudy recognized Beau Gannett and Sheriff Joe Pleasants. Fordyce told him that the other two were Colonel Munson and Attorney General Gilbert.

The hall was pretty crowded by now. Rudy and Fordyce stood up so they could get a better view of the proceedings.

If Beau Gannett was as angry as Fordyce had suggested, Rudy couldn't discover any trace of it in his demeanor. Beau looked entirely relaxed, sitting with legs crossed and arms folded, exchanging chitchat with the governor's men.

"Looks at his ease, doesn't he?" Fordyce murmured. "Wonder what he has up his sleeve."

Presently Beau got up and walked to the speaker's stand, raising his hand for silence. He introduced Gilbert and Munson to the crowd. Then he gave everyone a shock by telling of the shooting and killing of Lennart Holmgaard and the serious wounding of his sister, just hours ago.

Lifting his arms to silence the outbreak of startled reaction, Beau went on to announce that while the identities of the killers were still unknown, no effort would be spared to apprehend them. In the name of the Gannett Logging and Boom Company, he was offering a thousand dollars reward for information leading to their capture. It equalled the amount that the Gannetts had already posted for the capture of Axel Holmgaard.

Fordyce gave a cynical chuckle, underpitching his voice for Rudy's ears.

"Listen to that, will you! That cold-blooded attack on two poor innocent kids could have wiped Beau's plans to hell and gone. Instead, by being one of the first to learn of it—and now revealing it along with a big public denunciation of it— I guess he's damped in advance about half the sentiment there'd be generated for you Holmgaards otherwise."

But not all of it. Quite a number of men were trying to drown Beau out before he'd finished. A large segment of the audience was yelling bloody murder, even shaking fists at him, as he walked back to his chair.

Of those who remained silent, Fordyce remarked, he thought a lot were various locals whom Joe Pleasants had pressed into service as deputies. And these, he judged, were mostly restless malcontents who found a prospect of punitive action against almost anyone more alluring than the meager wage paid them by the county.

It was left to Sheriff Pleasants to introduce a short speech by Attorney General Gilbert, who somewhat mollified the shouters by stating that his mission was to mediate peaceably in the

344

Holmgaard affair. Exactly how he meant to do so was left unsaid.

Afterward Beau Gannett stood up and declared his absolute concurrence with the spirit of the governor's intent, and his promise to do all in his power to help Gilbert and Munson solve the impasse by any means short of bloodshed.

That brought yells of "Liar!" and "Damned hypocrite!" and the hubbub broke out afresh. Some people in the crowd were on the edge of coming to blows.

Rudy was still partly hung over. The rising hubbub of the crowd mingled with the stench of packed bodies and tobacco smoke made it worse. The aura of hatred and violence that pervaded the big hall was more intangible, but it fed into his nausea just as much.

Fordyce looked stimulated by all of it. His teeth were grinning and working around his dead cigar as he avidly scrawled more notes. He was *enjoying* this, Rudy thought, beyond any demand of lofty idealism.

He looked from Fordyce to Beau Gannett and back again, suddenly thinking, These goddamned hypocrites. What's to choose between them?

Feeling an excess of sick disgust choke up in him, he turned abruptly and walked out of the Armory. He leaned against its brick wall and let a night wind cool his sweating face.

A moment later, Fordyce exited and came over to him, frowning. "What's the matter, boy?"

"Nothing." Rudy straightened away from the wall, not looking at the older man. "I mean to go join my pa. If he's in a fight, my place is with him."

"The devil," Fordyce said softly. "I saw your face, Rudy. The way you looked at me. Like I turned your stomach."

"I guess it's turned, all right."

"Listen, boy—" Fordyce raised a hand to his shoulder.

Rudy stepped back from the hand, his eyes hard. "You'd better let go, Andrew. I've heard all your arguments. Or read them. I don't know who's right or who's wrong. What I know is that my brother is dead, my sister was nearly killed, and my father and mother are on the outs, likely for good. That's enough cost to our family for one moral campaign, don't you think?"

Fordyce's lips curled wryly around his cigar. "And I'm to blame. Is that it?"

"Sure. Me too. So is Pa. Beau Gannett. George Slocum. A lot of people, maybe. All I'm saying, Andrew, is that I'm sick of it."

"Sick of me?"

"Yes."

Rudy said it without thinking. There had been no need to think, and he did not regret saying it.

"Kind of sudden feeling, wasn't that, Rudy?"

"I guess it was."

"All right, I'll say it. Why?"

"I suppose it was seeing how damned happy you looked about the way things are going. I mean, okay, you're getting a great story out of it. But what happened to all those big ideals you were preaching?"

"All right, I get it." Fordyce looked very earnest. "Can I just say, you've taken me all wrong? Sure—I was pleased. But Jesus, boy, *not* because your kin was hurt or because I can capture a goddamn headline or two. No, sir—what I'm set up about is that all the shit Beau Gannett has pulled will kick back on him before very damn long. Hell, he's helped dig his own grave—along with those of all his kind—with just what he's said tonight."

"Has he."

"Sure." Fordyce tapped his notebook. "I've got it all down in good Gregg shorthand. Every damn word he said. Before I'm done, by God, I'll turn his own statements against him. Now. Does that convince you of my good faith?"

"No."

Fordyce rocked back on his heels and nodded his head slowly up and down. "All right, kid. If you get to see how wrong you are, you can always come and tell me. All will be forgiven."

Rudy felt a wordless flare of anger. His hand fisted, his arm tightened. He was close to hitting Fordyce, and only then realized the fury of his own reaction.

He turned on his heel and walked away, down the darkening street that led out of town.

Before long Rudy left the gravel highway and was trudging

346

along the old logging road, picking his way through the dark forest with a small flashlight. As he walked, he had a lot of time to think about how things had gone.

A damp wind combed through the woods, rustling among the branches. It seemed like ominous whispers of things to come. He shivered. Imagination. A hell of a thing to have too much of! It bored relentlessly at the underpinnings of purpose, and its fruit was fear. Having no strong moral convictions about what you meant to do didn't help matters.

Rudy was pretty sure that Elof, too, would be at the farm when he got there. Since the logging road swung past Tom O'Dea's cabin, Rudy paused to have a look inside. The log house was dark and deserted. Elof had abandoned his sickbed, and he would head for only one place: home.

Tramping through the night with his thoughts, pressing against a cool wind, cleared Rudy's head. As the dregs of his hangover faded, his mind went unwillingly back to last night's encounter with Beau Gannett . . . and Rachel. Thinking of it brought a burn of blood to his face.

The memory hung like a blot in his brain. He felt disgraced and angry and reckless. Was that why he was doing this? Ma had called his joining Pa and the boys "a wicked foolishness." Maybe she was right.

But you're not doing it because it's right, he told himself doggedly, and you're not doing it because you feel mean. You're doing it because you've got to. So quit thinking about it!

Rudy came off the logging road and halted on the edge of cleared land where the Holmgaard farm began. He stood for a moment watching the dark hulk of the house with its lighted downstairs windows. It was nearly midnight, and Pa and maybe the boys were still up. That meant they were ready for trouble.

For a moment indecision touched him. Here was his chance to fade away, if he wanted to take it. Once he crossed that yard to the house, there would be no turning back.

Then the decision was made for him. It was done abruptly and mundanely, as Otto picked up his presence and started barking crazily. The kitchen door opened. Nobody showed himself against the light, but Pa's voice made a stentorian boom:

"Who's out there?"

Rudy answered.

Axel came out of the door and into the yard, waiting in the flood of lamplight as his son approached, while Otto's frenzied barks turned to yaps of welcome. Rudy bent down to pet the pup, then walked on to where his father stood.

Axel's greeting was as gruff and belligerent as he'd expected.

"Well—you have come to fight them or me? Which is it?"

"I'm not fighting any Gannett's fight, Pa. You know that."

"I guess I should," Axel grunted. He dropped one arm around Rudy's neck in a brief, bear-rough hug as they walked into the house.

Arvid was sitting at the table. His arm was in a sling, but his color was good. He said a quiet welcoming word; he grinned as he got up and extended Rudy his good hand.

"What's the news from town?" Axel said impatiently. "How is Dani? You must know that."

Rudy told them that Dani was out of danger and, barring complications, should make a full recovery. Axel and Arvid exchanged glances of relief.

While he was talking, Elof came in from the parlor. He was leaning on Swan O'Dea, his arm circling her shoulders for support. Or maybe just for the fun of it. You never knew about Elof. But his face was sober as he listened to Rudy; then it broke into a lazy grin.

"Hello, Scientist," he said cheerfully. "I told Pa you would show up before long. He never believed it."

"That's a lie," Axel growled with no heat. He was eyeing Rudy with a perplexed scowl, as if not sure whether or not he was pleased to see him.

It made Rudy feel as if he were halfway shut out of things, and he resented it. He glanced back at Elof. "How are you?"

"Kind of rocky yet." Elof eased himself into a chair. "Dizzy spells, you know? They come and go. But I can hold a Winchester all right . . . if I got to. You reckon I will?"

Rudy told them as much as he knew about the situation in Winterfield. There couldn't be any doubt that the Gannetts and their followers meant business. He didn't have to add that any resistance to them would be a foolhardy act. Why mention the obvious? They all knew it and would fight anyway.

Unless Axel said otherwise.

All he did was tug at his beard and grunt, "We're ready."

Rudy glanced at Swan O'Dea. She had gone to the stove and was pouring steaming coffee into a cup. "That's fine, but what about her?"

Elof shrugged. "Well, I needed her help to fetch me here, Scientist. Then she vowed she'd stay. No way I could stop her, short of beating her off with a club, which I'm in no shape for. So . . ."

"I'm staying," Swan said quietly. She came over to Rudy and handed him the cup of coffee. Her bold look was faintly scornful. "Mind how you handle that; it's hot. Got any objections?"

Rudy grimaced. "None that'll do any good, I guess. But why?" He sipped the coffee and nodded toward Elof. "Is it on that lunkhead's account?"

"You can say that." Swan moved to Elof's side and rested a hand on his shoulder, eyeing all of them with the same scornful defiance.

Axel gave a humorless chuckle. *"There's* one that don't run out on her man."

"You ought to make her go, Pa," Rudy said. "It's no place for a—"

"What? A hot pant-half-breed?" Axel cut in harshly. "She's no kin of ours and no concern of ours neither." He glared at Rudy. "You're the one this is no damn place for."

It stung Rudy's temper again. "Why the hell not, Pa?"

"You're a boy with prospects. Andy Fordyce says so. You can't make no points for us getting your ass shot off. That's why." His voice softened; he nodded his head gently. "You ain't like the rest of us. Never have been. Never will be. Took me a long time to see that."

"There's a hell of a lot more you don't see!" Rudy said hotly. "I'm staying, Pa. I'm going to do my part."

"Ths ain't your part. Go back and help Fordyce get our story out. That's your part. That's where you ought to be."

Rudy shook his head dismally. He looked at his brothers. Their faces were neutral. God, was that how they all felt? That he was some kind of alien, or maybe freak, among them? And thought guiltily, What about you? Haven't you felt that way at times?

The hell with how anyone felt. He walked to a shelf and took down the Winchester rifle that he hadn't touched in months. Then he looked at his father.

"Pa. Like I said, the governor didn't send any troops. The only men he sent are his personal secretary and his attorney general—and they have instructions to parley with you."

"*Ja*. You said that."

"All right, will you do that much? Will you talk with those men?"

Axel grunted. "Maybe," he said.

⁂ forty-four ⁂

SELMA WOKE WITH a start. For a moment she couldn't remember where she was or what she was doing there. The springs of the narrow cot squeaked a protest as she sat up, then swung her feet to the floor. She sat on the edge of the cot, rubbing the grainy feeling out of her eyes with the backs of her fingers.

How long had she slept? She had trouble focusing even on that wisp of a thought. Her senses were coming alive by sluggish degrees. It was as if she'd been drugged to sleep.

Selma had taken no drug. She hadn't needed any.

One of the nuns had suggested that she and the children lie down for a while in one of the vacant rooms. Long hours in the waiting room, the grinding tensions of those hours, had sapped her energies to the dregs. Gratefully she'd accepted the offer, she and the twins following the nun to a room containing a bed and a small cot. Selma paused only long enough to install the twins in bed and then remove her shoes before collapsing on the cot. Her last memory had been of the door closing softly.

Not that she'd had any intention of dropping off to sleep.

She'd thought she might rest for a half hour, maybe an hour, then return to the waiting room.

It was a natural impatience. Not for a moment had she doubted Dr. Mueller's assurance that the operation on Dani was a great success. The young surgeon's pleasure could hardly be faked. All the same, it would be a while before Selma could see and speak with her daughter.

"You need some rest yourself, Mrs. Holmgaard," the doctor had said. "Why not get some? We'll let you know as soon as it's all right to see her."

Sitting on the cot's edge, she stared dully at her stockinged toes, trying to will herself into motion.

Gray daylight seeped cheerlessly into the room from one small window. She had slept too long. Five hours? Six? The sleep had not refreshed her. She was groggy and a little sickish. Her clothes felt creased and sticky next to her flesh, in the way that garments did after you'd slept in them all night.

Move! Selma told herself.

She worked her feet into her shoes and rose and moved sluggishly to the washstand. Filling the basin with lukewarm water from the pitcher, she bathed her face and neck and wrists, then rubbed herself harshly dry with a rough linen towel. Now she was coming back to life a little. She woke the sleepily complaining twins and washed their faces.

The three of them left the room and went to the desk in the foyer, where a nun, her eyes glistening with sympathy, told Selma in a heavy German accent that *nein—nein*, so sorry she was, but the *doktor* had left orders—nobody could yet the daughter see.

Selma returned to the familiar, now hateful confines of the waiting room. It was empty. Even Adam Gannett had deserted his post, and Tom O'Dea was gone too. No doubt they too had needed sleep.

Less than five minutes later, however, O'Dea came striding in.

Selma's pulse gave an unexpected bound. O'Dea was like a fresh gust of wind in this place. Black-bearded and burly, with that wide chalky grin (whether it was real or assumed for her benefit) splitting his broad face. Just the sight of him made her feel better. But he had a seedy and tired look too, and she suspected he'd been up most of the night.

Seating himself on the bench at her side, O'Dea confirmed as much. Then he reached in his coat pocket and pulled out some sandwiches wrapped in oiled paper.

"Here . . . I brought this from an eatery. How long since you've had a bite to eat? Come now, mistress—you need to keep up your strength."

Selma bit into a thick beef sandwich with reluctance. Then she was surprised to realize how hungry she was. Her stomach had been so queasy through yesterday and last night that she hadn't given a thought to eating.

While she devoured the sandwich, O'Dea told her that young Gannett had left the hospital several hours ago. This after word had come that his mother had been suddenly taken ill again. For a time the old lady's health had seemed to improve. But last night, unexpectedly, she had suffered a paralyzing stroke.

Shortly afterward, he, O'Dea, had gone out to learn whatever he might about the activities of the Gannett posse. What with all the heated debate that had gone on at the Armory, the big party of armed men hadn't set out for the Holmgaard farm until after the middle of the night. Talk had it that by this time, they had turned into quite an unruly lot of scuts. Some were passing bottles back and forth. The whole crew had been afire with its own black zeal, practically straining at the leash by then.

"It's little better than a lynch mob they were," O'Dea said grimly. "I wish I had better to tell you."

Selma bowed her head and shut her eyes, pressing a palm to her hot forehead. After the middle of the night? By now those men would have arrived at the farm. By now, probably, her husband and her sons would be shooting . . . and being shot at.

Ah—*min pojkes!* she thought blindly. My boys, my boys! What is happening with them?

O'Dea's big arm slid around her and she dropped her head against his shoulder, wanting the bulk and comfort of him close to her and not thinking beyond that. It was enough that he was here. The misery that filled her mushroomed beyond even the relief of tears.

Exactly as if he'd read her thoughts, O'Dea said gently, "I'm sorry it ain't one of your own that's with you now. A stranger's bein' can't count for much."

"You're not a stranger anymore, Tom." Her words formed stiffly, as if someone else had spoken them. "It's just . . ."

"Aye. They're your own. And them with such fine concerns elsewhere! Still . . . if Mr. Holmgaard had set foot in town as ye'd wish, he'd be arrested on the spot. Why put his leg in a trap?"

Selma threw back her head; her eyes flamed. "He did that long ago! He saw the trap and he stepped into it knowing—"

"Hush." O'Dea's arm gave her a brisk squeeze. "Sure . . . I reckon he did that. But men get set up in queer ways. Aye, they do. Take me, now—"

"Frau Holmgaard?"

A nun had appeared in the doorway, speaking softly. "Your daughter you now can see. She asking is for you."

The preparations made by Axel and his sons were simple enough.

Plenty of ammunition was on hand; a good supply of water had been brought in from the outside well. With men on watch all the time, there was no need to keep Otto chained in the yard to raise an alarm. As the pup would be in the line of fire outside, Rudy unchained him and brought him into the house. Otto was overjoyed by his liberation and newfound privilege; he raced around the rooms, capering wildly.

Rudy had made his decision. It wouldn't do him a lick of good to think about what lay ahead for him . . . for all of them. Four men and a girl wouldn't stand a chance against a small army of locals and out-of-towners.

So how would it end? That's what he didn't want to think about. He tried not to.

A misting rain started up a few hours after midnight. About the time it ceased, first daybreak was starting to pale the eastern sky. A watery gray light was dispelling the darkness as the first of the posse men came straggling out of the dripping trees that overhung the old logging road.

They didn't remain out in the open for more than a few moments. Somebody out there was giving them orders. They were quickly dispersed behind whatever cover was available: boulders, trees, clumps of brush.

Obviously none of them was eager to try crossing the open land that surrounded the house. Not straight off, they weren't.

Axel and his sons watched intently from the front windows. Otto, catching their mood, paced back and forth behind them, softly growling, his hackles bristling. After a few minutes someone stepped out into sight and waved what looked like a white handkerchief tied to a stick.

"Truce flag, Pa," said Rudy.

Axel squatted by a window, rubbing his beard. "I know what it is," he growled.

"Sure. Anyway, I told you—"

"Don't tell me again," Axel said harshly, and rose to his feet. His rifle was in his hand; a pistol was holstered at his hip. "All right, come on. We'll go out and talk to 'em, you and me."

The man holding the truce flag was Sheriff Joe Pleasants. As Axel opened the door and stepped outside, Rudy following, Pleasants came on across the clearing. Attorney General Gilbert and Colonel Munson flanked him, one on either side.

The groups met halfway between the woods and the house.

Pleasants performed the introductions. Then Munson took a sealed envelope from his pocket and held it out to Axel. "A personal message from the governor, sir. He directed that I hand it to you and no other."

Axel took the envelope and barely glanced at it before handing it to his son. Planting his fists on his hips, he narrowly studied the governor's men as he said, "Read it."

Carefully, Rudy broke the envelope's seal and took out a single piece of letterhead stationery, folded twice. He read it aloud slowly, for the letter was handwritten in a crowded script.

"'State of Wisconsin. Office of the Governor. Madison, Wisconsin. September 14, 1910. Mr. Axel Holmgaard, Winterfield, Wisconsin. Dear Sir: You are no doubt aware that Sheriff J. M. Pleasants of Sayer County has warrants for your arrest, charging you with assault and intent to kill. I am informed that Chief T. L. Baird of Winterfield also has a warrant for the arrest of your son, Elof Holmgaard, for the alleged murder of Shadrach Gannett of that city. Some persons believe that your continued defiance of the law arises from a fear that you and your son will not be given fair trials and furthermore that you have no means to employ counsel to defend yourselves. As governor of the state, actuated by a desire to prevent further bloodshed, I send Attorney General Gilbert and O. G. Munson, my private secretary, to represent me and to promise you and your son my full personal protection, fair trials, and counsel to represent you. If you and your son still refuse to submit peaceably to the orderly processes of the law, the responsibility of any bloodshed and loss of life must rest upon you alone. I am very truly yours, J. O. Davidson.'"

Axel gave a soft grunt of contempt. "Huh. That's about what I expected."

"Mr. Holmgaard—" Gilbert spoke in a quiet, positive voice. "You could do far worse than accept those terms. As matters stand, you have a great deal of public sympathy on your side. The killing of your son and near killing of your daughter have added to that sentiment. You should realize that these things alone will ensure fulfillment of any guarantees the governor offers you."

Axel turned his head and spat. "Maybe. And just maybe them terms of his ain't enough."

Munson said crisply, "I'd say, sir, that the terms are more than lenient. Considering that your own actions have precipitated much of what's come about, including the attack on your children—"

"Colonel, I'm sure Mr. Holmgaard is well aware of what's at stake in this matter." Gilbert cut his colleague off with firm diplomacy. "It might be possible, after all, for the governor's office to move for dismissal of some of the charges against Mr. Holmgaard. Contingent, of course, on his surrender to, and cooperation with, officers of this county."

"Careful there, Frank." Munson gave the attorney general an outraged stare. "That's pretty much exceeding your authority, isn't it?"

"I don't think so, Colonel. I'm empowered to speak for Mr. Davidson on any matter pertaining to a criminal complaint."

"What about my boy Elof?" Axel demanded. "Where will he stand, then?"

"My office will conduct a full impartial investigation of the circumstances surrounding the murder your son is alleged to have committed. You have my personal assurance."

"Yeah. And my land the Gannett company has flooded. What about that?"

Gilbert shook his head. "I am sorry. I have no authority to discuss a civil action."

"And you can't give me no promise for sure about getting them warrants on me lifted."

"I am afraid not."

"Well then, I guess you are shouting in the dark."

Axel sounded almost unconcerned. He turned on his heel and tramped back to the house.

Big Joe Pleasants' fleshy jowls wobbled to his tolerant, deprecating nod at the governor's men. "You see? I told you fellas before that you was wasting your time."

Rudy looked at the sheriff and the state men and shook his head slightly, then followed his father. He felt a leaden sickness in his belly. The die was cast. All he could do was go along.

⁋ forty-five ⁋

AXEL HAD NO special ideas about how to handle a defense of the place. His battle plan was an obvious and commonsense one. The house had four sides and four men to defend it—one to a side. Since some of the surrounding land was higher than the immediate area around the house, they'd be on more equal terms with the besiegers if they took their positions at upstairs windows.

Axel assigned Arvid and Elof and Rudy to windows that faced respectively to the east, west, and south. Regarding the north-facing side as the most vulnerable, he took that position for himself.

It occurred to Rudy that he owned a set of binoculars he'd obtained several years ago for the purpose of nature study, saving his money for nearly a year in order to purchase them. He hadn't used them in some time; maybe they would be useful now.

He dug the field glasses out of a box of his possessions that was stored in Elof's and Arvid's room. Then, with Otto claw-clicking nervously along behind him, he went to the north window where Axel had taken his post.

"Pa?" he ventured.

"*Ja.*" Axel was staring out the window, grim-jawed.

"You know these glasses of mine? I thought maybe I could kind of go around from room to room on every side. I can get a nice close view of what those guys out there are doing. Maybe even get an idea of what they're planning to do. Would that help?"

Axel turned his head and looked at Rudy now.

"*Ja.* Maybe it would. All right, boy. You go and do that."

Rudy grinned and got Axel's flicker of a smile in return. At last he'd come up with a suggestion of something that pleased the old man, if only a little. He felt rather foolishly warmed as he circulated through the rooms of the upper floor, training the glasses through the windows on one side and then another.

Just now the posse men were keeping a cautious distance. They were spreading out around the house and outbuildings, staying behind cover as much as possible.

Nobody, unless he'd taken leave of his senses, was going to try getting in close to the house without he put some thought and care into it. The land was cleared for a good distance all around the place, and it was either flat or lightly rolling. The only natural cover in all that bare expanse was some big stumps and a few good-sized boulders. There were also the barn and root cellar not too far from the house. To reach any of these, a man would have to run through a hail of gunfire.

Moving from one room to the other, Rudy could single out their activities clearly through the powerful glasses.

Some of them were working up toward the wooded rise that lay north of the house, between it and the fields. If a man could slip around back of the rise and come up through the trees, he could fire at the house from their shelter. Still, it would be a long shot from the rise to the house.

Others went downriver a ways and crossed the dam and got into the trees that grew densely on the bank opposite the Holmgaard house. This put them in a little closer, but it was still a testy range for the Winchesters and Savages with which Rudy guessed most of them must be armed.

He reported these movements to Axel, who merely grunted. "Seems there ain't nobody wants to go out on a limb right away," he said. "Well—"

The first shot fired by a posse man cut across his words. A tinkle of broken glass sounded from downstars.

Axel jerked out a chuckle. "There's shooting for you. Busted a window on the wrong floor."

As if the opening shot had been a signal, others of the posse opened up at the house. The first round of shooting was scattered. Another downstairs window shattered; the other slugs rapped into the house siding.

"I don't want none of you shooting back unless they make a rush at the place," Axel growled. "You pass the word to your brothers. And keep your head down. *Forsta?*"

"Okay, Pa."

"Another thing." Axel swiped a hand across his jaw, scowling as if he were undecided about something. "When you figure you got to shoot, you only shoot close to 'em. None of you shoot to hit anything unless I tell you. You got that?"

"Sure."

Rudy hurried back through the rooms, making only a token effort to keep low. He told Arvid what Pa had said, and then went to Elof's post.

Elof was crouched by his broken window, grinning widely at Swan, who crouched beside him and was saying fiercely, "No! I'm not sorry I stayed. I want to be here, no matter what."

"That's my girl!"

Elof cut off her words by yanking her to him and giving her a loud, smacking kiss. Then he grinned at Rudy in the doorway. "Hey, Scientist! Ain't it great? Some real excitement for a change!"

"What kind are you talking about?" Rudy asked.

Elof roared.

Rudy gave him Axel's message and returned to his own post at the south wall.

Quite a few posse men were working through the line of jack pines between the house and the dam. Rudy fixed his glasses and brought some of the faces into close focus. He could identify a few of them.

Most of the local guys would have joined the posse for the

360

fun of it. And he could tell from their faces, talking and grinning and laughing, and from the bottle that was being passed around, that they were out for a high old time and nothing else.

Damned fools. It was the kind of fun that could get a man dead before he knew it.

Rudy smiled a little at the thought. Maybe he was as bad as any of them. He was conscious that a quiet excitement had ignited in him. There was also the fear, of course, but somehow it only put an edge on the pleasurable fever of danger.

He pushed up the window sash, levered his Winchester, and took aim.

He emptied the magazine into the ground in front of and around the besiegers. He fired so close to one man that he actually saw a splinter fly from the nearby jackpine that his bullet hit, opening up the fellow's cheek. With a shocked yell, the man dived for the ground.

The posse men settled down in fresh positions and returned his fire.

As Rudy's last spent cartridge rattled to the floor and he began to reload, he fumbled a shell and dropped it. Just as he bent to pick it up, a bullet exploded the window. A shower of glass rained over him.

Otto gave a terrified yelp and shrank into a corner of the room.

Rudy hugged the floor, his heart pounding wildly. If he hadn't been bent over just then, he might have taken that slug in the face.

Now he was aware of shots being fired from other quarters, too. A din of gunfire filled the rooms as Axel and the boys began shooting back.

Sober and careful now, Rudy made another round of the upstairs floor. Arvid was calmly and phlegmatically firing out of his own broken window, keeping the posse men on that side pinned down. Then Rudy checked the opposite side where Elof was. The room reeked of burned cordite from all the shooting.

As Rudy crouched beside Elof, a man who was daring or dumb or drunk made a wild dash from the edge of the woods west of the house toward a huge stump almost halfway to the barn. An instant blaze of gunshots from Elof made him dive for the shelter of a rock that was a considerable distance short of the stump.

Elof grinned at Swan and Rudy. "Gee, too bad for that fella. Now he's stuck smack where he is, and I just bet he pooped his pants."

Still, the man's example goaded a few others into trying the same. Two or three at a time made short runs from the woods to a stump or a rock, but staying at a range where they weren't running too much risk.

Rudy took all of it in as he made a constant circuit of the rooms, keeping his own side protected and always pausing in his rounds to make a quick report to Axel.

One bunch of posse men worked in closer by way of the blocked Gannett log drive that had filled the flowage for quite a distance above the dam. The mass of jumbled timber didn't offer shelter comparable to that provided by trees and stumps and rocks. Yet by slipping into the jackstraw tangle of logs downstream and then working upriver through it, a man could get closer to the house than by other means. A lot of them did, and not a man was hit.

Rudy judged they were emboldened by the obvious fact that none of the defenders was shooting to kill—yet. But the Holmgaards had no trouble defending all four sides of the house. Without shooting to hit anyone, they still kicked up dust close to their besiegers. And did it rapid-fire when they felt like it. There were several windows on each side of the house, and its occupants never stayed at any one of them very long. No matter if a posse man directed a blistering fire at a window he saw someone fire from. A moment later one of the Holmgaards would shoot back from another window.

Circulating through the rooms with his high-powered glasses, Rudy picked up a few things that seemed almost farcically amusing—in a grim sort of way. One fellow was making a spectacular dash across the jumble of river logs when he slipped and fell, knocking himself cold. Another man, while laid up in what he fancied was secure cover, was lighting his pipe when a ricocheting bullet carried away both the pipe bowl and his left thumb.

By the end of several hours the clapboards of the house were riddled to shreds by bullets; some of the slugs had gone clear through the walls. There was hardly a shard of glass left in any of the windows.

Nobody in the posse had taken a direct hit as yet, and they were getting impatient to finish things off. It showed in their increasingly reckless moves from one shelter to the next, running in spurts across the open or inching clumsily through the tangle of river logs.

Gradually they were closing in on the house.

Axel made a decision that the posse men had to be shown he was prepared to play for keeps—if it came to that. He put a slug through the arm of a man who tried to get too close and sent him stumbling back to cover, shrieking at the top of his voice.

"Maybe," Axel said through his teeth, "they will know we are not playing pat-a-cake now." He looked at Rudy, who had just entered the room. "You pass the word. Tell the other boys what I did. Tell them—"

He broke off speech, taking quick aim as another man made a reckless run that brought him nearly to the barn. Axel's bullet dropped him like an axed steer.

Swiftly Rudy trained his glasses on the fallen man. He'd been hit hard, that much was plain. He was rolling on the ground, face twisted in agony. It was a face Rudy knew.

"Pa, that's Monty Harp, the sheriff's deputy."

Axel said nothing. He settled his eye along his rifle sights as two other men came running out. But they were looking only to pick up Harp and carry him to safety. Axel did not shoot again; his face had an iron set.

"Go tell the boys what I did," he said harshly.

Rudy paused at Arvid's post and told him, then made another hasty check of his own side. Afterward he joined Elof once more and gave him Pa's message.

"Yeah?" Elof was peering with squinted eyes out his window. "Well, ain't much doing on this side right now. Pass me them glasses of yours a minute, Scientist."

Rudy handed him the binoculars and Elof brought them to bear on something outside. "Uh-huh," he murmured. "Well, I be damned."

"What is it?"

"Bunch of guys standing back in the trees yonder. None of

363

'em's offered to take part in the shooting. So I wondered who—" Elof thrust the glasses at his brother. "See for yourself. Look at that break in the trees. No, more to your left. See 'em?"

Rudy nodded. He saw a half dozen strangers, all in city clothes, and they were talking to Big Joe Pleasants and the governor's men.

"Well," said Elof, "that guy in the funny plaid coat or whatchadinger—"

"It's called an inverness."

"Yeah. Anyway, he's Floyd Gibbons."

"Floyd—You mean *the* Gibbons? The reporter with the *Minneapolis Tribune?*"

"Uh-huh. You always read his stuff, didn't you?"

"Who hasn't?" Rudy lowered the glasses. "You sure that's him?"

"Yep. He was pointed out to me at that big auto race I went to a couple years ago. He was covering it." Elof grinned. "So the great Floyd come all this way to cover us. Well, well."

Above all the sporadic pop of gunfire came a yell of pain, followed by savage curses.

"Jesus!" said Elof. "Was that Pa?"

"Stay here. I'll have a look."

Not even thinking about ducking low, Rudy hurried to reach his father, shards of glass crunching under his feet. Axel, still swearing in a mixture of Swedish and English, had pulled back from his window. He was wrapping a bandanna around his right hand; the cloth was already staining with blood.

"Pa—"

"Get over to the window, damn it! Keep a watch! I got to tie this off. *And keep your head down!*"

Rudy hunkered by the window, his eyes just clearing the sill.

"Pa. I think there's at least six reporters on the scene. Maybe more."

"What's that?"

Axel said it so gently, yet so intensely, that Rudy turned his head to meet his father's stare. "I don't know for sure, Pa. But it seems like it."

He explained what he and Elof had seen. That the men were

well-dressed in a citified way. That one was Floyd Gibbons. Which argued that the rest of them, too, were from big-city newspapers.

"Bedamned," Axel said softly. He stroked his beard with his uninjured hand. "I tell you what now, boy. You get yourself a dish towel or something, anything that's white, and you step outside and wave it. You got that?"

Rudy gazed at him in disbelief. "Pa?"

"You heard me. Do it! We're giving up. We are throwing in the towel." Axel chuckled at his little pun. "We are surrendering. You tell 'em that. All right? They would plug me on sight, I think. And maybe your brothers. But a lot of 'em know you. And tell your brothers to quit shooting."

Bewildered, Rudy did as he was told.

Rummaging through the kitchen, a broken-up mess from all the posse lead, he couldn't find any ungrimed towels. But he located a clean pillowcase in Selma's linen supply, and that would do as well.

He attached it to a broomstick and crouched by the kitchen door, waiting. As he'd expected after the Holmgaards ceased fire, there was a slack-off in shooting from outside. The besiegers had called a puzzled pause of their own.

When he judged the moment was right, Rudy took advantage of the pause to edge open the door, thrust out his improvised truce flag and waggle it. He kept it up until Big Joe Pleasants' stentorian bellow rolled across the yard.

"Okay—come outside! Nobody'll shoot. Just see there's nothing in your hands but that flag."

Rudy swung open the door and stepped into the yard. He felt as a naked man might feel: all exposed. Worse. He felt like the biggest target in the world.

But it should be all right. Pleasants was rapping out orders for everyone to hold their fire, and he sounded like he had a solid control over his men.

When he saw the sheriff's great bulk emerge from the trees and start across the open toward him, Rudy walked to meet him. They hauled up facing one another.

"Well?" Pleasants demanded.

"Pa is ready to give himself up, Sheriff."

"Yeah? Why's that?"

Rudy shook his head. "I guess you will have to ask him that."

"All right. You fellows come out one at a time, hands over your heads and no guns in 'em. Got that?"

"Yes, sir."

"One thing you better know." Pleasants paused; then the hard edge in his voice bit deeper. "Monty Harp is dead. He's one of them you shot. Now he is dead."

Rudy's mouth went dry. "I . . . I thought he might be."

"Yeah. Well, I leave it to you whether to tell your old man that. Will it make him surrender more easy? Or not?"

Rudy didn't know. He felt sick and hollow-bellied now. The excitement was past; the game was up. And it had cost a man's life.

"Maybe you'd better tell him, Sheriff. After he gives up."

❧ seven ❧

The Trials

❧ forty-six ❧

THE NORTHERN WOODS were pleasant at this time of year. Heat and humidity had waned with the shortening August days. Most of the insect pests had disappeared after a night or two of frost, and there had been several such nights. But the days were crisp to warm, and the first banners of fall color were touching the trees. The rich odors of earth and wood mold swept the soft autumn breeze.

Ordinarily Selma Holmgaard and Tom O'Dea were two people deeply aware of nature's signs. So much so that they could become absorbed in them to the exclusion of everything else. Today they hardly noticed them at all. And the two of them had little to say as the buckboard jolted slowly over the ruts of the old tote road, except for O'Dea's occasional word to the team.

Going home, thought Selma. I am going home.

She tried to squeeze an atom of pleasure from that thought. Oddly enough, she could just manage to. She had grown to care for the new home as she had for the old one. It was the straw on which she could pin a forlorn comfort when everything else was gone. And just about everything was.

O'Dea, on the seat beside her, turned his shaggy head to fix her eyes with his curious, searching blue ones. Selma put out her hand and closed it briefly, gently, over his thick muscular hand where it held the reins. His bearded lips stirred in a faint answering grin, and he put his attention on the road again.

Touching his hand, she thought, cost her only a gesture. Of more than friendship, less than love? She didn't know for sure. But the affection she had come to feel for him was genuine.

What a mainstay he had been over the past few days!

At least the worst of it seemed over with, but that wasn't saying much. It was like the difference between getting your whole hand burned and having only one finger burned. Thank God all were alive but poor Lennart. And he had never been a happy boy or, as a man, one with the prospect of happiness, even the little that most people could find in this wretched world. Maybe, as she tried so often to tell herself, Lennart's youthful death had been a blessing to him.

Dani would live. And she would have her Adam. Fitting enough, for Dani was the real Eve. She had not lost her capacity to be happy, but she had learned a healthy realism.

Also, Rudy and Arvid, thought the lawyer to whom she had spoken, should not come off too badly. True, the killing of Deputy Harp injected an uncertainty into any prediction of the trial's outcome. But there were mitigating circumstances. Rudy and Arvid had followed their father's lead.

The bullet that had slain Monty Harp could have been fired only from the north side of the building. Axel had given his sworn statement that he alone had defended the north side. Whether it was true or not, this statement would take the boys off the hook. Axel alone would be charged with first-degree murder for that killing. So, the lawyer said, he did not think Rudy and Arvid would pull very stiff sentences.

But Elof. To lock the freedom-loving Elof away for life would be a cruelty worse than death.

Axel? To hell with Axel!

When Selma thought of what he had brought on them, the anger that rose in her was so black and fierce that it nearly gagged her. It left her unable to think clearly about anything else where Axel was concerned.

She thought of how he had looked in the newspaper photos that had occupied a double-page spread in the *Winterfield Daily News*. And nearly all those photos had featured him—in the sheriff's custody, in the county jail, talking to reporters. For a man whose conversational trademark had always been taciturn grunts, he'd grown remarkably garrulous—whenever a journalist with a poised pencil was around. You'd think he had won a major victory instead of losing all . . . and dragging his own flesh and blood down with him.

One brief visit with her sons had been all the sheriff would allow, and Selma had spoken with them through the bars of their cells with a guard looking on. But that had been enough to assure her they were all unharmed.

It was almost beyond belief (according to the news accounts) that anyone could have survived the devastating hail of lead that the posse had poured into the house. Yet the boys and Tom's daughter and Otto had emerged without a scratch. Axel's only injury had come from a ricocheting bullet that had embedded fragments of lead in the web of flesh between his right thumb and forefinger. Selma had felt pleased when Dr. Hammerstein told her that his removal of the lead particles had caused Axel quite a lot of pain and that his hand had swelled up like a balloon.

O'Dea brought the team to a halt with a word and pressure of the reins.

Selma gave him a questioning look. Then she realized they were just below the hill where O'Dea's rambling log house stood in its cover of dark pines. She supposed he meant to make a brief stop at his cabin for one reason or another.

But he didn't stir from the wagon seat. He hunched forward and settled his elbows on his knees, head down, as if pondering.

"Tom?"

"Look at that place." O'Dea gave a brusque nod toward the house. "A hermit's retreat if ye ever saw one. Ain't it?"

"I don't know," Selma said a little bewilderedly. "I never thought of you as a hermit."

"I been one all the same. Living in retreat from the world.

It's well enough, all this freedom of mine, but it don't warm a man's bed or his heart. Not worth a damn it don't."

She felt heat in her face. "Tom, will you drive on?"

"In a minute. I've something to say...that I couldn't before. Maybe it's too early to say now. But who's to know what tomorrow will bring? You might just up and pack off to live with that sister in Ohio you've talked of...and never say a word to me. And I could say nothing while your husband was in the picture. This is a kind of between-times, then. And maybe my only time to talk up."

Selma did not look at him. Her hands twisted together in her lap. "I wish you wouldn't, Tom."

"Why? It's not still Holmgaard, then?"

"No—no. But you know very well what a lot of other things there are, I am still *married* to Axel. And there are the children."

"Not children. Save for the little girls, and what'll they be doing for a father now? The rest are grown. Ready to take up lives of their own. As it should be. And a marriage...a marriage can be ended in name as well as in spirit. You can't hold onto what's been, mavournin. Try and you'll only hurt yourself. Don't be doing that to yourself. And me."

Selma looked fully at him now. "That's not how you talked when we met. As I recall, you talked about keeping your feet loose and your fancies free. That was just a few months ago."

O'Dea pursed up his lips, nodding speculatively. "So it was. A man can change in a day or in a night, come to that. You and me and your mister, now. We all lived the way we did long enough to raise up kids, and I reckon we none of us changed much in all that time. But mavournin...we've *changed*. I have and you have, and Holmgaard...hasn't he changed all to blazes?"

"Changing doesn't mean feeling different about someone, Tom. I mean, it might come to that, but—"

"Ah, might it not?"

O'Dea shifted his bulk so that he half faced her. "From the first I felt a pull between us. Nothing I could put a name to, but it began to ride me day and night, like a demon out of Sheol. Thought I might strike it off me back if only I could

372

seduce you. Then I'd be free again. And I tried, God help me, you've got to say I tried."

The soberness of his voice broke as Selma began to smile.

"Well, blast me. Is that funny, woman?"

"In a way. Well, no. No, it's not funny, Tom. Do you still want to seduce me?"

O'Dea's brows pulled down; he eyed her suspiciously. "No," he said at last. "Only after the fact, you might say."

"Fact?"

"The fact that I've come to a feeling for you, damn it! I tried not to let it happen. But I couldn't help meself. Christ, Selma! You can't be that blind you'd think a man'd be at a woman's side as I've been by yours, if not for loving her?"

"I'm grateful for that," she said slowly. "But I can't promise anything right now. And I don't think you can. You've been a wild man of the woods most of your life. Even if you really have . . . that feeling you say for me, I don't think you can change how you are."

"It ain't the feelings that change, mavournin," he said gently. "It's the man, I can tell you. I am sort of an expert on Tom O'Dea. Loving the wild places, now. For him, that's a thing that's always been. Always will be. Only he never found anything he could care for more. Now he has. And that's you."

Almost before his last words were out, Selma said quickly, "I could never live your way, Tom."

"I know that. But I can live yours."

"Could you?"

"Yes. I can show you. Take nothing on faith. I *will* be showing you."

They said no more for the rest of the ride.

Selma spent most of it turning O'Dea's pledge to her over in her mind. Even if he did show her he could change, how could she be sure it would last? Axel had been a staid family man all those years. Now look at him. She was no longer the unworldly teenager who had wed Axel Holmgaard. Experience had brought a practical cutting edge to all her considerations.

If she were her own sole support, raising up the twins by herself would be miserably hard. Over the past three days, she had thought mostly of her three sons in the county jail. Yet she could do nothing for them. It was the two little girls and Dani who had taken up nearly all her time and attention.

No question but that Miss Rachel Merrick's generosity had been a godsend. She had urged Selma to take lodging in her rooming house, and Dani must be moved there when she was discharged from the hospital and needed a place to convalesce. Selma had been overwhelmed by the proposal. Even if she were Rudy's friend, what did this woman owe any of them?

But Selma had had little choice. She could not run the farm alone, and she wanted to be in town, close to Dani and her sons. Of Winterfield's six hotels, three were run-down rattraps; the other three charged day-by-day rates that she couldn't afford. Just hiring a good lawyer for the boys would eat up what savings she had left. So, reluctantly, she'd accepted Miss Merrick's offer, on condition that she, Selma, discharge the debt with domestic work. Even Otto had returned to his former home.

But soon, hopefully, they would not have to fall back on Rachel Merrick's charity. If one good thing had come out of Axel's stupid fight and Fordyce's press campaign, it was to rally hundreds of people all over the Middle West to the support of Axel's wife and kids. Selma had firmly rejected offers of financial assistance. But the aid tendered by friendly "neighbors" (of whom the nearest was miles away) was in a different case, she felt. That kind of help might enable her to keep the farm in operation and go on living there.

At least Selma hoped so. In the three days that had elapsed since the shoot-out at the place, she had thought of it often and achingly. How had it come through the siege? She wasn't satisfied with O'Dea's assurance; she wanted to see for herself.

As they came off the logging road into the clearing, everything looked much the same as ever.

At the woods' edge a lot of empty cartridge cases were scattered around where the ground had been trampled by the feet of many men. It gave you some idea of how fierce the shooting must have been. But from here the house and other buildings looked intact and secure.

From the pasture, one of the several Holmgaard cows lowed softly, and Selma glanced at O'Dea. He winked and nodded in assurance. He'd come here every day to be sure all was well with the cows and horses, pigs and chickens.

It wasn't till the wagon drew near the house that she made out how the siding had been literally riddled with bullets. All the windows were blank staring holes. Selma scrambled off the wagon seat and ran to the kitchen door, which hung askew from one hinge.

On the threshold she came to a dead stop, sickened by what she saw.

The Holmgaard men had done all their firing from the second story. So the besiegers must have fired a lot of shots through the first-story windows just for the fun of it.

Apparently bullets had found nearly every precious thing that Selma owned. With a little cry she dropped to her knees, groping for the fragments of a figurine her mother had cherished. In a kind of horrified daze she wandered through the rooms, glass and china crunching under her shoes. The old organ . . . the new gramophone . . . dishes that had been treasured for generations. All broken, all gone.

It was the sight of her father's favorite chair, which had caught a storm of lead from a facing window, that tore the last shred of Selma's composure. Its leather upholstery and even its wood frame were a bullet-battered ruin. With a moan she buried her face in her hands.

Gentle hands on her shoulders. She twisted away from O'Dea's touch, whirling to face him.

But the lashing, furious words trembled on her lips and died unspoken. O'Dea had assured her that surprisingly little damage had been done. But what could *he* know? What did any man know? They never saw these things with a woman's eyes.

She bit her lips, fighting back tears; they spilled hotly down her cheeks. She leaned into the haven of O'Dea's arms, and only then gave way to the wrenching, bitter sobs.

❧ forty-seven ❧

DANI DIDN'T JUST look better every day, thought Adam Gannett; she looked prettier, too. He supposed he was hopelessly prejudiced, but he thought she was about the loveliest thing he'd ever set eyes on. Sitting beside her bed as they chatted in the hospital's afternoon quiet, he thought for the hundredth time how lucky he was.

"Did I ever tell you," she said suddenly, "that at times you get me blushing all over?"

"Remarkable if true."

"I mean, I *feel* that way."

Adam nodded gravely. "How do I manage that?"

"Looking at me the way you are right now. That's how."

"I guess I can't help that."

"I guess I'm glad."

Dani lay slightly propped up by pillows, her pale hair fluffed out around her face like a shimmering smaller pillow. Against the whiteness of sheets and a regulation gown, her skin had a glow of blood-warmth. For an invalid she looked healthy; her eyes were radiant.

"I shouldn't be so happy," she murmured, squeezing his hand. "The way things are, it makes me feel sort of guilty."

"Well, most of it shouldn't work out too badly. Your pa and brothers have a lot of public support for their stand. They won't come to trial till November, and by that time they should have a lot more."

"I know. Everything could be worse, couldn't it? But there's Elof—" Her hand tightened around his. "Adam—what about when it's all over? What about us?"

"I've thought about it. A lot."

"What, then?"

"Dani, I don't think we can make any kind of life for ourselves in these parts. Not and be together, we can't. Not with all the bad blood between our people. That's a kind of wound that never heals."

"I suppose not."

"So, as soon as you're on your feet—and after the trials are over, of course—I believe we should be married. A quiet out-of-town ceremony performed by a j.p. That way, word will get around we didn't just run away together—but it will get around slowly. By then we'll be gone."

"Where? To the Northwest?"

"Yes. I've written to friends in Oregon, inquiring about prospects there. For an experienced lumberman with a little capital to invest, prospects are pretty good. Will you go with me, Dani?"

"We'll go wherever you say. Anywhere." She was silent for a moment. "It's . . . just hard to think of not seeing any of my family again for a long time. But you're right. I can't bear all the fuss that's been kicked up. Now I know how a goldfish feels."

"Sure. We'll be well away from it, both of us."

Dani's clear eyes searched his face. "What about your mother? She's been awfully sick . . . and knowing about us won't do her any good. I'd feel terrible if anything worse happened on our account."

The stroke that had felled Letitia Gannett three days ago had left her half paralyzed, almost incapable of speech. She might live for years, even make a partial recovery. But probably she would be invalided for the rest of her days, and Dr. Mueller had warned that she must be spared any emotional upsets.

"No concern on that score," Adam replied. "She knew how I felt about you long before that stroke, and she knows I'm an off-ox in our family. Mother is quite realistic. She'd not place an unreasonable blame on you for Shad. Or anything else."

He rose to his feet, then bent over to kiss her. "I have to go now, dear. Visiting time is nearly up. I ought to drop in at Lydia's room for a few minutes."

"Won't she be dismissed from the hospital pretty soon?" Dani asked.

"I believe so. She was doing very well when I last saw her."

Physically, at least, that was true enough, Adam thought morosely as he walked down the corridor.

A woman's morale couldn't be at its best when her husband didn't give a rap about her welfare. Beau had been badly shaken by his wife's accidental fall down a flight of stairs and her losing the baby. But he'd paid Lydia only one visit while she was hospitalized; after that he had come no more.

Perhaps this was as much in accordance with Lydia's wish as Beau's own. Adam was nonplussed as to why that might be. He knew only that during his own calls on Lydia, she had been oddly reticent, even cold, to any discussion of Beau. What had caused her to change toward him? Beau had been savagely bitter about the loss of his child. Maybe that was it. He might have made some callous mention of it to Lydia's face.

The door of her room was open. Adam stepped inside and halted in surprise.

The Gannett maid, Emilie Gautier, was standing by a dresser, on whose top some garments and toilet articles were laid out. Emilie was packing these neatly away in a portmanteau. The smile she gave Adam was rather cool.

"Good afternoon, m'sieu."

"Hello, Emilie."

His gaze moved to Lydia, who was seated on the edge of the bed. She looked so slender and frail that it seemed she might break at a touch. She wore a brown suit and a matching hat and veil with no dash of bright color to relieve them or the waxen paleness of her face. In her own shy way Lydia was not unattractive, but she always went out of her way to minimize her possibilities.

"Hi, Lyddie. I gather the good word of dismissal has come, and you're preparing to go home."

Lydia slipped off the bed and came over to him. "Hello, Ad." She raised on tiptoe and kissed his cheek. "Yes, home. But not back to your beloved manse."

"Oh?" A bit puzzled, he said humorously, "If you're leaving us, I hope you're not planning on swiping our maid away."

"That is her decision, Ad," Lydia said quietly.

Puzzled, Adam glanced at the French girl. "Emilie? What's this about?"

"I am leaving your family's service, m'sieu," Emilie said primly. "I 'ave give your mother notice. Madam is going to her family in New York. Where she goes, I am going."

This came as no particular surprise in itself. Emilie had always been devoted to Lydia's welfare. What Adam hadn't guessed was that Lydia would take so drastic a step.

"Lyddie, I'd reckon this is not just a visit to your folks. Is it?"

"I am going home," Lydia said firmly. "And that is home."

"Does that mean you're leaving Beau for good?"

"Well..." She hesitated. "I don't know. We'll have to see how things work out."

"I guess I had to be hit on the head with it," Adam said. "I didn't realize things had gone that sour between you."

"I don't..." A hint of color stained her cheeks. "I don't feel any differently about Beau. It's only that...the situation has become impossible."

"I understand."

"You do *not*, m'sieu!" Emilie snapped out the words. She threw down an article of clothing she'd started to pack, then swung to face him, fists balled on her hips. "Do you know what that so-fine brother of yours did to her?"

"Emilie!"

"I am sorry, madam. *Oui*—I promised you I'd say nothing to anyone, but it—it is too much!"

"What is it?" Adam said sharply.

Emilie began to talk, stumbling over the hot out-spill of her words, sometimes resorting to gestures. When she'd finished,

Adam felt a sickness that seemed to reach to his bones. He had tried to divorce himself from his family's machinations, and now he realized how Dani had felt. To cut off your people when they were in trouble was hard to do.

Lydia watched him with worried eyes, moving her hands like small birds, biting her lip. "Oh Lord. Why did you have to, Emilie?"

"I *had* to, madam! What your 'osband did to you . . . and this of the gon he hid. That, at least his *brother* should know!"

Shad's gun.

The gun Shad had often carried with him. The gun that Elof Holmgaard had sworn Shad had pulled on him. The gun nobody had been able to turn up. Beau must have spirited it away . . . just as Elof Holmgaard had insisted.

But why hadn't he disposed of the pistol? Buried it or sunk it in the river or quietly restored it to Shad's effects at home to make it obvious that Shad hadn't packed a gun that night? Beau must have been uneasy and undecided, perhaps a little panicked. Whatever other charming qualities we Gannetts have, Adam thought dully, we've never been what you'd call practiced frame-up artists. So he hid the gun in that lamp globe till he could be sure what he wanted to do with it. It must have seemed the safest of places: the last place anyone would look for such a thing.

And Lydia had lost her child. That couldn't be undone. But what of Elof Holmgaard?

"Lyddie," Adam said gently. "Are you going to let that boy go to prison for life?"

"What do you expect me to do? Stand up in court and testify against my husband?"

"But Beau's not the one on trial. You can go to Tom Baird and make a statement and sign it. Or Emilie can. Either or both of you. You can tell how you found a gun that Emilie identified as Shad's inside a lamp globe in Beau's room, and how he reacted to it. That's all you have to say. But it might save young Holmgaard from a charge of first-degree murder."

"And then what? Then what, Ad? Will Beau be arraigned for what he did? Will I have to testify against him?"

"The law says you can't. Not against your husband. But Emilie—"

"No!"

"I will do what Madam tells me to do, m'sieu," Emilie said softly. "Only that."

"And I will tell her to say nothing." Lydia's thin cheeks burned with defiance; her eyes held on his. "Could *you* do it, Ad? Could you do that to your brother? Oh—but you're in love with Elof Holmgaard's sister. Maybe it would be easy for you."

Wearily, Adam scrubbed a hand over his face.

"I don't know, Lyddie," he said quietly. "I'm not in the position, am I? I can't testify to what either of you saw. You're the only ones who can do that."

⚛ forty-eight ⚛

ON A RAW, blustery day in early November, Elof Holmgaard went on trial for the killing of Shadrach Gannett. At mid-morning of that day, Rachel Merrick paid a visit to the county jail to see Rudy. A lone, sleepy-looking sheriff's deputy was on duty in the front office. He told her that, sure, she could see the Holmgaard kid, if she didn't mind him standing guard while they talked.

The deputy led Rachel to a small cubicle just off the cell block, a room whose only furnishings were a long, rough table and two benches flanking it. He told her to wait there. She seated herself at the table, folded her hands on it, and gazed at the bare wall.

A strong residue of guilt had made her feel that sooner or later she would be obliged to see Rudy, to talk with him, and she'd kept putting it off.

After the shoot-out and the jailing of the Holmgaards, a kind of circus atmosphere had pervaded Winterfield. Reporters from all over had converged on the northwoods town, creating a hurly-burly that was like nothing its residents had ever experienced. Axel Holmgaard's bold action had fired the imaginations of people everywhere, and all of them read into it whatever significance they cared to. That ground swell of sympathy had generated a larger demand for news. It had seemed, and still seemed, as if the public would never get its fill. Naturally, the public at large was more interested in the tribulations of "the little man" than in any defense his wealthy foes might present. So the Sayer County Jail was besieged by hordes of Holmgaard sympathizers, sensation-mongering journalists, and the quirkily curious.

It had given Rachel, who was quietly repelled by the spectacle, her excuse to stay away from the jail . . . and Rudy.

Today, however, the cynosure of public attention was the county courthouse, not the county jail located in back of it. Rachel thought she might have a chance for a quiet talk with Rudy—perhaps the best chance she would get.

I owe him that much, she thought.

Perhaps he would refuse to see her. It would be a relief; then she would not have to face him. She could assuage her conscience with the knowledge that she had tried. Even as the hope crossed her mind, the deputy appeared in the doorway with Rudy, whose wrists were handcuffed in front of him.

"Sit across from the lady, kid," directed the deputy.

Rudy sat on the bench opposite Rachel. He smiled at her. "Hello, Rachel."

The deputy said brusquely, "Just a minute, ma'am. I better look through that purse of yours."

She handed him the little reticule, and Rudy winked at her and said soberly, "That's using the old bean, Harve. She could be smuggling in a whole cake with a file in it."

The deputy gave him a look of sleepy disdain, rummaged briefly through the reticule's contents, handed it back to Rachel, and took up a position by the door, his burly arms folded.

"It's good to see you," Rudy said.

His smile and manner were so easy and friendly that Rachel was disconcerted. Feeling the warmth creep into her cheeks, she lowered her eyes.

What had she expected? That he would pine away on her account? He had lost a shade or two of his outdoor tan, but weeks of confinement would account for that. Otherwise he looked no different, except for a total lack of self-consciousness. For the first time he seemed to have shed the last unsure fluxes of adolescence.

I don't know if I like him this way, Rachel thought. Suddenly it was she who felt callow and unsure.

All the things she had wanted to say to him, homilies she had silently rehearsed for days, seemed banal and ridiculous. She'd carried a mental image of him as hurting and haunted, in need of assurance that she, wiser and older, could provide. She had steeled herself to tell him that she was only human and that he must learn not to set women on pedestals. She would play out a wistful little drama with herself occupying center stage and telling herself how dreadfully difficult all this was for her.

Obviously Rudy Holmgaard didn't need anyone's homilies. But it didn't make Rachel feel an iota less flustered. For a moment she almost hated him. Then a genuine relief flooded her. Everything would be all right with him.

She returned his smile. "Tell me how you've been . . . how your family is."

They talked quietly for ten minutes. Rudy said that he and his father and brothers had been isolated from one another in separate cells. Selma had kept them supplied with news, and she was doing well back on the farm, thanks to the generosity of "neighbors."

Things didn't look at all well for Elof. A clear worry broke through Rudy's gravity as he said it. He guessed that he and Arvid should come off a good deal better. Maybe even his pa would, depending on how things went. No, he didn't know the exact date that all of them would be brought to docket, only that it would be as early as possible after a verdict had been rendered in Elof's case.

When she rose to leave, Rachel said, "Is there something I can get for you? Anything that you need?"

"Just the outside of a jail," Rudy grinned. "Guess I still have a few friends around. That's worth more than anything else. I'm glad you came."

The words were casual and sincere, nothing more.

Rachel was glad to be out on the chill, windy street again. Back in the heart of a bitter November day, walking underneath a webbing of bare, leafless branches against a gray-steel sky, her heels clicking along an ice-flecked sidewalk, a cutting wind on her face. Somehow the cruel weather served to numb a curiously unexpected pain.

Rudy did not love her any more. She couldn't have hurt him as deeply as she had believed, and she was glad of that. All the same, a sense of loss gnawed in her.

Rachel walked home by the shortest way, cutting through the alley to her back door. Her own warm kitchen was like a haven. Lotte was out on shopping errands, and it was nice to have the lower floor of the house to herself for an hour or so. Rachel brewed up a pot of tea and, while waiting for it to steep, stood in front of the big Monarch and soaked up its heat. The newly installed doorbell rang as she was pouring the tea.

Rachel answered the door. On the porch stood a small, colorless young woman whom she took for a door-to-door solicitor of some sort. Then she noted the fine sealskin coat the woman was wearing.

"Good morning," Rachel said.

"Miss Merrick? I am Lydia Gannett. May I come in?"

"Oh?" Rachel's mind went blank with surprise. "Yes . . . please."

She stepped aside to let Lydia enter, noting in a detached way that her cheeks were pinched with cold. "You must be almost frozen," she said distantly. "Would you care for some hot tea? I was just having a cup."

"Thank you."

Rachel took the woman's coat and showed her to the front parlor, then returned to the kitchen.

Her mind was in a whirl. She had never met Beau's wife, had never seen her even from a distance. Currents of gossip had it that Lydia Gannett had returned to her former home in New York some two months ago, directly after her release from the Winterfield hospital. And the gossip-mongers had begun to speculate that she'd left Beau permanently. The rift must have its roots in the act of brutality that had cost Lydia her baby. Yet Rachel guessed she was the only person outside the Gannett household who knew the truth—and Beau would not have revealed that to Lydia.

Then why had Lydia come calling?

By the time she served the tea, Rachel's demeanor was composed and pleasant. She poured tea without a tremor of hand; she made light chatter about the weather and inquired after the health of Letitia Gannett.

Lydia sipped her tea. "I couldn't say. I haven't seen my mother-in-law in a couple of months. Nor my husband. Nor any member of his family."

"Oh? You're just back in Winterfield, then?"

"Since yesterday. I have taken rooms at the Statler House for my maid and myself. It seems to be the most respectable hotel in town. I doubt if Beau or any of his family is even aware I am in town. Nor do I particularly care whether any of them is or not."

Lydia finished her tea and set her cup and saucer on the service tray.

"Uh, more?" Rachel asked.

"Please."

As she refilled the cup, Lydia's soft, impersonal gaze inspected her in much the way that one might size up a piece of merchandise. Rachel knew that look in a woman's eye: It was unsettling to have it turned on her. Long ago, gossip had informed her that Beau's wife was a shy, retiring person who rarely called on her social peers and was seldom seen at any social function. Unheard-of behavior for the wife of a leading citizen. Odd. For to Rachel's eye, Lydia Gannett appeared very serene and self-possessed.

"You are very beautiful," Lydia said abruptly. "I had heard that you were."

"Oh, well. To misquote Mr. Clemens"—Rachel gave an uneasy laugh—"I'm afraid that reports of my incomparable looks have been exaggerated."

"They haven't been," Lydia said matter-of-factly. "To the contrary. But I'm sure you're curious as to my reason for calling on you."

"Well . . ."

"So am I." Lydia smiled a little as she picked up her cup and saucer. "But then, I'm not even sure of why I came back to Winterfield. There is the trial, of course . . ."

"Trial? You mean Elof Holmgaard's?"

"Yes. I thought I might look in on the proceedings. I haven't decided yet. But that's neither here nor there."

Lydia tilted the cup to her lips, permitting Rachel a bewildered moment in which to wonder what interest the trial of Elof Holmgaard might hold for Beau Gannett's wife. Then Lydia added, "I did go over there, but the courtroom was so crowded I didn't venture inside. I decided to call on you instead. After all—I think our meeting is long overdue, don't you?"

Rachel's face tingled; she dropped her gaze. "Perhaps it is," she murmured.

"You know, it's the strangest thing. I have always thought that if I ever met you, I would like you. And I believe I do."

"I . . . well, thank you. Certainly you have little reason to like me."

Lydia said gently, "I think it is the other way around, Rachel. But thank *you*."

How very civilized, Rachel thought obscurely: this pleasant and candid exchange between two women who loved the same man. How open-minded of both to reduce a touchy matter to a dialogue of simplified courtesies.

"Since we are being frank, Lydia—may I ask you something?"

"You may ask, at least."

"You aren't certain why you returned to Winterfield. Can you tell me, then—" Rachel hesitated, her face warming again.

Lydia smiled. "Let me guess. Is my marriage to be dissolved?"

"Yes."

"I can understand your curiosity, my dear. But I'm afraid I haven't the answer to that, either . . . as yet. And if Beau *were* free again—what then?"

Rachel shook her head. "I don't know. I suppose it would depend . . . on a lot of things."

"It would," Lydia said calmly. "And would you have a clear field then, do you think?"

"Perhaps. I don't know that I'd take the advantage, even so."

"You don't love him now?"

"That is not the question. I . . ." Rachel paused for the space of a heartbeat. "I am not a child any longer. I have a better idea of what I wish to do with my life."

"And you've a grave doubt or two about the wisdom of casting it with Beau's? Well, that's wise." Lydia's lips thinned away from her teeth in a smile that was no smile. "I can even contribute a doubt from my own experience. Do you know that I recently lost a baby? Of course; the whole town does. Well, for your private information...I lost the baby because Beau knocked me down in one of his lovely tempers. I ran from him and fell down a stairs."

Rachel said, "I know."

Lydia set the cup and saucer down with a clatter. Her eyes grew large in her white face. "You *know! I* knew. And Emilie and Beau. Nobody else. Then...*he* told you."

"Yes."

"*He* came to *you?*"

With a burn of shame beating into her face, it was all Rachel could do to hold the younger woman's aching stare. But it was Lydia who had turned this meeting into a challenge. Very well—if she were so eager to unearth sorry truths.

"Yes. He came to me."

⚱ *forty-nine* ⚱

SELMA AND TOM O'DEA came into town on the day that
Elof's trial was convened. They found seats in the courtroom
before it got too crowded. Before long, however, Selma found
herself wishing she had stayed home.

J.E. Byrd, the expensive lawyer that Axel had retained for
Elof, was unable to make any headway against the prosecu-
tion's array of witnesses and the apparent facts of the case.
Nobody except Elof and Swan had seen Shad Gannett pull a
gun on Elof. Constable McCrary and others who had come on
the scene moments later testified that no gun had been found
in the vicinity of the body. Beau Gannett testified that both he
and his mother had ordered Shad to break off relations with
the O'Dea girl, as her reputation for promiscuity was getting
him a bad name. As far as he knew, Shad had done so. More
testimony by several people who knew her served to point up
Swan's immoral nature. Therefore (the prosecutor managed to
insert on separate occasions) testimony of Elof Holmgaard and
Swan O'Dea to the effect that Shad Gannett had accosted and

threatened them seemed highly questionable. That being so, what of the rest of their story?

Mr. Byrd put in his swift objections, and the judge properly sustained them. But what was the good, Selma wondered. The jury was drinking in every word. You might as well shut the pasture gate after the bull had got out.

That was how it went until early afternoon, when the judge ordered an adjournment. Tomorrow, no doubt, each side would present its summation to the jury, and a verdict would be given. They shouldn't be long in reaching it.

As he was led away, Elof grinned and winked at his mother across the courtroom. Selma tried to smile back, but she felt queasy as she and O'Dea got up and went out. The reporters were at her before they reached the courthouse steps, belaboring her with questions. But O'Dea shouldered through, swinging his stocky powerful frame in a way that quickly cleared their path.

They climbed into the spring wagon and drove north out of Winterfield. Not till they were well away from the town's activity did Selma break silence.

"There is no hope, Tom. Is there?"

O'Dea ruminatively chewed the stem of his unlighted pipe. Then he took it from his mouth. "If I gave you a good word, you'd not believe it."

She touched his hand. "It wasn't very good for you, either. Listening to those things they said about Swan."

"No. It was bad. No great news to me, but bad all the same. Funny. I think the girl has changed. She's head over heels about your lad, now. It's him and no other, for her. And *now* her dirty linen gets turned out in public." He shook his head, wearily. "Jasus."

"Tom—"

Selma hesitated. A ferment of indecision had ended for her, and she did not know how to tell him what she must. But somehow it had to be said. Now.

"If I can get Axel to agree, I am going to sell the farm. The girls and me will need the money. Then I will go to live with my sister Hedvig."

"Whoa!" O'Dea threw his weight back on the reins, in his

abruptness of pulling up the team. He looked at her, his brows drawing down. "When did this come to ye?"

"Just now. But I think it started when you and me went back to the farm...and so much I cared for was all gone, smashed to pieces. I guess it was too much. It was the last straw." The words left her in a rush of acid bitterness. "I don't have a home anymore!"

"It's a far piece from this place," O'Dea said quietly, "Ohio is."

"Yes."

"And there will not be anything for us? You and me?"

"I don't think so, Tom."

She looked straight at him, and O'Dea looked away. He knuckled a fist across his jaw, rubbing it till the flesh reddened. "All right," he murmured. "This is no time to belabor it. But see here, mavournin. Do one thing."

"What?"

"Even if Holmgaard goes along, don't be jumping so quick to sell that farm. Hold off a while. Go to your sister's if you must, but don't sell out yet."

"What else can I do?" Selma said impatiently. "Axel and the boys will be in jail, the girls and me will be gone. What do you want me to do? Just let the place go to weeds and rats? Then it will be no good for anything."

"It will be if you leave some 'un to take care of it."

Firmly, she shook her head. "No. The 'neighbors' have been generous. So many people have been. But I can't go on letting them take care of our place and land. It's not right to ask that."

People had been too generous. Various sympathetic folks had pitched in this fall to harvest the crops, cut and store the hay, put in a winter's supply of firewood which Selma didn't expect to need—now. She could not afford to pay them, even had they accepted pay, and she wouldn't consider imposing on them any further.

"Suppose," O'Dea said gently, "one took on that job unasked."

"You, Tom?"

"Me, Selma. I can hold the place down alone through the winter, anyway."

"But why? I told you—"

"Aye. But you might be changing your mind. Stranger things have happened. And I got a couple good reasons for wanting to. One's to keep a link between you and this country. If Tom O'Dea has to mail you regular reports on how the farm is doing, you'll not be forgetting it. Or him."

Selma couldn't help smiling. "As if I could forget you! What's the other reason?"

"Why, I told you I'd be showing you what I can be in the way of a respectable husbandman. Can't think of a better way than taking on the care of your place."

"Tom, that's asking too much of you, it's—"

"I told you there'll be no asking," he said sharply. "If you think anything of me, let me do this. What d'ye say?"

She bobbed her head once, up and down, almost meekly.

O'Dea said, "That's settled, then," and gave the horses a loud word, putting them in motion again.

Next day the two of them returned to Winterfield. The crowds and traffic along the main street were even worse than yesterday. But now it was almost noon, for Selma had dawdled in getting started this morning. Out of a sense of duty to her son, she would come to see him sentenced, but she shrank from the prospect.

At this late hour, however, they would probably not even get close to the packed courtroom, much less find seats inside. There were other things they had to do in town. Selma felt a relief in that fact. They could perform those errands, then go to the trial when it resumed after the recess for lunch.

On her next-to-last visit to Winterfield, Rudy had asked her to collect his belongings from his quarters above the newspaper office. Some of his stuff he wanted put in storage at home, some of it brought to him at the jail—as he expected to be there for a spell. This would be a good time to take care of it.

O'Dea had errands of his own; he left her at the door of the newspaper office. Selma felt inside her reticule for the key Rudy had given her, at the same time peering through the half-frosted window. There was a light burning at the shadowy rear of the long room; someone must be inside, and maybe the door was unlocked. She tried it, and the latch clicked open.

She walked the length of the room to its back. Stepping around the tall cabinet into the typesetting alcove, she found Andrew Fordyce seated on his tall stool in front of the typecases. A dead cigar was clamped between his teeth; he slapped type into a stick with dizzying speed. He looked up, a little startled. Then he took the cigar from his mouth, grinning widely.

"Hi there," he said jubilantly. "I just *had* to get out a special edition! Say, isn't it great?"

"If you say so," Selma said coldly. "Don't bother getting up. I just came to get Rudy's things."

She started to turn away, but Fordyce dropped off the stool. "Say—" He planted his hands on his narrow hips, peering at her intently. "Aren't you set up over the news? Don't you even *care?*"

"About what?"

"Why," he said softly, "I guess you haven't . . . er, weren't you in court this morning?"

"I have only now come to town. What?"

"Your boy Elof. He's been acquitted, that's all. The jury brought in a verdict of not guilty. Reason of self-defense."

Selma just looked at him. His form seemed to quiver in her eyes as though she saw him through a watery film. Her knees felt weak.

"Here you are," Fordyce said solicitously. He yanked the stool away from the typecase. "Sit right here. Quite a surprise, huh? The jury didn't even retire to consider their verdict. But then, nobody expected they'd have to. Not after . . . say, you all right?"

Selma fumbled out a handkerchief. *"Ja.* Just fine. Not after what?"

"Well, when court convened this morning, it looked like old Elof's goose was already cooked to a turn. And just like that, bang, the defense produced a surprise witness. She turned everything upside down."

"She?"

"Yep. A girl name of Emilie Gautier. Little French gal, very cute, used to be a maid in the Gannett household. . . ."

Not quite believing, Selma heard him out. Of how Emilie Gautier had as good as verified Elof's and Swan's story. Then

393

Lydia Gannett herself had taken the stand and upheld the girl's story in every detail.

"Took real guts for her to do that," Fordyce observed. "She's quite a meek little soul. Or used to be. By God, I don't know, but she must have really gone on the peck at her husband."

"Then why didn't she talk up before now?" Selma demanded. "Why?"

"Anyone's guess. The Gautier girl is her maidservant now, and that'd explain why *she* kept quiet. But all either of 'em would admit to under cross-examination was that they'd hushed up out of misguided family loyalty. I suppose there's more to it, but who knows? Oh my," Fordyce added with an exultant chuckle, "what a hullabaloo it created. You should have seen Beau's face. God, you ever see a man's face turn actually *gray?* I never did before. He got up and walked out of the courtroom before his wife's testimony was halfway done."

"And Elof is . . ." Selma let the words trail. "No. He is not free yet."

"Afraid not. He went right back to the clink. But he's absolved of first-degree murder, that's the main thing. Naturally he'll have to stand trial on the remaining charges, same as his pa and brothers."

"And what about Beau Gannett? I suppose nothing will happen to him?"

"Not likely." Fordyce's grin faded; he picked a fleck of tobacco from his tongue and scowled at it. "Oh, he concealed evidence, and the court will have to bring charges against him for that. But you mark me, the son of a bitch—I beg your pardon—will never see the inside of a jail."

"Why not?"

"He's *rich*, that's why not. Christ, Mrs. Holmgaard, haven't you learned anything from all this? Wealth and privilege! That's the whole game in this cherished legal system of ours. Of course that blue-ribbon reputation of his will never be the same again." Fordyce's grin was returning now. "He's been shining himself up to be a citizen of solid sterling. It's all gone to pieces now. That's something."

With a feeling of repugnance, Selma stuffed the handkerchief into her reticule and slid off the stool. "If you will excuse me—"

"Wait a minute, please." Fordyce held his hands out palms up. "Let's lay our cards on the table. You've fought me from the first. Maybe in the light of what's happened, you still think I was wrong."

"*Think* you were wrong! Why, you—"

"Now wait! What's done is done. But if you'll take another look at how things stand *now*, think it over objectively, you'll see the worst is over, it's in the past. From here on, you and I can work together. To *help* Axel and the boys."

Selma gave him a wintry stare, not replying.

"See, I've kept a record of all that's happened. I'm going to write it up as a book. Sort of a socialist tract that tells a real-life story. If I could get some good quotes from you, the loving-and-dedicated-wife sort of thing, it would—"

"I am leaving him," she cut in icily. "That is all you got to know."

Again she started past him; Fordyce held out a peremptory hand.

"Now just *wait*! All right, you're leaving him, that's your privilege, but you don't wish him ill, do you? And what about your sons? Mrs. Holmgaard, look: If this book is played off right to the great reading public, it can become a best-seller. Now—"

"Don't shake your finger in my face, please."

"Sorry. As I was saying—I've got out petitions on your husband's behalf, I've deluged Wisconsin newspapers with letters to the editor, I've harassed the lawmakers in Madison every damn way I can think of. But a book, a well-done and properly promoted book, could take the whole damn country by storm. The iron couldn't be hotter. This is the time to strike!"

"M'm. I see. Maybe you could even sell that kind of a book to a lot of rich people. Say, maybe *you* could get rich too, eh?"

"Damn the money!" Fordyce flared. "You think I give a damn about taking the loot those goddamned capitalist robber barons have sweated out of the blood and guts of the laboring poor to line *my* pockets? Think again, lady! What I do care about is the cause. And that's what every goddamned cent I make will go to. Socialism and the revolution!"

Fordyce sank onto the stool, wiping a hand across his brow. "Let me tell you something. I marched on Washington with

Coxey's Army in '94 . . . when I was twenty-one years old. We were trying to get federal help for unemployed men. God, that was a time! The time of my life. But that kind of youthful idealism shrivels up in a man. Oh, I've kept up my 'Red card'— my membership in the Socialist Party. But the more I've got settled in, the more I've tended to settle for swatting a few puerile local flies. It eats the inside out of a man. Takes his heart away. Turns him into a full-fledged cynic. Well, I've got my insides back, by God. I know who I *am* again. That's what fighting for your husband—and all of you, whether you believe it or not—has done for me. And I'm damned grateful for it!"

"I am glad," Selma said tonelessly. "We're grateful too. For all you've done for us."

"Sure. Go ahead, make a mock of how a man feels. What he tries to live by. You've a deadly aim with that kind of dagger, Mrs. Holmgaard. You used it on Axel every chance. But he was too strong for you, wasn't he? Not like Rudy."

Selma nodded. "Oh yes . . . you went to see Rudolf, didn't you? To get him to write some kind of 'personal account' for your 'cause,' or your book, or whatever. And he turned you down flat. He's sick of your cause, Mr. Fordyce. He is sick of you."

Fordyce's satirical grin took on a sour twist. "Uh-huh. Said he only stuck with me as long as he did out of loyalty to his family. Guess that kind of loyalty doesn't extend to a man who gave him the best damn break he ever had. That kid really has a blind spot where 'family' is concerned. The magic word."

"And you, Mr. Fordyce—you have no blind spots. How nice."

"Oh, I don't know, Mrs. Holmgaard. I can't say for sure about me. Nobody's motives are entirely unmixed, are they? Not mine, not Axel's, not even yours. I'm sorry about Lennart, about the sorrow you've had. Believe that or don't. But it wasn't all me. There were a lot of other things. The Gannetts. Your husband having a wild hair up his ass. That Christ-awful family loyalty all of you swear by. And that mean shrewish tongue of yours. Maybe even that had a part in it."

Unable to use her, no longer troubling to ingratiate himself with her, he was free to strike out and hurt. But Selma was past being touched by anything he said or did.

396

She smiled. "It's nice in this country in the fall, Mr. Fordyce. That's when all the snakes go to cover. And here you are in your hole. But it's no place for me or mine. So now I will take Rudy's stuff away, if you don't mind."

Selma had sworn she would stay away from town for as long as the trial of Axel and the boys went on, but she found she couldn't. Her anxiety for her sons drew her to Winterfield nearly every day.

Fordyce redoubled his efforts to sway public opinion. He made two trips to Milwaukee, where he gave fiery speeches at the Freie Gemeinde Hall to audiences of prominent socialists and other foes of big business, including the city's socialist mayor, Emil Seidel. Fordyce's fund-raising campaign was a smashing success. Word reached the socialist comrades in faraway California, and Jack London himself sent a handsome contribution. "Fighting Bob" LaFollette expressed a cautious sympathy for the Holmgaard cause, but for one political reason or another declined to get directly involved.

Contributions to the defense would have enabled Axel and the boys to post bail for their release, but Axel refused to accept it and directed his sons to sit pat too. Again Fordyce took issue with him, arguing it would be better sense for him to get out and stump for his cause in public. But Axel had his own notions of how to conduct his affairs. He was going to sit right smack in jail and—what was that dandy phrase Fordyce liked to use?—martyr himself.

The trial lasted nearly a week. Defense attorney J. E. Byrd did a heroic job of trying to muddy the waters, but it did no good. The jury spent several days reaching a verdict. When they did, however, it was unanimous. Axel Holmgaard was found guilty of murder in the first degree. Arvid Holmgaard, Elof Holmgaard, and Rudy Holmgaard were found guilty as accessories.

At once Byrd made a motion for a new trial. On the same day, Judge Neilson passed judgment on the prisoners. Axel Holmgaard was sentenced to "imprisonment at hard labor for the balance of your natural life." His sons were to serve six months apiece in the Sayer County Jail.

Sheriff Joe Pleasants and one deputy would accompany the prisoner to the state prison at Waupun.

Axel was in a jaunty mood on the morning they were to depart. Despite gusts of snow and a biting January wind, a large crowd of his supporters gathered at the railroad depot to see him off. The train was late, and Axel was able to bask in the cheers and fanfare at his leisure. People lined up to shake his hand. He kissed so many babies and pretty girls that you'd have thought he was running for office.

The reporters and photographers had another field day too.

One cameraman came up with the notion of snapping Axel and the sheriff in a comradely pose. Being in a jovial frame of mind himself, Big Joe Pleasants agreed. The two posed side by side on the platform, an arm around each other's shoulders, grinning into the cameras. The resulting photos made the front pages all over Wisconsin.

Nearly everyone found them amusing, except for an inexplicable number of voters in Sayer County. Enough of them to cost Big Joe Pleasants his next election.

🐾 fifty 🐾

SELMA CAME TO town that morning, but did not go near the depot. She pulled the spring wagon to a stop in front of the courthouse and sat for less than a minute watching all the hubbub that surrounded Axel's departure a couple of blocks away. Then she descended from the seat, took a cloth-covered wicker basket from under it, and spoke to Otto. He sprang out of the wagon bed and trotted after her, around the courthouse to the jailhouse at the rear.

She went to the front desk and told the beefy deputy behind it that she'd like to visit with her sons. Agreeably, he heaved to his feet and circled the desk, lifting a bunch of keys from his belt. Then he hesitated, looking at Otto.

"Maybe I better keep that dog here while you're visiting, ma'am."

Otto exposed his front fangs and rumbled gently.

"Maybe you better not," said Selma. "I don't think he likes you very well."

The deputy grunted and sidled carefully around Otto, and led the way to a staircase off a side corridor. Thinking of the isolated cells at the back of the first-floor cell block where Axel and the boys had been held, Selma said, "Wait. Aren't they down in this place?"

"No, ma'am. Them cells down here we use to detain the real hardcases. Which you might say your menfolks counted as, for a while. All your boys pulled was a six-month sentence, and they stand in a good way to get that reduced. So we moved 'em to our second floor—the 'dorm,' we call it. Made 'em nice and comfy. This way, please."

They went up the stairs to a big sheet-metal door which the deputy unlocked and swung open. Selma saw that the second floor was one big room containing a scatter of neatly made up cots. It resembled a sort of haphazard army barracks, except for the barred windows that admitted plenty of daylight on all sides. Clothing was hung from hooks on the walls; open-shelved cabinets held whatever miscellaneous belongings the inmates were permitted. It was a bare-looking place all the same, but an improvement over the concrete-floored cells down below, where she had feared the boys might take pneumonia.

Rudy and Arvid and Elof were relaxing on their cots. All came over to greet and hug Selma, and pet the ecstatic Otto.

"Hope you brought us some of them good sinkers of yours, Ma," said Elof, lifting the white cloth that covered the basket. "Let's see—"

"Hold on there." The deputy took the basket from Selma and began poking around in the assortment of baked goods it contained. "I better just have a look at this here."

Wonderingly, Rudy shook his head. "She didn't bring a file with a cake in it, did she, Harve?"

"Say, these here are nice-looking doughnuts, Miz Holmgaard. Mm. They sure smell good."

"Won't you have some?" Selma asked graciously.

"Sure, if you insist." The deputy had snared five doughnuts almost before his words were out. He handed back the basket and munched a doughnut as he went out, saying amiably, "Knock on the floor when you want out," before he closed the door behind him and locked it.

"That fat slob!" Elof peered into the basket, outraged. "Ain't three sinkers apiece left for us."

"Now there's an improvement," his mother said dryly. "I can remember when you would have said that to his face."

"Yeah, and pull another month in this charm school," Elof said sourly. "How's things going with you, Ma?"

They talked about the usual things.

Now that the trials were over, Dani would wed Adam Gannett. That would be next week, and only Selma and Tom O'Dea would be present as witnesses. The newlyweds would leave at once for the Pacific Northwest. The boys had mixed feelings about their sister marrying a Gannett, but all agreed that Dani's happiness came ahead of anything. And Adam seemed a pretty sound apple in a bad bushel.

One subject they all skirted around was Axel. Everything had been said on that matter that could be said. The boys were downhearted about the break between their father and mother—a break so clean that neither party seemed to have regrets.

Even Elof commented on it.

Selma eyed him tolerantly. "Maybe you better just worry about keeping out of trouble when you get out of here. That should be a full-time job for you. You got any plans, you and Tom's daughter?"

Elof muttered, "I dunno." Then he burst out, "Damn it, Ma! Everything's gone bust! Our whole family . . . everything is changed. Christ!"

Selma laid a hand on his shoulder, saying gently, "I know."

Elof hated to grow up. But he had little choice now. What could she say to a son who had never listened before? Nothing much. What happened to him when he got out was up to him.

The boys introduced her to the only other inmate who presently occupied the "dorm," a soft-eyed, very polite young man who was serving a year for refusing to pay alimony to his former wife. Then Elof and Arvid drew off to let Selma and Rudy talk alone.

It had always been that way: She was concerned about Rudy as she was about nobody else, and her other sons had always understood it and accepted it. They stood by a south window and looked out through the bars, speaking quietly.

Watching his dark, close-to-handsome profile that faintly brooded now, Selma wondered where his life would take him.

He was very young yet—he had lots of time. Sometimes, lately, it was hard to remember that about Rudolf.

Otto whined softly and pawed at her skirt. He sat looking up at her intently. Selma bent down and rubbed his head.

Straightening up again, she looked out the window, following Rudy's gaze. The train was pulling out. Buildings between here and the depot hid the line of cars from her view, but a grimy banner of smoke marked the locomotive's progress.

It was going away. Everything was gone.

Selma clenched a hand around one of the window's iron bars. She bent her head, a sob swelling in her throat. No. She would not cry. She unclenched her hand and pressed it to her mouth.

Rudy touched her shoulder. *"Mor?"*

"Ja, sure. I'm fine. Rudolf...I was such a fool."

"No, *Mor.*"

"Ja. I wanted so much to keep us together. And I couldn't."

"It was the same with all of us."

"But you kids were raised to think so," Selma said bitterly. "That was my doing."

"I don't reckon. We just naturally picked it up from you and Pa. It seemed right and good. I still don't think it was wrong."

"It's not wrong while it's good, Rudolf. But when it goes bad, nothing can be worse. It's easy to blame your pa for what's happened. But if we had all just stood up to him at the first..."

"We're a crazy bunch," Rudy said soberly. "Pulling against each other all the time and trying to stay together too. I guess it just couldn't work out."

"Huh! I guess not." Selma fumbled out a handkerchief and blew her nose. "You know what Fordyce said? He said I let your pa down."

"To hell with what he said. I don't believe it for a moment, if that's what you're thinking."

"I wondered if you might be. *Tack sa mycket,* Rudolf."

"Anyway, *Mor*—Byrd has already moved for another trial for Pa. The state supreme court's pretty sure to grant the appeal. If it doesn't, Pa's friends can still work for an early commutation of his sentence through the governor's office. And he's got a lot of friends now."

"Isn't that funny," Selma murmured. "Always before, he hardly had any."

"They'll keep right on plugging for him. People aren't about to let this issue die. I think he'll be out of prison in a few years."

"I won't be waiting for it," she said quietly. "I won't wait for him."

"I know, *Mor*," said Rudy. "It's all right. Whatever you do is all right with us. . . ."

As she left the jail, Selma was pensive. It's not all gone, she thought. Not when you have kids that can feel that way about you. We are still a family. If we're apart, it doesn't change the feeling. That is what counts.

Tom O'Dea was standing by the spring wagon, hands plunged in the pockets of his mackinaw coat, his back turned against the windy whisks of snow. Otto gave him a feisty bark of recognition.

"Came to town to get some groceries," O'Dea greeted her. "And here I see your wagon. You should of let me drive you in."

"I didn't want to bother you. I just came to see the boys."

He nodded, shifting from one foot to the other. "So now Holmgaard is gone, eh? On that train."

"I guess he is. I didn't see it off. Tom . . ." She turned her eyes down, gazing at the icy patch of street between them. "I have changed my mind. I will stay on at the farm."

She looked up to see a slow grin crinkle the flesh around his eyes. "And you'll still be needing a man to help out," he said.

"The boys will be around to do that. At least for a while they will."

"Sure, after they get out of the clink. But till then, there'll be Tom O'Dea. I'm hoping there will always be him. Can you change your mind a little more, Selma?"

She tried not to smile back. Failing not to, she managed to make her reply serious. "I need time, Tom."

"Why," he said gently, "that's all I really asked."

❧ Author's Note ❧

THE READER MAY doubt that the events of this novel could have taken place in the prosaic Middle West of the early twentieth century. But they did.

The story of John F. Dietz, a firebrand farmer who, with his sons, defied a powerful lumbering concern in northwestern Wisconsin is a well-documented one. It unfolded between the years 1904 and 1911, complete with frontier-style standoffs and shoot-outs that would seem far less incongruous to the Old West of a few decades before (an observation made by more than one newspaper of the time).

Natives of Wisconsin who are still alive can vividly recall, from their far-gone youth, the popular notoriety that was achieved by the exciting series of events that culminated in Dietz's capture and trial. Reporters from far and wide converged on the scene. At the time, a paperback book of Dietz's exploits, *The Defender of Cameron Dam*, sold widely through the Middle West. A two-reel motion picture, *The Battle of Cameron Dam*, was filmed on location in 1913.

The major episodes of this novel are based on the Dietz family's incredible resistance. However, they have been fictionalized and compressed within a year's time for dramatic convenience. Some of the *dramatis personae* had their counterparts in real life. Similarly, my embattled family of Holmgaards corresponds roughly to the Dietz clan. But the characters and their interrelationships are products of my imagination. None of these is designed to reflect the personality of any person who ever lived.

Aside from the usual source works with which one attempts to reconstruct the conditions of a period and place, the nonfiction book which has almost exclusively provided the background for this novel has been *The Battle of Cameron Dam*, by Malcolm Rosholt. I am also indebted to Mr. Rosholt for his suggestion that I write a novel based on the remarkable saga of John Dietz.